Praise for INFERNO

'It's bloody brilliant, even better than Vendetta if that's possible ...
It's exciting and violent and sexy and heartbreaking. Loved it!'
LOUISE O'NEILL, author of ONLY EVER YOURS

'Darker, sexier and more dangerous than ever before ...'
MELINDA SALISBURY, author of THE SIN EATER'S DAUGHTER

'It's the best, best, best YA romance-slash-Mafia action film that
you could ever HOPE FOR ... IT WAS SO GOOD. SO GOOD.'
LAUREN JAMES, author of THE NEXT TOGETHER

Praise for VENDETTA

'A grimy, tense, crime/gang thriller with a dynamic cast of
characters; Vendetta brings drama and realism to a dark story
of grudges, revenge and passion.'
ALICE OSEMAN, author of SOLITAIRE

'I stayed up until Late o'clock finishing Vendetta ...
It's AWESOME. Great fighting. Great kissing.'
C.J. DAUGHERTY, author of NIGHT SCHOOL

'A vibrant new twist on Romeo and Juliet.
Full of energy and intrigue!'
LUCY CHRISTOPHER, author of STOLEN

'Fan-freaking-tastic ... I honestly can't say enough
good things about it! I would read anything Cat Doyle
writes after fluing through Vendetta'

VICTORIA

D0795151

A MESSAGE FROM CHICKEN HOUSE

Vendetta was one of the most thrilling debuts I've ever read, and I knew that, like the in very best series, it was destined to get even better! The stakes are twice as high in *Inferno* – and it's twice as exhilarating, twice as romantic and twice as 'I'll just read *one more* chapter'-y. Catherine Doyle has created a world so incredibly real, it's like you're watching it on a TV screen. It's a world where the villains are bad, but some of the heroes are even worse . . . and you're never really sure who's on which side. Just prepare yourself – you'll need the third one right away . . .

BARRY CUNNINGHAM
Publisher
Chicken House

INFERNO

Catherine Doyle

Chicken House

2 Palmer Street, Frome, Somerset BA11 1DS
www.doublecluck.com

Text © Catherine Doyle 2016

First published in Great Britain in 2016
Chicken House
2 Palmer Street
Frome, Somerset BA11 1DS
United Kingdom
www.chickenhousebooks.com

Cover and interior design by Helen Crawford-White
Cover photographs: girl © Aleshyn_Andrei/Shutterstock;
boy © Stefano Cavoretto/Shutterstock; key © Everything/Shutterstock
Typeset by Dorchester Typesetting Group Ltd
Printed and bound in Great Britain by CPI Group (UK) Ltd, Croydon CR0 4YY

The paper used in this Chicken House book is made from wood grown in
sustainable forests.

1 3 5 7 9 10 8 6 4 2

British Library Cataloguing in Publication data available.

ISBN 978-1-910655-23-8
eISBN 978-1-910655-34-4

For my mom

PART I

'I shall know you, secrets
by the litter you have left
and by your bloody footprints.'

Lola Ridge, 'Secrets'

CHAPTER ONE

THE POLICE

The detectives hitched themselves shoulder to shoulder at the end of my bed. I could feel them studying the bruises that were pooling under my eyes.

'Miss Gracewell, can you tell us how you sustained your injuries?'

I side-glanced at my mother, making my most subtle *oh-crap* face. What was I supposed to say? Point into the hallway in the direction of the Falcones and shout, 'The murderers are thatta way!'?

Gently she laid a hand on my shoulder. The game was *omertà* and the objective was not to get killed for snitching. The word flashed in my head like a neon sign: *omertà, omertà, omertà.* The vow of silence, and we were all bound up in it. *Don't die, don't die, don't die.*

'A fall,' I lied. 'Unfortunate, really.'

'A fall,' repeated the first cop, Detective Comisky. His moustache was twitching like a big grey caterpillar. His partner, Medina, had dark beady eyes. They were bulging, hoping. I could almost taste it – their need to prove themselves, to catch a Mafia assassin – or two, or ten. They were close, in a way. Between the endless fleet of mafiosi milling freely in the hospital corridors, Jack's dead henchmen at the warehouse, and my admission into hospital alongside the bullet-wounded Falcone underboss, things were already pretty suspect.

'Are you certain about that?' Comisky pressed.

I clamped my mouth shut and nodded, trying to ignore the distant well of panic inside me. Maybe speaking to the police would have been the right thing to do, but we knew that having Nic watching over me in my hospital bed was not enough to keep the others at bay if we tried to compromise their freedom. Sure, I had saved Luca, but Valentino could hardly let it pass if I broke the sacred rule of *omertà*.

'Very well, Miss Gracewell,' said Comisky, his tone decidedly icier. 'Can you, instead, tell us how you came to be brought into this hospital with Gianluca Falcone?'

I feigned a frown. 'Was I?'

His frown was much more convincing. 'Miss Gracewell, do you have any information about the warehouse shoot-out in Old Hegewisch two nights ago?'

'I don't know what you're talking about.'

'Miss Gracewell, can you explain your relationship with the Falcone family?'

'The who?'

4

'Miss Gracewell, can you tell us what you know about your father's relationship with the Falcone family?'

'Excuse me?' That one got me right in the throat. My words went all wobbly and I struggled for the right level of nonchalance. Beside me, my mother bristled. Why would they bring that up? They were trying to rattle me, and it was working.

'Detectives, if you could leave Sophie's father out of this, I'd appreciate it,' she interjected, buying me some time to compose my thoughts. For a moment, she seemed completely unruffled. Sometimes I forget she has dealt with the police before. She had watched them take her husband away.

Unpleasantness twanged in my chest. I wished my father were with us. I wished we weren't so marooned without him. He had left us to face everything alone, and it had almost killed us. Still, I was determined not to let the detectives see how much it bothered me. I was determined not to let them know my weakness.

The cops flicked their attention briefly to my mother, and then ploughed on, undaunted by her request. 'Miss Gracewell, did your father have something to do with this?'

I didn't miss a beat that time. 'My father's in jail, detectives.'

A patronizing smile lifted the caterpillar moustache from Comisky's face. 'That's not what I asked.'

I felt very cold all of a sudden, and my mother, so unwavering just moments ago, had gone deathly quiet. If I looked at her too long, I could see the ashen skin beneath her sparing make-up. Her fingernails were chewed so close to her skin they were bleeding. Secrets. Lies. They had nearly destroyed us. I lifted my chin and levelled the detectives with my gaze. 'Well, that's your answer.'

Detective Comisky puffed up his chest and released a deep grating sound. Medina stifled a yawn. He was obviously the smarter of the two, since he looked like he wanted to go home and take a nap rather than continuing to beat a dead horse. Already I was finding their visit exhausting. Talking is difficult enough when injured, but lying is infinitely harder. Maybe it was the tail end of a morphine crest, but my mind was wandering and I was starting to think Detective Comisky looked disconcertingly like Maurice from *Beauty and the Beast*.

He withdrew a small black notepad from his shirt pocket and flicked it open. He pulled a pencil from behind his ear and tapped it against the paper. 'Why don't we try the truth this time, Miss Gracewell?' he said, looking up at me again. 'Perhaps I should explain exactly why your cooperation with the law will be in your best interests . . .'

I kept my expression steady. *I saw nothing. I know nothing. They will discover nothing.* As it turns out, I needn't have worried about how they were planning to persuade me because they were interrupted, ceremoniously, before they could try.

The door to my hospital room was flung open and a figure breezed in with such misplaced casualness it felt almost like we were expecting him. His attire was impeccable as usual: a bright grey suit that shimmered underneath the fluorescent lights, and patent shoes that click-clacked as he walked. He had slicked his silver hair behind his ears. I almost gagged as the smell of honey wafted into the room, clinging to my skin, my hair, my brain.

I hadn't seen him since the warehouse, and I had been hoping I would never have to see him again. But unfortunately for me and my pulse, we were bound up in this investigation together, and as the Falcone *consigliere*, Felice was not about to let it go on unsupervised by him any longer.

'*Buongiorno*, detectives,' he offered, sweeping around them in an arc and coming to stand mid-way down my bed. The air was thick with that dreadful cloying sweetness, and I wondered if I would ever again smell honey without experiencing the accompanying sense of certain death.

Felice laid a hand on the side of my bed, his fingers curling around the bordering bars. I felt myself stiffen at his closeness. It brought back unwelcome memories of being tied up in his huge bee-infested mansion right before Calvino, his brother, beat the crap out of me. I shifted away from him. On the other side of my bed my mother squeezed my shoulder.

'It's OK, sweetheart,' she whispered, but there wasn't an ounce of conviction in her voice. The last time she had seen Felice Falcone, he was pointing a gun at her head. If she thought I couldn't feel her hand shaking on my shoulder, she was wrong.

'Mr Falcone,' croaked Detective Comisky, his cheeks rouging. 'I'll have to ask you to leave. We're conducting a private interview with Miss Gracewell.'

'Whatever for, Detective Comisky?' Felice's smile, while fake, was a lot more practised than that of his adversaries.

'Well, we—' Detective Comisky faltered. He shut his notebook and shoved it back into his shirt pocket, but kept the pencil clamped in his hand. 'I don't recall telling you my name, Mr Falcone.'

Felice raised his almost invisible brows. 'But you know *my* name, detective. Is it that strange that I should know yours?'

Detective Comisky blanched. Felice seized his surprise, stepping closer to him. 'Walter Comisky,' he mused. '342 Sycamore Drive, I believe. Beautiful residential neighbourhood. Those quaint brick houses, and then there's that fabulous park on the end of your street. I expect your girls adore it.'

Detective Comisky rolled his shoulders back and made himself stand a little straighter. He was a half-head shorter than Felice but he jutted his chin to account for the difference. 'They do, Mr Falcone. Now if you could just—'

'And your wife must *love* that backyard. So much open space for her gardening. All those beautiful hydrangeas, and I've always adored long-stemmed daisies. It's Alma, isn't it?' He flashed another thirty-two-tooth grin.

'No,' said Detective Comisky, with obvious relief. He hiked his belt up, returning a small, not-so-practised smile that flickered underneath his moustache. 'It's not.'

Behind him, Detective Medina's expression had crumpled.

'No, no, no.' Felice rubbed his temples as though his mind had betrayed him. 'That's not your wife, Walter, that's Detective *Medina's* wife . . . isn't it, Doug?' He peered around Comisky, making a show of his sudden interest in Detective Medina.

It took several long seconds before Detective Medina responded. 'I don't see why that m-m-matters in a p-p-professional investigation, Mr Falcone.'

My mother squeezed my shoulder a little harder, and beneath the sheets I squeezed my leg to stop it from shaking. Felice was a master of intimidation and it was hard not to feel the horror in the detectives' faces as they realized exactly what was going on. Here was a cat sharpening its claws in front of two quivering mice.

'It matters,' clarified Felice, without taking his eyes off his prey, 'because maybe I have a gift for her. Both of your wives, in fact. Alma and . . .' He made a show of tapping his chin thoughtfully, but there wasn't a person in that room who didn't believe he already knew the name of Detective Comisky's wife. 'Rose!' he whooped, feigning excitement in his fake *Aha!* moment. 'How could I forget? Rose. Beautiful, like a flower. Beautiful like her garden. They fit together seamlessly.'

Detective Medina raised his hand to his chest, rubbing at it with casual slowness, but there was a real possibility he was having a heart attack. I pictured Felice stepping over his body, being careful not to scuff his shoes. *Ugh.*

When Felice spoke again his voice was low. 'Perhaps your wives might like a jar of my home-made honey? I could have it delivered to them, it wouldn't be a problem . . .' He trailed off, letting the sentence, and everything that went unsaid in it, hang in the air.

The pencil snapped inside Detective Comisky's fist.

Felice smirked.

I sank deeper into my sheets. I remembered the jar of honey Felice had sent to Jack, and exactly where it had led us all. By the looks on the detectives' faces it was clear they knew exactly what that black-ribboned jar meant. In the underworld, he was 'The Sting', and his honey brought death.

'That's all right, Mr Falcone,' said Detective Comisky, shifting to the side so he was no longer standing between Felice and the doorway. He gestured at the door. 'We don't want anything from you. We want to proceed with this private interview. If you would please leave now.'

Felice threw his hands in the air, clapping them together once. 'Of course,' he said with blithe indifference. 'I have to be with my nephew anyway. I heard all your questions this morning tired him out, and I would hope you don't plan on doing the same thing to this poor girl. I'm quite sure she needs her rest, and even more sure that this investigation is an utter waste of your precious time, which could be spent more productively elsewhere.' He left the room without so much as a backward glance.

My mother released her grip on my shoulder and exhaled in a choked puff. My palms were slick with sweat even though Felice hadn't looked at us once when he was in the room.

'Well, then,' said Detective Comisky. 'We'll resume.'

The interview was concluded a couple of minutes later. That was on Day Two. Two days since my life had flipped upside down and changed everything I thought I knew. There were so many things that haunted me, questions woven inside the nightmares. And there were people, too. People I never wanted to see again, people I never wanted to meet, and people who still owed me answers. And though I didn't know it at the time, there was someone just like me, trapped on the other side of that world, trying to get out.

CHAPTER TWO
THE MAFIA QUEEN

At first my mother refused to leave my side. She just watched me, statue-like in her chair, blood-red eyes drooping with tiredness as she clutched my hand in hers and told me it would get better. Her voice shook as she said it, and I wondered at her reluctance to be apart from me – was she afraid of leaving me by myself, or was she terrified of being alone?

When she could barely open her eyes from exhaustion or speak without yawning the ends of her sentences, she agreed to go home and sleep. It was almost over. The next day I was getting out. After that I would never have to set foot in a hospital room again.

The sound of her retreating footfall was replaced by Nic's surer steps. He was returning from his brother's bedside, where he spent the other half of his time, his guilt splitting him in two.

'Hey,' he whispered. He leant over me, subtly assessing the bruises, like he always did. Maybe he didn't want me to feel self-conscious about it, or maybe he didn't want to remind me where they had come from.

'Hi.' I was lying down, feeling the weight of my tiredness on my lids. He looked as exhausted as I felt. 'I'm trying not to fall asleep.'

'Sleep if you need to, Soph. I'll be here.' I didn't notice him move, but I felt the soft pressure of his fingers as he brushed my hair from my face.

I didn't want to sleep – sleeping meant dreaming and dreaming meant nightmares, and then before I knew it, I'd be awake and screaming all over again. I shook my head, but I could feel the threads in my brain going slack. 'You should go,' I told him, my tongue thick in my mouth. 'Visiting hours are over.'

I caught the quirk of his lips as he pressed them against my hand, smiling. He had zero respect for visiting hours. Among other things. 'I'll wait until you fall asleep.'

I let my eyes close as the feeling of safety surrounded me.

'I'm sorry,' he said softly. 'Forgive me, Sophie.'

I wanted to. It was easy in times like this, when I was too tired to think, too distracted to remember. It was easy to listen to him whispering to me, his fingers stroking mine. If I thought too much about those hands – what they could do, what they had already done – then I wouldn't have been able to hold them, to let them trail softly along the bruises on my face.

If 'sorry' could have made it all better, I would have walked right out of the hospital and never looked back. But deep down I knew the boy who watched over me with quiet attentiveness was the same boy who had put a bullet in my uncle in the warehouse. And yet when Nic looked at me with those gold-flecked eyes, it was hard to ignore the flutter in my stomach, the weakness in my arms when I tried to push him away.

The line between right and wrong was a dark, blurry gap, and I had fallen down inside it.

When I woke up screaming, there was something hovering in the blackness – a strange winged shape upon the walls. I tried to blink it away, but the form grew crisper, taller. Real. I strangled my screams and sat bolt upright, crushing myself against the pillow. 'Who the hell are you?'

Either this was the creepiest nurse in history, or I was about to get murdered. She edged closer to me until the half-light from underneath the door flickered along her frame. I had only seen Elena Genovese-Falcone twice before – once in Valentino's portrait of her, and once in a newspaper article about the funeral of Don Angelo Falcone, Nic's father. She had been in Europe when Nic and his brothers had first moved to Cedar Hill.

In person, she was statuesque. Her frame was narrow and crisp around the edges – a consequence of tight-fitting, tailored clothes. The tip of her nose swooped upwards into a point and her dark hair was wound into a bun. She was gripping the bars at the end of my bed. If we were in a superhero movie, she might have ripped them right off, the way she was tensing her fists around them.

'So,' she said. '*You* are the Gracewell girl.'

Her voice was plummy, and edged with a faint Italian accent. It wasn't a question, more of an accusation, and I had the sudden sense of being caught in a trap. Which was stupid, considering that was my name and she hadn't exactly jumped any hurdles to figure it out.

'Yes,' I said, a tremor tripping through my voice as I reached for the bedside light and flicked it on. 'That's me.'

The room lit up and I felt marginally more confident. I could probably duck and roll if I needed to, but as far as I could see she wasn't brandishing a weapon. Unless you counted the patronizing smirk. The light had enveloped her harshly, illuminating a made-up face with high cheekbones and a pointed chin. Her hooded eyes were a familiar searing blue.

I smoothed the greasy wisps of hair away from my face. Let her take a good look at what her family did to me. Let her see the yellowing bruises, my swollen cheeks. I would stand my ground – I would show her I wasn't afraid. Even if I was totally and completely terrified. 'May I ask what you're doing in my room at this hour, Mrs Falcone?'

If she was surprised by my knowledge of who she was, she didn't let it show. I guess any halfwit could nail a game of 'Spot the Falcone'. Just look for the shampoo-commercial hair or those I-might-murder-you eyes.

Her lips reset into a thin line. 'You and I have a problem.'

'And what problem would that be?'

She straightened, folding her arms across her chest. *Well.* She was tall. 'You have done *something* to my sons.'

14

Sheesh. Talk about being selective with information. 'If you're referring to Luca, then yes, I did do something. I saved his life.'

'Something *else*,' she clarified with cool indignation. 'Don't try and be smart with me.'

I guess saving her son was not going to earn me any brownie points. 'I have returned to a *disastro*. Nicoli is pre-occupied. Distracted. You have gotten inside his head, like a worm.'

I slow-blinked at her. 'Did you . . . did you just call me a *worm*?'

'That's what you are. An American worm.'

'I am not a worm.' That was a particular combination of words I never thought I'd have to say. Was this how mobsters insulted each other? If I was braver, I might have called her a dung beetle and stuck my tongue out. 'I'm a girl,' I added for further clarification, feeling a little bit like an indignant two-year-old.

'A *stupid* girl,' she hissed. She was way too close now. I could see the shine on her Botoxed forehead. 'You should have minded your own business.'

'Don't you know what happened?' I asked. 'Don't you have any idea?'

She stared through me, nonplussed. My voice grew a little stronger and I pressed on, trying to make her see sense. 'Do you think I enjoy being in this hospital bed? Do you think I like my face being this shade of yellow and purple? I was dragged into your family's twisted games. I never wanted to be a part of any of this.'

'Then perhaps you should have stayed away from my son.'

I could feel my pulse in the tips of my ears. *Calm down, Sophie. Calm down.* 'Perhaps he should have stayed away from me.'

'And Gianluca!' She threw her hands in the air. '*Mio figlio!* So weak now. *Cos'è successo?* she asked the ceiling. 'This girl . . . this girl . . .' She shook her head, frowning as her sapphire eyes roved over my face. 'A beautiful nothing. You have broken them.'

She had careened right through my threshold for rude crap. I had to deal with enough inescapable unpleasantness when I was sleeping; I was not about to let someone berate me when I could do something about it.

'*Broken* them?' I felt anger rise inside me. I let it sweep me up and make me strong. 'I saved Luca's life. Any normal mother would be grateful for that. They would thank me, not break into my room in the middle of the night in the *hospital* where *your family* put me. Where the hell is your patient etiquette?'

'Careful,' she warned.

'I *am* careful,' I said. 'At least I *was* . . . until—' I stopped. What would be the point of blaming her angelic sons? Her denial was so thick it blinded her. 'If you can't see that all I ever tried to do was help your sons, even after all the bad things they did, then that's *your* problem. Now get out of my room before I call the nurse!'

Elena Genovese-Falcone exhaled in a hiss. She leant over me, the way Nic sometimes did, but the effect was very different. She brought her face so close I could see the capillaries in her eyes. I flinched away from her, cursing my instincts for making me look weak.

'I will leave when I have said what I came here to say. Don't forget, *saccente*, you lie here in safety because of my son's command and nothing else. I know *exactly* who you are – who your father is, *what* your vermin uncle is, and everything they owe us.'

'We don't owe you anything any more.'

'Those eyes,' she said, drawing back from me as her voice fell deadly quiet. Mutinous wrinkles appeared above the bridge of her nose. 'They are soulless.'

'Please just leave me alone.'

She just stared at me, like I was a puzzle she suddenly had to work out, like there was something written inside my pupils. After a heavy silence, she whispered, as though she was confiding something in me, 'I know there's more to you than you would have me believe.'

'No,' I said, exasperated, my head shaking from exhaustion and denial. 'What you see is what you get.' *Unlike – oh, I don't know – every freaking person in your family.*

Her lips twisted. 'Somehow I doubt that.'

'What did you come for?' I demanded. 'To insult me? To finish what your family started?'

'I came to tell you to stay away from my sons, or the next time we see each other, I won't be so careful about where I put my hands.'

'You wouldn't hurt me,' I ventured. Valentino wouldn't let her. 'Not after what I did in the warehouse.'

Her laugh died in her throat as quickly as it formed. 'Girl, I would put a bullet in my sister if I ever came across her unprotected, so what makes you think I wouldn't do the same to someone I have met only once?'

I had a sudden vivid impression of her choking me. The

thought made me swallow more audibly then I meant to.

'You're not meant for this world,' she added, like it was the worst possible insult.

'You say that like it's a bad thing.'

'We are born, not made. Dynasty and ambition made me who I am today. It brought me the life I wanted, the stature I have been owed since birth. The Genovese women are survivors; we have the blood of Sicily in our veins, entire families who work beneath us. It will never be like that for you. You will never be anything more than a passing distraction for my son.' She turned from me, and stopped with her hand on the door. She was in darkness. I decided now that I had met her I much preferred her like that – an indiscernible shadow. 'He would never choose you over his family.'

Seized by a mixture of bravery and anger, I hurled my response at her back. 'What's to say I would ever choose him over mine?'

'Please,' she said, throwing the word over her shoulder. 'You have no family left to speak of, and we both know it.'

White-hot rage ripped through me and I imagined leaping from the bed and pulling her hair out by the roots. 'You don't know anything about my family or my loyalty,' I gritted out. 'So just get out.'

She left a tinkle of laughter behind her and I fell back against my pillow, panting. I was flooded with adrenalin; terrified and angry and confused and wishing I had been braver, wishing I could stand my ground in front of the Falcones without feeling the creeping arrival of my impending doom. *Damn them. Damn her.* In a different world we might have gotten along. But in the stark light of day, between two families who would hate each other for ever, I was nothing more than a troublesome, interfering *Americano* – and she was the Mafia queen from hell.

CHAPTER THREE
GOODBYE

'You know, when I was going through your closet this morning, I had this horrifying realization that four pairs of sweatpants are more than enough for any one person in their entire lifetime.'

'Well,' I said, taking the sweatpants from Millie and balancing on her arm as I hiked said pants up under my hospital gown, 'those are obviously the words of someone who's never eaten an entire pizza and had their jeans betray them. You can never have enough sweatpants.'

'Sweatpants are basically just pyjamas.'

I wagged my finger at her. 'Socially acceptable pyjamas. *Socially acceptable.*'

She crinkled her nose in disgust, and I had to stifle the sudden urge to hug her. I was getting that a lot lately – this crazy appreciation for my best friend, who had been there for me more than ever since the warehouse. Plus, I was in a marginally good mood (all things considered) because I had just been discharged, my mother was waiting in the parking lot, Millie was helping me get dressed, and I was finally going home. Even if my life would never be the same again, at least I would be far away from IV drips and lurking Falcones. Especially the female variety.

I slipped out of my hospital gown and shimmied into a tank top and flip-flops. My hair was greasy so I wound it into a high ponytail, scraping the stray strands away from my face. I chose to minimize my general sense of bleakness by not looking in the mirror.

'Here,' said Millie, passing me a tub of strawberry Vaseline. 'This might help.'

'Thanks.' It was like trying to fix a bullet wound with a Dora the Explorer bandage, but I smeared some on my lips anyway.

Millie grabbed my overnight bag from the bedside locker and smoothed the sheets one last time to make sure I hadn't left anything behind. 'You ready to go?'

I did a cursory once-over of my hospital room. *Ah, the times we shared.* 'I am *so* ready.'

'Soph?' My name coincided with a knock, and my heart rate doubled as Nic came into the room.

'Oh,' said Nic, taking in Millie and me at once. He raked his hand through his hair, ruffling what was already ruffled. 'Hi, Millie. I didn't know you'd be here so early.'

'Nic,' she said, faux-smiling so I could see every transparent link of her braces. 'What a displeasure.'

Up until then, I had somehow, miraculously, kept them

apart since the warehouse. My feelings for Nic might have been a complete mess, but Millie's attitude to him and the rest of his family was pretty clear-cut.

'Right,' he said, no longer sure of where to put himself. 'It's good of you to help Sophie like this.'

Millie's laugh was cold. 'Thanks for the positive reinforcement, Nic. I'm surprised you even recognize the act of helping others.'

Nic shoved his hands in his pockets and relaxed his shoulders with a sigh. He looked at me. 'I just came to say goodbye.'

'So, is your stupid, pathetic, arrogant brother here somewhere?' Millie interjected. If her anger at Nic was a storm, then her attitude to Dom was a hurricane.

'Which one?' asked Nic.

Millie snorted. 'I guess there *is* quite a list. I'm talking about Dom, King of the Assholes and Overlord of the Douchebags.'

'Oh—'

'General of the Jackass Army,' Millie cut in.

'He's—'

'Admiral of the Idiot Navy. Captain of—'

'I get it,' said Nic, a hint of exasperation creeping into his voice.

'Just making sure,' said Millie. 'I know you and I live on *completely* different planets, with different rules about who gets to randomly kill and endanger people, so I figured I'd spell it out for you.'

Nic didn't take the bait. 'Dom's down the hall in Luca's room.'

'Well, tell him not to come near us. I would hate to risk drowning in his surplus hair gel.'

'OK.'

'Also, tell him he's an asshole for using me to *spy on my best friend's family.*'

'I'll pass on the message.'

'Mil,' I interjected, 'can I please have a second with Nic before we go?' The last second we'd probably ever have.

'Fine. But first, can I ask one last question?'

Nic splayed his hands in surrender. 'Go ahead.'

'If I offered you a candy bar would you punch me in the face in gratitude?'

'What?'

Millie feigned contemplation. 'I'm just wondering how you usually return a favour. You know, the way Sophie saved your brother's life and then you went ahead and shot her uncle.'

Oh, what's that? Why, it's the elephant in the room.

Nic's gaze flicked to mine once more. It seemed to say, *Please put me out of my misery.* 'I'm trying to make it right,' he said quietly.

'Can you unshoot someone?' asked Millie. 'I hadn't heard of that.'

'Oookay,' I said, shooing Millie towards the door. 'Just one minute, Millie. Please.'

'Sorry, but that felt good,' she sighed. 'I had to do it.'

'I know,' I said. She disappeared into the hallway and I shut the door after her.

The room felt so much smaller now that it was just Nic and me. I had to sit on the bed to catch my breath. That's the trouble with broken ribs; even standing becomes problematic after a while.

'So . . . that was awkward,' he offered, coming to stand in front of me, his knees almost touching mine. The strain of the encounter was indented above his eyebrows. 'I guess she hates me.'

'She's just protective,' I offered, not quite meeting his eyes, or he'd see what I really meant: *Oh man, she hates you with the fire of a thousand suns.*

'That's the funny thing,' he said, without smiling. 'So am I.'

'I know.' I echoed the sadness in his voice. 'I know you are.'

The silence stretched out, the heat between us keeping us there, like two magnets just shy of touching.

'So,' he said, his voice quiet, 'I should probably leave you alone now.'

I prickled under the heat in his gaze. It was strange how, even now, after everything, he could make me feel so laden with emotion. I wasn't sure if I liked or hated how on edge he made me. 'Yeah,' I said, getting to my feet and heaving through the surprising effort it took. He stepped back to give me room, his hands outstretched to steady me if I needed them. 'You should probably get lost. I would like to survive until my prom at the very least.'

He didn't smile. I wasn't smiling either. I was still partially hunched over, the lingering discomfort in my ribs making it hard to stand up straight. My face was a collection of pooling bruises – fluorescent yellow bleeding into faded purple that formed blotches underneath my eyes and along my jaw. I couldn't speak more than a few sentences at a time. This was how he'd remember me.

We lingered halfway between the door and the bed. This

was the moment we had been speeding towards since the day I found out who he was – this was the moment we said goodbye. And now it was here, I just wanted it to be over.

'So,' I said, turning from him. 'I'm going to take off . . .'

'Soph.' Nic tugged at my arm, pulling me around to face him.

'Don't,' I said, suddenly afraid of our proximity and how it shot through my emotions like an arrow. 'I have to go.'

His fingers brushed my chin. 'Look at me.'

I looked at him, past the dark eyes, the olive skin and the careful swoop of his hair. I made myself look at him, I made myself *see* him. There was blood on his hands. The fog was clearing, and I couldn't ignore it.

My phone buzzed in my pocket. Millie and my mother were waiting for me. I placed my hands on Nic's chest, feeling the hurried thump of his heartbeat as I pushed him away. 'Look, Nic, what you did in the warehouse . . .'

'I know,' he said, his eyes closing. 'You'll never forgive me.'

'You'd be a fool to ask for my forgiveness, knowing that you're still going to go after him.'

He didn't deny it. He didn't say anything at all. He wasn't finished with Jack, and his feelings for me weren't going to change that. He would never choose me over his family.

'Goodbye, then,' I said.

'Goodbye, Sophie,' he whispered unsteadily. '*Bella mia.*'

He pulled away from me, out the door, and by the time I made it into the hallway he was already disappearing into Luca's room, back to his brothers, back to their world.

CHAPTER FOUR

THE CUT

Aside from the obvious injuries – a swollen nose, some thorny ribs and a general pervading sense of my own mortality – Jack's beef with the Falcones had gifted me something else, too, only I didn't find out about it until I got home.

Post-traumatic Stress Disorder: post-traumatic stress disorder (PTSD) is a mental health condition that's triggered by a terrifying event — either experiencing it or witnessing it. Symptoms may include flashbacks, nightmares and severe anxiety, as well as uncontrollable thoughts about the event.

Great. I stared at my faint reflection in the laptop screen as the words settled in. I looked like a very sad, very sleep-deprived panda.

Everything had changed, and being back in my house and sleeping in my own bed only made that more apparent. Sophie Gracewell, one-time expert at sweeping things under the rug and reigning queen of the ignorance-is-bliss hypothesis, had disappeared. Or been killed, I guess, given the circumstances.

Before Nic, before everything bad that had happened, I was just sort of *there*, existing, but not really *living*. Everyone around me had their lives and hobbies and friends and passions, and I had a dead-end job, a dead-end future and a friend who would go so much further than me after school. I was Sophie, but that's all I was. Bored, aimless, mostly alone. And then suddenly I wasn't. I was part of something bigger, a player in a world that lived and breathed passion and danger, and it was wrong, and scary, but it was more than just existing, and now that I had experienced it, it was hard to shut off. It was hard to leave it behind.

Every noise made me jump, every screaming nightmare demolished my throat, every pleasant moment was squashed by harder, stronger memories of darker ones. I couldn't stop to smell a flower without my brain going: *Hey, this is a nice rose, but also, remember that time you saw a guy get shot in the chest?* I couldn't even watch *Aladdin* any more. *Yeah, this genie sure is charismatic but on a slightly different note, do you think blood is stickier when it's warm and still inside a person's body, or when it's drying all over your hands an hour or so later?*

When I stood in my room amidst old DVDs and books and clothes and all the other comforts of my old life, I felt completely unlike myself. Something new had taken hold of me. It began as a pinch, an uncomfortable twinge in the pit of my stomach that twisted into something darker. It wasn't my ribs. It was fear. I was afraid, and the fear was relentless.

And the solution?

If you believe you are suffering from PTSD, we advise you to seek help from a qualified health professional.

The solution was to tell a therapist about the night my mother and I almost got shot in the head by a bunch of trigger-happy mobsters, and the lingering irrational urge to make out with the boy who had tried to kill my uncle directly after I stuck my hands inside his brother's chest cavity to save his life.

I'd rather go on a picnic with Hitler.

Instead I replaced my preferred hobby of watching Netflix and eating ramen noodles with a couple of new games called shadow-watching and street-staring. You don't really notice how many shadows there are in the world until you start being afraid of them. I spent hours at the windows looking at shapes go by, watching pedestrians to see if they were watching me. I studied every car on the street with manic interest. After a time I saw the same one cropping up over and over – a blacked-out Mercedes with black rims. I convinced myself someone was watching me. When I went outside to check, it was gone, rolling down the street and disappearing from view – whoever it was, they were just going about their life.

I missed my father more than I thought possible; his absence was like a physical ache in my chest – this haunting sadness that I couldn't shake, this face that was never far from my mind. I needed him and he wasn't there. Sometimes, the anger surfaced and I would curse him – how could he have left us? How could we possibly face this without him?

I started to dream of him – of that fateful Valentine's night a year and a half ago. My mother's screams rose up through the floorboards, and before she crashed into my room with news of what he had done, I heard her, somewhere far away, shouting in a voice thinned by hysteria: 'He got him. He got him!' Was my mind playing tricks on me, or was this fresh new horror lifting the veil on all the other things I had squashed down to the bottom of my memories? 'He shot him!' And then it was my voice, screaming into a void inside an impossibly expanding warehouse, looking for Jack in the blackness and knowing he was already gone.

During the day, I called every number I had ever had for my uncle. I left messages with old acquaintances. But there was nothing. The Falcones were gone, too. Millie said their house was deserted now. There was no sign of them ever having existed in Cedar Hill, nothing except for the memories seared into my brain.

And something else, too.

One morning, when I had beaten the sunrise, and was pacing around my room, attempting half-heartedly to tidy it, I came across the shorts I had been wearing that night at the warehouse. I held up the frayed denim, and Luca's switchblade dropped on to my bed.

Oh. I picked it up and traced the letters. *Gianluca, March 20th.* It was heavy, the crimson falcon swooping across the handle like it was going to unstick itself and take flight. I sat down on my bed and stared at it. I had his switchblade. The proof that he had set me free against his family's wishes – that he, of everyone, had done the right thing in that one moment. I had one last piece of the Falcones sitting in the palm of my hand.

It felt good. I had an unexpected surge of confidence holding it. I guess it reminded me of the confidence he'd had in me. Plus, it was a weapon, and a weapon meant protection. I slid the pad of my index finger along the sharp edge of the knife, revelling in the feeling of metal on skin, the quiet sureness it gave me.

I started to carry the switchblade with me everywhere, like it was some depraved comfort blanket. I ate in the kitchen with my mother, the knife tucked into my shorts, pressing against my hip. At night I kept it under my pillow, curled in my fingers. When Millie came over I thumbed its edges inside my pocket. In moments of idleness I flicked it open, measuring its sharpness against my palm.

I thought about using it, wondered what it would feel like to pierce someone's flesh. Sometimes I really freaked myself out. I used to fantasize about moving away from Cedar Hill and starting a new life as just an unknown girl in a big city, working on film sets, holding a boom mic, adjusting a shot, or helping to run lines with Liam Hemsworth while he fell hopelessly in love with me. Now I was fantasizing about chopping Felice Falcone's finger off and laughing in his face. *God.*

It happened almost ten days after leaving the hospital. I had been looking out the window – counting the black cars that rolled too slowly down my street, my eyes vibrating from exhausted concentration. Now I was nearing the edge of unconsciousness, where I knew sleep would come whether I willed it to or not.

My mother hovered in the doorway to my room, a mug cupped between her hands. She raised it in offering.

'No, thanks.' My words slurred.

'It's chicken noodle.' She bit down on her smile to keep it from shaking. 'You haven't had anything all day.'

Hadn't I? Had *she*? 'So tired.'

She edged into the room, setting the soup down on the nightstand. 'Sophie, please. I'm worried about you.'

I shook my head, squishing my cheek into my pillow. 'Don't be.'

It was almost like a ritual: *Won't you eat a little more, Sophie? Won't you have a bite of this? Do you want to talk about it with someone? You're not trying, Sophie. Please just try.*

Her blue eyes were wired with red. She seemed tired, too. I felt her hand on my arm. 'Will you drink some of this at least? It will help you to sleep well.'

'You have it,' I said, feeling myself sink. 'Please.'

She stroked my hair, her voice quiet. 'I will. I'll have some too.'

I couldn't lift my head even if I wanted to. My lids drooped shut and I fell, down, down, down into the blackness that was waiting to envelop me. The shadows swooped. The gunshots rang out.

I woke with a start. It was dark outside but my curtains were still open. The moon was high and full, the stars casting streaks inside my room. Everything was silent. I wasn't screaming. I wasn't sweating. I hadn't woken myself up and my mother wasn't there, fretting by my bedside like she usually was.

She's asleep, I realized with such a flood of relief it took me another second to notice the searing pain in my hand. I flicked on the light and stared in horror at the blood on my sheets.

The switchblade was open on my pillow, the knife slicked with my blood. Even the handle was stained, darker beads of crimson sinking into the grooves in the inscription. There was a three-inch gash running across the palm of my right hand. I had cut myself in my sleep!

It was bad enough to drench my sheets and wake me up. It was bad enough to give my mother a horrible jolt if she walked in just then. This was the only uninterrupted morsel of sleep she had gotten in weeks, and I sure as hell wasn't about to ruin that.

I grabbed a T-shirt and tied it in a knot around my hand. I flicked the switchblade closed and stashed it in my drawer. I flipped the pillow over to its unbloodied side and crept downstairs. Every creak was a miniature heart attack, but my mother's bedroom stayed silent as I descended. I would disinfect the wound, wrap it up and come up with an excuse for the injury tomorrow.

The kitchen door was ajar and the light had been left on, but it wasn't until I reached the door that I heard the crying. I peeked through the crack. My mother was sitting at the table, her feet curled around the chair legs. She was dressed in her pyjamas, but it was easy to see she hadn't been sleeping. Her head was in her hands and her breaths were coming in violent, heaving gasps.

My heart felt like it was crumpling in my chest.

I pressed my hand on the door, and then stopped myself. There was blood all over me. I had become so obsessed with arming myself, even in sleep, that I had ended up stabbing myself. And now my bed was covered in blood and here was my mother thinking she had seen the worst of it already. She couldn't see me like this. It would only make it a hundred times worse.

I reeled backwards.

I crept back upstairs, where I washed my hand in the bathroom sink and wrapped it in strips of cotton wool. In the mirror, a grey-eyed wisp stared back at me. Where had the blue gone? In the half-light, I couldn't help thinking of Elena Genovese-Falcone's words to me. I supposed I did look a little bit soulless. I felt a little bit soulless too.

I found a spare sheet in the ironing cupboard and spread it over my bed, covering the bloodstain on the mattress. I buried myself beneath the duvet and lay on my back, looking at the ceiling as my hand pulsed. When the tiredness came, I stuffed the duvet in my mouth and prayed that when I woke up screaming my mother wouldn't hear it.

CHAPTER FIVE
THE DOLPHIN PHILOSOPHY

'Hey, Paranoid Patty, can I come in?'

I opened the front door and Millie bounded through it, shaking her head at me as she slid her oversized sunglasses off her face and on to her hair. 'You're like something out of a bad horror movie, peering through your sitting-room curtains like that. It's the middle of the afternoon!'

'There was a car . . .' I started, and then instantly gave up. 'Never mind. Come in.'

She padded after me into the sitting room, where I was watching old re-runs of *America's Next Top Model*. Tyra Banks was on-screen berating a model for being disrespectful and not 'caring enough' about the opportunity. She was so angry it looked like her eyes were going to pop out of her head, but the model was just staring through her, totally checked out. I could kind of relate to that feeling.

'God.' Millie crinkled her nose at the screen and then turned in a slow swivel back to me. 'What's this all about?'

'Tyra was *rooting* for her,' I said, pointing at the screen. 'And now she's pissed 'cause Tiffany basically didn't give a crap, so it's become this whole drama.'

Millie was moving her index finger in a big circle, gesturing at the TV in its entirety. 'Soph, I meant gen-er-ally,' she said, elongating the word, so that she sounded extra British. 'You know I meant generally.'

'Did you know there's such a thing as a "smize", Mil? It's like smiling . . . but you do it with your *eyes*.'

'Uh-huh . . . Did you know there's such a thing as a sun? It's like fire, only it's a big round ball in the sky.'

'There's also this thing called the "booty tooch". It's something.'

Millie halted me before I could demonstrate, raising her hands in the air and whipping her hair across her face in a violent head-turn. 'Please. You know how uncomfortable second-hand embarrassment makes me. Where's your mum? Do we need to stage some kind of intervention here?'

'She's in the garden . . . it's her new hobby.' *Obsession* might have sounded a little harsh, if true. My mother was constantly planting new flowers. Sometimes she stayed in the garden so long she forgot to eat dinner. She forgot to work, too – maybe she didn't want to – and now our garden bloomed with ten shades of strange flowers and unruly shrubs, while her commissioned projects lay in unfinished piles of fabric around the house. I think she hated being

35

indoors the same way I suddenly hated being outside. I think she hated idle moments of stitching or sketching when her brain would bring her back to that night in the warehouse, to the sound of bullets and the smell of blood. She had the garden, I had the switchblade, and I had no right to judge her obsession.

'At least one of you is getting some vitamin D.' Millie flung open the curtains and I recoiled like a vampire, flinching at the sun's invading rays. 'You'll go see-through if you get any paler.'

'I'm fine.' I was surprised at how genuine I sounded. I couldn't remember the last time I had slept properly. The slash from Luca's blade was still fresh and pulsing, and every couple of hours, my heart would do this weird thing and seize up, and then my breathing would quicken and I'd get the sudden sense I was about to die.

'Very believable,' said Millie. 'You are *not* fine. You are in deep denial. And pretending this fear doesn't exist is not beating it, it's accommodating it. And it has to stop, OK?' She had her hands on her hips. She was definitely not smizing. 'Bad things happen. And then you get over them. That's how it goes. I know this whole situation has been . . . unfortunate.'

I decided not to bother ladling out any more lies. My best friend could see right through me – even if she couldn't hear it in my voice, she'd see it on my face. I sank back into the couch. 'You know, I've been thinking lately.' That was pretty much *all* I had been doing. 'My whole family is unlucky. What's to say I'm any different from the rest of them? Did you know that my dad lost both his parents in a car accident when he was only sixteen? They were deadbeat alcoholics and one day they drunk-drove themselves into a barrier on the interstate. Jack and my dad went to live with their grandmother and *she* ended up dying of cancer, basically leaving them out on the street. My mom's dad died on her birthday and then her mom died of a broken heart a couple of years later. That's literally what they told my mom. Her heart just . . . gave up. My only uncle is a *freaking drug dealer*, who could be dead right now for all I know, and my dad's in jail for *shooting* someone . . . Sometimes it feels like I'm being circled by something that's just waiting for me to put one foot out of line. It's like it's inevitable.'

Millie unstuck her hands from her hips and sat down next to me. 'What's inevitable?'

I shrugged. 'My destruction?'

'Your *destruction*?' Her eyebrows had reached full arch height. '*Really?*'

'OK, maybe that was theatrical. But you know what I mean.'

'That is ridiculous. Seriously. So your dad had shitty parents. It happens. And his granny dying of cancer? So did mine. That's a crappy fact of life too. He and Jack were on their own from a young age and that's probably why Jack ended up dealing. We know why your dad shot Angelo Falcone. It was an accident. And if he hadn't shot him, who knows? Angelo probably would have murdered Jack. I'm sorry you don't have a large family and that all that bad stuff happened, but the universe is not against you. You're not, like, doomed, or whatever. This isn't a *Game of Thrones* episode. You're good, OK? You've come out the other side.'

'I just wish it felt like that.'

'It will. Eventually. You just have to *try*.'

'I know,' I conceded. She was right. Of course she was. I just wasn't really dealing in logic, so it was hard to see it.

'So,' she said, leaning back with a triumphant smile now she felt she had gotten through to me. I let my gaze drift back to the window now that the direct sunlight had stopped assaulting my retina. 'With all that in mind, I was—'

'Mil,' I shrieked, bounding from the couch and gluing myself to the window. Outside, a black Mercedes was crawling by my house again. *No one* drives that slow. Not even in a residential zone. 'Get your ass over here and tell me this car is not the most suspicious thing you've ever—'

'Dammit, Gracewell.' She yanked the back of my T-shirt and dragged me away from the window. 'Listen very carefully to what I'm about to say.'

'Can you just humour me and take a look—'

'Persephone Elizabeth Gracewell, *listen* to me.'

'All right,' I said, refocusing. 'I'm listening.'

She inhaled a giant breath and did a slow-blink. 'OK. Have you ever met my mum's friend, Emily?'

'The millionaire from London?'

'She *married* a millionaire,' Millie corrected. 'She's from the same estate as my mum.'

I tried to act like the distinction mattered to me. 'OK, what does she have to do with anything?'

'Trust me,' Millie said, moving close enough so I could count her freckles. 'Emily has everything to do with this.'

'I'm listening.'

'So the first thing you need to know is that Emily is a total bitch. And these days she has way more money than sense.'

'You better not be about to compare me to Emily,' I interjected.

'No, I just don't want you to feel sorry for her.'

'It already seems a little one-sided.'

'Some people are just assholes, OK?' Millie said. 'Like, one time Emily tried to get with my dad at a party, *in front of* my mum, who's supposed to be her *friend*. The last time she came to visit us, she hit on Alex. Major no-no. Do you see what I mean?'

'Um, I suppose,' I reasoned. 'But in a wider context? No. Not at all.'

'So, Emily went on this cruise a couple of years ago,' she continued. 'She likes to flaunt how mega-rich she is now – if there was a cruise ship made of gold, she'd be on it. Anyway, at one point on the cruise, which I can only imagine was all kinds of boring, she got to go out and see the dolphins close up. There was a group of them on this little speedboat and they were riding along and the dolphins got so excited they started chasing the boat. After a while, they came level with the boat and were jumping out of the water at the same speed. Emily was loving it, snapping photos and flooding her Instagram while she stood as close to the side as she could. All her captions were like "OMG best day ever", "Ahh, this one is definitely smiling at me. I think he fancies me!" and "Free Willy LOL", which is annoying because Willy was a freaking orca and you know I hate when old people overuse text abbreviations.'

Millie paused to assess my reaction.

'Right,' I said. 'So . . . this is all still very vague . . .'

'Well, you won't believe what happened next,' she said,

shaking her head. 'One of the dolphins overshot the mark. He jumped out of the water and ended up headbutting her in the face. He knocked her clean out.'

'*What?*'

Millie's eyes went impossibly large. 'Yeah.'

'Wow,' I said. 'That is really not how I saw that ending.'

'So,' she said, stepping back from me and lacing her fingers in front of her. 'What are your thoughts?'

'Was the dolphin OK?'

'Yeah, he went right back on swimming.' She grinned, before adding, 'She had to get a second nose job, though.'

'Right,' I said, still trying to figure out the point of the story. I never was that good with metaphors in English class, but this one seemed particularly obscure. 'And the reason you told me this story is because . . .'

'Because, Soph, life is unpredictable. One minute you're sipping champagne on a boat deck and laughing about how rich you are and the next minute you're getting hit in the face by a dolphin. Shit happens, OK? No matter where you are or what you're doing, you are still susceptible to the uncertainty of life. You can't just roll yourself up in bubble wrap and close off the rest of the world. My *point* is that you need to get off your ass and come back outside before we lose the tail end of this summer and get sucked into the oblivion that is senior year.'

'Well,' I said, feeling very much like I had just had my ass handed to me. 'I can't really argue with that.'

'No you cannot. The Dolphin Philosophy always prevails.' She raised her palm in the air. 'Now let's get you back to normal, OK? Up top.'

I high-fived her and she grabbed my wrist. 'Hey, where did this bandage come from? Did you cut yourself?'

Oh, yeah. That. 'Accidentally . . .' I hedged. 'I sort of fell asleep with Luca's switchblade in my hand.'

'As you do,' she deadpanned, moving her suspicious gaze from my hand to my face. 'You really need to get rid of that.'

'I will,' I lied. The thought of relinquishing it brought an uncomfortable twinge to the base of my spine. It was in my pocket even then, resting heavy and sure against my thigh. I liked it. I needed it.

'The sooner we get you out of this house the better. Tomorrow night, OK? How does bowling sound?'

'Like fresh hell.' I withdrew my hand and pulled the sleeve of my shirt over it. 'I'd rather take a dolphin to the face.'

'You should be so lucky,' she retorted. 'The movies, then?'

'Only if we can watch that one with the robot who falls in love with the human who made him.'

'Sophie,' she whined. 'You know I can't relate to non-human love stories. That's why *The Princess and the Frog* was so problematic for me. They spend way too much time as frogs.'

'Mil, if I'm going to re-enter society, I'll be damned if it's not to the backdrop of a futuristic romance that transcends both scientific engineering and biology to conquer impossible odds for true love.'

'Fine,' she conceded, with an eye-roll. 'I'll suffer this one for you.'

'Oh, cheer up. It'll be fun.' I patted her on the arm, trying to force some enthusiasm. 'Smize.'

CHAPTER SIX
THE GIRL WITH PURPLE HAIR

Millie drove us to the movie theatre in her new car, a second-hand Toyota Matrix she had been drooling over and saving for all summer. Despite the fact we almost crashed at several intersections, and she had absolutely no respect for the speed limit, we made it in one piece. I got out, feeling marginally strengthened by the fact that fate must be back on my side.

Friday night wasn't exactly the best time to go to the movies. The whole place was wedged with people and every time someone brushed against me, I jumped a little. I did my best to loosen up, but it was hard to let go completely without scoping out our surroundings every couple of minutes.

Millie and I trickled into the line at the concession stand.

'Are you getting popcorn?' she asked.

I was looking over my shoulder. I felt shivery, like something was amiss. I tried to relax. I was too aware of my heartbeat, and my palms were slicking with sweat. *Focus. Calm down.*

Millie prodded me. 'Helloooo.'

'What?' I stroked the switchblade in my pocket. I hadn't wanted to bring it with me, but the idea of going to the movie theatre had just felt so huge at the time. I needed it to keep my anxiety under control.

'Popcorn,' said Millie, snapping her fingers in front of my face. 'Full disclosure: there will be rivers of butter on my popcorn. Lakes, in fact. I'm getting popcorn with my butter, OK? Is that what you want to hear? I'll be drowning in a vat of my own buttery shame. And don't you dare look at me with those judgy eyes, Sophie Gracewell, don't you dare judge me.'

'*Moi?*' I protested, clenching and unclenching my fist around the switchblade and offering her a blithe smile. 'I would *never*. I actually think that decision is very inspired. I may even copy you.'

Millie twirled her hands. 'And *that* is why I'm the trailblazer.'

I bristled as the woman behind me brushed against my back. I stood a little straighter, and flicked my gaze over my shoulder. Not a threat. 'And what am I?' I asked Millie, keeping up with the flow of conversation while my brain whirred.

'You're the sarcastic one.'

'So you get "trailblazer" and I get "*sarcastic*"?'

'OK, then. You're the one with the little face dents.'

'I prefer the term "dimples". And that's still terrible.'

'Fine.' She studied me in quiet contemplation. 'You're . . .'

'The moron who walks herself into danger?'

'You're the moron who walks herself *out* of danger!' She clapped her hands in celebration. 'That's a good one, actually. You're slippery.'

I moved my gaze over her shoulder. A woman with plum-coloured hair was hovering across the foyer. It was cut short, styled into a severe bob with the heaviest bangs I'd ever seen. My recent love affair with *America's Next Top Model* had attuned me to hairstyles, and as far as dramatic cuts went, this one was hard to miss. It covered her eyebrows and hung low over theatrical eye make-up.

Millie noticed my distraction. 'Cute boy?' She followed my gaze. 'You're being woefully obvious.'

'See the girl with the purple hair?'

Millie turned her whole body around. 'Who? Lego-head over there?'

I pinched her. 'Stop being so obvious. I swear she's watching us.'

'She probably can't even see us through her fringe.'

'I'm serious. There's something up with her.'

Millie rolled her eyes. 'Soph, *come on.* We've been over this a hundred times. Nobody is out to get you. You're safe.'

We edged closer to the till. 'Just hear me out,' I said, still keeping an eye on the purple-haired girl. She was pacing now, looping around the theatre in a circle. If she was trying to play it cool, she was failing; I was on to her. 'She was in the parking lot the same time we were. She was staring at us so hard I thought she was going to hit on you. Then she was standing behind us the whole time we were getting our tickets, and now she's lingering here but she hasn't bought one thing.'

Millie was gaping at me. 'Soph, has it really gotten this bad . . .'

'I know what you're going to tell me. You're going to tell me it's a movie theatre and there's loads of people here and that's the whole point and I'm being paranoid . . .'

She nodded along with me.

'But Mil, the more I think about it, I'm pretty sure she was driving a black Mercedes in the parking lot. That's the same type of car that's been driving by my house!'

Millie opened her mouth like she was going to say something. She stopped, closed it, and swallowed. She sighed. 'OK, well, what do you want to do about this? Do you want me to go over there and talk to her? Would that make you feel better?'

I thumbed the closed blade in my pocket. 'Just watch her. Let's see what she does.'

'OK,' she resolved, looking around. 'I don't even know where she's gone.'

'She's by the windows over there. Don't look now. She's doing something on her phone.'

'Right, well, just forget about it for now. I bet she's just waiting for a date, or an adequate hairdresser.'

The couple in front of us moved off. We took our place at the counter. Millie ordered our food and we made our way to the screen, carrying obnoxiously large buckets of popcorn.

I waited for Purple Hair to follow us in, but she didn't. I kept my other hand in my pocket, clenched around the closed switchblade. Calmness trickled over me. Deep down I knew I was just being paranoid, but outings like this would help it ease over time. I just had to push myself. After a while my heart rate settled to a steady pace. I popped a handful of popcorn into my mouth and revelled in the taste of butter on my tongue. The lights dimmed and the screen flickered to life.

Afterwards, we used the restroom because the movie had, against all odds, managed to emotionally obliterate Millie.

'You don't have to look so smug about it,' she told my reflection, as she scrubbed the mascara tracks from her face.

'You wept,' I said, triumph stretching the smile on my face. 'You wept like a *baby*.'

'Oh, excuse me for caring about the love story. You didn't tell me she was going to have to murder him in the end.' She sniffed. 'I mean, she *dismantled* him.'

'Yeah, well, sometimes robots go bad. Besides, I thought you said you couldn't connect with non-human love stories anyway, so why are you getting all weepy about it?'

'You didn't tell me he'd be a *hot* robot! I was picturing the gold guy from *Star Wars*.'

I laughed and the feeling was an airy tickle in my chest – something I hadn't felt in a while. I wasn't thinking about the switchblade or the warehouse or the paranoia. I was thinking about my best friend and how funny she was without even meaning it, and I might have kept laughing if we hadn't run into the purple-haired girl the second we left the bathroom.

She was hovering in the foyer, like she had never left. Suspicion surged inside me – uncomfortable and suffocating. My throat went tight. She was standing by the windows, slumped casually against the wall, her phone in her hands, but her gaze was roving.

'I see her,' said Millie, under her breath. 'So before you start freaking out, don't. Her movie's clearly just finished, and we're going to the car anyway, so just ignore it.'

God, was I that obvious?

I side-glanced at her as we shuffled by. At closer range I noted that she wasn't particularly scary. She was young and short – about my height – and she chewed on her lip with a self-consciousness that didn't exactly terrify me. She was on the phone, and it looked like she was having an argument. Maybe she had been stood up. Maybe she had been waiting this whole time for a date or a friend. God, she was *so young*. I was suddenly highly embarrassed by my jumpiness. I could feel my skin flooding with patches of red. What the hell was wrong with me? It was worse than being afraid of my own shadow. *She* was probably more afraid of *me* at this point. I had been staring at her non-stop for most of the evening. And I was the one with a knife in my pocket.

'I think *I'm* freaking *her* out,' I whispered to Millie.

'Oh, you definitely are.'

In the parking lot Millie had to dig through her purse to find her keys. 'Why do they make them so easy to lose in there?' she huffed. 'I swear, if this isn't the most annoying thing about driving I don't know what is.'

'Just put your key in a separate pocket or something.'

'Great idea. If you could just mail that to two hours ago that would be great.' She dropped her bag and crouched beside it as she rifled through it.

The lot was almost empty now. Our movie had been the

last to finish and the remaining cars were thinning out, leaving open spaces lit up in circles from the street lamps.

Purple Hair was jogging towards her car. When she stopped, she turned in my direction. We stared at each other for a second before she looked away. She leant against her car, just like I was, and started examining her fingernails. I watched her in sulky silence. Her Mercedes had black rims. After a couple of seconds, she flicked her gaze up again and started walking towards me. I felt myself tense. Either she was going to yell at me for staring at her or admit to her stalkery.

Millie sprang up, key in hand. 'Suck it, universe!'

Purple Hair, who was less than twenty feet away now, froze mid-step and swivelled abruptly, marching back towards her car. She flung the door open and jumped in.

What the hell? Was I going insane? Was I supposed to know her?

Was she a Falcone?

I shook myself out of my delusions before they took me over completely. Most of this was in my head. *Focus. Breathe.* We got in the car and Millie revved the engine, humming to herself as she adjusted the air conditioner. The black Mercedes was behind us as we made our way out of the lot, I decided not to say anything this time. We drove with the radio on and I almost bit through my fingers.

'Weird,' Millie said finally, when we were turning into Cedar Hill fifteen minutes later. 'I swear that Mercedes has been behind us the whole way.'

'I told you!' I flooded with triumph. 'She's stalking us!'

'What?' she said, narrowing her eyes at the rear-view

mirror. 'Is that Lego-head?'

'She's been behind us the whole way.'

'Huh.' Millie flicked an indicator at the last minute and turned up a side street. The Mercedes followed. 'You know what? I think you're right. There's something up with this chick. Let's see if we can lose her.'

'Mil, don't do anyth—'

Millie slammed on the brakes and turned on to another side street with a deafening squeal. I was thrown, shrieking, against the side of the car. She crushed the accelerator and we sped down the street, taking a last-minute turn on to another residential row of houses and zigzagging around the neighbourhood.

After twenty minutes of what Millie called 'stealth driving' around Cedar Hill, we doubled back and pulled up outside my house. I got out, feeling a passing urge to kiss the pavement.

'Told ya we'd lose Lego-head!' She was cackling to herself. She didn't really feel threatened. Suspicious maybe, but only mildly, and I could tell the chase was for my benefit. She offered me a brace-filled grin as she pulled away. 'See ya tomorrow for phase two of our rehabilitation plan!'

My mother greeted me at the door. 'How was it?' Her tone was anxious but her expression was going for enthusiasm. 'Was it fun? Did you have fun?'

I felt a sudden urge to hug her, but I stifled it. I didn't want to freak her out. 'It was good,' I said. 'I had fun.' I kept the memory of the black Mercedes wiped from my expression.

She smiled, a whisper of relief in her response. 'I'm so glad, sweetheart.'

I wondered how long she had been watching the driveway, waiting for me to come home. 'What did you get up to?' I asked. 'Did you see the girls?'

She waved her hand around as I shut the door behind us. 'I didn't get around to it,' she said airily. 'I did some gardening instead. Watched some TV. Did you eat?'

'Popcorn. A mountain of it.'

She laughed, ruffling my hair. 'Well, you're definitely back to your old self!'

I kept the threads of panic bound up in my throat. 'Yup, I'm feeling much better.'

She rested her hand on my shoulder and I touched my head against hers. She smelt of lavender and peppermint. We went into the kitchen, both of us walking carefully on eggshells.

That night I lay awake in bed imagining a car rumbling down my street, every hour, like clockwork.

CHAPTER SEVEN

THE SHADOW IN THE GARDEN

I was lost in a thick dreaming fog when Nic's voice floated into my consciousness.

'Sophie?'

The sound perforated the vision, filling up the endless space around me.

'Are you here?'

The Nic in my nightmare wasn't speaking to me. He was standing, like he always did, over the dying figure of my uncle, as blood coated the floor beneath them. I was across the blackness, leaning over Luca, with my hands pressed tight against his torso. He looked the same as he always did, as I had come to remember him even in my waking moments – paper-white and utterly still. I knew every shadow on his face, the quirk of his lips, the length of his lashes. I stared at him every night in this dream while his blood lapped around my hands. When I tried to call out, the sound always vanished into a puff of nothingness. And Nic? Nic never spoke to me. He wasn't speaking now, either. He wasn't even facing me.

'Sophie? I'm sorry, I know it's late.'

But still, that voice, so insistent, so familiar . . . Where was it coming from?

'Sophie?'

I sat up in bed, half expecting Nic to burst out of my closet. I grabbed my phone and flung open my curtains, peering into the garden. Below me, Nic was lit up by the sensor light above the kitchen window. He was waiting for me with all the innocence of someone who didn't know any better. But Nic did know better, and being in my garden at 1.12 a.m. meant he was way out of bounds.

My window was already open. 'Nic?'

I was still groggy with sleep, halfway between incredulity and reality, and my heart and my head were doing a thousand flip-flops a minute.

He raised his hands, palms facing outwards. 'I know,' he said. 'I'm breaking all the rules.'

'The only rule,' I hissed back, conscious not to speak too loudly and wake my mother. Since she hadn't shooed him out of the garden already, she wasn't downstairs.

'Come down?' he said, his eyebrows lifting.

'What's happened?' I asked, the dregs of sleep leaving me. 'Has someone been hurt?' A sea of possibilities rushed through my mind.

'No,' he said, lowering his voice to a less audible whisper. 'It's nothing like that. No one is hurt.'

I could almost hear the *yet* in the pause that followed.

'Oh.' I hadn't realized how hard my heart had been thumping until it dulled again. 'Then what is it? What's going on?'

His smile was tight. 'Can you just come down, please? I'm starting to feel self-conscious.'

I knew I shouldn't. That was a no-brainer. But it's hard to avoid something when it's right in front of you . . .

'Stop weighing it up, Sophie. Just come down, I have to talk to you.'

His expression, steeped in moonlight, held a level of anxiety I hadn't come to associate with Nic. He was rattled. Something had happened.

'Fine,' I conceded, curiosity and something else – something mutinous – pushing me from the window. 'But only to see that you're all right.'

I grabbed the switchblade and shoved it in the pocket of my sweatpants. It settled me, and as I descended the stairs with light footfall I relaxed in the feeling of it thumping against my leg.

The night was surprisingly cold. Now that I was close to Nic I could see just how jumpy he really was. There were rims of darkness underneath his eyes, and he shuffled uncomfortably on his feet as we stood apart from one another.

'What's going on?' I asked.

'I miss you,' he said in one long, heavy sigh. 'I hate not knowing what you're doing or if you're OK . . . after everything that happened. It doesn't feel right.'

The more I studied him, the more dishevelled he appeared. His hair was more messy than tousled, curling strands brushing across his forehead and dipping into his eyes. There were days of stubble shadowing his jawline. 'This is what we agreed,' I said softly. 'This is the right thing.'

The only thing.

'I don't like it, Sophie,' he repeated. 'There should be another way.'

How easily he could compartmentalize everything – separate the girl he wanted from the family she came from. For me, everything came in one big jumble. 'There isn't another way,' I told him. 'And if there was, it probably wouldn't be the right one. You can't just come around here, Nic. It makes it harder for both of us.'

He was scrutinizing me. Eventually he dropped his shoulders and his fists went limp at his sides. 'So this is really what you want?'

I knew I should say 'yes', but somehow I couldn't. 'I don't know,' I told him truthfully. 'I just know I don't want to be afraid any more. I don't want my mother to be afraid either . . .'

He nodded, a frown twisting on his lips. 'But you're not afraid of me.'

'Maybe not of you,' I said, feeling out my answer. 'But I'm afraid of what you've done. Where you come from. You know that.'

He raked his hands through his hair. He seemed so out of it, so tired.

'I've never seen you like this,' I said, pulling back.

'Stress,' he said, exhaustion softening his voice. 'I'm stressed.'

'Stress?' I repeated, studying him.

He raised his face towards the sky, to the blanket of stars

that stretched overhead. 'Yeah,' he said. 'Family stuff.'

'And you never think about leaving it behind? For college? For normality?' *For good?*

He simply shook his head. I remembered his mother's words: *He would never choose you over his family*. It was true, and I knew it. Nic would never leave the family, not for me, not for him, not for anything. The only way out was in a coffin.

When he spoke again, his gaze was no longer on the stars and his voice was barely more than a whisper. 'Do you remember the last time we were here together?'

'Everything was different then.'

'You let me kiss you,' he said, his gaze unwavering.

'Even though you shouldn't have.'

I felt the warmth of his breath in his response. 'I never could follow the rules when it came to you, Sophie.'

'We should have followed them, Nic.'

He shut his eyes tight, inhaling sharply. 'Don't say that. Please.'

'It's the truth.'

He fell silent, and I felt compelled to fill up the space.

'You moved house,' I said, changing the subject. I was trying to ignore the intimacy that still lingered between us, trying to remind myself why I should be upstairs in bed, away from him.

'Did it surprise you?'

'No, it's not that. It's just strange to think of the Priestly mansion empty again after it was so . . . full of life.'

'Yeah,' he said, clearing his throat. He stuffed his hands in his pockets, and in a flicker he was boyish again, a grin pushing against his cheekbones. 'Do you miss me, Sophie?'

I looked away from him, at the new flowerbeds blooming in the darkness – my mother's anchor to her sanity. An anchor she needed because of this boy and his family. 'I don't want to talk about this,' I said quietly. 'Please, Nic.'

He flinched. 'OK,' he said, his voice small and quiet now – barely as audible as the branches rustling around us. 'Look, I know I shouldn't have come here tonight, but I was worried about you. I wanted to see you, and sometimes when I get an idea in my head it sort of has to play itself out. It doesn't mean I'm not still aware of everything that's happened, all the pain you've suffered because of me. Because of my weakness.'

I could almost pinpoint it – that feeling of falling back into him. Already, I had inched closer. I could sense his warmth pressing against the air, his eyes the only thing I could focus on. It was dangerous. It was the opposite of what I was supposed to be doing. 'If we can only be together at night, hidden like this, whispering so no one can hear us, then we shouldn't be together at all.'

'There's always the future, though.' His lips parted, his breath hitching as the idea took over him.

I pressed my thumb into my palm and felt the dull sting of the blade's cut, trying to clear my mind. 'There will never be a future where my father didn't kill your father. Where you didn't try and kill my uncle.' My voice hardened. 'After I screamed at you not to do it.'

He shook his head angrily. 'There *will* be a future, when this is all behind us.'

'Behind *you*, maybe,' I told him, stepping back so that my

back grazed the stray branches of a bush. 'But not behind me.'

He came towards me, pushing the warmth back into the air. 'Do you want to talk about it, then? I'll talk about it until my voice runs out. Do you want me to tell you I'm sorry a thousand times? I *am* sorry that it hurt you and that it changed the way you look at me. I hate that you look away when I try to get your attention. I hate that you pull away from me when I get close to you. I hate that I can see the moment when you remember your uncle and your voice turns cold. I hate that what my family stands for drove a wedge between us. I hate that that's how we were brought together. I hate that I'll always question whether it would have worked if we had been from the same world. I hate that I hurt you, but I had to do what I did. I can't apologize for that. Jack would have killed Luca. He would have killed me. It was about my family. It was about protection. It's no different to what your dad did.'

'What the hell does that mean?' I reeled from his final words. 'You can't compare the two like it will get you off the hook or something. You know what my dad did was an accident. That was different.'

'Was it?'

Had the wind stopped blowing? Suddenly I was back at Felice's house, staring into Valentino's cold cerulean eyes, listening to him question everything I knew about my father, about his intentions, about his *soul*.

Venom dripped from my answer. 'What's that supposed to mean?'

A shadow flickered across Nic's face, bleeding deeper into

the pools beneath his eyes. He ground his jaw and swallowed the words forming in his throat.

My voice went deathly quiet. 'Do you have something to say?'

'Never mind.' He shook his head. 'I'm tired. I didn't mean to take it out on you.'

'You're not the only one who's tired, Nic.'

'I know,' he said, switching back to the Nic I was used to. Calm, quiet, focused. He lifted his arm as if he was going to reach out to me, but then caught it in mid-air and curled his hand into a fist again. 'It's hard seeing you and knowing it can't last. I just . . . I had to.'

'Yeah.'

'I guess we can't go on pretending the warehouse didn't happen.'

I shrugged. 'He survived. You all did. For that, at least, I'm thankful.'

Nic unclenched his teeth. 'Do you know where he is?'

'What?'

'Do you know who's hiding Jack?' he repeated, his voice softer. Honeyed. As if softness could ever mask his meaning.

I blanched. 'Nic, this is not something I'd ever discuss with you.'

Something happened – so quick I almost missed it – but his chin snapped up, and his eyes flashed with something. 'Just give me something, Soph, so we can be prepared. Please.'

'No,' I cautioned. 'Don't put me in this position.'

'Is he with the Marinos? That's what Valentino thinks. But I said there's no way they'd take him in. It's Eric Cain, isn't it?

He's got connections with the Irish mob in Boston. Or are there more? Has the Golden Triangle Gang re-banded?'

'Is that why you came here?' I asked. 'To sweet-talk me into revealing my uncle's hiding place?'

'No,' he said quickly. 'Of course not.'

'Then why ask when you know how sour it will make things?'

'Because if we don't know who's hiding him, we don't know who might be coming for us.'

'Has your family been following me?' I asked, as the purple-haired girl dropped into my mind. 'Do you think I'll lead you to him or something?'

'What are you talking about?' he countered, bewilderment creasing his forehead. 'Of course we haven't. I promised you we'd never do that again.'

'And yet here you are, still trying to get information out of me!'

Nic muttered an Italian curse. 'Come on, Sophie. I was just asking.'

I turned from him. 'I'm going inside now.'

'Wait.' He skirted around me, his frame suddenly wide and tall in the doorway. 'This kind of went off-track.'

'Did it?' I asked, crossing my arms in front of me. 'Or did you just forget to be less obvious about it this time?'

He took a step, and before I knew it, his hands were on my arms. His shoulders slumped, defeated. 'I'm an idiot. I'm the world's biggest idiot. I just wanted to see you.'

I knew if I stayed this close to him for another minute, if I let my defences drop any further, then *I'd* be the world's biggest idiot. 'Goodnight,' I said, sliding out from beneath his grip.

By the time I'd shut and locked the kitchen door behind me, he was gone and the sensor light had flickered out. I pressed my forehead against the window and wondered how badly he had wanted to see me tonight and how deeply he needed to know about Jack. Had it been desperation or long-ing that drove him to me?

CHAPTER EIGHT

THE MANSION

The next phase of my mildly successful social rehabilitation was to meet Millie at the diner after her morning shift ended. I had texted her about Nic's garden visit right after it happened. The entire incident was, in my best friend's measured response, a 'giant no-no', a mistake that necessitated 'further and immediate action'. I wasn't sure how I was going to get the Falcones out of my head, but I was glad she was willing to help me.

It was surprisingly difficult to navigate the familiar streets of Cedar Hill, counting the breaths as I heaved them out, trying to make myself look ahead instead of at the pavement.

I clutched the switchblade, trying not to think of my mother who was still at home, tethered to our house. I tried not to replay the watery smiles, the shifting gazes, the way she kept looking past me for the possibility of danger.

At the end of Lockwood Avenue, I stopped walking and peered up at the turrets of the old Priestly house. The driveway was empty and a chain hung around the gates, linking them closed. I pushed them as far apart as they would go and slipped through. I still had time to kill, and even now, after all this time, there was something about the house that called to me. It was time to say goodbye to it for good.

Stray leaves littered the porch. I had to stop myself from brushing them away. They would only gather again. The back garden was as it had been during my last visit. The grass was almost as tall as my knees, and chunks of old fountain and wooden tables were strewn across the lawn. I pressed my nose against the patio doors, studying the kitchen. The last time I was here Valentino was sketching at the table, Felice was pontificating about an Italian murderer and I was hovering in the middle of a lethal family rivalry without knowing it. The family crest was hanging somewhere else now.

I stumbled backwards. My throat had grown tight, and out of habit I clutched at my ribs. I couldn't tell if my visit was helping or not, but the sudden sense of closure was overwhelming.

I circled the house again. In the driveway I stared up at the old turrets, feeling a stirring sadness in my bones. It felt peculiar, standing alone in the grounds of a place that had brought such great passion and grave danger into my life. Jack's dealings with the Falcones were forged long ago in the underbelly of Chicago, but my time with the Falcones had taken root here, in the driveway of this lonely old mansion.

I pulled Luca's switchblade from my pocket and rotated it

in my hand. Underneath, the jagged cut in the centre of my palm glowed red. This knife was the last piece of them. I could leave it here with the rest of my memories, but somehow it didn't seem right. To drop it in a place they would never revisit seemed like cheating. I would return it to Luca, or at least to somewhere he would find it.

I stuffed it back in the pocket of my shorts and turned for the diner, trailing my fingers along the tree bark as I retreated down the driveway.

I saw it then. Outside the black gates, halfway down the other side of the street, was the black Mercedes. I craned my neck and stood on my tiptoes. Black rims! There was no mistaking it; the car was back and it was getting bolder, following me around in broad daylight.

I marched towards the end of the driveway. Down the street the car door was flung open and the girl with purple hair emerged on to the footpath. She was wiry but small, wearing low-rise jeans and a black tank top. *A Falcone*, I thought. There were definite shades of Elena Genovese-Falcone in her. She had to be one of them, a spy probably, which only added another lie to the pile Nic had built already.

This had gone on long enough.

I squeezed myself through the gap in the chained gates again. It was harder this time because I had an audience, and I was vaguely embarrassed of my squishing cheeks as I slid them against the metal. My attempts at intimidating her wouldn't exactly thrive after my compacted-chipmunk display. She waited, propped against her car as I surged towards her. I might not have had any official karate training, but I was damn scrappy – if I needed to, I could probably kick her in the face at least once if she tried to come at me.

'Persephone!' A shout rang out behind me. I almost stopped but I registered the voice in time. Mrs Bailey, Cedar Hill's resident gossip merchant, was not about to mess up my showdown with whoever this nosy Mercedes chick was.

Purple Hair actually looked taken aback as I stomped towards her, but still, she made no effort to approach me. She simply waited, and the arrogance of it just made me angrier. *Get out of my life,* I wanted to yell. It would be easier to say it to her than to Nic, because I couldn't look at him without remembering the intensity in his kisses, or the way he looked at me. But this girl was just a straight-up pain in my ass and I would have no trouble telling her exactly where to go.

I could hear Mrs Bailey bustling her way up the street behind me.

'Persephone Gracewell!' The wail was shriller this time – half car alarm, half dying cat – and somehow, *somehow*, it stopped me.

I skidded to a halt.

Purple Hair peered around me, at the commotion. From her vantage point, she couldn't see Mrs Bailey and Mrs Bailey couldn't see her, and I was stuck in between them both, wondering which was the greater annoyance in my life.

'Mrs Bailey,' I laboured, turning around. 'I'm kind of in the middle of something.'

Mrs Bailey was pottering up the street as fast as she could. She was shiny with sweat. Her cropped hair was flopping into her eyes and her dress was bunching around her ankles, threatening to trip her.

She grabbed on to my arm, gasping for air like she was drowning. 'There. You. Are.'

I mentally ran through the checklist for CPR in my head, just in case. I didn't particularly like Mrs Bailey, but I wasn't above trying to revive her if she collapsed at my feet. 'Is everything OK?'

She removed her grip from me and clutched at her heart. 'I've. Been. Looking. For. You. For weeks!'

I was still acutely aware of the girl behind me. Time was of the essence. I was about to hand out a much-needed lesson in Inappropriate Snoopery. After all, I was the expert. 'Can you hang on just a sec, Mrs Bailey?'

'Why? Where are you going?'

When I turned around, Purple Hair was back in her car. Mrs Bailey blinked over my shoulder at apparent nothingness.

Crap. I started towards the Mercedes. 'Hey!' I yelled. 'Wait!'

She revved the engine and pulled away from the curb. I tried to run after her but I fell short, stumbling and panting. 'Hang on! I want to talk to you!'

The car sped off down the street, squealing around a faraway bend, and I had to swallow the string of curses welling up in my throat.

I doubled back towards Mrs Bailey, already feeling fed up with her company. She had the *worst* timing.

'Who was that in the car?' she asked.

Count to five. Calm down. Do not punch her. 'I don't know.'

Her face changed, and she remembered why she had stopped me. 'You haven't been at work in weeks, Persephone. I've barely seen your mother. I thought you were an apparition when I saw you just now.'

'Well, I had an accident,' I told her. 'I'm sure you heard?'

She cocked her head, running her gaze along my stiffened frame. She lingered over the faint swelling around my eyes, stared for too long at the faded bruises near my jaw. 'You look dreadful,' she informed me.

'I've missed this.'

'You look like you have jaundice.'

'Yeah, well you know how it is . . .' I trailed off, gesturing at myself and searching for the words I needed. 'One minute you're standing on the top of the stairs playing on your phone, and the next minute you're hurtling down them, toppling over yourself . . . and just generally . . . hitting your face off stuff . . . repeatedly . . . until it bruises . . . a lot . . .' I flashed a sheepish smile. *That ought to do it.*

Mrs Bailey ignored the flimsiness of the lie, waving it away on the wind. 'What a terrible business, Persephone.'

I shrugged haplessly. 'I bruise like a peach.'

'Indeed,' she muttered.

'Was there something else?' I asked.

She was staring at me – at the old bruises around my jaw. I had tried to cover them with make-up, but clearly I had failed. My skin was still pretty Simpson-esque. I smoothed my hair down and brought it in front of my ears so that it fell around my face – a fashionable yeti.

'Have you been keeping to yourself, Persephone?'

'I should go,' I said. 'I'm supposed to meet Millie.' I side-stepped around her, but she tugged at my arm, pulling me back.

'I wanted to say something to you.' She started fidgeting with the folds in her dress. 'I wanted to tell you that if you were feeling upset about . . . well, about anything, perhaps I could help. I'm going to church tomorrow morning. It's a good place to find comfort.'

The surprise inside me swelled. 'Thanks,' I offered, aiming for politeness. 'I'll give it some thought.'

*

I was almost at the diner when Millie called me. 'Hey, I was thinking I would just meet you at your house. There's no need for you to come to the diner.'

'I'm pretty much here,' I told her. I crossed the street, leaving the library behind me and scanning the diner lot. She was standing outside, her purse on her shoulder, her phone pressed to her ear. 'I can see you!'

'Oh.' I watched her face fall. 'OK, then . . . listen, before you freak out—'

'Mil,' I interrupted her. 'Is that what I think it is?'

I was across the street, and she was staring at me, and I was staring at the corner of the lot, where a black SUV was facing the diner.

'Ehhh.' She followed my gaze, not that she needed to, since she was clearly already aware of its presence. 'No?'

'You've got to be kidding me.'

'Just ignore them, Soph. Seriously. The goal is to cut contact, remember?'

'They're outside my diner!'

Millie had started unlocking her car and was gesturing at me to join her. But I was making strides towards the SUV. The window buzzed down before I had a chance to slam my fist against it. Dom poked his head out. Unlike Nic, he was the picture of health. His shiny hair was thick and slicked back, and his skin was smooth and olive, like he had just been on a relaxing two-week holiday in the Caribbean.

'Gracewell. Nice day, isn't it?'

'What the hell are you doing here?'

I was distracted by a moving blur behind Dom's head. Gino ducked around his brother and continued his manic waving. 'Hi, Sophie. How are the ribs?'

I rehinged my jaw. It was hard to know whether he meant to be rude or inquisitive with his question, but either way, I wasn't impressed. 'Fine, Gino. Now answer the question.'

'No can do,' said Dom. 'But don't worry, it doesn't involve you.'

'My family owns this diner.'

'OK,' said Dom, cocking his head. 'In that case, I suppose it involves you slightly. But not directly.'

Well. This added a whole new layer to the timing and strangeness of Nic's visit. It was getting harder to believe he had just wanted to see me.

Gino was tapping out a rhythm on the dashboard with his fingers, but I couldn't hear any music inside the car.

'Don't stress about it,' said Dom. He had stopped paying me any attention and had taken his phone out to play a game on it. Hint received. I tried to see around them, into the back, to check if they had weapons, or just for a clue as to what the hell they were doing there. Surely it wasn't just for Jack. He wasn't about to come strolling into Gracewell's in the middle of the day. My uncle was dumb, but no one was *that* dumb. 'Unless you have Jack Gracewell in your pocket,' Dom droned without looking up, 'you can take off.'

'Shouldn't you be off drugging and kidnapping someone,

Dom? I know how you like to do that.' I imagined throttling him and the thought made me feel warm and fuzzy inside.

He bared his teeth at me. 'Careful now, Gracewell.'

My cheeks started to burn. A hand brushed my shoulder and I turned to find Millie beside me. 'They've been here all week,' she said. 'I was waiting for the right time to tell you.'

That got Dom's attention. He flicked his gaze up. 'Millie,' he offered, with a curt nod. Gino was still tapping on the dashboard, his chin jutting in and out with the rhythm.

'Dom,' she hissed. 'You're looking greasy as ever.'

'Still juvenile, I see,' he returned. He glanced at his phone again, drawing his finger across the screen and flicking at something in the game he was playing.

'Shut up, Dom,' I said, jumping to Millie's defence.

'So snappy now she knows we can't touch her,' he muttered to Gino.

'Let's just go. Let them have their secrets.' Millie tugged me away. I went willingly. Dom's aftershave was overpowering and his attitude was making me want to punch him. 'Oh, and, boys?' Millie shouted over her shoulder. The window was already buzzing up, but they definitely heard her when she shouted, '*Vaffanculo!*'

'You've been brushing up on your Italian, Mil?'

'I got an app,' she said, opening her car door and smiling as she slid in. 'I knew it would come in handy.'

We pulled out of the lot and I watched the SUV sit motionless as it hovered across from the diner, waiting for something. So they had one car at the diner and one car trailing me. And one boy popping up in my back garden. *What the hell are they up to? What secrets do they think I have?*

69

'So are you ready for the next phase?' Millie asked. 'Do you have the switchblade with you?'

'Yes . . .' Hesitantly at first, I pulled it out of my pocket.

'So I was reading up about this, and we have to get rid of it, but in, like, a symbolic way. The switchblade is really the last thing you have that connects you to the Falcones, right? So when you leave that behind you, you'll be emotionally distancing yourself from all the pain they caused you. Are you with me?'

'Uh-huh . . .'

'So traditionally you're supposed to burn these things, like, in a ritual or something, but I googled it and you can't really burn a knife.'

'Did you really have to google that?'

'What you *can* do,' she said, ignoring me, 'is throw it in a lake where it'll never be found again. And then it will be gone and hopefully some of the memories and stuff will go with it. I know it's a long shot but it can work for some people, and since you can't really risk going to therapy or whatever, I think it's worth a try.'

I stared at the switchblade, at its grooves and flourishes that had become so familiar to me. At the name that I read at least ten times every day. 'I don't want to throw it in a lake, Mil.'

Millie slammed on the brakes and the car came skidding to a stop. 'Are you serious? Come on, Soph. You know it's got to go. You cut yourself with it. You're too dependent on it.'

'It's not that,' I told her. 'I just think I should return it to him. It has value. It's a sentimental thing.'

'Pfff, and you think Luca Falcone is sentimental?'

I held it up to the sunlight and watched it reflect in a

hundred different directions. 'I do, actually.'

'Fine,' she said, pulling the most illegal U-turn she possibly could. 'Let's go and give it to his idiot brothers, then.'

'No! Are you crazy? Then they'll know he set me free!'

'Oh yeah.' She started manoeuvring the car back around again, taking advantage of the quiet street to pull another tragic turn. 'Well, then?'

'The mausoleum,' I said. 'Mrs Bailey mentioned going to church earlier and it got me thinking about the Falcones and their beliefs. Their father is buried in Graceland Cemetery. If I leave it there, then one of them will find it eventually.'

'Ah,' said Millie, a smile brightening her features. 'Leave it in the grave. I like it.'

'You do?' Relief flooded me. Sometimes it was difficult to tell whether my thoughts were rational or completely insane.

'And,' she added, 'by traipsing through a graveyard, we can get a nice little gander at where you'll end up if you don't cut Nic and his family *out of your life*!'

'Mil, can I ask you something?'

'Sure.' She turned out of Cedar Hill and we started heading towards the open road.

'And please be honest.'

'I am a pillar of integrity.'

'Are you or are you not reading a Dr Phil book right now?'

'That man is a saint, Sophie Gracewell. A damn saint.'

A laugh bubbled out of me. 'The things you do for me.'

'Tell me about it,' she sighed. She revved the engine and the car sped up, setting a steady course for the cemetery.

CHAPTER NINE
THE CEMETERY

Graceland Cemetery was enormous; almost one hundred and twenty acres of constructed landscape that had been growing since 1860. Now it was a Who's Who of Chicago's most important figures. We got the Falcone mausoleum's location from the main office and chose the most direct route to the lake at the north end of the cemetery. It was bordered by clumps of shrubs and weeping trees. Along the edges, the water was dotted with elaborate stone mausoleums with plaques etched in bronze above them. Some of the names were familiar to me; that's how I knew we were getting close. We stalled in criminal territory – between the Marinos and the Genoveses – and I pulled out the map again.

'Crime really does pay,' said Millie, releasing a low whistle.

'The question is, which of these Mafia families would I have to marry into to get a sarcophagus?'

We stopped at the inked circle on the map and Millie pointed at something in the trees. 'I bet it's right on the lake. Prime cemetery real estate. Classic Falcone, eh?'

We made our way along the hidden path. When the branches of overgrown trees tapered away and the way widened, we found ourselves standing on the edge of the lake. There, secluded by the surrounding trees, and poised along the waterfront, was the Falcone mausoleum.

'Holy crap,' muttered Millie. 'How many gangsters are in this thing?'

The mausoleum was a gargantuan structure made of unblemished white stone. On either side of the main chamber, decorative Roman columns marked a small square courtyard filled with hundreds of long-stemmed red roses.

Two weeping angels guarded the entrance to the mausoleum and above the double bronze doors, the Falcone crest had been erected. Thick block letters were etched into the stone:

CASA DI FALCONE
LA FAMIGLIA PRIMA DI TUTTO

We stood, dwarfed, in front of it.

I pulled the switchblade from my pocket. 'Should I leave it on the steps?'

'I guess.' Millie frowned. 'It could get stolen, though.'

'We can't break in,' I said. 'Look at those doors.'

She made her way up the steps and started jiggling the

horseshoe handles. With a deafening thud, the door yielded, and she heaved it open, her mouth dropping into a perfect O as she swivelled to face me.

I sprinted up the steps. 'Oh my God!'

'We're breaking in!'

'We're going to get in so much trouble!'

'OK, wait.' Millie composed herself. 'Maybe you should go in first with the switchblade and put it somewhere. I'll keep watch, then when you come out, we'll swap, so I can see what it's like inside.'

I was already slipping inside. My pulse was racing and I couldn't wait any longer. The darkness was pulling me in.

Millie closed the door behind me. It thumped against the stone, sealing me off from the outside world. There was a sudden absence of warmth, and a staleness in the air. I felt peculiar, as though I was not only stepping into a tomb but into the past as well.

CHAPTER TEN

THE MAUSOLEUM

I waited for my eyes to adjust to the dimness. At the end of the passageway, a crescent-shaped stained-glass window sprinkled rays along the ground. At my feet, sparkling shades of blues, greens and reds streaked towards me. On either side of me, tombs were inlaid into the marble like drawers, with stately black handles on either side. They were all marked with a simple plaque, engraved with gold lettering. A corresponding Roman numeral accompanied each name on a separate line.

I brushed my fingers over the inscriptions as I shuffled along, listening to my footfall against the stone floor.

A heavy bronze door had been pushed open at the end of the passageway. The room beyond was dusky, illuminated by a handful of errant rays coming from the window behind me.

I froze in the doorway.

Someone was sitting on a marble bench in the middle of the room. He had his back to me – facing towards another wall of tombs, where Angelo Falcone's inscription seemed to glow brighter than the others.

Like a statue cursed to life, Luca turned to face me.

'Oh.' That was all I could come up with. Seeing him again, alive and so close, his blue eyes blazing in the dimness, caught me completely off guard. Something was snaking around my stomach, clenching and unclenching, as the memory of our last moments together came flooding back.

'Sophie,' he said with unexpected casualness. 'What brings you to my family's grave?'

He remained seated, his hands resting on black jeans. His face was still paler than it should have been, but he sat straight with shoulders squared, which made him seem tall and strong, as he had been before. *Before I had my hands pressed against the wound in his side.*

I cleared my throat. 'Um, hello.'

He let the silence linger, watching me. I fixed my attention on his boots – shining silver buckles gleamed across black leather. The boots of a soldier.

'I was just . . .' What was I just? 'I thought I'd come by and . . .'

I snapped my head up, searching his face for the answer. His eyebrows lifted, disappearing under strands of black hair. 'You were just . . . ?' he prompted.

I pulled myself away from the memories, from the past. Wasn't that the whole point of my being there? To forget. *The switchblade.* I fished it out of my pocket and held it between us. 'I came to give you this.'

He flicked his gaze over it, slow, appraising. His brows drew together. 'How did you know I'd be here?'

'I didn't,' I said. 'I was just going to leave it outside somewhere you would find it. But then the door was unlocked and I thought—'

'You thought you'd trespass into my family's inner sanctum.'

My cheeks were getting hot. I brought my hair around my face to cover them. 'Something like that . . .'

He stood up and came towards me. He wore his injury well, but it changed the way he carried himself, dipping him slightly to one side. I could smell his aftershave and see the small lines underneath his eyes. Did he know how well I knew his face now? It was burnt into my brain from that night. I knew the length and thickness of his lashes. I knew the ones near the corner of his eye were pale, while the rest were jet black. I knew the line of his cheekbone, and where it curved above his jaw. I knew too much.

Luca brought his fingers to his lips, pulling my attention to the small scar above them. 'You're telling me you came all the way to Graceland Cemetery to give me back my knife?' He was trying to find the lie in my words.

'It's an important knife.'

'It is.'

'And I shouldn't really have it.'

He plucked the knife from my hand and rolled it over. He looked up, frowning. 'There's blood on this.'

'Is there?' I leant closer until I was almost nose-to-chest with him. I couldn't see any blood.

'Here.' He pressed his fingernail against the base and I stared until a tiny brown spot came into focus. It was just inside the *L* in the inscription.

I pulled back, grimacing. 'I thought I cleaned it all.'

When I looked at him again, his face had clouded over. I stepped back, suddenly conscious of how close we had been standing.

'What did you do with it, Sophie? Did you hurt someone?'

'Don't you think that's a tad hypocritical considering you're an assassin?'

'That's different. I'm trained. You're . . . you.'

I threw him a withering look. 'I know you think that's some sort of insult, but I'm choosing to take it as a compliment.'

'Take it as you like.' He dropped his voice. 'Who did you stab?'

'*Fine*,' I relented. 'If you *must* know, I may or may not have accidentally stabbed myself when I was sleeping.'

'Ah,' he said, like the answer to some great riddle had been revealed to him. His face relaxed and he resumed blinking. '*That* makes sense.' He closed the blade and slid it into his pocket. 'No more switchblade for you.'

'I didn't want it anyway,' I told him, my tone petulant. 'I'm clearing out my life of everything that's been harmful to me.'

'So *that's* why you came,' he said, circling around me and turning to look at the walls again. 'To clear out the assassins once and for all. *Symbolically*.'

'Yes,' I said to the back of his head. 'I'll have you know it's a form of therapeutic healing.' His hair had grown since I'd seen him last. It was still shaggy, but stray black strands swept across his neck now. He was wearing a grey T-shirt and

78

from the back I could see a glimpse of a silver chain disappearing beneath it. I wondered what it was. I wondered why I cared.

He glanced at me over his shoulder. 'And here I was thinking you wanted to see me again.'

My body erupted in violent incredulity. '*What? Why* would I want to see you again? We're not even friends. Honestly, Luca, you're so full of yourself.'

He turned around on the heel of his boot, amusement colouring his voice. 'I'm joking, Sophie. Don't have a coronary.'

'You have a terrible sense of humour.'

'Maybe it's too complex for you.'

'Don't make me regret saving your life,' I teased, wiping the smirk off his face and shining a light on that Big Thing we had been so expertly avoiding.

'Oh yeah,' he said, feigning a sudden memory flash. 'That.' He wound his fingers together. 'I'm not sure I ever thanked you.'

I raised my eyebrows, expectant.

'Thank you,' he said, acting shockingly earnest, before flipping his accent into a rolling Italian lilt, and adding, '*Grazie, sinceramente.*'

'It's OK.' I waved my hand around in the air. 'I got your flowers.'

Luca's face screwed up. 'What? I didn't send you flowers.'

'Oh, that's right,' I deadpanned him. 'You didn't send me *anything.*'

'Ah,' he said. 'I see what you did there. Maybe I'll reconsider.'

'I imagine it will be a cold day in hell before Luca Falcone gives anyone a bouquet of flowers.'

The corner of his lips twitched. 'It's not really the Falcone style.'

'I guess there's nothing so sweet as honey,' I said, only dregs of joviality left in my voice now.

That really did shut him up. He turned around and let his attention settle on the wall again. He didn't gesture for me to leave, and even though I should have, I didn't. I lingered, without really knowing why I wanted to hang out in a dusky tomb with a bunch of dead murderers and someone who had once made my skin burn with hatred. Someone I used to fear. I guess I didn't feel any of that any more. When I pressed my hands against his body in the warehouse and felt his blood, warm and sticky, on my fingers, he became something else to me . . . human, breakable.

'So . . . nice place you got here . . .' I came to stand beside him. We faced the wall and I read the plaque directly in front of us.

GIANLUCA FALCONE
DECEMBER 7TH, 1923 – MARCH 20TH, 1995
CXIII

'Your namesake,' I said.

'My grandfather.'

'He died on the day you were born?'

He turned to look at me. 'Creepy much?'

'It's written on your knife!'

'OK, stalker. Relax.'

'You are so incredibly annoying.'

He shrugged. 'So I'm told.'

'You should come off that pedestal every now and then.'

He grimaced. 'But I like my pedestal. I can see everything from up here.'

'I bet the view's even nicer from your ivory tower.'

'It is,' he said, solemnly. 'I'd invite you up some time but it's only for really intelligent people who have a great sense of humour.'

'Then you must be squatting.' I turned back to the plaque, renewed curiosity flickering in my mind. 'Did your grand-father get to see you?' I asked. 'Before he died that day?'

'Yes. Valentino and I were born early in the morning.' Luca's voice changed, losing the tinge of arrogance that made it haughty. His family was not a laughing matter. 'My grand-father held me in his arms for an hour. He wasn't so interested in Valentino. I don't know if it was because of his defect or because I was the less screechy of the two of us, but my grandfather convinced my parents that he and I were kindred spirits. He said he *felt* it. I'm not so sure. How kindred can you feel with a scrunched-up baby who can't even see properly? Anyway, after he gave me back to my mother, he walked right out of the hospital and dropped dead on the street.'

'Oh,' I gasped, feeling my face crumple. *That took a dark turn.* 'Was it a heart attack?'

Luca's smile was rueful. 'Sophie Gracewell. Naïve as ever. They hit him twice; once in the head, once in the heart. Twin bullets, to represent Valentino and me.'

I clutched at my stomach. Despite my best efforts to remain composed, I was starting to feel a little sick. I focused on the letters in front of me, following their elaborate curves. 'Who shot him?'

I could feel Luca watching me. 'The Marinos.' In his mouth, the name *Marino* sounded like a curse word. Nic had spoken about them in that same tone when he had asked me about Jack in the garden. 'We call them the Black Hand. You could say we have a . . . colourful history with them.' He stopped, his head dipping like he was staring at something on the ground, and quietly, emotionlessly, he added, 'It had been a long time coming.'

'What exactly does *colourful* mean?'

Luca shrugged, still staring at that same spot. 'That we're always killing each other.'

'Ah,' I said, feeling horrified and doing my best to hide it. 'Of course . . .'

'We were in a truce at the time . . . or at least we were supposed to be, but they were still harbouring resentment for something that happened several years before that. And with the twin thing, I suppose the symbolism was too great to pass up.'

'The twin thing?'

'Yes,' said Luca, looking up again, but not at me. His gaze roved around the room, tripping over his ancestors' tombs. 'In the eighties, during the second blood war between our families, my grandfather ordered the killing of Don Vincenzo Marino and his family. It was a drastic move, but he thought that would cripple the Marino dynasty and end the blood-shed once and for all. The Falcones got Vincenzo and his wife, but their sons weren't there. They were twins. No one knows where they went – seems like they just disappeared into thin air. After that, Vincenzo's younger brother, Cesare, took over, but he was an incompetent boss. The family didn't respect him the way they respected Vincenzo. Just like my grandfather had planned, the Marinos were weakened without strong leadership, and Cesare agreed to a truce.' He heaved a sigh. It was heavy and filled with regret, as though he had been there to witness it all.

'But the bloodshed didn't end, did it?' I asked quietly.

'The Marinos endured the terms, at first, but they obviously didn't swallow them – maybe the twins' survival gave them courage, or maybe it was my mother's sister, Donata, who changed things. She married Cesare Marino when she was barely twenty years old. He was almost twice her age, but she didn't care. Donata was hungry for money, for the power she couldn't find in her own family.' His expression soured as his mind turned to his aunt. 'The Genoveses were on the way out, and I guess you could say the Marinos had an opening.'

'And she took it,' I supplied. I considered the idea of marrying some random forty-year-old mob boss for money and power, and it made my skin crawl. What twisted brand of ambition would make someone want to do that? I remembered Luca's mother's words to me in my hospital room: *The Genovese women are survivors; we have the blood of Sicily in our veins, entire families who work beneath us.*

Luca nodded. 'Donata became more of a boss than her husband. Within a couple of years, she was running the whole operation. The day Valentino and I were born, Donata sent her Marino *soldati* after my parents, out of some sick, delayed retribution.' At my look of confusion, he clarified, 'Soldiers.'

'Soldiers?' I repeated in a voice much higher than normal. In my head I pictured an army of mafiosi marching towards a hospital, and bringing death with them. I swallowed hard. 'But why?'

'Donata wanted to orphan Valentino and me, the same way the Falcones orphaned the Marino twins. She wanted to kill her own sister.'

'That's ruthless,' I said. 'I mean, they're *sisters*.'

Something unreadable flitted across Luca's face. 'They're Genovese,' he resolved, as though that would explain everything. It didn't, but I stayed silent and after a moment, he picked up the thread of conversation again. 'My grandfather got a tip-off that the Marinos were going to move against us, so he met them on the streets outside the hospital that day and they took him instead.'

'God,' I said.

'Yeah,' said Luca. 'He paid the ultimate price in the end.'

'For killing the Marino boss and his wife?' I thought about the wife. Had she been someone like me, ushered into the family by her feelings and naïvety, or was she raised the way Nic's mother and her sister were? Did she marry Vincenzo Marino willingly, knowing what might one day happen to them?

'For ordering it,' Luca clarified. 'The hit on Vincenzo Marino and his wife was Felice's. His first. Well, first and second.' A bitter smile twisted on his lips. 'If you ever want to piss Felice off, mention the missing Marino twins and he'll go so red you won't recognize him. The ones that got away,' Luca said with mock wistfulness. 'Only Felice would lament the failure to kill a couple of kids.'

'He ruined their lives,' I said, bitterness overtaking me at the thought of Felice's stupid face. His leering grin. His murderous eyes. 'Wasn't that enough?'

Luca shook his head. 'There's a long history between our families, Sophie. It doesn't come down to a couple of murders, not of their boss, not of my grandfather. We've been warring with the Marinos since Sicily. It started with land, and land became profit and drugs and arms, and territories, and revenge. There have been losses on both sides.'

'I don't see how that excuses anything.'

Luca's voice hardened. 'I never said it did.'

'Nic told me once that you never go after members of the Mafia culture, no matter what they've done.'

Luca's laugh was mirthless. 'Nicoli says a lot of things. That doesn't make them true.'

'So he lied.' I tried to keep the surprise from my voice. I know Nic was more than capable of being dishonest, but when he had sat beside me in his sitting room, pouring out the secrets of his lineage, he had seemed so sincere.

Luca's forehead creased. 'I think it's less about him lying to you and more about him lying to himself. The Marinos have always been different from the other families. We've never shared a history of respect with them.'

'Are you still at war . . . in a "blood war"?' I amended, wondering at the sick turn in my stomach, at the way my panic flared at the thought. How strong were the Marinos now? How close were they to the Falcones? Just how bloody was a blood war?

'No. Not for a while now.' Luca's face was pale and drawn; he looked tired of standing, tired of talking. He sat down, tucking his boots under the bench and leaning forward. He steepled his fingers in front of his lips, thinking. I was struck by the memory of Valentino – how alike they were in that moment, one in my memory, the other beside me. I stayed standing, curious now that I was steeped in their history. I circled the room, scanning names I couldn't pronounce and Roman numerals that made no sense.

'That's good, I suppose, that there's peace,' I said.

I couldn't see Luca's face, but the back of his head jerked, and he snorted. 'A truce is only as good as its sincerity. Once my mother's sister has rebuilt her wealth and the Marino membership, she'll come out of the woodwork.'

'Maybe she won't. Maybe she wants peace too. That's what most people want.' Well, most sane people.

'Peace or not, there's an old Falcone saying: "Never turn your back on a Marino".'

'Ah, a family saying,' I said. 'Kind of like "A Lannister always pays his debts".'

He swivelled around, re-planting his feet on the ground closest to me. He cocked his head. 'What?'

I raised my hand to him. 'Don't act like you've never seen *Game of Thrones*, Luca. Nobody likes a liar.'

He rolled his eyes. 'Trust you to lower the seriousness of the conversation.'

'I was *contributing*,' I countered. 'It's not like *I* have a family motto to offer.'

'What a shame,' he said drily.

'If I did, it would probably be something like "When all else fails, play dead".'

'That's idiotic.'

'Tell that to possums. They know what they're at.'

'Well, it's nice to know I don't have to worry about you when you're out there on your own.' I could almost taste the sarcasm in the air.

My laughter surprised me. It hung in echoes around us, making the room seem bigger and colder.

Luca's eyes grew in surprise, two sapphires sparkling in the dimness. 'What's so funny?'

'Just the thought of you worrying about me. Or, well, anything, really.'

He narrowed his eyes. 'How low your opinion of me is.'

I circled the bench, zeroing in on his grandfather's inscription. I could sense him turning with me, following my movements. How long had we been in here by now? And why was I so eager to traverse the walls of history in his company?

'They were hoping I would be just like him,' he offered into the silence. I pressed my lips together, surprised at his willingness to surrender information to me, to want to talk to me about something real, something important. 'Gianluca Falcone was the *capo di tutti i capi*, the boss of all bosses. My grandfather had marked me that day in the hospital, before he died.'

'Do you *want* to be like him?' I asked, turning to study him.

A subtle tilt of the chin, and then, quietly, he said, 'Isn't the answer obvious?'

'He sacrificed himself so that you would have parents to raise you.'

'One right doesn't remedy a thousand wrongs.'

'You should write a book of quotes.'

He wasn't smiling. I supposed it was obvious then. Glaringly obvious, if you knew where to look - Luca had abstained from the role handed down to him by his father, the role they all wanted him to undertake. He had given it away, but not entirely. He was still the underboss. Conflicted, dreaming, but ultimately trapped. What was there to smile about?

'What do all the numbers mean?' I read his grandfather's Roman numeral aloud. 'One hundred and thirteen? Is it some kind of ranking system?'

Luca stood up, the earlier exhaustion fading from his face. 'You can read Roman numerals?'

'I'm pretty smart, I'll have you know,' I said. 'Not a nerd, like you. But smart, in the ways that matter.'

He traced the number with his forefinger. 'This is my grandfather's kill count.'

The room seemed to darken all of a sudden. I stepped backwards and stumbled against the bench. *One hundred and thirteen people. One hundred and thirteen funerals. One hundred and thirteen grieving families.* So that was what it meant to be the boss of all bosses. Suddenly Luca's words took on a whole new weight. He was Gianluca II, his grandfather's prodigy; the butcher's legacy. 'And your family *want* you to be just like him?'

'Yes, they do.' An emotionless answer.

'And, just *how* like him are you already?'

Luca glanced sidelong at me, his lips twisting. 'You really think I'm going to answer that?'

I moved away from him, to another, sparser wall, where there were just two plaques and I didn't have to think about Luca's Roman numeral. Or Nic's. The sign on the right was Felice's, his death-date yet to be marked. The sign on the left simply read:

'Who's this?' I asked.

Luca came to stand beside me. His arm brushed against mine. I could feel the static on my skin. 'This is Felice's wall.'

Between the plaques, a ruby encased in silver had been inset into the stone. Protruding from the silver in swirling calligraphy were the letters F on one side, and E on the other. Beneath the ruby it said *Sempre.*

Luca brushed his fingers along the words, translating. '*Always.*' And then in a quiet voice, he added, 'Felice wanted to be interred next to his wife.' He traced the ruby, reverentially, softly. 'He engraved her tomb the day he engraved her ring. Every dime he ever earned went into those two rubies and then one of them went with her and it broke his heart.'

'Where?' I asked, looking for dates and failing to find them. She wasn't dead. Yet.

'She disappeared. She was eight months pregnant with their daughter, and one day she went out and never came back.'

'Why?' I asked, though in truth it was not hard to imagine. Felice was, after all, a terrible human being.

'He's never said.' Luca shrugged. 'He still believes she'll come back to him some day.'

'Do you?'

His mouth hardened into a thin line. It sharpened his cheekbones and the clean cut of his jaw. 'He's a fool.'

'A romantic, maybe,' I tempered, wondering at how bad things must have gotten for an eight-month-pregnant woman to walk out on her husband. Still, being married to a sociopath is no easy feat.

'No,' said Luca. 'A fool.'

I got the sense the topic was closed. I let it be, thinking on Felice with fractionally more empathy than before. Emphasis on fractionally. I guess no one can be painted with just one brush. There is light and shade in all of us, pain and hardship, and some of us rise from it while others are darkened by it. *Evelina*, I thought, *wherever you are, you are probably better off.*

Luca sat down on the bench again, his legs stretched out and crossing at the ankles. He was watching me. 'You're pale.'

'I'm always pale.'

'You're translucent.'

'It's the lighting.'

'You can go now,' he offered in what I assumed was his attempt at politeness. It needed work. 'Millie will probably combust if you leave her out there any longer.'

'How do you know Millie's out there?'

His laugh was low and breathy. 'You're kidding, right? I could hear you coming from a mile off. You bring a whole new dimension to the word "unsubtle".'

Why was I still stalling? I backed into the doorway, studying him the way he was studying me – unashamedly. But what was he looking for exactly? I watched the way he slumped his shoulders, the way his elbows balanced on his knees, how his dark brows cast shadows over his bright eyes. In that moment he looked exactly the way I had been feeling. Tired, defeated. Alone. Troubled. 'Do you . . . spend a lot of time in here?'

He cocked his head. 'Why? Are you worried about me?'

'No!' I practically shrieked.

'Good. I'd hate to think you were going soft.'

'Never.' *Well, that's where giving a crap gets you.* With as much haughtiness as I could muster I marched through the doorway, but something stopped me and I dug my heels in. I couldn't help it; I had to know. I peeked around the doorway, curiosity bubbling up inside me.

He was still staring in my direction.

'Why didn't you ask me about my uncle?'

'What?'

'You didn't ask me if I knew where Jack was. But you must be wondering. Especially, you know, after what happened.'

Without so much as blinking, he said, 'I already know where he is.'

My jaw dropped. 'Why didn't you tell me?'

'Why didn't you ask?'

I came back into the room, my energy spiking. 'Where is he?'

'Well, we don't know *exactly* where he is yet. But we have a pretty good idea of who he's with.'

'Who?'

'You better not go looking for him.'

'Of course not,' I lied.

'You're lying. It's written all over your face.'

'I'm not lying, I'm just stressed!'

Luca thought about it for a moment. 'Isn't it obvious?' he asked, his voice half-sigh, half-frustration. 'Where is the one place that Jack would go, the one place he would seek refuge from us?'

Oh. *Oh.* Well that explained the little history lesson earlier.

Luca watched the realization dawn. He pulled his lips back, revealing the feral tips of his canines. 'And if he is there,' he said, 'if they *are* truly aiding and abetting a known Falcone enemy, then, once again, the truce is broken.'

'Shit.'

'The question is,' Luca said, leaning back on his palms and hunching his shoulders, 'if we're right about where Jack is hiding, what exactly is Donata Marino getting out of the arrangement?'

'So you really haven't been following me, then,' I muttered. I didn't mention Purple Hair. If she was his enemy, the news would just unsettle him. I already had enough to worry about now, without confirming the Marinos had gone ahead and danced all over whatever truce they had had with the Falcones.

Luca's eyes widened. 'What?' He stood up. 'Why would you say that?'

I backed up a little. Now was not the right time to be pouring fuel on the fire – breaking open that old wound before I knew what it even meant. Besides, I could be wrong . . . I *could* be. Purple Hair could be anyone. 'It's just . . . with Nic showing up in my garden the other night, I was wondering if there was a plan or something . . .' I trailed off.

Yup. That ought to smooth things over.

Rage flashed across Luca's face as he took a step towards me. 'Nic did *what*?'

Or not.

'Um, never mind,' I said, turning into the main passageway. 'I have to find Millie.'

Luca cut in front of me. 'You need to tell me about this.'

'Why?'

He blinked at me. 'What do you mean "Why"?'

'Why do you care?'

'I care about the movements of my brother when they go against explicit family orders *and* when they endanger someone else. Don't be so smug about it, Sophie. This is serious.'

'Oh, *I'm* smug because I won't tell you my personal business? Well, excuse me.'

'Sophie, this isn't a game,' Luca warned. I could tell he was fighting to keep his voice level. 'Don't be so stupid.'

Stupid. Stupid. *Stupid.* Why the hell was he always calling me stupid?

'Oh, this isn't a game?' I repeated, seeing red. 'You think I don't know that? Did you forget who else was in that warehouse with you? I remember every damn second of that night!'

'Then take this seriously!'

'I couldn't be taking it more seriously if I tried,' I hissed, raising my palm so he could see the jagged cut. 'I haven't slept in weeks. My mother is a *zombie.* Don't you dare preach to me about the seriousness of all this. You have no idea what your family has done to me. And I don't care who you are, you have no right to demand to know my business!'

He came closer, tension rippling from him. 'I have a right when it involves my family.'

I had to tip my head back to look at him. 'You're not *my* underboss, Luca. I don't owe you a thing.'

I pivoted around him, expecting resistance, but he let me go, his expression crumpling with something I couldn't place.

'Oh, so you yell at *me* about everything that happened!' he shouted after me. 'But you meet him in your garden like some pathetic reincarnation of *Romeo and Juliet*!'

I swatted his words over my head as I marched away from him.

'In case you didn't realize, Sophie, that play was a *satire*! You're not meant to aspire to it!'

'The way you're talking right now, you're aspiring to my fist in your face!' I yelled over my shoulder. I reached the door but he was there in a flash, sliding in front of me. He was so tall. So broad. So immovable. 'Move,' I hissed. 'Or I swear to every god and planetary system I will hit you in your smug face.'

'Sophie,' he said. His voice was deceptively controlled, but his blazing eyes told a different story. 'You saved my life. You threw your body on top of mine to stop Jack from killing me. So don't think I'm not grateful or appreciative of what you did when I tell you that you are acting like a complete *moron*.'

He caught my wrist before my hand connected with his cheek.

'Don't,' he growled.

'Let go of me,' I huffed.

He released me, and my arm fell to my side with a dull thud. I took a gasping breath.

Luca's gaze was hard and shining. I felt like it was crushing me. Whatever he was about to say, I sure as hell didn't want to hear it. I pushed past him and heaved the door open, bounding down the steps.

Millie was lying on the grass by the lake, taking a selfie. 'Well, *finally*,' she groaned, clambering to her feet. 'What the hell took you so— Holy crap, Soph. Watch out! Luca Falcone is behind you!'

'I know.'

'Oh.' She started circling us. 'Wait a second . . . What's going on here? What were you two doing in there for so long?'

I led the way through the trees. Millie trailed after me.

Luca followed us. 'I don't know how many times I have to say it to you before you get it through your skull!' he pressed. 'He's not good for you, Sophie!'

'Whoa, whoa, whoa!' Millie jumped in front of me. I halted, and behind me Luca skidded to a stop. 'Is there some kind of . . . *jealousy* going on here?'

Luca rolled his eyes. '*Per l'amor di Dio.* Don't be ridiculous.'

I started marching again. 'Maybe it's OK to care about someone and to have them care about you,' I snapped. 'Maybe the world won't end. Not that you'd know, of course, because you don't need anyone when you have your precious, arrogant self!'

'Yeah, that must be it. I'm bitter and alone and I don't know what love is. And you're living in your little world of denial and it's going to end up putting you in the ground because I guarantee no matter how long you hang around him, when the chips are down, he'll choose his family over you.'

'Holy Moses.' Millie was huffing beside me. 'What the hell happened between you two?'

Luca's string of Italian curses filtered into hurried English. 'My brother's idiocy has, once again, rubbed off on your best friend.' He wasn't even panting, unlike me and Millie, who were marching so fast I was fighting the urge to clutch my ribs and double over. 'Or maybe it's the other way around.'

'OK, that's it!' I skidded to a halt and closed the distance between us. I prodded him in the chest. 'Luca Falcone, if you say another word about me—'

'What?' He swatted my finger away. 'What are you going to do to me?'

All the anger bubbling inside me collided. I squashed it, speaking calculatedly and slowly as I stared at the shards of turquoise in his eyes. So I was stupid, naïve, moronic – he had told me a thousand times already – but at least my conscience was clear, and he had no right to judge me when *his* wasn't. 'I'm not a fool, Luca,' I said, my lip curling. 'Don't treat me like one. If you had let me finish instead of flying off the handle, you would know that I sent your brother away when he came to see me. No matter what I feel about him or *ever* felt, he looks at the world and sees murder and bloodshed, and I deserve a life with love and peace. I've been through *enough*. I've seen *enough*.' I could feel my voice cracking, so I pushed harder, so he wouldn't hear it. 'The truth is, he's broken,' I said. 'You all are.'

Luca faltered backwards. It reminded me, for one horrifying instant, of the moment he had been shot in the warehouse. His shoulders slumped, his arms went slack and he just stared at me. I had wiped the sneer off his face, and still my throat was wobbling. Water was pooling in the backs of my eyes.

Millie tiptoed into the space between us. 'Ooookay,' she said. 'For reasons unclear to me, that got a bit heated. Let's just take it down a notch, and discuss this like adults.'

I didn't notice how hard I was panting until I tried to catch my breath.

'Forget it,' said Luca, turning from us. 'I'm done. You're on your own, Gracewell.'

'Fine. Good.'

He disappeared through the break in the trees.

'Sophie.' Millie dropped her voice. 'I think you have a problem.'

I swallowed another offending quiver and mashed my words together. 'I know. I'm pretty sure the Marino Mafia family have been following me.'

'I'm talking about a different kind of problem.'

A single tear slid fast and hard down my cheek. I wiped it away. 'The switchblade is gone,' I said. 'So it's done.'

She was still staring at the trees. 'This is not what I meant by closure.'

PART II

'The enemy is within the gates;
it is with our own luxury, our own folly,
our own criminality that we have to contend.'

Marcus Tullius Cicero

CHAPTER ELEVEN

THE BLACK HAND

I spent the rest of the afternoon at Millie's, purposely not talking about what had happened in the cemetery. The switchblade was gone and I was trying to ignore the emptiness it had left behind. We made cookies and watched Harry Potter movies back to back until guilt at leaving my mother in the general gloominess of our house began to eat away at me. Real life was waiting at home – the shadows on the wall, the screams in the night, the gaping hole where my father should be. I left as evening was falling, dragging myself out of Millie's distraction bubble. I was experiencing a sudden urge to stretch my legs and work off at least some of the sugar I had packed into my body, so I could at least try and sleep tonight.

The sun was beginning to dip, tingeing the sky with streaks

of pink and orange. It wasn't until I was passing the diner that I became aware of the black Mercedes trailing behind me. The traffic on Main Street had declined and now cars passed by in dregs.

I turned into the lot and stopped walking. The Mercedes parked several spaces away. The engine shut off and the girl with purple hair emerged. She flicked her hair from her face but the bangs held steady, drooping over her eyes. There was a forced casualness about her stance – her arms hung limply by her sides, but her hands were clenched in fists.

She rounded the car and came towards me. I squared my shoulders to appear bigger than I was. We were almost the same height and she was slight, too. She stopped too close to me and I stepped backwards, away from her citrus perfume. It took a moment to find her eyes underneath the bangs and the black kohl powder she had over-rimmed them with.

'Sophie Gracewell,' she said, appraising me with unashamed forwardness. Her voice was a lot softer than I expected it to be. It struck me again how young she was – she couldn't be much older than me. She twirled her hands in front of her as though she was pointing me out to an invisible audience. 'God, I feel like I've been trying to get you on your own for, like, my whole life.' She smiled broadly, revealing two dimples so pronounced that it suddenly seemed impossible to be intimidated by her. Which was irritatingly misleading.

'That's funny,' I said, not laughing. 'I feel like I've been avoiding you for about that long, too.'

She nodded, her smile faltering as she heaved a sigh. 'I've been freaking you out, I know. I'm sorry.'

Her contrition disarmed me, and, softer than I intended to, I said, 'There's a right way and a wrong way to approach someone, you know.'

She started chewing on the corner of her lip, smearing her fuchsia lipstick across her teeth. She was wringing her hands and I realized she was as jittery as I was.

'I take it you're a Marino,' I said.

Her eyes went wide. 'So you've heard of us?'

'Somewhat.'

'All good, I'm sure.' She offered me a bashful smile, all doe-eyed, with those dimples again. There was a small gap between her two front teeth.

'So my uncle sent you?'

I crunched my palms into fists, feeling the sweat on my fingertips.

She shook her head. 'I didn't think you'd have figured it out.'

Poof! There goes the truce.

Thank God I hadn't mentioned anything about this to Luca.

The girl's grin betrayed a sense of lightness that was buried beneath the dramatic make-up and severe hair. 'How did you know that?'

'I guessed,' I lied.

She broke off into a chesty laugh. 'He said you were clever, but I think you had me figured out at the movie theatre. I'm sorry if I scared you. I was trying to get a minute to talk to you by yourself. No one else is supposed to know.'

It was hard to dislike her – as far as Mafia types went, she was surprisingly normal. I might have let my guard drop if I hadn't known her surname. 'What's your name?' I asked her.

'Can I know that, at least?' Anything to distract from the pulsing *Marino* in my head.

'Sara.' She feigned a curtsy and I found myself laughing before clamping my mouth shut. God, she was weird, too. What the hell was she doing running errands for my uncle? She should be out being a teenager.

'Sorry,' she said, seeing the bewildered curiosity on my face. 'I'm kind of new at this messenger thing.' Her expression turned sheepish. 'I'm supposed to just give you something,' she continued. 'I'm not really even supposed to talk to you.'

'Why?' My pulse kicked into high gear.

'Oh I don't know.' She smiled. 'In case I tip over and all the family's secrets come out.'

'Right,' I said, understanding perfectly.

'Anyways, your uncle wants to see you.'

'Not to be rude,' I said, 'but he could have called me and saved you all this running around . . .' *And creepy-ass stalking.*

Sara rolled her eyes so intensely her irises practically disappeared. 'That's what *I* said. The last thing I wanted to do was freak you out, but your uncle wanted to be extra careful now that he's got, like, a thousand hits on him. He was hell-bent on making sure you weren't running around with . . .' – she faltered and something dark flittered across her face – '. . . with people you shouldn't be,' she finished. 'It's important that the information reaches you and only you. It can't leak. At least not yet. I guess this was the only way to ensure that.'

'I see.' It all seemed so intense, so clandestine . . . so dangerous. They didn't want to shatter the truce yet. They obviously didn't realize it was already hanging by a thread. I swallowed hard. I felt like I had my finger in the dam, holding on to a secret that was swelling and swelling. 'So where is he?'

'I should go now.' Sara fished a business card out of her pocket and held it in front of me. 'Take it,' she said. 'Before they fire me!' She pulled an elaborate mock frown; it dragged at her cheeks, revealing razor-sharp cheekbones. Her eyebrows sank low over her eyes and I was struck then by how familiar she seemed. That expression – I had seen it before.

I gaped at her, forgetting the card hovering between us.

'What's the matter?' She smiled, revealing sharpened canines that spread into a generous display of white teeth.

'You look . . .' I shook my head. 'You reminded me of someone, is all.'

All the good cheer she had been exuding evaporated in that moment. Her expression soured and she stepped away from me, still holding the card.

'You insult me,' she said, dropping her hand.

'I didn't say anything.'

'The comparison was implied,' she said. 'I know exactly who you mean.'

I raised my palms in innocence. 'I'm sorry if I offended you.'

She held up the card again and this time I snatched it from her.

'Look,' she said. 'You shouldn't speak of a Marino and a Falcone in the same sentence. If you learn nothing else, learn that before you walk into Donata's club. And whatever you do, *don't* mention her sister.'

'A club?' I caressed the glossy card with my fingers, considering the ridiculousness of me parading through some Mafia club in the city amidst a whole *other* mob family. As if one wasn't enough. 'What's to say I'll even go?' I shook my head. 'I'm not sure I ever want to see my uncle again. He betrayed my mom and me. He doesn't deserve it,' I said, surprised at my willingness to confide in someone who had been unashamedly stalking me up until now.

Sara raised her hand to touch my shoulder but then stopped herself in mid-air, thinking better of it. 'I understand, you know. It's difficult being pulled in directions you don't want to go in. And even more so when it's your family holding the strings. But it will become clear to you, if you let it.'

Um, what? Part of me was curious. I couldn't help it. It was like this festering, buzzing thing in the pit of my stomach. 'I shouldn't go,' I said. 'It's not my world.'

She dropped her voice, even though no one but me could hear her. 'You will have to see him, Sophie. Better that you go on your own terms.'

A caution – a whisper of something else. 'What's that supposed to mean?'

She loosed a weary sigh. 'It means important things are happening and he will need to see you, one way or another, and soon. You should go to him or he'll come for you, and this place is not safe for anyone right now. Not even me.'

'You make it sound like I don't have a choice,' I said, feeling the chill in her words as they settled around me.

She offered me a half smile. 'You have the illusion of one, at least. That's more than I ever had.' Another failed smile, and then, 'Please don't make me do something I don't want to do . . .'

Before I could respond she was marching back towards

106

her car. I stood, speechless, as she sped out of the lot, leaving me wondering about the quiet threat in her final words.

I studied the card in my hands – it was crimson. In the middle a tree with swirling branches was printed in black ink. Underneath, the word EDEN was written in calligraphy. I flipped it over. There was an address, along with the phrase 'Lose Yourself'. Scrawled along the top, in my uncle's hand-writing, were three simple words: 'Sophie. Tuesday 11 p.m.'.

I shouldn't go. Jack had already gotten me in enough trouble. But if I didn't go to him, he would come to me. He would come *for* me, whatever that meant. And the further I could keep him from Cedar Hill, and my mother, the better.

Something was going on, and if I had to see him I was damn sure going to try and find out what it was. I was sick of being kept in the dark – so close to the things swirling around me, and still out of reach. Enough was enough. For my father's sake and my own, there were questions that needed to be answered, and I needed to know what my uncle planned to do next – to Nic, to Luca, to all of them, now that he was being sheltered by the Marinos, now that the truce was crumbling around them. I would accept the illusion of my free will and try, at least, to use it to my advantage in some way. Jack had shown up to protect my life once, maybe he would listen to me about the truce. If he walked away now, before any bloodshed – if he left town – he could prevent a war. And surely no one, not even my crazy, morally unhinged uncle, wanted a war.

CHAPTER TWELVE
THE INTERCEPTION

The thunder of feet against the pavement startled me from my thoughts. I snapped my head up just in time to see Nic racing towards me. I shoved the card into the back pocket of my jeans.

He skidded to a halt right in front of me. His eyes held a wild, frenzied look. 'What was that about?'

Surprise at seeing him was quickly replaced by bitter memories of my fight with Luca, and all the things that were said. Nic shouldn't be here. And yet he was, and this time it definitely wasn't for me.

I folded my arms and looked around him. 'Hmm? What was *what* about?'

Nic frowned in a very obvious I-know-you're-lying kind of way. 'I saw you talking to Sara Marino just now . . .'

'You mean your cousin?' Their bone structures were identical; she had Nic's cheekbones and Luca's mouth.

Nic levelled me with a dark look, funnily similar to the one Sara had just offered me in similar circumstances. 'Don't call her that. She's scum, just like the rest of them.'

Family politics can really feel like they're sapping the marrow from your bones. Especially when *somehow* you get caught in the middle. I was like a goldfish trying to navigate its way through two opposing schools of sharks. 'Where did you come from?' I asked, changing tack.

He gestured behind him, to the side street by the library across the road. Much more subtle than Dom and Gino's earlier stake-out point. But then again, they were idiots. 'Calvino and I were watching the diner.'

'Why?'

Nic narrowed his eyes. 'We think there's something in there,' he said, cagily. 'Something your uncle needs.'

'What?'

Nic clamped his mouth shut and frowned.

'Why are you giving me that dirty look?' I asked him.

'How long have you known he's with the Marinos?'

'I'm not getting involved in this,' I told him sharply. 'I don't know anything about anyone.'

'Do you know what this means?' he said, but I got the impression he wasn't really asking me. He was asking himself. The implications were huge. They were etched across his face.

'It doesn't mean anything,' I said. 'You don't know anything for sure. That girl didn't mention anything about Jack.' It was a brazen lie, but better than letting the anger escalate, better than fuelling the fire.

He pulled his hand through his hair, cupping the back of his neck. 'Do you have to be so difficult?' he murmured.

'Do you ever take a holiday?' I countered. 'Like, do any of you just wake up and think "Today feels like a pyjama day."? Or is it always, "Today is a good day for murdering and stalking."? Seriously, Nic. *Seriously*.'

He came closer, until I could feel the heat of his body.

'Seriously,' he echoed, his voice strained.

I stared at his chest. I didn't want to look at his eyes. 'You are so . . . frustrating.'

Nic loosed a loaded breath, and I caught the edge of his smile in a mistaken glance at his face. *Don't look at him.* 'I know that feeling,' he said, his murmur warming the shell of my ear. I wanted to scream, cry, shove him and then possibly make out with him. *Dammit.* It felt like my whole body was on fire. It occurred to me that I might be on the verge of having a breakdown in the middle of Gracewell's parking lot. The stakes felt too high all of a sudden.

What was he doing here? What the *hell* was Jack playing at? What was in that diner?

And *where?* I knew every inch of that place.

'Sophie, *ti prego*.' Nic's words were a quiet nudge. He curled his arm around me, pulling me into him. I pressed my fingers against his chest, feeling the quick *th-thump* of his heartbeat. Human, fallible. *Scared*, I realized. Scared of what was to come. Gently, he pressed his forehead to mine. 'Everything will be OK,' he whispered, his heartbeat galloping beneath my fingertips. 'Just tell me what she said to you.'

I made the mistake of looking at him. I could smell the

faint scent of alpine, almost feel the heady blissfulness of the last time we had kissed. I swallowed. 'She didn't say anything.'

He inhaled sharply. 'Fine, let's talk about something else, then.'

'Like what?'

His eyes were trained on my lips. His hand moved to the small of my back, the other cupped the back of my neck, pulling me into him. 'This,' he said gruffly.

He pressed his lips against mine, hard and searching. I shivered against him as his kiss grew stronger and more urgent. *No.* I made myself think. I made myself remember. He dragged his hand down my back, brushing his fingers along the waistband of my jeans. *No.* I pulled my lips from his just as he slipped his hand into my back pocket. I pushed against him, but it was too late; he was already pulling the card out from where I had tucked it.

He jumped back from me as I lashed out at him. He jerked his head and my fingers caught his chin. Quick, but not quick enough. His hand flew to his jaw.

His eyes went wide. 'Sophie.'

'How could you?' I gasped.

'I'm protecting you.' He shook the alarm from his face and flipped the card over, his dark eyes slitting as he read Jack's handwritten message to me. 'I had to do it.'

I glared at him.

'You weren't going to give it to me,' he said.

'It was mine! I didn't have to!'

'You don't know what you're dealing with here, Sophie.'

I had to curl my fingernails into my palms to keep from trying to slap him again. 'In that one kiss, you just cheapened everything we ever had.'

Alarm spread across his face. He stepped into our bubble again, his hands reaching out for mine. 'I didn't cheapen it. I did it to look out for you.'

I backed away from him. 'Just leave me alone.'

'You can't go see your uncle, Sophie. I don't care if you're mad at me, but you can't go into that club. That's Black Hand territory. It's not safe for you there.'

I gestured around me as I walked away. 'It's not safe for me anywhere!'

He matched my quickened pace easily. 'Listen to me. Donata Marino doesn't care about Jack. The Marinos never associate with anyone outside their family. They're using him, and if you get sucked into their world, they'll use you too. I'm asking you – I am *begging* you – do not go to that club.'

I didn't look back at him. 'It's none of your business what I choose to do.'

'I'll make it my business to go in there after you.'

I turned around. 'You wouldn't!'

He set his jaw. 'Try me.'

'You can't manipulate me like that,' I hissed. But he could and he was. I didn't want him following me into that club and going head-to-head with my uncle and all his new allies. There would be blood, and it would be on my conscience.

I started walking again. 'You were supposed to stay away from me.'

He followed me. 'That was before.'

'Before what.'

'Before I knew the Black Hand were involved.'

My mind was swirling with possibilities. How could I get rid of Nic from this scenario? How could I convince him not to come to that club? He wasn't going to give up.

'Let's make a deal, then,' I said, swivelling. I masked my features and lifted my eyes to his. I made them as wide as I could and nudged at my bottom lip with my teeth.

He watched me, unblinking.

I drew in a breath and with all the sincerity I could muster I made my proposition. 'I won't go to Eden if you promise not to go to Eden.'

He looked past me, contemplating. He drummed his fingers against his jaw. 'You promise?'

'I promise,' I lied.

'OK, then,' he relented. 'So do I.'

As I let myself in, a chair screeched in the kitchen and my mother rushed to meet me in the hallway. Her face was drawn tight.

My throat seized up. 'Mom? What's going on?'

She held up my pillow in greeting, the bloodied side turned towards me.

Crap.

'Sophie?' She padded towards me. 'What's happened?'

The cut on my palm burnt with the memory. The image of my mother crying by herself that night in the kitchen had been seared into my brain – the vision so like the version of my mother approaching me now, searching my face for clues. Guilt bubbled inside me. I blinked once, slowly, banishing the memories.

'Oh, yeah.' I took the pillow from her, held it by a corner and rotated it, forcing nonchalance. 'I had a nosebleed a couple of nights ago.' I flicked my gaze across her features, praying the lie would land. 'The doctor said it would probably happen once or twice, since my nose is still healing. It's not a big deal.'

Her eyebrows drew together, creasing her forehead. 'Why didn't you wake me when it happened?'

You weren't asleep. I shrugged. 'It was late. I didn't see the point.'

'The point?' My mother shook her head. 'You should have come to me, Sophie. You know you can always come to me.'

'It was just a nosebleed. It had almost stopped by the time I woke up.'

'Still,' she said. 'I'm your mother. That's what I'm here for.'

I offered her a half smile in the dimness. 'Please don't worry about it.'

'Sweetheart,' she mirrored my smile, her head cocked lightly to one side, 'it's a mother's job to worry.'

I had to crush an urgent need to hug her. There was something strange in the air, and it was making me feel like I might burst out crying at any moment. She was so small and tired, and yet even now, there was a constant ripple of strength in her. Strength for me. Strength I wanted her to keep for herself.

Get a grip, Soph.

'I'm fine, Mom.' There was a short silence. The pillow hung limply at my side. I debated doing an elaborate twirl, and decided that might be overkill. Instead, I lightened my voice. 'Everything is fine . . . except of course for this pillow, which, unfortunately, is not. I think it's time we put it out to pasture.'

She stared at the pillow, mock-frowning. 'Poor little guy.'

I held it up for examination. 'I'll miss him.'

'We'll get you a better one,' she stage-whispered, pretending to block her mouth with her hand. 'Bigger *and* puffier.'

I drew my eyes wide. '*Mother*,' I chastised. 'Have some *respect*. He can *hear* you.'

We laughed, and for a moment it felt real. She followed me into the kitchen, where I threw the pillow in the trash. 'Sayonara,' I declared, stuffing it into the can. I turned back to my mother. 'In the interest of honesty, I feel I should tell you I'll be stealing a pillow from your room in the next three minutes or so.'

She smiled even brighter that time. 'What's mine is yours.'

'In that case, I might also commandeer that tear-drop necklace with the emerald stone.'

'Except my jewellery, clothes, make-up and everything else I consider valuable,' she added with a wink. 'You may, however, help yourself to a small handful of my potpourri.'

'Wow.' I blew out an exhale. 'You generous lady.'

She picked up a mug from the table. The moment felt so wonderfully normal. I wished I could have wrapped myself inside it and forced everything else from my mind, but like all good things, it faded too quickly. I turned to go, and she gripped my arm, squeezing it just above the elbow. She eyed me over the rim of her mug, peppermint on her breath as she said softly, 'You know you don't have to pretend, sweetheart. Not with me.'

We watched each other in silence, the bloodied pillow just a couple of feet away, my father's absence filling up the space between us.

'Neither do you,' I said quietly.

Her gaze turned quizzical but she kept the mug high. 'I'm not pretending.'

'OK,' I conceded. 'If you say so.'

I left her nursing her tea, staring at something far beyond the kitchen window. Another life, maybe. One before my father, before me, when she was a budding designer in a city far away, with high hopes and big dreams. Not this small town, this stifled life, these blood-red memories pressing down on us.

CHAPTER THIRTEEN

EDEN

When I told my mother I was staying the night at Millie's, she nearly fainted with relief. Every step I took outside our front door was a small victory for her, and an entire night spent with my best friend was music to her ears. In her mind, I was coasting back to normality, and it didn't matter that I was leaving her behind. She pressed a twenty into my hand, 'for pizza, ice cream, whatever you girls need. It's on me.' I tried to give it back, but she clasped her hands behind her back and shook her head. 'You deserve to treat yourself!'

Oh, if only she knew. I swallowed my guilt – it was getting easier to stomach these days. I consoled myself with the knowledge that meeting Jack head-on would keep him from showing up unannounced at my house at some point in the future, which would be so much worse for both of us.

'Are you sure you'll be OK here by yourself?' I asked instead.

Her laugh was a short tinkle. 'Of course, sweetheart. I have plenty to keep me occupied. I'm putting up that new trellis at the back of the garden. I'm planting wallflowers!'

My mind flicked to her unfinished dressmaking projects, now long overdue. 'A trellis, eh? Cool . . .'

She swatted my arm. 'I don't just sit around and stare listlessly into the distance when you're not here, you know.'

'*What?* So you don't spend all your free time thinking about how much you miss me?'

'I replace my affection for you with my beautiful new plants,' she said, her voice teasing. 'They're much less sarcastic.'

'Just wait till they're teenagers.'

'Have fun,' she said, pulling me in for a hug. 'Talk about boys. Plan some adventures!'

When she pulled back, she was beaming so hard her lips were twitching. I grabbed my purse and tried to act like I really was going to an innocent sleepover at my best friend's house and not a Mafia den in the middle of the city.

I had second thoughts about Eden – big ones – but in the end Millie ended up convincing me.

'Whatever your uncle's doing, Soph, you could squash it before it's too late.'

'Something tells me it's already too late.'

'You'll have to face him one way or another. Isn't that what Lego-head said?'

'Her name is Sara.'

'All right, all right,' said Millie, waving her hand around. 'You don't have to act all kinshippy with her. She was stalking you, don't forget.'

She googled the nightclub. There were pages of paparazzi scandals involving local celebrities and alleged underworld figures. Donata was featured in almost every article, sometimes by her maiden name, Genovese, and sometimes by Marino. She was a tabloid darling, each piece hinting at an undercurrent of fear. No one dared speak ill of the 'Genovese Queen', as one newspaper called her. She was the great and fearsome femme fatale of Chicago.

Her affluence shone through the expensive stoles and designer dresses. Her dark hair was a mane of the world's finest extensions and her dramatic make-up airbrushed her expertly. But underneath the pomp and glamour she was a skeletal figure with a scrawny neck and severe features. She had that unmistakable Genovese ice – the same chill that Elena Genovese-Falcone had brought with her to my hospital room. The sisters were imprints of one another; each one surrounded by rival Mafia families, waiting to pick off the other. And Donata had a glittering night palace of her own making in which to plot.

Millie pressed the pad of her index finger on the screen, at an interior shot of Eden where everything was draped in white beneath a ceiling of chandeliers. 'We have to go,' she resolved. 'We just *have* to.'

'And what if I don't like what he has to say?' I countered. I had no doubt I wouldn't like it.

'Then we can just leave. And then it's done, Sophie. You'll

have heard him out.'

I was chewing a pattern into my lip, staring at the screen, my mind playing out all the possible ways this could go. How angry would I be when I saw him? How angry would *he* be? And Donata. What was her role in all this? If Elena was anything to judge by, I had seen quite enough Genovese ladies for one lifetime.

'Sophie, *look*.' Millie was tapping her fingernail on another picture, this time of a different floor, where everything was bamboo, and fire-lamps blazed around the contours of a pooling dance floor. 'It's the most exclusive club in the city. We *have* to go.'

The logistics of actually getting inside were still hazy. Millie had a pretty good fake ID. I didn't. If that crimson business card was my ticket into Eden, I was in trouble, because it was in Nic's pocket.

Stupid Nic.

We barricaded ourselves in Millie's bedroom and rifled through every single item of clothing in her wardrobe. 'If we want to get past the bouncers, we have to be sexy but not slutty. It's a very fine line,' said Millie, picking up and discarding a floral peplum dress. I examined a cream chiffon blouse. Millie snatched it from me and flung it on to the ground. 'I said sexy, not politician!'

After almost an hour of indecision, Millie chose a royal-blue strapless dress, a thick silver necklace and hoop earrings. I picked a black body-con dress with spaghetti straps and a lace hem. I borrowed a simple gold necklace and stud earrings, pairing the outfit with Millie's patent black ankle boots. Millie insisted on doing my hair and make-up.

'Voila!' she triumphed, spinning me towards the mirror.

I gaped at my reflection. I had been Barbie-fied. The dress was miniscule, and so tight it clung to every inch of me. My hair brought new meaning to the word 'volume' and the hairspray had turned it into a glittering blonde rock. My eyes were rimmed with so much black it was hard to find the blue inside them, and my lips had been lined and glossed until they shone at twice their normal size against my bronzed and blushed face.

'Well?' Millie wiggled her high-definition eyebrows at me through the mirror.

'I look like a hooker.'

She came to stand beside me.

'You also look like a hooker,' I told her.

'A twenty-one-year-old hooker?' she asked with big, hopeful eyes.

Eden was a sleek three-storey building on the corner of West Grand Avenue. It climbed into the sky in a display of black monochrome and tinted glass. On the corner, two bouncers and a severe-faced woman holding a clipboard were guarding a velvet-roped entranceway. Above them, 'EDEN' was imprinted in illuminated red letters that lit up the street below. The spiralling tree emblem from the crimson card stretched across the entire second storey.

My mind flittered across Luca and his disdainful thoughts of my intelligence. Oh, if he could only see me now. 'I never considered myself an idiot until this very moment,' I said, staring wide-eyed at Eden as we drifted towards it.

'Really?' said Millie, blinking heavily. 'But you've done *so* many idiotic things already.'

I winced.

'If anything, this is the least idiotic, because we're going into a public place and, most importantly, I am here!' She waved her hands in front of her. 'It's cool, you know. Some people just wait for danger to find them, but not you, you go after it. You say "Hey, Danger, bet you weren't expecting me. Suck it." You don't wait for the dolphin.'

'Huh?'

'The *dolphin*,' she emphasized. 'You don't wait for the dolphin to hit you in the face.'

'Oh.' I touched my head against hers as we reached Eden, smiling, despite everything, because I had found someone just as weird as me to be friends with. Smiling because I was doing my best not to freak out.

There were two lines of people trickling from the entrance; the first was a short one that moved quickly. The second line stretched all the way around the building and down the street and was moving at a snail's pace.

Millie flipped her hair over her shoulders and sashayed into the smaller, elite line. I went with her, pursing my lips to try and look pouty and important. The woman with the clipboard dragged her gaze along our outfits. A smug smile flitted across her thin red lips. 'Names?'

Millie had already pulled her ID card from her purse.

The woman didn't glance at the ID or her clipboard. 'Sorry, girls. You're not on here. You'll have to join the back of the line.'

Millie bristled. 'You didn't even check.'

Her smirk returned. 'Hon, I don't need to check.'

Millie released a sharp laugh. 'Excuse you? Perhaps you need a refresher course on who we are?'

The woman's expression faltered. She flicked her gaze to me. 'Your name?' she asked me.

'Sophie Gracewell,' I said. 'I have . . . an appointment with my uncle.'

An appointment?

Smooth. Real smooth.

She looked down at her list again. 'Sophie,' she muttered, flicking a page up so she could look at the one underneath it.

Millie poked her head forward so that it was almost right on top of the clipboard. 'He's a close friend of Donata Marino.'

She deflated in front of us. 'Miss Gracewell,' she said, unclipping the rope and standing back to let me through. 'My apologies. We're expecting you.' She eyed Millie with badly concealed contempt.

'I think you mean you're expecting *us*,' Millie said. Her smile was deliciously false. 'We wouldn't want a second mishap, would we?'

With a sigh, Clipboard Bitch stepped back to make room for Millie too. 'Ladies,' she said, 'welcome to Eden.'

CHAPTER FOURTEEN

THE AMBUSH

We combed the first two floors, scanning the dance floors and slipping between booths and drapes. We tried not to knock against glasses of Moët champagne as we shimmied between tables full of models and socialites and men in glossy suits. We downed a couple of vodka and sodas for courage before making our way up one last flight of stairs.

The third floor was smaller than the others. It was furnished entirely in dark wood and thick bamboo furniture, with gold flames casting streaks along the walls. A line of trees in floor-sunken pots climbed towards the ceiling, their spindly branches stretching overhead in waxed leaf canopies. It was like walking into a glamorous safari, only we were the animals.

Towards the far end of the room there was a small stage where a girl with cropped black hair and eye-assaulting sequinned shorts was crooning into a microphone. It was hard not to stare. She was such a train wreck, flopping across the stage and clutching the microphone like it was her life raft. The third floor was a lot quieter than the other two, probably owing to her.

Just behind the unhinged performer was a secluded seating area. It had been cut off from us by drapes and there was a burly bouncer standing in front of the entrance, scanning the small crowd. In the whole club this was definitely the hardest place to get to, and that's how I knew Jack would be in there.

We crossed the empty dance floor and were halted by the bouncer. 'Private area, ladies.'

I peered around him. There, surrounded by a bunch of people drinking and chatting animatedly with one another, sat Uncle Jack. My eyes were immediately drawn to Eric Cain beside him, easily discernible by his flaming-red hair. He was the one who had shot Luca. There were lines of white powder spread across the table and he was leaning forward, a rolled-up bill in his hand as he snorted it greedily, his crimson hair flopping in front of him. He snapped his head up and twitched his nose like a rabbit.

Jack threw his head backwards, his eyes tearing with amusement. The last time I saw my uncle he was bleeding out on a murky floor, and now here he was with a cigar in one hand and a drink in the other, laughing like he didn't have a care in the world.

I pointed him out to the bouncer. 'That's my uncle. I'm

here to see him.'

As if remembering some instruction, he stepped aside and ushered us through. Sara was the first to notice me. She was standing apart from most of the group, hovering, an uneasiness permeating her made-up features. She looked exactly how I felt. There was a tall reed of a man shadowing her. He was much older, with salt-and-pepper hair that curled tightly to his head. He had cat's eyes that tilted upwards at the corner and flashed amber in the dim lighting. His razor-sharp grin was overly curved and entirely mirthless. He was watching me. I looked away. *Focus.* Sara sidled over and placed a gentle hand on my uncle's shoulder. He pulled his gaze from his huddle and saw my eyes boring into him.

Jack got to his feet, and before I could stop him he was crushing me into his chest. His drink sloshed against my shoulder and his cigar flickered perilously close to my hair. 'I'm so glad you came, Sophie. I've been so worried about you.' I pushed him away. Jack gestured to another couch nearby and sat down again. He stubbed out his cigar, patting the space beside him in invitation. 'Please sit. There's so much to talk about.'

Understatement.

He looked better than I'd expected, considering the last time I saw him he was basically dying. He was slimline and well dressed in a dark-grey suit. His grey-brown hair had been cut short and he had shaved, making his face appear younger. He was paler than usual, his cheeks absent of their rosy flush, but his eyes were bright.

The woman on Jack's couch was poised along the edge, her bony fingers laced together on her lap. She was bird-like, with big black eyes rimmed in purple eyeshadow. Donata Marino. Donata Marino was staring at me.

I edged over to the seat. Millie stayed by the entrance, unsure where to put herself. *I'll find you soon*, I mouthed at her. I knew she would have wanted to stay, out of solidarity, but I had to talk to Jack without her. He would be reluctant to share his plans in her company and I intended to get all the answers I could.

Millie slipped behind the bouncer and into the paradisiacal surroundings behind us, while I lowered myself on to the couch, keeping closer to Jack than to Donata, who was perched on my left, the stronger of two evils. I felt the coldness of her stare on the side of my cheek.

Jack put his arm around me, encasing me in a cocktail of alcohol and sweat. 'Thank you for coming.' He was so sincere, so serious . . . so like himself, the kind uncle I remembered from my childhood. And yet when I looked at his surroundings, everything blurred again. The two sides of him did not add up, and the version that had walked into that warehouse was the one I had come here to confront.

'I almost didn't,' I said, ducking out of his grasp. 'And this isn't meant to be some happy reunion.'

Jack had the audacity to laugh. 'Aren't you at least glad I'm alive?'

'I never wanted you to die. I don't think like that.'

'I know,' he said. 'Otherwise you would have blown my cover in the warehouse. But you led that Falcone prick away from me and I owe you my life for that. You're loyal, Sophie, and I'm sorry about the danger I put you in. If I'd have known what would happen I would have sent you somewhere safe.

Trust me, I won't be making that mistake ever again.'

I pressed my lips together, waiting.

'We have a lot to talk about,' he continued. 'I hope once you understand my position, you won't hate me.'

He made it sound so simple, like the lives of scores of people weren't balancing on pinheads around us. Like he wasn't being sheltered by one of the most ruthless families in Chicago. I didn't even know what to ask first. There was so much to say, and yet now that I was here, sitting beside him, staring at him, I felt tongue-tied. 'Jack,' I said, expelling a pent-up sigh. 'How did it come to this?'

I looked at him imploringly, like a child asking if Santa Claus was real but not really wanting to hear the truth.

'I wanted a better life.' His answer was deceptively simple, and not at all what I was expecting. 'I wanted to rise above my station.'

'*This*, Jack,' I said, endeavouring to be more specific since his answer was so painfully vague. It shouldn't be this simple – the things he'd done, the drug trafficking, the killing. 'How did you come to be *here*?'

'I'm safe here, Sophie—'

'Do you know this will probably start a war? Is that what you want to happen?'

Jack hesitated, and for the first time he seemed unsure. But I got the sense it wasn't because of my question, but because of my knowledge of the truce, which I had betrayed by asking it. I hadn't been thinking of hiding anything from him; I was too hell-bent on getting him to stop hiding stuff from me.

He glanced sidelong at Donata. Something passed between them, a flicker of amusement, a quiet understanding. Her smile was spidery. 'Your niece knows more than I expected.'

I scrunched my hands in my lap as my cheeks flushed with heat. 'Isn't it common knowledge?'

Donata was still looking at Jack. She nodded, just once, her eyes slitting as she said, '*Fidelitate Coniuncti.*'

'Not yet,' he said, looking around him now.

There was definitely something between them, and it dawned on me with quiet revulsion what it was. I got up, suddenly feeling hot and sticky.

Jack sprang to his feet. 'Let me explain what happened, Soph.'

I turned on him, trying to ignore the icy wave of Donata's attention. 'How *can* you explain it?' My sudden shrillness roused some of the others from their conversations. 'You're messing around with drugs and the Mafia, and you're cosying up to her to save your own ass even though you *know* how dangerous it is, how many people could die if the truce is broken. What could you *possibly* say that would make any of this OK?'

Jack's sigh deflated his chest and made him seem smaller. 'It all comes down to money, Sophie. When I was a young man I had to ask myself, how can I use my talents to make sure I don't end up on the bottom rung of society, trying to climb out of poverty my whole life? Your father and I never got the chance to make a go of our lives in the right way. All either of us ever had was our own smarts and the ambition to do—'

I bristled. 'Do not involve my father in this. He has nothing to do with your depraved drug trade!'

Jack clenched a hand on my shoulder and squeezed it. 'Calm down. You're making a scene.'

'This whole thing is already a scene!' I hissed, pointing openly at the cocaine two feet away from us, at Eric's chomping jaw and guffawing laugh, at the girls pouring champagne on each other and shrieking in the corner. 'You shouldn't be here! You should be far away.'

Jack set his jaw. 'I'm not leaving you.'

'I insist that you leave me.' I edged closer, cutting Donata out of the conversation, and dropped my voice. 'And you should leave these people too, before it's too late.'

Jack shook his head, his expression suddenly drained of joviality. 'Sophie, we're in this together.'

'My family is not in this with you, Jack,' I gritted out. 'When are you going to get that through your head?'

'Your father built his entire livelihood and his family on the money *I* gave him for that diner. Gracewell's might be the culmination of Mickey's life's work, but it sits on my trade—'

'No,' I spat. 'Stop!' I was tired of being swayed this way and that by people with corrupt morals and pretty words. I was tired of hearing people out, of giving the benefit of the doubt only to have it thrown back in my face. This was not what I had come here for, to be leered at by Donata and her cronies, to be lied to by my uncle, to be terrified by the idea that I was tied to him, that someone like him was my anchor.

I turned from him, scanning the exit. Sara was looking at me. The man with the sharp grin was still hovering close by, watching her now. A shiver of unease shot up my spine. She dipped her head and smiled sympathetically. Did she have an overprotective uncle too? Had she been forced into this life the same way the Falcones were raised to be one thing and one thing only? Was she as ashamed of her family as I was? We were the same age, more or less. But she was here now, stuck, and I was determined not to be.

Jack stepped between us and brought his face close to mine. Our eyes – the same eyes – bored into one another. 'Sophie, we're family, you and I, and I want you by my side, where I know you'll be safe. It's where you belong.'

I blanched. 'I have a mother,' I snapped. 'A mother you almost got killed, and believe me, I'm not about to forget it.' Anger mounted, rushing and sizzling inside me. 'I came here to hear you out, but it was a mistake. I'm glad you're safe. I'm glad my father doesn't have to grieve for his little brother in prison, but I don't want anything to do with you. Not now, not ever. I'm saying goodbye. *For good.*'

I stepped back, but he stepped with me. His cheeks had flushed a rosy hue. 'Sophie,' he said, surprisingly gentle, yet intimidating. He was teetering on the edge of something, his eyes flicking from side to side, to Donata, to his cronies. 'There is no way out now.'

I lifted my chin, steel staring into steel. 'There is for me, Jack. You might have forged your allegiance,' I gestured pointedly to Donata, then swirled my hand around, encompassing the club, its hedonism and all the wrongness, 'but I stand with my mother, and *only her.*'

A veil of anger snapped Jack's features back into place. '*Only her?*' he asked, his eyes slitting. 'And what about the Falcones?' He spat the word.

There was an Italian curse from somewhere over his shoulder. Donata.

'I have nothing to do with the Falcones,' I insisted.

Jack arched an eyebrow. 'I was in that warehouse, Sophie. You're the key to their undoing; you're the answer to my freedom. And with the Marinos, we'll be able to do it.' His voice climbed in pitch and his eyes were manic, darting. 'We'll finally be able to rid Chicago of this festering wound of self-righteous fools. Mark them for every mark they put on you. We'll hang Valentino in his chair. We'll drown Felice in his own honey. We'll take Luca Falcone's head from his body.'

My stomach seized up and I clasped my hand over my mouth. So he *wanted* the war. He was orchestrating it.

I swirled around, scanning the numbers – the sheer amount of Marino family milling around us. They mightn't have been ready before, when the truce had come down, but they were ready now. Were the missing Marino twins here, too? Baying for revenge, all of them united in hatred?

Donata was laughing – it was a high-pitched screech of pleasure. I hated her. I hated her. I hated her. And I felt sick, so sick I couldn't stand another minute in their presence.

'I'm leaving.' I turned. 'This was a mistake.'

I pushed by the bouncer and marched on to the main floor. But I was stopped again, this time by Sara. I almost crashed into her. She raised her hands. 'Wait,' she said. 'Please.'

'I thought he cared about me, but he doesn't. I'm just a pawn.' I stifled the urge to cry, swallowing hard against the rising lump in my throat. 'I want to go home, Sara.'

'I know,' she said, tugging me to the side so all those hovering behind us couldn't overhear our conversation. Even Razor Grin was out of earshot, and he wasn't happy about it. 'But this isn't the way to make it happen. She won't let you leave if she thinks you won't even contemplate helping her.'

I glanced over my shoulder. Donata was poised on the edge of her dance floor, watching us. 'What would you have me do, then?'

Sara's sigh hung in the air. 'Just agree to whatever she wants.'

'Are you crazy?'

She edged closer so even her fuchsia lips couldn't be read when she spoke. 'I'm not telling you to tell the truth, just say you'll think about it or whatever. My mother doesn't like the word "no". You're not going to walk out of here smiling if you don't at least pretend to give her the respect she thinks she deserves.'

'Why are you helping me?'

She dropped her gaze and when she spoke again she was just a little girl in a thrumming, glitzy club where she didn't belong. And it hit me so clearly in that moment that I felt an intrusive and weird urge to hug her. 'Because I was you, Sophie,' she said, glancing over her shoulder. 'I wanted to study music, to see the world, to hang out with my friends, to do *good* things and be a good person. I still *am* you in a lot of ways, so I get it. There's this blood in us – people who think they can speak for us.' She started tearing her fingernails along her arms like she could scratch it all out of her if she tried hard enough. I grabbed her hands and pushed them away from her arms, to make her stop. They fell limp at her sides. 'You're lucky. There's another life for you. You've just got to be smart enough to hold on to it, to get back to it. And that means maybe you need to play the game—'

I was wrenched away from the girl with the kind heart and the big dreams. Five spindly fingers clasped around my wrist, long red nails digging into my skin like talons. I was twirled around until Donata's face was inches from my own and Sara's was lost somewhere in the crowd behind me. Donata's lips had twitched into what I supposed was her attempt at a smile. 'You and I aren't done.'

Her heavy-lidded gaze was steady on mine and I felt suffocated by it. Despite Sara's gentle presence, the friendly way she spoke, her unassuming nature, *this* was the real Marino family and I couldn't pretend to like them.

Jack was hovering behind Donata. His face had twisted and for the first time, he seemed uncomfortable. Still, he let her hold me like that, digging her nails into my skin until I felt her draw blood.

Donata threw her head back. 'Antony,' she called, bird-like in pitch. 'Antony, it's time!' I watched the faces behind her, their eyes snapping to the back of her head, but whoever Antony was – her son? A would-be torturer à la Calvino Falcone? – he was either too scared to answer her call, or maybe he wasn't there at all. 'Marco! Libero!' she called, but still, no one came to her aid. The music was too loud.

I kept my voice steady. 'I can't do anything for you right now. I have a pounding headache and I need to go home. Let me come back another day,' I added, taking Sara's advice.

Behind us, the singer was crying her way through a nineties pop song.

Donata Marino rounded on me. 'You can go when you've agreed to help us,' she snapped.

Jack stepped closer to me, around the side of her, keeping

his distance, like she was radioactive. 'Donata,' he warned. 'You're scaring her.'

She rolled her eyes, but he had managed to shut her up. He softened his voice, peppering it with gentle force as if to make up for Donata's aggression. 'There's something of mine in the diner, Soph, but the Falcones are watching the place night and day. It's too dangerous for us to go in. But not for you. You can help secure it. You can sneak in unharmed, and bring it to us.'

'Get it yourself.' The words were out of my mouth before the meaning of what he had said dropped into my stomach.

'There's a safe,' Jack cut in. 'And we—'

'No,' I hissed. 'No way.'

I really could have laughed right then. How insane did they think I was? They were both staring at me, waiting for me to change my answer. My head was so heavy. Suddenly it felt like the whole club had tripled in capacity. The dance floor behind me was filling up. People were starting to jostle against my back. The singer was screaming her next verse.

I could make out Millie through the crowds, fighting towards me. 'We should go,' she shouted, pushing her way closer. 'Something's going on.'

Jack was there in a flash, blocking my immediate exit. 'Sophie, I know it's not an ideal situation but there's a lot of money at stake. If we could just sit down and talk about all of this . . . Your dad would want me to help you. He would want me to keep you safe.'

'You're the one putting me in danger.' I stumbled backwards, into the crowds. They were closing in, stifling me.

Something struck me in the back and I crashed nose first

into my uncle's chest. Razor Grin and Eric Cain were at his sides, shouting, pulling him away from me. But Jack was fighting them. He was shouting too, his face turning crimson with fresh rage. 'How could you betray me? How could you do this to us?' It took me an extra second to realize it was me he was yelling at. But I hadn't done anything. I faltered backwards, away from his huddle, sinking into a scrap of shoving bodies.

I could hear Millie screaming, but there were other people shouting too – male voices. Voices I recognized. I was pulled backwards. Bodies pressed against me. I fell against someone, thumping the back of my head. A shoe clipped my ankle and I lost my footing, my heels giving way beneath me.

It all happened in a matter of seconds. I landed with a thump that knocked the wind out of my lungs, and then Nic appeared, circling above me. He lunged at Eric Cain, who was a flash of darting red hair and pale skin. Nic grabbed him by the throat and yanked him downwards, cracking his knee straight into his face. I could almost hear Eric's nose smash into pieces as he crumpled to the ground. Nic hurled his foot into his back, the force of the kick bending his body like an S. He slammed into him again and Eric's slim frame contorted and writhed out of view. He pulled his knife out. Vaguely stunned and winded, I thought, *I am about to witness Nic murdering someone.*

Jack sprang up, and Nic's attention snapped in two. He arced to the left and disappeared into a sea of faceless people, chasing my uncle. Felice Falcone's voice rang in my ears. He was somewhere close by, yelling instructions, calm against the storm. I scrabbled on the floor, my heels sliding as I tried to get up. Someone was brandishing a gun above me and I dipped backwards, cowering on the ground.

The crowds swelled until there was nothing but blackness overhead. I couldn't see Millie any more, couldn't find Nic or Jack. I was shouting but no one could hear me; no one was listening. I slid backwards, trying to get to my feet again, but someone knocked me to the ground. There was a rasping voice. Calvino Falcone, with his shiny bald head glinting underneath the lights. He charged over me, nicking my ankle with his shoe. I crawled in his direction, trying to free myself from the sea of limbs that were keeping me down, but he stopped abruptly and stumbled backwards.

I slammed my body to the right and he fell to his knees beside me. I reached out to use his shoulder as an anchor but he was too quick. He sprang up clumsily and threw himself at something. I was shoved backwards again. The blackness overhead enveloped me. Gino darted by, his gun pointed at someone I couldn't see. Then there was a shape – wide and tall, and careening backwards. Calvino fell on top of me and I was crushed against the floor. I lay winded, trapped and star-fished beneath his limbs.

Someone was screaming my name. I couldn't see properly. There was red everywhere. It covered the floor. My hands were coated in it. It was dripping around my ears. It stuck between my fingers and matted my hair in clumps. My shoes kept sliding on that thick, warm liquid, my eyes blurring with the sheer volume of it. I was gasping for air but everything smelt strange, like rust and salt, and my mouth tasted like metal. I was gagging as I tried to struggle free from Calvino's hugeness. Why hadn't he stood up yet?

And then it hit me. He was dead.

CHAPTER FIFTEEN

THE GETAWAY

I pushed against Calvino's lifeless form, trying to shift over six feet of bulky muscle. He rolled off me, landing face down on the ground with a thud. His hand was crushed underneath his body and his legs were sticking out at a strange angle. Blood pooled around us. It was all over my arms and legs, all over him. There were multiple stab wounds in his back.

My stomach lurched and I spewed vodka all over the ground. It mixed with the blood, glistening under the lights. With panic still flooding inside me, I stumbled forward and pulled myself to my feet.

Everyone was scattering. A smudge of faces streaked by me, their expressions contorted in terror. Millie was gone – they all were, Falcones and Marinos and Jack, and I was alone, steeped in Calvino's blood. I stumbled towards the stairwell, trying to escape the screams that were ringing in my ears. It took me a while to realize they were coming from me.

I hurtled down the steps, tripping over my heels. When I reached the ground floor, I was swept inside a stampede clamouring for the exit. I called out for Millie but I was stuck inside the swarm and she wasn't anywhere. I squeezed between shoulders and arms, pushing my way towards the front. If anything happened to her, I'd never forgive myself. I shouldn't have brought her here – I should never have come. I was a bad friend, the *worst* kind, and the more people that jostled against me, the higher my panic soared.

Outside, everything was hazy. The air was too thick and humid. Sirens wailed in the distance. I staggered across the street. The pain in my ribs was resurfacing and my whole body was convulsing. I clutched at my sides and pressed on, trying to put as much distance as possible between the club and me.

On the other side of the street, I started trying to make my way back to where Millie had parked at the start of the night, but I was disoriented; I couldn't remember. How much time had passed since then? An hour? Two? The blood in my hair was streaking down my face and dripping into my eyes, mixing with my tears as I gasped them out. I fished my phone out, doubling over on myself as old pains rushed through my body. The screen was blank – it was either broken or without battery. I shook it and tried again but it didn't light up. *Crap.*

'Millie!' I yelled, blinking through the red, shouting into the sky. 'Millie!'

I was yanked, crying and screaming, into an alleyway, and

pushed against a wall.

Luca's eyes pierced the darkness as he brought his face close to mine.

Then his hands were on me, his fingers running up and down my back as I stood shaking before him. It took me a second to realize what he was shouting.

'Where did they get you? Where are you hurt?'

My teeth were chattering so badly I could barely speak. I looked down at his hands where they were pressed against my body. I was covered in blood. Every part of my dress was soaked. He released me and my legs gave out. I flopped like a doll, half-bent at the waist, panting.

He took my face between his hands, his thumbs smearing the blood and tears together on my cheeks as he lifted my head. 'Sophie, you need to focus. I need to find the wound.'

I blinked a fresh stream of tears on to my cheeks. 'I'm OK,' I said, convulsing. 'I'm OK.'

'Come on,' he urged. He pressed his body against mine, anchoring me upright as he moved his fingers against my neck and back into my hair, searching frantically. 'Come on,' he breathed. 'Help me. I need you to help me.'

'It's not my blood,' I cried, grabbing his hands and crushing them in mine. 'It's not my blood!'

Luca faltered as my words crashed into him. Comprehension dawned, slowly lifting the panic from his features. He dropped his hands and stood back. 'I thought—'

Nic came charging into the alleyway, pulling Millie in tow. He barrelled into Luca, knocking him off kilter. 'I've got her,' he was saying. 'Did you find—' He stopped when he saw me. His eyes swelled and he cursed so loudly it made Millie scream.

Luca grabbed Nic by his collar and pulled him further into the alley. '*Calmati! Calmati!*'

Nic was still shouting.

Luca slammed him against the wall. 'It's not her blood! It's not her blood!'

Millie collapsed into me, winding her arms around my neck. 'Soph, I. Was. So Worried. I. Couldn't. See. You. Anywhere . . .' she trailed off, her words turning to sobs as I imprinted Calvino's blood on her.

The sirens were getting closer and Nic was pulling me away. I pulled Millie with me. 'We've got to get out of here. Now!'

'My car is back that way!' She pointed in the direction of the club, the crowds, the sirens, the chaos. Her face fell as she realized the impossibility of it all. '*Shit.*'

'Come on,' said Nic, tugging us with him.

We followed the Falcone brothers down the alley, both of us hobbling in our heels. The sirens split apart the night air as they got closer and closer. At the end of the lane we staggered into a parking lot.

Luca jumped into his SUV and started the engine. Before I knew what I was doing I was climbing into the back seat, wedging myself beside Millie and dragging blood across their leather seats. We needed to be anywhere but here. Nic got into the front seat and Luca took off.

'Take the back streets,' Nic told Luca.

'I know,' he ground out. 'Did you get him?'

'He was too quick.'

Luca cursed. 'I told Valentino it was a bad idea.'

'Better than them coming to us first.'

'It was the wrong territory.'

A scream from outside jolted me from their conversation. I pressed myself against the window, peering at the parking lot as we pulled away from it. Felice and Dom were dragging someone towards another SUV. A flash of purple hair streaked across my vision. Felice shoved her into his back seat and Dom threw himself in behind her, his hand snaking around her mouth.

We pulled on to a back street and I lost sight of them.

'What are they doing?' I asked, pressing myself against the window and leaving bloody handprints on the glass.

No one answered me. Millie was still crying. Nic and Luca were arguing in Italian. Jack was God knows where. We were speeding into the night, far away from the direction of Cedar Hill and the sirens at the club. And in the sudden calmness of the car, one very vital piece of information erupted inside my head.

'Calvino's dead!' The memory descended on me like a black cloud. 'He fell on top of me. This is his blood!'

My throat started burning. Millie pitched over her knees and vomited.

Luca and Nic had fallen silent in the front. They shared an uneasy glance, and then Nic turned around, leaning across the armrest.

'Your uncle is dead,' I said, hearing the horror warp my voice. 'He's gone. He's dead.'

Nic was so calm it threw me.

'Do you hear me?' I pressed. 'Do you understand what I'm saying?'

'We know,' said Nic. Simple, emotionless. But his face was

too placid. He was barely blinking, and I glimpsed a muscle feathering in his jaw. Luca's knuckles were white against the steering wheel. Millie was still retching.

Why did they have to come? They had ruined everything. Now someone was dead and it was only going to get worse. Everything was such a violent, steaming mess. That stupid crimson card. That stupid boy.

Nic was watching me.

'You broke your promise,' I said.

'And you broke yours.'

There was no accusation in his words, but they still stung. Every second seemed to pull him further away from the boy I had thought he was, and I was starting to wonder if I had tricked myself – if the feeling of needing someone, of *wanting* someone to want me in a world where everyone had turned their back on me, had masked the truth of everything.

'Did you mean it – at least when you said it?' I asked, my voice deceptively steady for all the commotion that was raging inside me. *Show me who you are.*

It was hard to find the warmth in his dark eyes now. They were hardened, absent of their golden flecks. 'No,' he said. 'I never meant it.'

Honesty at last. Even if it stung. Well, we could give each other that, at least.

'I didn't mean it either,' I said. I didn't want him to think he had gotten one up on me, even now, in the midst of all the bloodshed and horror. My pride was important to me, and his betrayal was irritating.

'I thought you did,' he admitted with a frown. 'But when I told Luca he was sure you'd lied.'

I glared at the back of Luca's head. So mistrustful. So accurate. Tears were streaming down my face. My vision was red around the edges. In my mind the image of Calvino careening backwards played over and over. I tried to blink it away, but it slithered back in every time my attention lapsed. Here was a new nightmare, waiting to play over the top of the warehouse one. Great. At least my mother wouldn't have to suffer this one along with me. The world is full of small mercies – I chose to recognize that one.

To Nic, I said, 'You would have come either way, though.' It was a statement, not a question. I knew he would do anything to get to Jack. To have the first move on the Marinos was obviously a no-brainer. Anything I did or didn't do was peripheral to that.

'Yes,' he said. 'We would have.'

I looked away from him, out the window, every molecule in my body still trained on those brothers, wondering what was next for them – for all of us. But I didn't want to talk about Nic's betrayal any more. We were both just a couple of liars with blood on our hands and agendas more important than our trust in one another.

It is what it is.

We were leaving the city, heading west and watching the city lights fade behind us. Millie was cowering against me in the back seat. 'Soph, I'm so scared. I really don't want to die tonight.'

'You're not going to die, Millie.' Luca spoke matter-of-factly from the front seat. His panic in the alleyway was a million miles away from his carefully controlled demeanour now. 'I think we all need to calm down.'

'I am calm,' said Nic. It was scary how emotionless they could act, how pragmatic they seemed to be at a time when it felt like the world was tipping over. For all I knew they could have murdered someone in Eden, and still I didn't have the guts to ask them.

'I'm not talking about you,' Luca returned. 'We can't send them back to Cedar Hill like this. They're in shock. *Qualcuno chiamerà la polizia.*'

I looked at myself and then at Millie. Our dresses were destroyed, our limbs were bloodied. 'We're a mess. Our parents are going to freak out.'

Luca nodded. Calm. Focused. 'We need to get you both cleaned up.'

Nic turned to his brother. 'It will take a lot. *Guardali.*'

Luca's grip on the wheel tightened, threads of red lining his white-knuckled hands. He kept his eyes trained on the road. 'I can't,' he said quietly. 'It makes me sick.'

'I didn't think she'd come,' Nic said.

They switched to Italian as the argument escalated.

'It's too late now,' said Nic, flipping the conversation back to English, either too weary or too distracted to stay angry. 'We have to deal with the evidence. Sophie is covered in it.' He threw me what I assumed was an apologetic glance, but it only made me more concerned about the 'evidence', and whether *I* constituted part of that as well.

Millie's hands were clutching mine so hard my fingers were turning purple. I didn't want her to let go. I wished I hadn't counted those stab wounds. They were printed in the backs of my eyelids: those pooling smudges.

Nic's phone rang. He turned away and his voice changed,

turning low and hurried, as he flipped into long strings of Italian. When he hung up, he released a heavy sigh. It was the closest thing I had seen to grief up until then.

'Valentino?' Luca asked Nic.

'Yes.'

'Did you tell him?'

Nic nodded. 'The boss is angry.'

'*Ci sarà del sangue,*' said Luca, shaking his head. Whatever that meant, it didn't sound good.

Millie pinched me. 'What's going on?'

Nic turned around again. 'Valentino knows you're here.'

'Is he angry about what happened?' I asked.

Nic looked away from me, out the window towards the passing trees. 'Yes,' he said quietly. 'He's angry.'

I got the sense that was a colossal understatement.

'Where are we going?' Millie asked tremulously.

Nic fell back against his seat with sudden, violent exhaustion. 'We're going to *Evelina.*'

Millie turned to me, her eyes wide and pooling. 'What's *Evelina*?'

Evelina was the name of Felice's runaway wife. And if *Evelina* was also a place, that meant it was his house. I thought about sugar-coating my response, but there was no point. We were sitting in a pool of Calvino Falcone's blood and speeding into the darkness with two assassins to the place where the Falcones had tortured me and held me against my will.

When I said the words they were strangely disconnected, as though my threshold for horror had caved in and there was nothing but blithe impassivity left. I had stopped

146

shaking. I was numb. 'We're going to Felice's house.'

Millie dug her nails into my hands. 'No, please. Make them turn around. I just want to go home.'

There was only one thing more horrifying than the thought of being inside Felice's house again, and that was the thought of seeing my mother react to my appearance. She would keel over. She certainly would never sleep again, and I couldn't watch her waste away from anxiety any more. And besides, it wasn't like they were going to let two girls steeped in Marino/Falcone evidence walk unaided back into Cedar Hill, so why pretend we even had a choice?

'It's going to be fine,' I lied, patting Millie's arm.

'Shit,' she said. 'We're going to hell.'

In that moment, with her pallor drained by fear and our trembling hands entwined beneath blood that wasn't ours, it really felt like we were.

PART III

'This is the law: blood spilt
upon the ground cries out
for more.'

Aeschylus, *The Libation Bearers*

CHAPTER SIXTEEN

EVELINA

I had only ever seen Felice's house once – on the night I was kidnapped by the Falcones. Being back again was like being plunged into a nightmare. Poised at the end of a winding driveway lit up by iron lamps, it was an architectural feat. Unblemished stone climbed across three stories, protruding into the front lawn in a circular balcony supported by a row of Roman columns. The roof was domed. Four black SUVs surrounded the front entrance. His precious bees were around the back somewhere, quiet and hidden in the darkness. I was glad of that, at least.

I had the vaguest sense we might die, but I didn't mention it to Millie. We held hands as we crossed the driveway. The gravel was crunchy underneath our heels. I remembered that crunch. I had heard it once before, when I had left this place, but that felt like a lifetime ago now, and the bruises had only just begun to fade.

A faint pricking feeling in my eyes made me realize I was crying. I wasn't even aware of it. The tears felt like rain, born of something outside of myself and far from my immediate awareness.

A crystal chandelier lit up the foyer, and on the ground, the Falcone crest greeted us – a crimson falcon poised for flight. I tried not to stare at it. It brought back too many unpleasant feelings and I was already at capacity. Up ahead, the stairway split, winding towards the second storey in mirroring steps.

The quiet was eerie. Did they know about Calvino? Would Luca or Nic have to tell them? I was conscious of every droplet of his blood on my skin. We climbed the stairs, our heels click-clacking off the marble as we followed the boys up and up. On the second storey, Luca and Nic led us to a room at the very end of a dimly lit hallway. The door was already ajar. Leather couches sat either side of a grand fireplace. The local news was playing on a giant muted TV. The headline was flashing:

ONE DEAD IN EDEN MOB FIGHT. POLICE ARE ON THE SCENE.

Valentino was in his chair by the fireplace. His attention was trained on the TV, so I could see only the side of his head – close-cropped black hair and a sharp profile. Beside him, squished side by side on the couch, were three boys; the first I recognized as CJ, Calvino's twelve-year-old son. He was the one who had filmed my torture, thirsty for his dad's approval.

He was staring at a fixed point on the floor. The other two boys were younger than him – no more than nine or ten – with rounder faces and fair hair. They had the same eyes, though, and their mouths bent the same way. Even though there was a yard of space on the other side of them, they had crushed themselves together. They were crying. I wondered where their mother was. I wondered if they had one – or had she, like Evelina, made a run for it while she still could?

'Wait out here,' said Nic. 'We'll be back.'

He crossed in front of Luca and entered the room. Luca lingered, keeping Millie and me under his attention for a moment longer. His brows lifted and in the silence I realized my teeth were chattering. I unhinged my jaw to stop them.

'Relax.' Another beat under that azure gaze. 'It's going to be OK.'

I believed him, that's the strange thing. He was earnest, at least in that moment, and I remembered the last proper words I had spoken to him. *He's broken. You all are.* It occurred to me, as I quivered in someone else's blood, that I had walked myself into danger for the shred of hope I had for an uncle I wished would change but never would, and I realized we were both broken, he and I. We were a couple of fractured lines, running parallel to one another, stuck in families that wouldn't ever truly let us go. And I was sorry for hurting him.

'OK,' I said quietly. Millie didn't say anything, but I could feel her shaking beside me, trying to hold on to herself. 'We'll stay here.'

Luca stalked into the room while Millie and I hovered outside the doorway, teetering alien-like on the edge of something we were caught up in but not a part of.

The brothers crossed the room and rounded the couch. Valentino was still staring at the headline. It had changed:

DONATA MARINO TAKEN INTO CUSTODY. MORE TO COME.

Luca clapped his hands on the younger boys' shoulders. '*Questo è un giorno triste*,' he said softly. His face clouded and for the first time I could see grief creeping to the surface. The boys looked up at him, their eyes shimmering. A moment passed between them and I got the overwhelming sense that to these kids, Luca was someone important. And not just in the Mafia sense.

Nic bent down beside CJ. His voice was hard. 'We will have our revenge.'

Without lifting his eyes from the floor, CJ nodded.

Luca dragged his brother upright by the back of his neck. 'Can't we have one moment of peace, Nicoli?'

'This is not a time for peace. It's not what's best.'

'And what's best for Sal and Aldo?' asked Luca. '*Sono bambini.*'

The youngest boy blinked his big eyes. 'Me and Sal aren't babies,' he said, affronted. 'We *want* to talk about revenge.'

I glanced sidelong at Millie, our faces screwing up with matching levels of shock. We had never heard a child talk like that. Not even in movies. It was jarring, and yet in that room just then it seemed so . . . casual.

Sal didn't look as convinced as Aldo. His face was blotchy with his tears and his lip was quivering violently.

'You see?' said Nic to Luca. 'This is what's best.'

Luca shook his head.

Valentino pulled his attention from the news. They were showing footage of the club exterior now. There were fire trucks and ambulances on the scene. Onlookers had gathered around it and the front entrance was cordoned off with police tape.

He turned to his brothers. 'Can you two stop arguing? I'm trying to find out what happened.'

'We know what happened,' said Nic. 'We were there.'

Valentino rounded on his brothers. He pulled his hands from the wheels of his chair and cracked his knuckles. 'Oh, you were?' he asked, his voice acidic. 'Then maybe you can tell me how you screwed up so spectacularly and managed to get one of our finest members killed in action? Maybe you can tell me how you marched into that club with a contact already on the inside, the element of surprise on your side *and* five armed assassins, and still *somehow* failed to kill a sitting duck?'

'They were armed!' Nic said. 'There were too many people in the way and Calvino went back for Jack after we pulled out. What could I do about that?'

'You could have gone for Donata!' Valentino snapped. 'You had them in the palm of your hand and they both got away!'

Nic's anger rose to match his brother's. 'You don't know what it was like, Valentino. You weren't there.'

'It's not my job to be there! It's *your* job!' Valentino clasped his hands around the arms of his chair and hoisted himself up, balancing on his good leg so he could be closer to Nic. I was surprised by how tall he was. He jabbed his brother's chest. '*You* said it would work. *You* cased the place. We put our trust in *your* intel and it failed. You've made me look weak, Nic. *Un pazzo incompetente!'*

'You're not a fool, Valentino.'

'Tell that to the Marinos!' he hissed.

Nic lifted his chin and, defiantly, he said, 'We're still stronger than them.'

'Are we?' Valentino's voice fell deathly quiet. He bared his teeth, sharp canines ripping into a savage smile with no mirth. 'What makes you so sure, brother? We don't know what Jack Gracewell traded for their protection. We don't know what weapons Donata Marino has.'

He released his stance and slumped back, landing heavily in his chair. It was jarring to witness him so unhinged. Tonight had removed his mask of careful impassivity and it was unsettling for everyone. Aldo's sobs turned to hiccups. He and Sal were cowering so hard they were sinking into the couch.

Valentino's shoulders slumped as he looked away from Nic, scowling. 'Calvino has died and Jack Gracewell walks free still. *È una disgrazia.'*

'We did our best,' said Nic.

Valentino growled at his brother, his features turning feral, the way I had seen Luca's many times before. 'It wasn't good enough, do you understand? Your best wasn't good enough.'

'Stop shouting at me!' Nic replied. He turned to Luca, his expression imploring. 'Tell him to stop!'

'Valentino,' said Luca, calmly. He clasped his twin's shoulder, and Valentino sat a little straighter, strengthened by the gesture. 'This isn't helping. What's done is done. We

156

need to stick together, not tear ourselves apart.'

It occurred to me that I had never seen the Falcone twins side by side before. On the surface they were so alike – the same bright eyes and stern expressions – but when they spoke, they broke apart. This time it was Luca in command of himself, controlled and practical, as Valentino shook with rage, turning dangerous at the threat of what lay ahead. There was a world of difference between them, but I knew what they were: two halves of one whole. The boss and the underboss, united, in that moment, in their loss.

After a heavy silence, Valentino waved his arm in half-surrender. 'It is what it is,' he conceded. 'We must look forward.'

Millie and I had gotten used to being invisible by now. We had shuffled closer without meaning to, listening with eagerness as they argued back and forth.

It was Aldo who spotted us. Wiping his nose with an over-used tissue, he pointed through the doorway. 'Who are they?' he asked, tugging at his brother's sleeve.

Sal cocked his head. 'I don't know.'

Aldo's eyes grew. 'Is that . . . is that . . . blood?'

I looked down at myself. *Uh-oh.*

Valentino followed Aldo's gesture, and our eyes met. He dropped his face into his hands, his reaction muffled by his fingers. I was expecting a mild explosion but his response was weary. 'Luca, *why* would you bring her in here looking like that?'

CJ lifted his head. He lurched forwards, bending over his knees. I thought he was going to be sick but instead he cradled himself, his fingers clutching at his sides as he stared down at the floor. He was probably smart enough to know it wasn't my blood.

Luca looked at me sharply and I had the sudden image of him strangling me.

'Sorry,' I mouthed, hands raised in supplication. Millie and I backed away, into the semi-darkness of the hallway. We waited with our backs pressed against the wall and our hands squeezed tight while the conversation turned to angry Italian murmurs inside the room.

In the distance, down the marble stairs, we heard the purposeful clacking of heels. At the end of the hallway, coming at us like a bird of prey, was the crisp figure of Elena Genovese-Falcone. Her face was shadowed by the darkness but she glided with purpose, her black dress pooling around her. She was so like Donata and yet the idea of them once playing together as children seemed impossible. She was every bit the Falcone queen, marching through her dark castle. It was hard to decide who was worse between her and Donata, but they both definitely had a seat waiting for them in the pits of hell.

I pulled Millie against the window at the end of the hallway. Part of me wanted to open it and jump out into the garden. I'd take a thousand bees over Lucifer any day.

Elena came to an abrupt stop outside the room. She turned on the heel of her boot and pinned us silently with her eyes. Her lip curled, and in that plummy voice she said, 'Did I not tell you to stay far away from my sons, girl?'

Millie gulped. I gulped.

She gestured at Millie, one wiry finger tracing her outline. 'And now it seems you have multiplied.'

I felt an unexpected rush of indignation course through me. 'I *was* staying away from them,' I protested. 'Maybe you should have told them to stay away from me.'

Millie pinched me. *Shut up.*

Elena flashed her teeth. 'You think I didn't?'

'W-we d-don't want to be here,' said Millie. 'It wasn't our choice. We were in Eden when it all kicked off and we got caught up in the . . . in the hustle. We just want to go home, Mrs Falcone.'

Elena pitched forward and got right in my face. 'Rubbing shoulders with my sister, were you, little Gracewell?'

I shook my head. 'Of course not—'

'Were you laughing about how your father slaughtered my husband?'

'What? No, I went there to see my uncle—'

'And what exactly has your uncle bargained with my sister for her protection?'

'I–I don't know,' I stuttered.

'Really, we don't,' Millie added.

'Drugs? Money?' she continued, watching us closely for any signs of betrayal on our faces. 'What does that man have in his diner that would open the gates of my sister's dynasty?'

My exasperation peaked, and too exhausted to reign in my annoyance, I half-shouted, 'I don't know! I don't know anything about it!'

I blinked and her face was an inch from mine. 'I think you're lying.' Closer still, until Millie was axed from my periphery. 'I think there are lies in those eyes.'

I blinked hard – to hide the lies? Perhaps that's what she thought, but the truth was that I was experiencing an overwhelming flurry of rage and I was *this* close to slapping her right in her face to get her away from me.

'Secrets,' she hissed, pulling back from me at last. 'We all have them. And, girl, I will find yours and when I do, my sons will see you into the next life. If you're a spy, I will find out.'

'She's not,' interrupted Millie. Elena double-blinked, reminded that there were two of us.

Millie's words came flooding out. 'Neither of us are spies, actually. We're not good at subtlety, to tell you the truth, so if we were you'd have found us out by now. We just want to go home and watch movies and go back to school in a couple of weeks. Please don't kill us or ask someone to kill us or hurt us. We don't care about your sister, I didn't even talk to her at the club, which was really overpriced and kind of creepy, and even though I saw her in the crowds I thought she looked kind of haggard and definitely not as glamorous as you but then again I'm sure she's like twenty years older than you and you got all the good looks in your family.'

Elena opened her mouth to interrupt, but Millie ploughed on, oblivious, silencing whatever she was about to say.

'Sophie didn't even really talk to her either, you see it was Jack she went to see because he gave her a card, but you probably know that because your son stole it which is fine because he was looking for Jack so that's totally his prerogative, but Sophie only showed up because she thought her uncle was going to apologize and try to make everything right but obviously he didn't, he made it way worse, which means he's just totally evil, and we know that now and we'll never make the mistake of trusting him again, I promise you Mrs Genovese, erm, Falcone, Your Eminence, ma'am. We're sorry. We're not spies.'

Millie's panting filled the silence. Elena's mouth stretched in a joker-like grin, all teeth and no lips, and something that sounded like a snort of amusement rustled the air between us.

She raised her finger and pointed it at Millie's forehead, and just when I thought she was about to poke her eye out, she said, 'You, I like much more than her. You, I believe.'

I watched in silent shock as Elena disappeared into the sitting room, her dress cascading behind her.

'Holy crap,' breathed Millie. 'Holy crap, she's scary.'

'Yeah,' I said, incredulity mixing with fierce gratitude for my best friend. 'And you managed to disarm her.'

Inside, the Falcones spoke in tones that rose higher and higher.

Elena: 'Felice has returned.'

Nic: 'I can do it.'

Luca: 'No.'

Valentino: 'It's not about doing the right thing. It's about doing the intelligent thing.'

Elena: 'They've broken the truce.'

Valentino: 'It's my decision.'

Luca: 'Don't worsen the situation, Valentino.'

Valentino: 'We need to show solidarity in this.'

The conversation dipped to low Italian murmurs.

After a while, Elena left the room with CJ in tow. Her arm was resting along his shoulder, pulling him against her as she strode along the hallway. Luca and Nic emerged next, ashen-faced. Something was definitely wrong. Even more wrong than it already had been.

Luca walked ahead of us. 'Follow me. You can shower and get cleaned up in here.'

He led us into a bathroom halfway down the corridor. It had a gigantic marble-fitted bathtub and gold faucets. The business of killing really was so lucrative. Nic disappeared into a different room.

'Where did your mother go with CJ?' I asked Luca.

He opened a cupboard and dropped two bath towels on to the countertop by the sink. 'Shower quickly, get dressed and then we'll take you home. The sooner the better.'

'Why?' asked Millie, getting in on the suspicion. 'What's happening?

Nic returned with a pile of clothes. He dropped them at our feet. 'These belong to our cousins. Some of it should fit.'

They shared a glance as they shut the door behind them. Millie and I pressed our ears against it but we couldn't hear anything. The wood was too thick.

'What's happening?' she asked. 'Are we in trouble?'

I pressed harder, until it hurt my ear. 'I don't know.'

She took out her phone. 'Should we call the police?'

'And say what?' I looked down at my bloodied self. 'I'd be implicated, Mil. We both would. My mom wouldn't be able to handle it. It would destroy her. We barely made it through the warehouse.'

'But we'd be safe,' she said in a quiet voice. 'Wouldn't we?'

'You mean if we brought a patrol of police cars to the Falcone compound . . . ?' I trailed off.

'Right,' she muttered in agreement. 'I wonder how long that would last.'

We showered quickly, first Millie then me. We towel-dried

our hair and got dressed. I squeezed into a pair of black jeans and a T-shirt that was a size too small for me. The tennis shoes were too small, too, but I crammed my feet into them until the ends of my toes curled and chafed.

We unlocked the door and emerged to the distant sound of screaming.

Luca was sitting on the ground, his knees pulled up against his chest. He shot to his feet. 'Are you ready?' Clipped tone, shoulders tense.

'What the hell is going on?'

'Don't worry about it.' He slipped behind us and ushered us downstairs, his hand against my back, pushing, insistent, as we descended the marble stairs. Nic was lingering by the open door, his gaze flickering back and forth to the other end of the foyer. Luca guided us towards the entrance and the darkness beyond it. We were being herded.

Another shriek reverberated in the air. It was louder down here – it was coming from somewhere at the back of the house. It had to be Sara, but it all felt so devastatingly familiar, like I was listening to a distant memory of myself, screaming just as she was, begging for my life.

What Sara said at Eden was right. She *was* me, and not in a good way.

I rounded on the Falcones. 'So this is what you do? You bring defenceless girls here and torture them?'

I moved backwards, towards the screams, but Nic pulled me into him, clamping me to his side. 'Sophie, don't,' he urged, keeping his voice low. 'We're taking you home.'

Millie tugged at my arm. 'Can we just go home, Sophie?' She was crying again, the last dregs of her mascara smudging beneath her eyes. God, she was ruined, and it was my fault. She wouldn't sleep again for a long time. But how could she walk away so easily? How could she stomach the guilt of leaving someone behind like that? She didn't know what was happening. She didn't know what was in store for Sara. But I did. Sara didn't deserve this. She was *good*.

'We can't just leave her here!' My teeth were chattering again. When did it get so cold? The dampness in my hair was chilling me.

Luca was stony-faced, but his jaw was tight. Nic was calm, feet planted firmly beside me, ready for the exit strategy, ready to deposit the potential snitches far away from the crime currently taking place.

Another ear-splitting shriek rang out.

I shook Nic off and pushed by Luca. He tried to block me but I shoved him away. He stumbled, caught off guard, and without formulating any semblance of a plan, I started sprinting towards the noise.

CHAPTER SEVENTEEN

REVENGE

I weaved towards the back of the house. It was like a sinister treasure hunt: follow the desperate wails. But Nic and Luca were both faster than me and I didn't know the layout of the mansion. Luca caught me halfway through the kitchen. He circled me, blocking my way through.

Behind him, the kitchen continued through an archway, widening into a glass conservatory that jutted on to the garden patio. Felice's beehives dotted the lawns beyond. I could see movement – people – and when the next scream rang out it felt unbearably close.

'Move,' I said.

Luca started to push me backwards. 'This isn't your concern, Sophie.'

Sara screamed again.

I gritted my teeth. 'I said *move*.'

'What exactly are you planning to do?' asked Luca, playing for time, moving to the side slightly so that my view was blocked. 'You know you can't get involved in family business.'

'I'll call the police, Luca. Don't think I won't.'

He grimaced. 'You know where that would get you.'

I did know. In the ground. 'How could you let this happen again?'

Nic took a step towards me, blocking out Luca. He was obviously going to try and reason with me. He made his voice go soft, a whisper of intimacy, a moment shared between us. 'Sophie, you both need to get back to safety and forget about all this. We should have brought you somewhere else, I know that now, but it's too late to change it.'

His eyes were dark like molten chocolate. Lips, slightly parted, breathed warm air into the space between us. Nic had gotten the Eden card from me by acting like this. Two could play that game.

I looked at my feet, biting my lip in false reflection. 'I don't know . . .' I murmured.

His shoulders dipped and he relaxed his stance. I pivoted around him, shooting for the double doors. I skidded into the conservatory. Outside, a sensor light was bathing the garden in harsh white light. I was just close enough to catch a glimpse of Sara Marino's purple hair when she screamed again.

In a millisecond, everything fell into place. There was a whole fleet of Falcones. I recognized Dom, Gino and Elena, but there were others – women with long, dark hair, polished men in suits, young teenagers, and even an old man bent over a walking stick.

Valentino was seated in the middle, his head tilted at the scene, his fingers steepled in front of him. On the grass, Sara was on her knees. Her hands were bound behind her back. Her head was lolling forwards, a stream of blood falling from her lips.

CJ was standing on one side of her; Felice was on the other. They were like chaperones, but there was nothing protective about their behaviour. Felice had a gun in his hand and he was brandishing it above her head. He was gesticulating at his rapt audience, his lips curving into his cartoon smile. This was his theatre, and she was his show.

I reached the glass door and my fingers curled around the handle. I pulled it and it swung open with a soft whoosh. Luca flung his arm around my waist and clamped his other hand against my mouth as he pulled me against him. We froze like that, half-in, half-out of the Falcone mansion.

He brought his lips close to my ear. 'Don't say a word.'

His breath shivered all the way down my spine.

Felice was speaking. 'For Calvino, our fallen brother, and for everything he stood for . . . justice, honour, morality . . . we will have vengeance. We will make Donata Marino suffer as we have suffered.' He brought the butt of the gun down and smacked it across Sara's face. It knocked her sideways and she stayed that way, whimpering into the grass.

Luca's hand stifled my reaction. He was trying to drag me backwards, but I was writhing against him. 'Let me handle this,' he urged. 'You'll only make it worse.'

Felice handed the gun to CJ, but when he spoke, it was to the line of Falcones watching him. 'My boy, it is time for you to avenge your father. You must step up now and become the man he raised you to be.' He peeled his lips back, his teeth glistening like fangs in the moonlight. 'And what better way to begin than like this? After all, *l'uccisione è personale.*'

Dom was actually clapping. Somewhere down the line, a girl hollered her approval. The others stood in silence, waiting for Calvino Junior to do something.

I was being hoisted away from the scene. I tried to catch Millie's eye. She was free to act; free to do something. But she was statue-like and bug-eyed as she watched the garden scene unfold. Her skin had taken on a distinct green hue, and it looked like there was a very real chance she would keel over.

Come on, Mil. Snap out of it.

In the garden, CJ was holding the gun limply in his hand. He looked around him, as if searching for something in the family. No one came forward. No one told him to go upstairs and grieve with his little brothers. They just stood there, waiting. This was his test, and he had to pass it.

Sara's cries spluttered into the earth, her fingers fisted in the grass. She was too weak to stand, too frightened to turn her face towards the Falcones.

I was still grappling with Luca. I tried to bite his hand but I couldn't get the right angle. Licking it wouldn't do any good. We weren't in middle school.

'Come on!' said Felice, gripping CJ by the shoulders. He pressed the heel of his shoe against Sara's side and pushed. She faltered, swaying to the side. 'I was just a few years older than you when I made my first kill,' said Felice to CJ, but it was loud enough so everyone could hear him, so everyone could bask in his glory. '*Two* kills,' he corrected himself. 'I wiped out the Marino boss and his whimpering wife with just two bullets. And now here we are, in another generation with the truce broken once more and another Marino cowering at our feet. You can do as I did, and cripple that insidious family, take the boss's jewel from her arsenal.' He raised his gaze to the crowd, a lazy smile flitting across his face. 'Poetic, is it not?'

CJ, who had been looking up at Felice with wide, unblinking eyes, snapped his head back into place. Something seemed to click inside him. He got down on his knees and leant over the girl. His mouth twisted, cruel and biting, and I saw shades of Felice in him – a whisper of the man he would become if he did what was expected of him tonight. CJ raised the gun high above him, like he was going to shoot at the sky. And just as Luca managed to swing me around, away from the scene, he brought the gun down hard. There was a crack, and this time Sara's scream was a raw, animalistic screech.

'*Bel lavoro!*' shouted someone.

'For Calvino!'

'*Tale padre tale figlio!*'

Felice's voice rang out. 'We have only just begun.'

My tears were falling over Luca's hand. He was half carrying me from the room. There were more whoops coming from the garden. They would kill her, right there in their self-made amphitheatre.

I had to do something.

I made myself go limp. My legs dragged along the floor and I flopped over Luca's arm like a rag doll. We dipped towards the ground together.

'Sophie?' He tried to hoist me up.

I didn't budge. My fingers were brushing against the floor and my legs were bent outwards from each other. In that moment, Luca made two crucial errors. He made the mistake of believing me, and he propped me against a chair.

I leapt from the chair, slid across the conservatory floor and screamed at the top of my lungs.

Everyone in the garden turned around. There was a sudden cacophony of muttering. Sara was lying on the grass, one cheek facing the sky, her face so badly swollen I could barely make out her eyes. CJ was standing again, the gun dangling by his side. He was glaring at me.

Felice stepped off the grass and stalked towards me. Valentino turned around. His icy gaze bored holes in me. Whatever bravery had just coursed through me was spent. I clamped my fists together so the Falcones wouldn't see them shake.

Luca came to stand in front of me and raised his hands to Valentino. 'Sorry, brother,' he said. 'I'm taking them home. She got lost.'

Luca made to pull me away again, but I stalled. Trouble or no trouble, I had come this far and I still wasn't dead. I shoved him out of my way so we could stand side by side at the entrance. I pointed at Sara. 'I've come down here to get her. We're all going home together.'

Sara heaved her head up, and I saw her eyes grow wide above her swollen cheeks. She didn't speak – she couldn't – but I could read the desperation in her eyes, I could feel it in the fear that pulsed between us as we stared at one another.

Help me.

I will.

Felice broke the stunned silence. He threw his head back at the sky and released a laugh, the sound forcing itself from his throat like he was choking. He made a show of wiping the tears from under his eyes; even in his manic amusement I could feel his grief as though it was gripping me by the throat. 'This girl has a death wish, Valentino. She seems to constantly exhibit this unyielding desire to be killed.'

'Maybe we should grant it, then,' said Elena. 'Since she keeps getting in the way.'

I could feel Nic behind me, bristling. He moved around us and stepped into the garden to where his mother was standing with her arms folded. 'We're going,' he told her. 'Don't say things like that. She's not going to be a problem for us.'

She closed her eyes. 'Oh, Nicoli,' she said. '*Sei un pazzo in amore.*'

Felice tutted. 'Our Nicoli, I truly thought you had a better handle on your affairs. You're so much more . . . effective when she's not around. Look at you now, standing on the periphery of something you should be *directing.* Your cousin needs you. Show him how to use the gun. Show him the pretty tricks you can do.'

'*Basta!*' Valentino raised his hand in the air. 'This is not a situation any of us should be making light of, Felice. I'd caution you, *once again*, to remember your place in this family.'

The mood was souring, and fast, the sharp edge of the Falcones' collective grief cutting into the air.

'You mean my place in this *nursery* you're running? This is, *yet again*, another juvenile matter that has been ill-handled. You are like young volcanoes – constantly erupting with these

171

ludicrous emotions. When was the last time an *Americano* got free rein to run around this house? *Giammai!'*

Valentino's voice fell deadly quiet. 'And what concern is that of *yours?'*

Felice was nonplussed. 'I show concern in matters that undermine the status of this family, nephew.'

There was a collective intake of breath.

Valentino bared his teeth. It seemed for a moment like he was going to launch himself at Felice and tear his throat out.

A man with thick, jet-black hair stepped out of line. He was tall and broad, but moved with a strange fluidity, almost like a dancer. He was the perfect mixture of Angelo and Felice – lithe and narrow, with warm, dark eyes. 'Felice, remember to whom you're speaking. You should amend your tone accordingly.'

'And your words,' added Dom.

Felice addressed the tall man with venom. 'I don't need your caution, Paulie. I remember. He's our brother's *child.'*

'He's your boss,' said Luca, forgetting about me and stepping into the garden to join the others. He stopped beside Valentino. It was a telling show of solidarity: the underboss and the boss, side by side, united against the *consigliere. Cracks*, I realized. *They're everywhere.* No wonder Felice's wife had run a mile. 'You would do well to remember the Falcone order, Felice.'

Felice's smile was mirthless. 'How could I ever forget? Angelo's decision to—'

'Enough.' Valentino cut him off. 'You've displayed enough theatrics for one night.'

'You insult me,' said Felice, turning dangerously quiet. 'I

have lost my brother tonight. Avenging his death should not be considered a display of theatrics.'

Valentino's tone was cutting. 'We will speak later, in private, when you don't have your audience.'

A ripple of unease travelled through the waiting Falcones. There was a sudden chill in our midst and instead of mistrustful eyes being trained on me, they were directed inwards, at each other.

Sara Marino and CJ were forgotten on the grass. Now the attention was deflected from him, CJ didn't seem interested in the girl or the gun. He looked like he'd rather be anywhere else in the world.

'Enough of this,' said Elena, coming to stand beside Luca and Valentino. They were cut from her cloth – the same bright blue eyes and high cheekbones – none of that golden warmth Nic had inherited from his father. 'Sort this nonsense out, we have our vengeance to exact tonight.'

Murmurs of agreement swept through the garden.

'You can't kill your sister's child.'

For a second I thought the words were mine; that they had sprung from my brain just as I had begun to conjure them. I might have convinced myself, if it wasn't for the faint British accent with which they were said. Millie came to my side and laced her fingers through mine. I could feel them shaking. 'Let her come with us.'

Elena's composure imploded. 'Enough, son! You *must* do something about them. The *Gracewell* girl, surely. The level of—'

It was Paulie who cut her off. 'Elena, you know this girl saved your son's life. Let us not spill more blood than is necessary tonight. It was not Angelo's way.'

There it was. My bargaining chip. 'You owe me a life, Valentino,' I called out, squashing my internal freak-out. I gestured at Sara. 'Her life for Luca's in the warehouse. Let her go.'

Valentino raised his brows, surprise twisting on his lips. 'That's not really how this works.'

'This is turning into a circus!' Felice had retrieved his gun from CJ and was standing on the grass again, tapping his foot. 'Let the boy shoot the Marino girl and be done with it.'

'No!' Millie and I both shouted. Millie had her phone in her hand now. It didn't go unnoticed by the rest of the Falcones. Even if they got to her before she could speak to an operator, a 911 hang-up was enough. Her plan was a lot braver than mine, but I wasn't convinced it was a smarter one.

Paulie started towards us and we stumbled back into the house.

Nic edged closer. 'Millie, don't.'

She lifted the phone to her ear. 'I'll do it if you don't let that girl go.'

'You also know you'll regret it.' His words were under-pinned by the terrible truth. If she broke *omertà*, she would forfeit her life, or that of someone close to her.

Nic stopped at the doorway. Paulie stood next to him, while the others peered through the glass. It was OPERATION: DISARM THE GIRLS.

'The girl is not going to die,' said Paulie.

'You're lying.'

He raised his hands in supplication. 'Valentino is sending a message to the Marinos. He won't kill Sara. They are cousins,

174

you know. Felice just gets carried away – he's grieving. He has given you an exaggerated impression of what's going on here.'

'I know he wants CJ to kill her,' I said. 'I know the truce was broken. But I also know that killing Sara Marino is only going to make this entire situation worse. She's innocent, and everyone in this garden knows it.'

There wasn't a single murmur of disagreement at that, but uneasy gazes travelled inwards, shoes now shuffling against the grass and frowns rippling through the crowd of Falcones.

Paulie's expression was serene. 'You and I both know that what happens to Sara is not Felice's decision. Valentino measures his decisions. Felice exaggerates.'

'Has he exaggerated her injuries too?'

'They're superficial.' There was something soothing about Paulie's manner, too. It was in the way he talked. I found myself wanting to believe him. 'She won't come to any harm.'

'She's already been harmed,' said Millie. She was still clutching her phone, and the Falcones were all staring at it like it was a bomb.

I looked into the garden. Valentino's face had settled into that veil of careful impassivity. 'I give you my word,' he said. 'If you leave now and promise not to alert the authorities, we'll release Sara. A life for a life.'

'How do we know that?' asked Millie.

'You'll just have to trust me.'

'We have nothing to base that trust on.'

A mirthless smile lifted his mouth from its hard line. 'Millie, you and I are having this conversation in front of a fleet of assassins who would end your life right now if I asked them to. There would be no witnesses and your bodies would never be found.' He snapped his fingers. 'Base your trust on that.'

'Send her home with us, then,' said Millie.

'We can't send her with you. She has to be escorted to Donata's people with a Falcone emissary. We are entering into strict negotiations.'

'Of the warehouse variety?' I asked.

Valentino pinched the bridge of his nose. 'No, not of the warehouse variety. Of the Sicilian negotiation variety.'

A part of me knew what those negotiations might be. They had someone the Marinos wanted, and the Marinos had someone the Falcones wanted. Jack. But I couldn't think about my uncle now – he knew the stakes, he had made his bed. My immediate concern was Sara, making sure she was safe, making sure she had a chance to live the life she dreamt of, to find the hint of freedom she had envied in me.

Millie and I glanced at each other. How could we know for sure, if they weren't prepared to guarantee her release to us? What did it even matter? We didn't have a bargaining position. We had a phone with six per cent battery, the flighty affections of Nic and the passing gratitude of Luca for saving his life once. The others could kill us if they wanted to. We were already pushing our luck.

'Don't get involved in this, girls,' said Paulie. He had the largest eyes I had ever seen. 'It's not your fight. This is not your world.'

Luca was on the grass now. He picked Sara up, sliding his arms underneath her elbows. She got to her feet, wobbling. He brushed the matted hair from her face and started speaking to her. She was crying. He held her against his side and brought her away from the others.

I turned to Nic. 'Are they telling the truth, Nic? Will they let her go?'

He closed the distance between us and took my hand, right there in front of his entire family and his horrible mother, and squeezed it. I was so stunned I let him. 'Yes,' he said. 'Valentino will let her go.'

I could see only him then – the golden flecks inside his eyes, the quiet sureness in the quirk of his mouth, all that warmth he exuded. 'Let me get you out of here,' he said. 'Let me take you home.'

Millie lowered her phone. It dangled by her side, a weapon re-holstered. She shrugged, even her smallest movements showing her exhaustion. 'I think I believe them, Soph. I believe Nic.'

Outside, Luca had started to untie Sara's hands. Luca would take care of her. Luca would set her free just as he had done for me when I'd been kidnapped.

'Yeah,' I said. 'So do I.'

CHAPTER EIGHTEEN

THE BODY

BODY OF MARINO TEENAGER PULLED FROM LAKE MICHIGAN

A BODY FOUND IN LAKE MICHIGAN has been identified as Sara Marino, the nineteen-year-old daughter of rumoured Mafia boss and tabloid regular Donata Marino (formerly of the now-defunct Genovese crime family).

Authorities arrived on the scene yesterday morning, after being alerted by a local fisherman who came across the body at the edge of the lake just after 8 a.m.

According to the Cook County Medical Examiner's Office, the cause of death is currently under investigation. It is not believed to have been accidental.

A family spokesman confirmed the loss to reporters yesterday evening, saying, 'We are deeply saddened to lose our beloved Sara. She was a creative and compassionate individual with a bright future ahead of her. We will stop at nothing to determine the events leading up to her death.'

The statement comes less than a week after the infamous Eden nightclub brawl, where a member of a rival Sicilian mob, Calvino Falcone, lost his life. Donata Marino, the club's owner, was taken into custody but was later released without charge. CCTV footage from the event was unavailable due to a systems malfunction in the nightclub. Police are appealing for witnesses to come forward.

Neither family has been forthcoming with statements. The FBI have pointed to the murder of convicted murderer Rico Falcone at Stateville Correctional Center earlier today as a possible sign of Marino retribution, raising further suspicion that a war is brewing in the criminal underworld.

The Marino crime family, known colloquially as the Black Hand Mob, is among the five largest Mafia families in Chicago. The hostility between the Falcones and the Marinos was famously brought to public attention during the Chicago crime spree of 1987, which was marked by the Falcone murder of Don Vincenzo Marino, boss of the Marino family, and his wife Linda Harris in their family home. Their sons, Vince Jr and Antony, disappeared after the attack. Over the course of the feud, many Falcones and Marinos lost their lives, while just three arrests were made. The blood war was reignited several years later with the suspected Marino murder of Don Gianluca Falcone outside Northwestern Memorial Hospital. Though recent times have seen a tradition of peace between Chicago's foremost criminal families, the events of this week point to the resurgence of their violent rivalry.

Sara Marino was the youngest of five children. Her brothers include Marco, Libero and Franco Marino, who is currently serving life in prison for murder. Her sister, Zola Marino, was recently released from prison after serving a six-year sentence for manslaughter. Sara was active on the Eden club scene and had recently deferred a course to study music at the University of Chicago. She did not have a criminal record.

Funeral details have not been released.

CHAPTER NINETEEN

RAGE

Those lying bastards.

I laid the newspaper back on the table. My mother was bustling around behind me. Grease crackled in the frying pan and the kitchen smelt like bacon. I excused myself and went upstairs two steps at a time. I locked myself in the bathroom and threw up.

I brushed my teeth and re-tied my hair, blinking at my pale reflection.

Why did you believe him?

You stupid girl.

Inside my bedroom, I stuffed the edge of my pillow into my mouth and screamed and screamed and screamed.

Those black-hearted, cold-blooded killers.

I could have wrung Nic's neck. How could he lie so

cavalierly like that? He was poison; him and his entire family. No one was safe from their crazed quest for retribution.

I rejoined my mother in the kitchen. She had made eggs to go with the bacon. She was humming to herself, her voice tripping over a melody I didn't recognize.

I sat down with shaky legs, the after-effects of being sick still stinging in my cheeks. In my mind, I pictured a blank white page.

On the far corner of the table, half-sewn piles of fabric competed for space. A ripped envelope peeked out from under the pile.

My mother set the plates down and sat beside me.

I pulled the letter towards me, scanning it. 'Our mortgage payment is overdue.'

She plucked the letter from my hand and refolded it inside the envelope. 'I'm working it out.'

'Are we out of money?' I asked, keeping my attention trained on her profile as she crunched on a slice of bacon. 'Is the diner in trouble?'

'It's just a misunderstanding,' she said, chewing through her words slowly and deliberately. 'Eat your breakfast. Don't worry about this boring grown-up stuff.'

Boring grown-up stuff. The newspaper was face down where I had left it, but the headline still pulsed against my brain. I blinked the words away, putting up that blank white page again. I forced myself to eat a forkful of eggs.

'I should go back to work,' I said.

My mother passed me the salt shaker. She had painted her nails again. Coral: summery and bright. She had forgotten to do her pinkie. 'Don't be silly. You should be out in the sun, having fun.' Her face relaxed in a placid smile. The crow's feet by her eyes seemed deeper.

'I should help out with money,' I said. 'I don't mind . . .'

'You don't need to put the weight of the world on your shoulders. I've got it under control.'

Have you? I wanted to ask, but I didn't. There was too much fear and anger raging inside me. It was a struggle to keep it in.

She tapped the side of my plate. 'Your breakfast is getting cold.'

I chewed on a slice of bacon, trying to ignore the restless feeling in my stomach, the thoughts pushing against my brain. I swallowed the headline and the image of Sara Marino's lifeless body pulled from a lake, and told my mother how spectacular the food was.

We talked about the garden and the new wooden trellis she had erected against the back wall. We talked about me going back to school soon. We didn't talk about the mortgage letter again, or all the half-finished projects. We didn't talk about Jack, or about my father. Lately, it felt like our conversations were defined more by what we avoided than what we discussed. That's the trouble with trauma – you wear it like a cloak, but to acknowledge it only makes it worse.

I ate what I could manage, tasting nothing but ash in my mouth. The coffee was too bitter; the juice was too red. My mother was picking at her plate, dissecting her eggs as I cleared my plate and excused myself.

It was overcast outside, but the humidity was unbearable. Even indoors, I felt stifled by it. It frizzed the ends of my hairs, sticking them to my neck. My T-shirt was warm; it clung too tightly around my arms.

Millie came by in the afternoon.

'Soph!' Her face broke, and she surged into me, wrapping her arms around my neck and knocking me backwards into the hallway. 'I can't believe they actually did it, I can't believe they went through with it.'

'I know.' The thing is, though, I could.

She looked utterly deflated. *I* had done this to her. I had pulled her down with me, into a murky, unforgiving world. Now we were like zombie versions of ourselves, trying to climb back out. But it's hard to forget the things you've seen once you've seen them, it's hard not to wonder about the people you're trying to leave behind, once you've gotten to know them. If the blood war had begun, with deaths on both sides already, then who knew who would be next? It's hard to ignore it, even if they're liars. Even if they're assassins.

I ushered Millie into the sitting room, where we sank into the couch. She brought her legs up and curled her feet underneath her. 'I can't stop thinking about it. We should have done more.'

'I shouldn't have believed Nic. He'd already betrayed me by showing up at Eden in the first place.'

'It's not your fault,' she said, her voice quiet. 'I believed him too.'

'I shouldn't have let him take that red card from me.' And that was the awful reality – they wouldn't have come if I hadn't slipped up that night in the parking lot.

'Nic took it from you,' said Millie.

'And I let him.' I thought of our kiss, the dark passion, the cloying sense of wrongness in it. 'I've been an idiot. I feel like

184

I've been waiting my whole life for something to happen to me, something to shock me into living. I couldn't wait to fall for someone, to feel *loved*. But this is not what I expected. This is not what I wanted. Everything is so messed up.'

Millie was silent for a while, chewing over her words. She leant forward and knitted her hands together. 'People rarely end up with their first love. It's, like, this stupid fairy-tale myth that they peddle to you in Disney movies. Did you know Snow White is, like, fourteen? If I ended up marrying my four-teen-year-old crush, I'd be stuck with Tom Peterson and his stupid bobble head. You're allowed to make mistakes.'

'I got involved with an *assassin*. And I guess I never real-ized how messed up he was until he made me that promise and then killed Sara anyway. She was his cousin, Mil. I can't get my head around it. How could I have been so blind?'

Millie shrugged, her eyes trained on a spot on the floor. 'I went out with Dom. The warning signs were there for me too. But I don't regret it, Soph. I learnt from it.'

I raised my eyebrows. 'What did you learn?'

She huffed a sigh. 'That I'm painfully shallow.'

Her candidness roused a small smile, a spark of amuse-ment inside the darkness that surrounded us. 'I wish I could tease you about that, kettle.'

'Sorry, pot,' she said, her smile as small as mine.

I flopped back into the couch and looked up at the flecked paint on the ceiling as I voiced the realization that had been unravelling in the pit of my stomach. 'I don't think I ever really knew Nic at all,' I said quietly. 'If I really understood him, I would never have walked out of that house and left Sara behind. I romanticized him,' I admitted, the painful truth almost choking the words out of me. 'And it killed her.'

Millie tugged my arm so that I looked at her. '*They* killed her. If we had tried to do more, there might have been three bodies in that lake and not one, and that's the hard truth, Soph.'

'Maybe.'

Millie's tone turned low and dark. 'And there's something else, too.'

I could feel my face going pale, the faint prickles of nausea from earlier coming back in full force. 'What?'

'When I was at work earlier, I found the safe. After what you told me Jack said in Eden, I knew there had to be something to it. So I went looking for it.'

'We've always had a safe.'

Millie shook her head. 'Not that safe. A different one. A *bigger* one. It's in those giant cabinets above the stove in the kitchen – you know, the ones that are really high up?'

I nodded. We never used them – they were too hard to reach.

'I wouldn't have noticed the actual safe except it's hidden behind a sheet of lino inside the cupboard. It was peeling at the corners so I pulled it away. It's massive, Soph, and *old*. It's all fancy around the edges too, so you just know it's chock full of stuff that shouldn't be in there. I'm guessing you need a big fancy key to get in, from the look of the lock. We don't have any like that at the diner.'

'He probably carries it with him.' My head felt very light all of a sudden, but I didn't really feel surprised. Jack had said there was a safe – only a small, naïve part of me had thought he meant the one we always used. Of *course* there was another one – a secret one, full of things only he knew about. 'That's what the Falcones are watching the diner for.'

Millie nodded. 'I'd bet anything that whatever Jack needs is still in there. That's what he wanted you to help him with. That's what he's bargained to Donata.'

'I don't have the key . . . or the desire to help him,' I added. 'He's poison.'

'Have you heard from him?' Millie was looking at me with cautious interest now. She was a little paler than usual. Her hair was greasy. Millie's hair was never usually greasy.

'No.'

'Do you think you will?'

We both knew the answer. I thought about that crimson card, about the stuff he'd yelled at me at Eden. He knew I was the one who gave their position away, but how could he have known it was an accident? 'Yeah,' I said, pushing my answer through a sigh. 'He'll be back.'

Millie's eyes grew wide with fear. 'What are you going to do?'

'The question isn't what *I'm* going to do. It's what *he's* going to do.'

I remembered the clawing feeling of Donata Marino's grip on my arm, how she had dug in as though she never wanted to let go. How Jack's anger at my betrayal had surged through the crowds that night. I remembered Sara Marino, nose pressed to the grass at Felice's mansion as it glistened with her blood. Images of her waterlogged corpse pressed against my brain, demanding to be seen. I already knew what my course of action would be when Jack came back.

Deny deny deny.

CHAPTER TWENTY
THE CONVERSATION

The Kardashians played on a mindless loop in the background as all the things we had seen in the last week choked the conversation from us. There was more to come, and yet there was no predicting any of it. All we could do was stay away and hope against hope that when the storm came, it would pass us by.

The house phone rang, and my mother's footsteps sounded in the hallway. I strained to listen, noting the rarity of the phone ever ringing at all these days. A new client? I hoped so. My mother dropped her voice, so I lowered the volume on the TV. Millie was scrolling mindlessly through Instagram on her phone, looking at pictures of someone else's food.

'. . . left it all to me and it's not fair.'

OK, definitely not a client, then. She was never usually rude to clients. In fact, my mother, interminably polite, was really only rude to one person.

I muted the TV.

'. . . just up and leave like it's nothing!'

Her voice had risen, her pitch rousing Millie from her scrolling. She snapped her head up and I put my finger to my lips.

'I have to clean this up again, and how am I supposed to do that? There's no money.'

'Who's that?' Millie mouthed.

I shrugged, keeping my finger at my lips.

My mother dropped her voice again, and the words that reached me this time were disjointed, plucked out of sentences so I couldn't find their meaning.

'. . . since that night . . . normal . . . the truth . . . promise when I thought . . . any more.' I got up and crossed to the door, easing it open a notch. I still had to strain, but the words came together now, and I held my breath so I could hear them all.

'. . . not fair on either of us. I have to.'

I peeked out. My mother was standing in the hallway. She was leaning against the bathroom door, one hand twined in her hair, the other clutching the phone. 'Fine!' she hissed. 'But it's not right. I don't think it's right!' She dropped her head and brought her hand to her eyes, rubbing them. 'I'll send her,' she said. 'But we're not done talking about this. Not even close.'

By the time she had hung up, I was standing in the hallway, my eyes burning holes in the back of her head. She turned around and instead of surprise, there was defeat in her reaction.

'Sophie.' Her arms fell limply to her sides. 'Oh, Sophie, I'm so tired.'

I took a cautious step towards her. 'Was that Jack?'

She blinked dumbly. 'That was your father. He wants you to go see him tomorrow.'

Surprise bubbled in my mind. 'Why?'

'Because he knows what happened with the Falcones,' she answered flatly, frown lines rippling along her forehead as she conceded, 'I told him.'

'Why?' My horror seeped through my voice. Why would she do that, knowing there was nothing he could do to change it? Why worry him needlessly when she was so worried herself? And then I pinched myself as guilt wrapped around me. She wasn't coping, that was why. And once upon a time, he had been her rock. Maybe he still was, even though animosity lingered between them. Maybe she still needed him just as much as I needed her.

She raked her hair away from her face. Her defences were down and she was too tired to put them back up. 'Because I wanted to make him see.'

'See what?'

Her gaze shifted past me to where the sun was pushing through the hall window. 'That everything isn't OK,' she told me plainly. 'That it hasn't been OK for a long time.'

'No,' I said, quietly, feeling a strange sense of relief at unveiling the truth we had been so carefully avoiding. I didn't realize how badly I had been craving it. 'No, everything isn't OK.'

But, why, I wondered, did he want to see me and not her? I studied my mother's slumped frame, and saw in her what he probably had heard in her voice – weakness. *It's me*, I thought. *I'm the one who has to fix this.*

As if a switch had flicked inside her, my mother snapped her head up and her gaze became hard and shining. 'You know, despite everything that's happened, I love your father very much,' she said, her words woven through a heavy sigh. 'I love the life he built for us. I love the daughter he gave me. I love our family.'

'That's good . . .' I ventured, ineptly. She hadn't spoken so openly or tenderly about him in a long time. The words were warm, but there was something beneath them . . . a barb, a sadness.

'I miss him, Sophie,' she admitted. 'I miss him every day.'

Tears spiked behind my eyes, her sudden candour jarring. 'Me too, Mom. I miss him too.' *I miss us. I miss our family.*

'But sometimes . . .' She shook her head, slowly, her gaze drawn to the ground between us, to another time and place, to something I couldn't access. 'Sometimes I feel like I might just explode.'

She turned from me abruptly and stalked through the kitchen and into the garden, where she disappeared into her flowers.

I watched her go. I had come to know that feeling all too well.

CHAPTER TWENTY-ONE
PRISON

The bus to Stateville Correctional Center was airless, the seats dank with years of enmeshed body odour. I curled up by a window near the back and flicked through the playlists on my iPod. I listened to Joshua Radin and watched Chicago fade into remoteness.

I arrived early in the afternoon. My hair was flat against my head where I had leant against the window to sleep. I wound it into a ponytail. My clothes were sticky. The humidity hadn't broken yet and the heat outside was stifling. The sky was overcast, a thick blanket of blinding white pressing down on me. The air was charged, the ends of my hair floating with static.

A storm was coming.

Inside Stateville, the meeting room smelt like disinfectant.

Three prison guards lined the walls, watching with glazed indifference. I tried not to catch their eyes, afraid they might see through me and find out the things I knew.

My father shuffled in to meet me. He was a little slumped over, like the act of keeping his head up required too much energy. He was still wiry and thin, with greying hair that flicked out behind his ears and dipped into big, grey eyes. They used to be bluer, like the ocean.

He lifted his head and his smile lit up his features. For a passing moment, he could transform himself into the father I used to know outside of these walls. 'Sophie, it's so good to see you.'

I wasn't allowed to hug him, so I struggled with what to do with my hands. I settled on an awkward wave/salute.

We sat down. I was studying his face, his neck, his hands – any part of him that I could see – searching for signs of injury. He was studying me just as closely. It threw me a little. The bruises on my face had gone now, and the swelling around my nose had disappeared. I was paler than usual, but other than that, my injuries no longer marked me. Still, he knew about them now, so it made sense that he would try and search them out.

There was a crack running down the back of my plastic chair. It dug into me and I shifted, trying to get comfortable. There was no point. I folded my hands on my lap, searching for the right words. How should I begin? How much should I say?

The discomfort on his face mirrored mine and I almost smiled at how similar we were. He dipped his head and gave me a *look*. The room around us faded, until it was just the two of us, secured in our own little bubble. He dropped his facade and his face crumpled.

His words tumbled out. 'I know what happened, Soph. Your mom told me.'

'Yeah, well,' I said, lacing my fingers together in front of me. 'Jack's an asshole.'

Grief etched itself into the planes of his face, pulling them down until he looked old and weary. 'I'm so sorry. That's all I can say. I am sorry all of this has happened to you. I'm sorry your life was in danger and I wasn't there to help you. I'll never forgive myself.'

Something settled deep inside me, burning, and I had the sudden urge to clutch at my stomach and rip the feeling out.

'You don't have to say sorry,' I said, sounding angrier than I had meant to. But I *was* angry with him, about what had happened, about the mess he had made for all of us. 'It didn't have anything to do with you.'

He dropped his head into his hands. 'You've been through too much. And I wasn't there. I'm never there.'

I looked at the crown of his head, where tiny white hairs were beginning to sprout beneath the grey and brown. 'Dad, I'm fine.' *No thanks to you.* I didn't say it though, I couldn't be cruel.

He lifted his head. 'You're not fine. And neither is your mother. She's terrified, and I don't blame her. I'm trying to give her advice but she won't listen to me. She's angry at me, Soph. And she has every right to be, but she's not coping and I'm worried about her.'

'You and me both.'

I asked the question that needed to be asked, the one

flashing at the front of my brain. 'Have you heard from the man of the hour?'

'Not yet.' My father's breath whistled through his nose. When he spoke again, his words quivered with anger. 'The things he's done, the position he's put you and your mother in. He was supposed to keep you safe in my absence, not risk your lives.'

'Did you know?' My fingernails were digging into my hands, making crescent shapes in my skin. 'Did you know what he was up to all that time?'

'No.' I had barely finished my question before he snapped out his answer. 'Of course I didn't know.'

'Did Mom fill you in on everything?'

'As much as she could,' he said. 'But I don't want to talk about that, I want to talk about my girls.'

'Well, I want to talk about the drugs and the Golden Triangle Gang and everything else that's put us in hot water. I want to talk about everything you missed.' So I did talk about it. I told my father everything that had happened up until the warehouse shoot-out – I told him about Jack's shadiness, about the drugs and the gang he had been a part of, how he walked my mother into the warehouse, how he stood over me and tried to kill the Falcone underboss. I talked until my voice nearly ran out. I talked until I was sure I had toppled Jack over in my father's mind, until I was sure he saw the cold, hard truth about his little brother.

Then I let up, breathing long and deep, as a small weight shifted inside me and I felt less bound up than before.

My father, who had been listening intently, unblinking as he watched me, straightened in his seat. 'Soph, I promise I'll make him pay for endangering you and your mom,' he said. 'I'm so disappointed in him – in his choices, in the path he's chosen. I should have cut him off long ago.' Compared to all the words I had just hurled at the space between us, his answer felt like nothing, but I could see how his face had changed, how everything in his brain was slotting into different places. He was completely wrung out. He scrubbed his hands against his forehead. 'But I can't get to him. I don't know where he is or what he's doing.'

That was the moment. Indecision flickered inside me. To tell or not to tell. To stir or not to stir. But I needed guidance. A plan for when Jack came back – I needed my father to intervene so I wouldn't have to. So I decided to give him this chance to step up and protect us, the way he'd said he would. 'I know where he is,' I said, without batting an eyelid. I sat back in my chair, instinctively pulling myself away from him in case the force of his reaction was too great. 'Jack's with the Marino crime family.'

'No,' he said, quickly. 'No way.' Well, that answered the question of whether he had heard of the Marinos before. 'Jack would never be so stupid. He would never openly consort with the Marinos.'

'He is,' I insisted.

My father shook his head.

I pressed on, determined to push Jack from whatever pedestal my father had placed him on. 'I don't know what he's offering Donata Marino but he's with them, I swear. He's not even hiding it.'

'God,' my father exhaled. He looked like he was about to pass out. He raked a hand through his salt-and-pepper hair.

'After everything. To do something so dangerous. What is he *thinking*?'

It didn't really feel like he was talking to me any more, but since I had the answer, I figured I'd supply it.

'Protection,' I said. 'That much is obvious. The Falcones want Jack dead, so he's hiding with the one family who will happily go against them.'

My father's eyelids fluttered at half mast. He looked genuinely ill rather than angry. I slid my hands across the table as close to him as I could without touching. I willed my strength into him. 'Do the Falcones . . . do they know where Jack is?' he asked.

'Yes.' My brain flashed with scenes from Eden. 'They've known for about a week. There was a . . . showdown of sorts . . . It was on the news,' I tacked on, deciding that telling my father I was actually there would be the world's stupidest mistake. He'd freak out, even more than he was now. 'I know Jack was there, though . . . someone I know saw him.'

He recoiled from the information, his eyes growing wide. 'He was at the Eden shoot-out?'

'You heard about it?'

His eyes were darting, panicking, as he processed the information that his only family in the whole world apart from my mother and me was now in the middle of the city's most dangerous blood war. Jack was courting violence and murder, and my father couldn't get to him – he couldn't be the protective big brother he was used to being. Jack was on his own.

'Of course I heard, Soph. Donata Marino's *teenage* daughter was just murdered by the Falcones.' My father indicated

197

behind him in the general direction of the prison. 'Franco Marino is serving his sentence here. He howled the walls down. A Falcone was murdered in his cell yesterday morning, but nobody's talking.' My father composed himself, his mouth turning hard. 'Listen to me, Sophie, I need you and your mother to leave Cedar Hill immediately.' He lurched forwards, his hands thudding on the table. 'Leave the house, leave the diner and get as far away as you can.'

'What?' I hissed. 'But that's your place. That's *our* place. I can't just leave it.'

He grabbed my hands and squeezed them. 'Soph, right now, I need you to leave it behind. And I need you to do it tonight.'

A prison guard shouted at us to separate. I snapped my hands away.

'When you get home, pack your bags, pack your mom's bag, get in the car and drive.'

I could have crushed the table beneath me. Here was the father I needed, the man who wanted to keep us safe, and he was stuck behind bars barking orders at me. I was so frustrated, so scared. And I felt utterly alone. I was starting to feel wobbly, like my head wasn't properly attached to my neck. He had just asked me to do the impossible. We had no money, no destination. All we had in the whole world was our house and the diner. That was it.

'Mom won't leave. She's just getting her life back on track.'

'She's not.' His expression turned grim. 'She's not sleeping, she's not eating properly. Her conversations are erratic. She's having flashbacks. She's afraid to leave the house. She's not holding it together, Soph.'

Every word was like an ice pick in my heart. If he had managed to tell how shaken she was without even seeing her, then maybe she was even worse than I thought. 'She won't listen to me,' I repeated.

'You're the *only* person she'll listen to. You're her reason to get up in the morning.'

'Dad,' I said, half-hushing him. I watched the veins in his temples bulge. 'You're panicking. You just need to calm down.'

'You don't understand,' he said, clenching and unclenching his fists. 'You don't understand how powerful these families are, how close you are to everything now Jack's tied up in it all.'

'I do understand,' I insisted, my own voice turning hard to match his. 'Trust me, I get it.'

'Then leave,' he urged. 'Before it's too late.'

'And what about you?' I asked, knowing he wasn't safe in prison after all. Even inside, they could get to each other if they wanted to. A dead Falcone attested to that. And if Jack slipped up, then who better to punish for it than his only brother?

'I'm keeping my head down, Soph.' He dipped his head as he said it, too.

'Five minutes!' shouted a guard.

Dammit. There was never enough time.

'Promise me, Soph.' He took my hands in his.

We were yelled at for contact and I pulled away, scrunched my hands into fists.

'I—' I paused. I was thinking about Millie, about the diner, about my bedroom, about the garden that was just beginning to look like a garden, about my school, about my father stuck inside these dangerous walls . . . 'I'll try.'

'You won't *try*,' he snapped, the urgency of everything catching in his mood. 'You'll do this for me, Soph. This whole shitstorm has only just begun. If you stay in Cedar Hill, you'll be swept up in it. You need to lie low until they burn out from coming at each other. Until a boss is dethroned, until there's a ceasefire. Until they get the hell out of your town.'

He was right. This was the advice I had come for – what I needed. I had allowed myself the illusion of walking away, but I hadn't taken any steps; I had only shut my eyes. The truth was, I was stuck between the two sides of this Mafia war, caught up in their murders, in their plans, in their anger, and my heart clenched fearfully for both of them. Something was coming. I could feel it, as though the earth was bubbling underneath my toes, and sooner or later it would burst through.

'OK.'

The guard was calling time on our meeting. All around us, chairs were screeching away from tables. We stood up. 'I don't know when I'll get to see you again, Dad.' I felt a sudden overwhelming sense of desperation at the thought of being so far away from him. My breathing started to hitch and I had the most unpleasant sensation in the backs of my eyes.

He pulled me into a hug. 'I love you, Soph.'

'I love you, too.' They were wrenching him off me and pushing him into line. I stumbled backwards. I didn't notice the tears until they started dripping down my neck. My palms were sticky and it felt like there wasn't enough space in my lungs to inhale.

I ended up outside the prison without remembering how I made it there. The humidity enveloped me, creeping into my hair and underneath my clothes. My legs felt like lead as I walked.

I sat down on the bench and waited for the bus. The air was heavy and it wasn't just the promise of rain. Jack and Donata were on the move, and that meant I had to be too. I couldn't be a sitting duck.

I was so caught up in a stream of anxiety and fear, trying to come up with the right thing to do and the best way to tell Millie – how we would afford it – if we even *could* do it – that I wasn't paying attention when the bench creaked and someone sat down beside me. He slid an arm behind him and lazily tilted his body towards me, until the sudden flash of black hair and olive skin in my peripheral vision, coupled with the familiar waft of his aftershave, struck me.

'Sophie Gracewell, fancy meeting you here.'

CHAPTER TWENTY-TWO
SPARK

'So,' Luca said. 'Do you think you and I will ever run into each other in a movie theatre or a shopping mall, or will it always be prisons and cemeteries for us? Is that our thing?'

Where was that goddamn bus?

Anger surged inside me, but if I opened my mouth to say the things I really wanted to say I'd explode, and right now I just wanted to be at home with my mother, coming up with a plan. I folded my arms, like that could keep it all inside me. 'I do *not* want to talk to you, Luca.'

I could feel the cold prick of his stare on the side of my face. I watched his hands in my periphery, picking at a thread in his dark jeans, settling and unsettling on his lap. 'I didn't kill her, Sophie.'

I turned away so my ponytail whipped out behind me and almost slapped him in his face. 'You may as well have.'

'No.' His voice turned hard, and I imagined frustration drawing his brows together. 'You do not get to paint me as a guiltless monster. Don't give me a label I haven't earned. I have enough deserved ones already.'

I didn't answer. After a couple of seconds he got up, rounded the bench and hunkered down on the other side of me so I was looking right at him. His hands gripped the wood beside my thigh. Every time I tried to look somewhere else, he jerked his head and held my gaze. 'Look at me. Listen to me.'

'Don't tell me what to do,' I snapped. 'How many times do I have to tell you: I don't answer to you!'

'I don't care who you answer to. I just need you to know this.' He raked a hand through his hair. 'I tried to release Sara. Valentino wanted her as a bargaining chip, not collateral damage. She was still a teenager.'

'She was innocent,' I said, hearing the faintest quiver in my voice.

'Yes,' he said. '*Una innocente.* She wasn't supposed to die. OK? I promise.' His voice turned to a growl. '*I promise.*'

I swallowed hard. There was something earnest resonating in Luca's promise – a realness that was always absent from the ones Nic made – but still, how could I believe him? Sara was dead and Luca was an assassin – convincing and dangerous. He was a rose with thorns, just like his brother. I had fallen for that before.

'Did she jump into that lake by herself, Luca?'

He fell back on his haunches, a shadow falling across his

features. 'CJ just snapped. Delayed grief, or whatever. Felice had riled him up and then he had the gun pointed at her and she was gone and I couldn't help her and I have her blood on my hands, and I know that. I *know* what Sara was at her core – she was nothing like the rest of us. Believe me, I hate myself for playing a part in her death, for not being able to stop a twelve-year-old with a gun, a twelve-year-old who shouldn't even *have* a gun, the same way I couldn't stop my brothers when they were twelve, so you can take your anger and hatred and pile it all the way up on top of mine if you want . . . but don't for a second think it's not eating me up inside.'

He got up and crossed back to where he was sitting, but this time he didn't look at me when he dropped on to the bench. He dipped his chin to his chest and stared at his hands, and I saw in him the boy I had seen in Valentino's portrait a long time ago. The person he really was – someone at odds with his life and trapped by a family much bigger than his dreams and desires. Grief surrounded him, and the only thing to do was keep on killing until the tallies were even. But that was the thing: they never would be.

I relented, not wanting to twist the knife any further, knowing now that he was already twisting it himself. 'You're not a monster.'

I caught the curl of his lip, the way his teeth nipped hard on it as though to draw blood. 'What would you know?' he said, his voice quiet.

'I know you're kind,' I said, feeling a strange urge to comfort him, to soothe the emotional wounds he was inflicting upon himself.

'Only in comparison to the others.'

204

'No,' I said, feeling surer now that what I was saying was true. 'You're like her.' I remembered the last conversation I had shared with Sara, the way her eyes blazed when she spoke of a different life, another kind of existence she would forever be denied. He must have seen that in her, too. That's why he picked her up that night, why he wanted to set her free. 'You have the same heart.'

He snapped his head up and his eyes were so blue I almost lost my train of thought. 'Are you trying to make it worse, Sophie?'

I offered him a sheepish smile. 'I'm actually trying to make it better.'

'You are not doing a good job.'

I shrugged. 'It's not exactly my forte. I'm good at changing the subject, though. Speaking of which, what the hell are you doing here?'

'My grandfather's brother was murdered in here yesterday.' He gestured behind him. 'Paperwork. I got the short straw.'

'I heard about that.' I tried to ascertain his level of grief but he seemed calm, his expression matter-of-fact. 'I'm sorry.'

He tipped his head back so he was staring at the sky. 'I'm sure you can guess what I'm about to say.'

'"It is what it is,"' I said, fighting the urge to roll my eyes. 'It's a pile of crap, is what it is.'

'You're so eloquent,' he murmured.

'You were right about the war,' I said, wishing he would look at me and engage with the actual seriousness of his possible impending death.

'Donata's getting stronger by the day,' he sighed. 'There are rumours that the missing Marino twins have resurfaced. They're rallying.'

I felt myself go pale. 'What?'

'Marino morale is high.' Luca paused, chewing on his lip, before adding grimly, 'and that is never a good thing.'

'Where are they?' I asked, wondering at the scope of revenge that was no doubt on their minds. Felice must be quaking in his expensive leather shoes.

Luca dipped his head further back, a groan of frustration catching in his throat as he exhaled. 'If I knew that, I wouldn't be lounging on this bench right now, Sophie.'

'Are you worried?' I asked, thinking of Donata and her troops, of all the ways she could hurt the Falcones. 'About this . . . blood war?'

'Yes, I am.' He turned his attention back to me. 'But I'm not worrying about my family, Sophie.'

'Me?' I ventured.

'I don't know what you were doing in Eden, or what your uncle wanted from you. I expect you won't tell me anyway, but as long as Donata has access to you, as long as she feels you owe her something, you're in trouble. I don't know what your uncle bargained for that protection, but I'd bet it had something to do with you.'

The air was pressing down on us, and I could feel my back grow sticky with the rising humidity. 'But what could I offer her?'

His jaw tightened, drawing hollows beneath his cheekbones. 'I don't know.'

'I can't give her anything.'

He inched forward, so subtly I barely noticed it, until I

could make out the scar above his lip. He narrowed his eyes and asked, 'Are you sure about that?'

Heat erupted inside me. I felt like I had been caught, but I hadn't done anything. I knew about the safe, but it wasn't like it had anything to do with me. It wasn't like I was going to do anything about it. 'Yes,' I said. 'I'm sure.'

'Valentino's looking into you, you know.'

Alarm spread across my face. 'Why?'

He turned and flopped back on to the bench, exhaling at the sky. 'My mother's been in his ear.'

'Oh.' *What a charmer she is.* 'Well, he's wasting his time.'

'Donata's going to come back for you.' He said it casually, like it was a conversation about the weather, but it stuck in my throat and I gulped it down, knowing it was true.

'I'll be OK,' I told him. An image of my mother and me cramming our car full of trinkets and duvets popped into my head. 'I have a plan.'

'What kind of plan?'

'The secret kind.'

He pulled himself up. 'Sophie—' He stopped, chewing on his words.

'Yes?' I prompted.

He frowned at the ground, his lips twisting. He was considering something.

'What is it, Luca?'

I was about to poke him when he returned his attention to me. Hesitantly, as if the idea was still forming, he said, 'If you need help, you can ask for it.' At my surprised silence, he splayed his hands. 'I mean you can come to us, Sophie. If you need to.'

I almost fell off the bench with shock. 'What?' I asked, my eyes bugging out of my head. 'Are you kidding?'

'Why would I joke about something like this?' His expression was stony. 'I know what Donata Marino does to people who won't bend to her will. You don't.'

'A month ago your family was actively trying to murder me.'

'I know.' He paused, his fingers drumming below his bottom lip. 'But things are different now . . . We can protect you.'

'Reluctantly,' I pointed out, reading his obvious hesitance.

He shook his head. 'The process will be difficult,' he told me plainly. 'I don't offer our protection lightly. But I offer it nonetheless.'

My shock faded a little, bewilderment rising in its place. I didn't know exactly what he meant by process, but I could plainly see his offer was real, and important.

'Why?' I asked. 'Why would you want to protect us? It wasn't that long ago that you hated me.'

'We didn't know you then,' he said, before adding, almost begrudgingly, 'We didn't *care* about you then.'

I clamped my hands together on my lap and felt their clamminess. Something squirmed inside me. 'So, you care about me now,' I said, meaning to make a joke of it, but it came out soft and low and full of something guttural that made me embarrassed. 'Why?'

We both knew what I was really asking. *What changed your mind?*

Luca angled his body towards me, lost in quiet consideration. We were so close, if I edged forward I'd be right under his chin. Why would I edge forward? What was up with me today? When he spoke I could feel his breath on my cheeks, the only moving air in our bubble of stifling humidity. 'Because I don't know anybody like you. You're like . . . a rare artefact. And it would be a shame if you got broken.'

Amusement spluttered from me in the most unattractive way. 'Are you really comparing me to an antique right now? Oh my God, you *nerd*.'

He started laughing, and the carefree melody of it swept me up until I was laughing too, and it was absurd because our families were being threatened and murdered and there we were squished together in a hundred-degree heat outside a maximum security prison, and we used to hate each other and now we were laughing so hard I had tears in my eyes.

He composed himself first, but it took a while and I was left choking my laughter into silence. 'What I *meant* was,' his face twisted into a quiet smile that felt secret and deadly, 'you're a bright spark, Sophie. And I don't want anyone to snuff you out.'

'Oh.' Well I couldn't make fun of that. Was I supposed to say something back? Wasn't that how compliments worked? The silence was growing and suddenly his words felt heavy and important and he was so close to me and I was perspiring and panicking, and . . . and I said, 'And you're kind of like a snowflake.'

Oh, Jesus Christ.

He masked his fleeting surprise with a quirked eyebrow. 'Excuse me?'

'Nothing,' I said quickly. 'I didn't say anything.'

'No, no,' he said, rounding on me so his face was too close, his eyes too searing, his smile too irritating. 'I'm a *snowflake*, am I?'

'Shut up. Seriously.' I pulled wisps of loose hair around my cheeks. 'Shut up.'

'I think you were trying to tell me I was special.'

'Icy,' I said. 'I meant you were icy.'

I could practically taste his glee. I was floundering, and he was relishing it.

'And unique, in that you're uniquely *annoying*,' I added. 'God, you're annoying. That's what I meant.'

'If I'm annoying, then they haven't yet invented a word to describe you.'

'Shut up. I'm perfect.' I stuck my tongue out.

'I suppose you're not the worst.' He removed himself from my personal space and refixed his gaze to the sky. His arms stretched out behind him, his fingers brushing my shoulder, but he didn't seem to notice. 'But goddammit you are stubborn, Sophie Gracewell.'

'I'm not stubborn. I'm persistent.'

'No. You're stubborn.' His smile turned rueful. 'And you make terrible decisions. Especially in life-or-death situations. It's like you always choose to do that one thing you're definitely *not* supposed to do.'

'I do not!' I protested.

'You know that saying, "If everyone was jumping off a cliff, would you jump too?" Well, I seriously think you would.'

'So you are basically telling me I'm stupid, is that it?'

'No,' he said in a measured voice, like he was actually trying not to offend me. 'I'm saying you are ruled by your emotions. And I'm afraid there'll come a time when the smart thing will be to walk away from a dangerous situation, and you won't do it, because your emotions will stop you.'

I rolled my eyes. 'Well, *excusez-moi* for having emotions. It's not my fault you're lacking in that department.'

He stared at me, his expression suddenly unreadable. 'I have emotions, Sophie, but I don't let them rule me.'

'Whatever,' I said haughtily. 'I am very capable of making smart decisions, I'll have you know.'

He frowned at me. 'Why did you come to Eden, then?'

'Why did *you*, Mr Double Standards?'

'It's different for me.'

He was beginning to annoy me – this holier-than-thou thing he had going on. He turned his attention from me, lost in his own world. For the first time that week I wasn't thinking about all the danger swirling around me, or all the things I still didn't know. Instead, I was thinking about how annoying Luca was. I was thinking about his superior attitude. That smug smile he had. The weird musicality in his laugh. I was thinking about how his hair swooped behind his ears in that stupid careless way. I was wondering about his eyes and whether their intense blueness ever caught him off guard when he looked in the mirror. I wondered if he was vain. He didn't seem vain, but I never did have a proper handle on his character. It always seemed to change just when I thought I had figured him out.

He was looking at me again, his lips stretched wide so his smile was all teeth.

I slow-blinked. 'What?'

'You realize you've been staring at me for the past five minutes?'

'No, I haven't,' I said. 'I was staring into space. I was thinking about stuff.'

'If I didn't know better I'd say you were getting lost in my eyes.'

I sprang to my feet. 'Oh my God, I was not. You are so full of yourself.'

In the distance the bus was rolling to a stop and I thanked the universe for small mercies. I was going crazy. He was making me crazy and I had to get out of there.

He eyed the bus with unconcealed disgust. It was really old, and even from outside you could just tell it smelt of sweat and broken dreams. 'Do you want a ride back to Cedar Hill?'

I was already carrying myself away, hiding the pink in my cheeks. I waved over my shoulder. 'No thank you, Zoolander. I'll leave you to your vanity.'

'You'll melt on that thing. It's from the Stone Age.'

I twirled my fingers in a queenly goodbye as I got on the bus.

My face fell. The driver was wearing a wife-beater. A half-smoked cigarette lolled from his mouth and he was tapping a sign that read '*Air conditioning on board this bus is temporarily out of service. We apologize for any inconvenience.*'

I backed down the steps, swallowing my pride as sweat beaded on my forehead. I whirled around to find Luca leaning against the bus stop, smirking, in his award-winning role as the actual personification of *smugness.*

I skipped over to him. 'Sooo . . . about that ride you offered . . .'

'I knew you'd come crawling back.' He turned on his heel,

his amusement flying over his shoulder. 'How do your words taste, Sophie?'

I stuck my tongue out at the back of his head as I followed him to his car. 'The air conditioner was broken.'

'So your pride is worth the price of having cool air on your face?'

I wiped a stray bead of sweat from my brow. 'Hey, Luca?' He glanced over his shoulder, an eyebrow hiked up. 'Shut up.'

CHAPTER TWENTY-THREE

BLUE VIOLETS

Luca's car was spacious and cushy, and the air conditioning was heavenly. I lay back and sighed happily as a cold
breeze feathered my face. For an instant there was
nothing else but that feeling of welcome relief, dissolving the
sticky hotness that had been crawling up my back all day.

'This is amazing,' I groaned. 'I can't believe I was going to
take that bus.'

We were on the highway and Luca had one arm lolling
easily on the armrest between us and the other resting atop
the wheel of the car. We were going fast but it didn't feel like
it. It felt . . . safe.

Luca side-glanced at me. 'You are easily pleased, Sophie
Gracewell.'

I shrugged. 'I'm trying to concentrate on the small things

right now, and this small thing is nice.'

He nodded, his attention refocusing on the rear-view mirror. 'That's a good philosophy.'

'Thanks,' I said. 'I just came up with it.'

He frowned, adjusting the mirror and dropping his speed. He muttered something, but I couldn't catch it.

'What is it?' I sat up.

A horn sounded behind us. I turned to find a car weaving erratically three vehicles back. It was black, but other than that, I couldn't make anything out. One thought pounded out all the others, as the word *Marino* rang in my head.

Luca sped up again and I was flung against the seat. '*Cazzo*,' he said. 'Sophie, get down.'

He grabbed the wheel with one hand and reached under his seat with the other, pulling out a handgun. My eyes grew to twice their size. 'Luca . . .'

'I said get down!' he shouted.

He weaved towards the side of the street.

The strange car was two cars back now, swerving from one side of the highway to the other. Oncoming vehicles were honking as it veered into their lane.

I slunk to the ground, resting my head just above the seat. Luca kept the gun cocked in his hand, his eyes narrowed at the rear-view mirror. He opened the window, and the sound of hollering filled up the car.

My knees were shaking against the floor, my hands gripping the seats so tight my fingers had turned white.

'Don't get up,' he warned. 'Whatever happens, don't get up.'

The erratic car overtook the one directly behind us. I could hear it even though I couldn't see it. The shouting got louder. Luca pulled towards the side of the road, his jaw clenched tight. He was watching the side-view mirror, then over his shoulder, gun outstretched as he pulled the window down, and then . . . and then it was over.

The car behind us backfired, chugged and sped up, leaving the sound of five frat boys laughing and shouting in its wake as it passed us.

Luca pulled his firing arm back. '*Dio.*' He stowed his gun down the side of his seat and fell back against the headrest as he eased us into the middle of the highway again. I crawled back up, one hand clutched over my heart, the other dug firmly into the armrest between us.

'Oh my God,' I gasped. 'I really thought we were dead.'

Luca's knuckles were marble-white against the steering wheel. 'I thought it was . . .' His words caught in his throat, and he cleared it, shaking his head so that his hair fell across his eyes. He swept it back, leaving his hand on his face, and sliding it down across his lips. 'I thought it was the Marinos,' he said, his voice muffled by his fingers.

'So did I,' I breathed.

This was the first time I had seen concern etched so freely across his face, and it made my stomach twist with fear for what was to come, not just for me but for all of us. That was a test run – a false alarm – but it was a very real reminder of the kind of world now moving around me. His world. His fate.

'In an alternative universe, we could both be dead right now,' I realized.

'Don't say things like that.'

I looked at my hands, feeling the weight of everything

pressing down on me again.

Luca eased off the highway at the next exit and pulled into the parking lot of a Dunkin' Donuts. 'Coffee,' he said, scrubbing his hand across his forehead. 'I need a gallon.'

Adrenalin had surged through every part of me, and now it was seeping away, making me shake as I tried to centre myself. It was strange. We almost died. And yet, there was no danger, not really, in the end. I felt stupid for overreacting, and yet at the same time I felt lucky to be alive.

'Sophie?' We were in the drive-through line and Luca was staring at me.

'Hmm?' My smile felt watery.

'What do you want?'

Oh, I dunno. To live a life where I'm not constantly expecting the untimely deaths of those around me. 'Nothing,' I said, half scanning the menu outside without reading it. 'I'm fine.'

Luca's voice darkened. 'You're not fine.'

I pinched my fingers to give myself something to do. My heart was still ramming against my ribcage. I was still thinking about the gun Luca had pulled out, about the car that had sped by us. 'I'm just having a moment.'

Luca scanned the menu as we inched by it, one hand on the wheel, the other elbow propped on the open window frame. 'OK,' he said. 'I'm going to make an executive decision and get you a doughnut with rainbow sprinkles, because you seem like somebody who would like that.'

I felt a white-hot flash of indignation. If he was trying to skirt over the bizarre-ness of what had just happened, patronizing me was not going to help.

'I'm not a child,' I said. 'You don't have to get me anything.'

I was feeling the dim heat of embarrassment flaming in my cheeks. Luca had been prepared to defend us both with his life just now on the highway, and me? I'd been crouching like a scared rat beneath the glove compartment. What the hell was wrong with me? How long would it take for my legs to stop feeling like jelly? I had seen so much already. I should have been braver, stronger. But I was a coward. I was useless.

We pulled up to the window and the smell of freshly baked dough wafted towards me. I clutched at my stomach to stop the growl and was reminded with a sharp pang that I was *starving*. Dammit, I wanted that doughnut. But I didn't deserve it. I didn't deserve anything. I was so sick of cowering.

'You should eat something.'

I was too angry with myself to respond. I shrugged and directed my gaze out the window while he ordered.

A couple of minutes later, we were on the highway again. Luca was drinking his coffee like it was water. The radio was on low and there was country music – something about a pair of boots and a truck – filling up the car.

Luca unwrapped a brown bag and placed a doughnut on the dashboard above the radio. It sat between us like an artefact in a museum. It was covered in rainbow sprinkles. The glaze was still dripping down the sides and the smell invaded my nostrils. Desire exploded inside me as my mouth filled with water.

Without taking his eyes off the road or saying anything at all, Luca nudged it half an inch across the dashboard towards me.

I lasted two minutes. Then I caved.

I stuck out a tentative hand, watching him in my periphery. He was focused on the road and humming softly under his breath. I snatched the doughnut and took a bite, revelling in the gooey sugar as it rushed over my tongue.

My brain was fizzing. Luca took another gulp of his coffee and I noticed with a frown that he hadn't gotten anything else for himself. Just a tall, bitter helping of caffeine. How typically Luca of him. I put the doughnut back on the dashboard and nudged it, ever so slightly, towards him.

His gaze flicked to the left, his lip quirking upwards for one passing second. Slowly, he reached his hand out and took it, taking a bite on the other side so that even in its punctured state, the doughnut and all that sugary glory was perfectly symmetrical. I watched him chew, fixated on the curve of his jaw. He blinked, slow and heavy, and I could tell he was enjoying it. I felt bad taking it away from him, but I was still starving, and this doughnut was literally the happiest thing that had happened to me in way too long.

I took another bite, joining with my first so the grooves aligned. A groan of pleasure escaped me and I closed my eyes, thinking only of the taste for that fleeting moment. God, it was good. I fought the urge to stuff the rest in my mouth, and put it back. Luca picked it up a minute later. He chewed in silence but this time he nodded, as though agreeing with my earlier groan.

We shared it that way – tiny bites – back and forth until there was just one bite left. I watched, feeling way too forlorn as Luca picked it up. It was his turn. We were almost home now. The rest of the ride had passed quickly, with sugar and smirks and side-glances as we slowly picked through one measly doughnut and expertly avoided the entire shitstorm that was swirling around both our families. We didn't mention Donata or Jack or the gun Luca had under his seat. We didn't talk about the warehouse, the blood war, the fact that we were at the start of something that was only going to get worse. We were both thinking about it, but our whole drive became about that doughnut and nothing else.

He took the tiniest bite and put the final piece back on the dashboard, leaving the last of it for me. He cleared his throat, and just as I popped the end of it in my mouth and swallowed without bothering to chew, he turned to me and asked, 'Better now?'

'It's a start.' I rubbed my fingertips on my shorts to get rid of the stickiness. 'Was that the first doughnut you've ever had?' I asked him.

Luca threw his head back and laughed so loudly I almost jumped in my seat.

He laughed and laughed. I could see all his teeth. I didn't realize how wide his smile could stretch, or how little crinkles formed beside his eyes when he was amused. I didn't know he could even laugh like that. It was so strange to see him untethered from his usual brand of seriousness.

I thought he might actually tear up with amusement, but after a while he just shook his head, shaking off the dregs of his laughter. 'Are you serious?' he asked, stealing a glance at me as we pulled off the highway. 'Was that a real question?'

'What?' I asked, my eyes wide and innocent. 'Why are you laughing so hard? Don't be so rude.'

He shook his head, still smiling, and I fought the urge to slam my fist into his knee to wipe the smile off his face. He was disconcerting like this. It made him too approachable. I was used to aloof-Luca, snarky-Luca. This Luca threw me off.

'Yes, I've had a doughnut before,' he said. 'I've also tried cake and pizza, and I've been on a swing set and played on a PlayStation. I did not grow up in a metal cage.' He laughed again, but this time under his breath. '*Dio, sei divertente. What a question.*'

I weighed my response. 'I wasn't trying to make fun of you. It's just . . . you just seem like such a . . . um . . .'

'What?' He flicked his gaze to me again. 'A killjoy?'

'I don't know,' I said, trying to salvage what I was about to say. But the thing is, that sort of *was* what I was about to say. 'Well, yeah, kinda. You're always so *serious* about stuff.'

The joviality seeped from his expression, but his voice remained light. 'I have to be serious about things, Sophie. It's my job. But that doesn't mean I don't know how to have fun. Or how to eat a *doughnut.*'

'OK, then,' I said, duly scolded. 'Consider me enlightened.'

He was still shaking his head. 'You really are something else.'

The mood had finally lifted. The tension from earlier had drained, and I relaxed in the easiness that took its place.

'Thanks for the doughnut,' I said, watching the expanses of green outside and enjoying feeling satiated. 'You were right. I love sprinkles.'

'I know,' he said. 'I'm always right.'

I rolled my eyes. 'Smart-ass.'

'So, are we even now?' he asked. He was watching the street again – country fields blurring into each other on either side of us, while trees jostled for space overhead. 'For you saving me in the warehouse, I mean. I figured the doughnut might make a good thank-you.'

'Oh, no, no,' I said, flopping back against the seat. 'Correct etiquette demands a bouquet of flowers. A doughnut, I'm sorry to say, simply won't cut it.'

Luca's exhale whistled through his nose. 'It's an impossibility,' he said, his words filled with mock regret. 'Surely the sprinkles made it a worthy thank-you gift?'

I shook my head against the leather. 'I don't make the rules, Luca. And if we're being technical, you really only gave me *half* a doughnut.' I grinned, revelling in his frown.

'OK then.' The car jolted to the side and Luca slammed on the brakes, pulling us into a mud ditch at the edge of the street. My body strained against the seatbelt as I lurched forwards. He pulled the parking brake and flung the door open.

'Where are you going?' I half-shrieked, undoing my seatbelt and whipping my head around at the same time. The place was deserted. There were no cars behind us – just fields and trees and muck on either side of us.

Luca was already out of the car, striding towards the field beside us. 'Wait there,' he called over his shoulder. He ducked through the fence and got lost in the grass. It brushed against his knees as he walked through it, bending low and scouring the ground. Clad completely in black, and with a switchblade sticking out of his back pocket, Luca ran his fingers along the grass.

He was completely and utterly out of his natural environment. And it didn't bother him at all.

I waited in the car with his keys and his phone and his gun

and the radio still on, and tried to figure out just what the hell he was looking for on this random dirt road.

He ducked back into the car a couple of minutes later, his cheeks tinged with the faintest circles of pink. He was holding a small bunch of flowers in his hand, dirt still clinging to some of their ends, heads drooping against one another where he had grouped them together in his fist.

He held them across the armrest between us. 'Here,' he said, not quite looking at me.

A bouquet. For me.

My jaw unhinged. I took them from him, my fingers scrabbling against his palm as he released them and I tried to keep the mashed bunch of blue flowers together.

'Thanks,' I finally managed, rotating them, checking that they were really real. 'You got me violets.'

'Is that what they are?' He was already easing the car back on to the street. I caught the hint of his smile. He so knew what they were. Nerd.

Something swelled in my chest. They were half-wilted, ripped from the earth and strewn with stray blades of grass that were probably covered with tiny bugs, but they were the first bouquet of flowers I had ever got. And they were beautiful.

'I earned these,' I said, beaming at my bounty as I held them in my lap.

Luca nodded at the road, his lips stretching to reveal a flash of white teeth. 'You definitely did.'

The start of the afternoon – the prison, the highway scare, the gun, the terror – faded with the fields behind us.

Luca dropped me off at the end of my street just after six p.m. I scooped my flowers up and hopped out, turning to wave them at him. 'Thanks for the ride.'

'You're welcome.'

I gestured down the street, in the direction of reality as it came creeping back in. 'Anyway, I'm sure you have . . . diner business to attend to.'

He shook his head, his expression turning sombre as his seriousness returned with thoughts of his family. 'I don't watch the diner, Sophie.' He sighed, just a little, and his brow furrowed. 'My responsibilities are closer to home.'

'Oh,' I said, realizing that Luca's presence in Cedar Hill really was just a favour to me. An act of kindness that had saved me from melting on that bus. 'Thank you for going so far out of your way for me.'

He raised an eyebrow. 'You don't have to seem so surprised.'

'Hmm,' I teased, pretending to consider him. 'Maybe you're not so bad after all.'

He leant across the seat, jabbing his finger in the air. 'If you tell anyone, I'll deny it. I have a reputation to uphold, you know.'

'Oh, you mean the whole asshole thing?'

'And speaking of reputations, don't do anything stupid,' he added, leaning back into his seat and releasing the parking brake. 'Fight your natural urges.'

I frowned at him. 'And it almost ended so well.'

He shrugged as I shut the door. Through the open window I heard him say, 'Well, then it wouldn't really be us, would it?'

He didn't wait for my answer and I didn't stand watching

his car as he took off, back to *Evelina* and the underworld. My thoughts skipped to the safe and all the secrets it held, to his brothers who were lurking somewhere nearby. I turned for home, my bouquet of blue violets held tightly in my hand.

There was a time, not too long ago, when I never would have expected eleven flowers and half a doughnut to lift my mood so high. But that was before Jack, before the diner, before the Marinos, before the Falcones. That was before my father told me to get the hell away from Cedar Hill.

My footsteps slowed as I realized that to honour my father's wishes, I would have to ask my mother to do the impossible. I was caught between them – between everything – and all the roads were hazy and grey, and I didn't know which one to choose. The sky was grey too, heavy with a distant rolling storm, and it pressed down on me as I walked, suffocating me slowly under its heat.

The violets were electric blue, and I held them tightly. I was still holding them like a perverse life raft for my sanity when I shut the front door of my house and found myself face-to-face with Donata Marino. She was perched, like a Gucci-fied vulture, on the threshold of our kitchen.

CHAPTER TWENTY-FOUR
ALLEGIANCE

In the giant game of human ping-pong that was fast becoming my life, Elena Falcone held one bat, Donata Marino held the other, and I was a small, white ball, whirring back and forth.

And I was so over all this.

My mother was hovering behind Donata, her hands curling around the kitchen sink edge as she leant against it. Donata was rigid, squared shoulders cutting her neck in half, hands fisted at her sides as she stood between us. She wore all black for her daughter. Sara Marino had been dead less than a week.

My body deflated in a mixture of shock and fear. The flowers went limp at my side, their blue heads drooping towards the floor. I forced myself to look at Donata as memories of her bony grip at Eden brought a phantom sting to my wrists. She moved aside, granting me entrance to the kitchen.

'Well, here you are, Ms Gracewell.' She lingered over my name as though it burnt her mouth. Her darkened lids fell heavy over bloodshot eyes.

'Sweetheart.' My mother said the word on an inhale. Her brow was creased, the sun-tanned skin rippling. She looked like she was trying to figure out a riddle.

I put the flowers on the countertop beside me, tossing them with forced casualness, the irrational part of me worrying that Donata might sense where they had come from, *who* they had come from. In that moment, those flowers felt as incriminating as a giant neon sign on my forehead flashing *FALCONE SYMPATHIZER.*

The atmosphere was strange – loaded, like the entire room was tilted on a knifepoint, waiting for the plunge into something darker.

'Mom?' My fingers clutched my phone inside my pocket. I was already unlocking it. 'What's going on? Did she hurt you?'

She shook her head. The circles under her eyes were moistened. 'No, sweetheart . . . she was just telling me about . . .'

'About my daughter,' said Donata, peering at me through black-rimmed eyes. 'I was telling your mother about what the Falcones did to my nineteen-year-old girl.'

'Dreadful,' whispered my mother. 'Those boys . . . it's just dreadful.'

'I was telling your mother how it might have happened to you . . .' Donata paused, calculated, waiting . . . and then, 'how it still might.'

'Oh, Sophie,' my mother said, falling head over heels into

Donata's manipulation. She pressed a hand to her chest. 'I'd lose my heart.'

'You're not going to lose anything,' I told her calmly. 'I'm sorry about your daughter,' I added, speaking to Donata and being careful to keep my features in check. I didn't want her to know I had seen Sara after Eden that night – how close I had been to saving her. How dreadfully I had failed. 'But I can take care of myself.'

Donata waved my words away, a manicured hand flying between us. My mother shrank further into herself. 'Let me cut to the chase. I'm here to tell you what the Marinos expect from you, Sophie.'

'The safe in the diner,' I answered, without even blinking.

'The money is no longer your concern,' she replied, unfazed by my knowledge of the safe. 'Your uncle thought you might remove it for us – but I think trusting you with that task given your current attitude is not such a good idea.'

So it was money. It must have been a whole lot, considering how hell-bent they were on getting back in there.

'We intend to retrieve the contents of the safe ourselves.' Her lips peeled away, revealing a line of yellowed teeth – a wolf waiting to pounce. 'It will be more . . . opportune this way.'

I narrowed my eyes. 'What's that supposed to mean?'

'It means we will no longer back down from Falcone threats. We are going to hang them with their own noose.'

The explanation might have been vague but the image was horrifyingly vivid. I tried to blink it away, to school my features so she wouldn't know how hard my heart was thumping, how it felt like it was climbing into my throat. I

228

shouldn't care. I shouldn't show it.

Her smile was tight, pinching the hollows in her cheeks. 'Their *soldati* are watching the diner. We know exactly how and where to get to them. When we take the safe, we'll take the heads of the Falcones who stand guard over it, too.' She inhaled sharply, her face reflecting some imagined glory. 'We are ready for them.'

'An ambush,' I whispered. I thought of Eden, of all the pain and rage it had caused when the Falcones had made their move. I imagined the scene unfolding: a couple of Falcones outnumbered and trapped at the diner with Donata and her Marino soldiers surrounding them. Dom's arrogance. Nic's blind determination. I shook my head, my eyes growing wide at her polluted scheme. How could she roll the dice again, and so soon?

'It'll be a bloodbath.'

'And you're going to help us,' she returned calmly, as though it had already been decided. 'You're their weakness.'

'*Me?*' I said, dread draining the colour from my cheeks. 'How?'

Her smile grew, shifting the sharp planes in her face until she appeared more skeleton than human. 'You'll see.'

'No,' I said. 'I won't see.' I pushed away from the counter and stood in the middle of the kitchen, heaving. 'I won't help you.'

She knitted her arms across her chest. She seemed so infuriatingly sure when she said, 'You will.'

I shook my head. 'You're crazy.'

'This will be your task. When we come back for you, you're coming with us. You'll help lure them into our trap.'

'I don't want a task,' I said firmly. Everything inside me told me to run, to hide. Everything was darkness and Donata, rage and ice, expectations and consequences. I could feel the walls closing in, my mother's muted panic pressing against me.

'If you do as I tell you when the time comes, you stake your allegiance with us and we'll take care of you.' Her eyes flicked to my mother. 'You'll be safe. Provided for.'

My mother hung her head. So she was shaming her. She knew about our money troubles, about my absent father, and she was using it as a weapon against us.

'If you don't kill them, they'll kill you.' She was still looking at my mother. 'It's only a matter of time now Jack is in the fold.'

'What's he offering you?' I pressed. 'Are you really so easily bought?'

The ghost of something sinister passed over Donata's face. 'If you fail to do what I'm telling you, then your allegiance is with them.' She snapped her fingers. 'And we will kill you.'

The flowers pulsed in my peripheral vision. I could never hurt the Falcones. Not in a thousand nightmares. 'Can't you just leave me out of this?'

Donata looked at my mother. 'It is my experience that in matters of life and death, everyone should know what's at stake.'

My mother raised her head. Her eyes were rimmed with red. She looked at Donata, shook her head, and sighed.

I didn't say anything. I wouldn't lie to her and agree to her demands, and yet I was afraid of refusing her. I needed her to leave so I could gather myself. So I could snap my mother out of whatever day-coma she was in. So I could find a way to warn Luca. I remembered Sara's advice to me in Eden – I had to pretend. I had to pretend so Donata would slacken her grip just enough so I could breathe. So I could *think*.

Donata shifted and a gun appeared in her hand. Before I could move, she was pressing it into my mother's jugular, lifting her to her tiptoes as she bent her backwards across the sink. I froze, a half-scream jolting from me.

My mother choked out a whimper.

Donata cocked the trigger, her eyes boring into mine as I stood stock-still across from her. 'How high do I need to make the stakes, Sophie?'

'Don't,' I pleaded. 'I'll do it. I'll do what you want.'

Donata pushed the gun harder and my mother choked again. Her eyes were bulging, the capillaries angry and red. Donata leant over her, and when they were nose-to-nose, she said, as calm as if they were old friends, 'Remember your promise, Celine.'

'I'll help you,' I said. 'I'll do what you ask. Just don't hurt her.'

Donata pulled back, slipped her gun into the pocket of her dress and smoothed the stray black tendrils around her forehead. My mother fell forwards, her hands circling her throat as she gasped for air. 'You are a cruel woman,' she heaved.

Donata straightened the sleeves of her dress. 'I have to be.'

'Leave my house,' my mother said. 'You've made your point.'

I followed Donata into the hallway, making sure she really was leaving. Her heels click-clacked with purpose, the sound pulling me back to the memory of her sister, Elena, as she thundered down the Falcone corridor at *Evelina*. What a twisted destiny the two of them had secured for themselves.

Donata turned on the threshold, her back towards the heaving sky and the heat pummelling against us from the driveway. We stared at each other. 'We'll be back for you.'

My stomach lurched, but I regarded her calmly. 'When?'

'Soon.'

'I'll be ready,' I lied. My mind was whirring with all the ways I could beat her. I wouldn't let her win. I wouldn't be her pawn.

Her voice turned weary, the pitch dropping as her shoulders dipped. She exhaled a sigh and her mask shifted, just a little. 'We're not the enemies, Sophie.'

The air was too warm; I could barely feel it as I sucked it in and forced another lie. 'I know.'

She lowered her voice then, and her words fell into something else – a plea. 'Girl, you might think you love one of them, but that is the Falcone game. Don't make the mistake my sister made. Angelo Falcone might have once been a shining star but he was violent and cruel. Do you know what he gifted to my sister on the night of their wedding? My father's death. Elena and my father never saw eye to eye, and her elopement with Angelo Falcone didn't help things, but to kill a girl's father simply to remove a nuisance from her life? That's no gift. Yet she was so wrapped up in his glittering eyes and his wealth, she fell more in love with him for it. You can curl your lip because your uncle and I deal in the business of drugs, but the game of murder for murder's sake is a twisted one. The path is dark and there is no going back.

'The next time you think about those boys, ask yourself

how many fathers, mothers, sons and daughters they have killed. Ask yourself who dumped my daughter's body into that lake? Who carved "*La nostra vendetta*" across her heart?' Her voice cracked and she stopped abruptly, covering her mouth with her hand and pressing her lids tight shut. '*Mia bella bimba.*'

'I don't—'

'You will help us destroy them,' she interrupted, 'and I will forgive you for the mystery of how Valentino Falcone knew where to send his *soldati* the night my daughter was taken from me.' She caught me by the wrist, pulling me into her until her perfume rolled over me.

'Yes,' I said, breathlessly. 'I promise.'

'For Sara.' For a passing second, she wore her grief plainly on her face – it aged her, made her human, and I felt something squirm inside me at the sight. She was being ravaged by her loss, and it was driving her to bloodshed and madness.

My throat was starting to quiver, making the words thick and heavy as I forced them out. 'For Sara,' I said.

'You must see sense.' She placed her other hand on my shoulder and squeezed it, as though to strengthen me, but all I felt was frightened and full of guilt. '*Fidelitate Coniuncti.*'

She turned from me and charged into the heavy evening, taking her place in her blacked-out convoy. It had appeared from nowhere but I knew it had been there, somewhere close by, all along. The Marinos wouldn't send their queen anywhere unaided. I wondered if Jack was with her now, sucking up to her like a lapdog.

A hand brushed across my back as my mother came to my side.

I watched as Donata drove away from us, my heart hammering violently in my chest. 'What's "*Fidelitate Coniuncti*"?'

'I don't know, sweetheart.'

A familiar surge of regret flooded through me. I should never have gone to Eden. I would go to my grave regretting that decision. Maybe Jack would have come to me in the end, but it would have been on my terms. It would have been on my turf. But now the choice was gone.

'What did you promise her?' I asked.

'Something I have no intention of delivering.'

I turned to her.

'I told her I would get you to cooperate,' my mother continued. 'She said she would hurt you if you didn't. I would have promised her the moon if it got her out of my house.'

'I'm not going to help her. I don't care what she wants. I'm not hurting anyone.'

She looked alarmed. 'Of course you're not.' She pulled me back into the darkness of the house. 'You're not getting involved in any of this. It's not our world.'

'Dad says we have to leave Cedar Hill.'

She nodded, a shadow passing across her face. 'I see now he's right. Sophie,' she tugged at my arm and took my hand in hers, 'you know everything I do is to keep you safe. You know I would die before I let anyone put you in danger, right?'

'Yeah,' I said. 'Of course I know that.'

'Good,' she said quietly. 'Because sometimes it's hard to know what the right thing is. Sometimes . . . especially lately, everything seems so fuzzy. But we have each other, and that's what matters. I'm sorry Donata Marino lost her daughter, but I have no intention of letting her gamble with mine. Not ever.'

I squeezed her hand. 'We'll be OK.'

She nodded, but her gaze was lost somewhere over my shoulder. 'We'll go away from here. I just have to find the money.' Her face crumpled but she caught it, stretching a smile as her eyes turned watery. 'I'll think of something, sweetheart.'

'Don't worry,' I told her. 'I already have.'

In the kitchen, I filled a glass and put the violets inside it. I placed the makeshift vase on the windowsill and swallowed my nerves. *We'll come back for you soon.* Soon the world would tilt into darkness. Just how soon was soon? I wasn't going to stick around and find out. Tomorrow my mother and I would disappear.

I pulled out my phone and dialled Millie's number. She answered on the third ring.

'What are you doing tomorrow morning?' I asked her.

'I don't know,' she replied, cagey as ever. 'Why?'

'I need a ride to *Evelina*.'

CHAPTER TWENTY-FIVE

THE LIE

When I woke up the sun had risen somewhere behind a thick sheen of dark clouds and even the air inside was crackling. I showered, washing off the fear and the sweat, and by the time I emerged again, freshly clothed in denim shorts and a tank top, I looked a little less like death-with-frizzy-hair.

I found my mother hovering in her room. She had changed into a tracksuit and white sneakers, and had clipped her hair back behind her ears. She stopped folding a T-shirt when I came in. I could never tell her what I was about to do. I couldn't explain my intentions because she wouldn't under-stand them, and she wouldn't let me go. Not after everything Donata had told her about the Falcones. She'd think me a lunatic for going to the murderers' palace.

'I've got to go out for a bit,' I told her. 'But I'll be back this evening.'

'Where are you going that will take so long? I thought you were just going to the bank . . .'

'Errands,' I said, keeping my voice lofty. I gestured around me at the air, hoping to distract her from the threads of suspicion that were connecting behind her eyes. 'I'll go to the bank and get my savings. I have to see Millie and let her know what's going on. And I want to pick up a few things too.'

'Oh,' she said, bewildered. 'Do you want me to come with you?'

'I think you should carry on packing, so we can get a head start.'

She was nodding at all the clothes that had spilt out around her. 'Yes,' she said, frowning. 'There's a lot to do.'

I stepped back from her, smiling without feeling the joy that was supposed to go with it. 'Exactly.'

Millie was already waiting for me when I flung the front door open. 'I hope you know what you're doing,' she grumbled as I got into the car. I had spent thirty minutes talking her around last night before I finally got her on board.

'I hope so too,' I said.

'You know you can always stay with me. I can ask my dad to lend—'

'Mil,' I cut her off. 'This isn't a vacation, it's a blood feud, and I told you a thousand times, I am not involving you.'

'What if they refuse to help you, Soph? Any bright ideas then?'

I flopped back against the seat, staring out the windscreen at the sinking grey sky. 'Then I guess I'm going to have to rob a bank.'

CHAPTER TWENTY-SIX
SANCTUARY

After a long ride from the city, we pulled up outside the winding driveway of *Evelina*. I was surprised we remembered the way so easily – but then again, it had become the setting of some of my most scarring memories.

'I'll be nearby,' Millie said as I got out. We'd agreed I would go in alone. It was safer that way, and I had already involved Millie way too much as it was. 'Text me every fifteen minutes. If I don't hear from you, I swear to God I'm calling the police and I'll take my chances with the consequences.'

'Thanks, Mil. I owe you a ton for this.'

She pushed her shades up her nose and sighed. 'I'll remember that if I ever need a kidney.'

I jogged up the driveway, pushing away the bubbles of anxiety as Millie pulled away and got lost, or hidden, somewhere in the surrounding countryside.

The doorbell rang inside the walls. The man who answered was the gentle giant who had tried to calm Millie and me down when we were here before . . . the Falcone who had lied right to my face about Sara's fate. Paulie. Still, it could have been worse. It could have been his brother. It could have been Felice.

He glanced behind me. 'Miss Gracewell. This is surprising.'

He had all the formal politeness of his brother but none of the slimy passive aggression. I studied his hand perched lightly on the doorframe. His fingernails were painted bright pink and yellow.

'I guess it must be,' I said, trying not to sound childish or vulnerable, both things I felt overwhelmingly in that moment. 'I was wondering if I could speak to Luca?'

I could see confusion breaking through, the wheels in his head desperately turning, trying to figure this all out. 'Would you like to come inside while I get him for you?'

'Yes, please.'

His loafers fell soundlessly on the marble as he disappeared down a hallway. The grandness of the house crept up on me, the echoing sounds of my breath seeming louder than usual. I studied the Falcone crest etched into the floor and the three-tiered crystal chandelier that hung overhead and cast rainbows along the double staircase. High on the wall in the far corner of the foyer, there was a picture.

In the photograph, Felice was wearing a suit, and beside him was one of the most beautiful women I'd ever seen. Her wavy chestnut hair was gathered high on her head in ruby-encrusted pins. She had wide blue eyes and creamy skin that belonged in a CoverGirl commercial. Clad in a lace wedding dress and clutching Felice's arm, she was beaming at the camera. It seemed very much like love, I had to admit, and somehow, the softness of her beauty seemed to soften him too. He didn't seem scary or evil, just young.

Evelina. Even in the photograph, the glint of her ruby ring caught my eye. It was just like the one in the Falcone mausoleum. Huge. *Expensive.* Red – the colour of love. The colour of violence. What had he done to drive her away? The letters F and E were carved into the bottom of the frame, the word *Sempre* glowing silver beneath them.

Always, I remembered.

What a lie.

Luca emerged from the hallway and stopped by the bottom of the staircase, keeping yards of distance between us. 'I must be irresistible. You can't stay away from me for more than twenty-four hours.'

I whirled from the photograph of Felice and his bride and took a deep, steadying breath. 'I don't really know how to even go about saying this . . .' I conceded.

He leant across the banister, his chin resting on his folded arms. 'Try putting one word in front of the other.'

His tone was teasing but I could feel him studying me. I drowned the urge to flip him my middle finger, and instead made the choice that meant there was no going back. I said the words that would make me a Marino enemy and push my life even closer to the knife-edge.

'Donata Marino wants me to help her kill your family.'

Silence enveloped us. Luca's expression didn't falter. He just stared at me, his eyes barely flickering in recognition.

I decided it would be best to add something, just in case there was any lingering confusion. 'I'm not going to. Obviously.'

He pulled back from the banister and stood straight, seeming so much taller then. He stopped when he was just a foot from me. He scanned me, briefly, but not quickly enough that it wasn't noticeable. Was he checking for a weapon?

'What did she offer you?' he asked evenly.

I shrugged. 'Safety, mostly . . . from your family.'

'From us?' he said. 'But we have no interest in you.'

Something about that stung me. I shook it off; he was right. That was the whole point: the Falcones didn't care about me any more.

'I don't know what she's thinking, Luca,' I admitted. 'She's going to hurt me and my mom if I don't help her. We have nowhere to go. We have no money to get away from them.' I cleared my throat to stamp out the quiver in my voice and then I thought, *What's the point?* Luca knew the truth. I was sick of trying to hide it. 'And I'm scared, Luca. I am really scared.'

'When?' he asked, his voice level. 'When does she intend to move against us?'

It hit me then. This was Luca in commander mode. This was Luca putting his duty before his emotions. He was keeping cool because he was trained to. I had no idea what he was really thinking or feeling. I tried to put myself in that mode too, but my heart felt like there was an iron fist around it, and I couldn't help thinking of my mother packing up all her stuff at home, waiting for me to come back to her with a plan, with money, with a way out.

'Soon,' I told him. 'She said she'd come back for me first. They're going to ambush your family at the diner. She wants me to help her.' I hesitated, embarrassed by the implication, by the absurdity of having to say the next part to his face. 'She thinks I'm a . . . Falcone weakness.'

Something flitted across Luca's face – a passing shadow, an unreadable emotion. His jaw tightened, but apart from that he barely blinked. 'Is that so?'

'Apparently.'

'And she told you all of this?'

'Yes.'

'Without provocation.'

'She wants me to help her,' I repeated, feeling the dim heat of embarrassment in my cheeks.

He narrowed his eyes. 'Does she know you have no experience with weapons?'

I held my palm up, the cut facing him. 'I would have thought that was obvious.'

He didn't smile.

'She's so angry, Luca,' I said, feeling the betrayal sing in my words. Donata would have my head for this. She'd have my head for even stepping through these doors, but if I was going to pin my hopes on anyone in this whole mess it sure as hell wasn't going to be her. 'Her grief is driving her crazy. She wants to destroy your family. Soon.'

Luca's eyes darkened. He studied me in the silence.

'That's all I got,' I said quietly. 'That's it.'

His concentration broke. I could see the mask shifting – the barrier coming down, unsmoothing his features. He scrubbed a hand through his hair, his fingers pulling at his temples as he closed his eyes. 'A bold move for the Marinos,' he murmured, a frown twisting on his lips. 'What is she playing at?'

'What will you do?' I asked, fear spiking in me at the idea of a retaliation, at how quickly the blood war was escalating. If Eden was anything to go by, it wasn't like the Falcones were shy of grand bloody gestures. Nothing was too bold for them.

He stared at me, his tone deceptively level when he said, 'I won't let her harm my brothers.' There was a short silence, then he closed whatever he was thinking off from me, and instead asked, 'What will you do, Sophie?'

I looked at the ground, at the majestic crimson falcon. Something crumpled in my chest and I felt the sudden urge to cry. I wasn't a Marino but I wasn't a Falcone either. 'I've said it now. There's no going back.' I paused, collecting myself, and then conceded, in little more than a whisper, what we both plainly knew already. 'She'll probably kill me for it when she finds out.'

Luca dipped his head but I decided not to look him in the eyes in case I projectile-cried all over him. 'Sophie, are you asking me for our protection?'

I knew when he offered me his help outside the prison that it wasn't without trepidation. I knew it wouldn't be easy – he had said as much – but I needed it now, and if it cost me my pride to ask him, to ask all of them, then I would give it, because my mother and I were desperate. This was our strongest option, and that, in itself, was terrifying.

'I just . . . I need somewhere for my mom and I to hide until this is over.' I paused, drilling down into what I really wanted. 'I need to disappear.'

'I'm not a magician.'

'No,' I agreed. 'You're more powerful than that. You're the Falcone underboss.'

He didn't deny it. He started chewing on his pinky nail, his expression turning contemplative. I zeroed in on the scar above his lip. Suddenly my shoulders felt impossibly heavy, weighing me into the ground. Why wasn't he answering me? Because I was crazy, that's why. But I had cast my die. 'I didn't mean to freak you out—'

'I'm not freaking out,' he cut me off. He wasn't, I realized. He was completely serene, calm like a lake, and I was choppy and stormy and desperate. 'I'm thinking about how I'm going to do this.'

'Do what?' I was halfway between him and the front door, in purgatory, and it was hard to tell which direction was hell.

A wry smile twisted on his face. 'How I'm going to convince my family to protect Jack Gracewell's niece and Michael Gracewell's wife.'

'Oh.' *Well, when you put it like that . . .* My face fell.

A laugh rang out, echoing along the walls and crawling up the back of my neck. Felice emerged from somewhere behind me. 'Isn't it obvious, Luca?' he said, his voice filling up the foyer. 'We have to call a Council.'

The sound of more footsteps carried into the foyer – this time from above us. Had they all been there, listening, this whole time? Nic and Gino appeared at the top of the stairs. 'What's going on?' asked Nic, peering over the balcony.

I waved up at him. 'Guess who,' I sang, feeling monumentally awkward.

He nearly fell over the banister. In lightning speed he

245

descended the stairs, coming to stand beside Luca. Gino trailed behind him. 'What's going on?'

Felice's laughter had tapered off. 'This girl is a one-woman show,' he said, without taking his lidless eyes off me. 'I swear she'll keep us all on our toes.'

I decided to bite my tongue. Impoliteness wouldn't get me very far.

'We're calling a Council,' Luca told Nic.

'No way,' said Gino disbelievingly. 'How come?'

Nic was looking back and forth between Luca and me, trying to figure it out. 'Why?'

Felice gestured at me in the most unnecessary dramatic way he could, as though I was his lovely assistant. 'Your *beloved* Persephone Gracewell has just switched her allegiance and snitched on Donata Marino. It appears she is in need of Sanctuary.'

'Sanctuary?' Gino spluttered an incredulous laugh. 'Holy shit.'

'Sanctuary?' I echoed, feeling the sense that I was missing the weight of the meaning. 'Is that a thing?'

'Yes,' said Nic, his frown twisting. 'It's a thing.'

CHAPTER TWENTY-SEVEN

THE FIGHT

Sanctuary was the order of extending protection and loyalty to someone not bound to the family by blood. It was the closest one could get to becoming a Falcone without being born as one. Luca told me it would take a vote – a majority verdict – to offer my mother and me the safety I had come seeking from them so casually. If approved, they would give us a safe house and enough to survive on until Donata Marino was silenced for good.

We stood in the foyer, the Falcone boys and me, presided over by Felice, as I was questioned about every solitary detail of my encounter with Donata. I told them everything I knew – or everything she had said, at least – not knowing how much of it I could really count on. Felice couldn't understand why she would put her faith in me at all.

I couldn't really understand it either.

'None of this makes sense,' he mused. 'Not for those Marino cowards.'

I had forgotten about Donata's final words – *Fidelitate Coniuncti* – and I stumbled over them as I relayed her message to me. Luca arched an eyebrow and Felice muttered, 'Interesting.'

'Is it a threat?' I asked. 'What does it mean?' I couldn't spell it well enough to google it. I could barely say it.

'It's Latin,' said Luca, uneasily. 'It's not a threat.'

Felice pulled out his phone, *consigliere* duties overriding his desire to question me further. 'I'll assemble everyone. Should be an hour, perhaps less. I'll speak with Valentino,' he added, directing the last part at Luca. 'He'll find this most strange indeed . . .'

'He's paranoid,' Luca answered. 'There's nothing in this.'

'I wouldn't be so sure.' Felice disappeared, his footsteps echoing down a distant corridor.

'What was that about?' I said.

Luca batted the question away. 'Don't worry about it.'

Nic was the only Falcone brother not frowning. He was relaxed, shoulders squared – a soldier, ready for whatever was coming. 'I'm glad you came to us, Sophie,' he said earnestly. His voice took on that low tone, like he was closing the space between me and him until it was just the two of us. 'It's not right what she's doing. But she won't be alive for much longer. We'll make sure you're kept out of all this, I promise. '

Dom had joined us by then. 'Don't make promises you can't keep, Nic.' He rolled back on his heels. 'The Council will decide.'

'I know that,' I said, addressing Dom and trying to keep the venom from my voice. 'I know this is kind of a long shot. I didn't think there would be so much ceremony involved . . . I just . . .' I turned with hopeful eyes to Luca. 'When you told me yesterday that I could come to your family if I was ever in trouble, I didn't think I'd ever have to take you up on it. But Donata terrifies me, and I'm sick of taking chances with my safety.' I added, 'I'm taking your advice. I'm being smart. I recognize I can't get out of this on my own.'

Luca had a hand over his mouth and was smoothing his fingers along his jaw, thinking.

'Yesterday?' said Nic. 'What was yesterday?'

'We ran into each other at Stateville,' I answered quickly, seeing that Luca wasn't feeling so inclined. His mind was elsewhere. 'He gave me a ride home.'

Why did I feel like I was justifying myself? Why did I feel like there was anything to hide?

Nic frowned. 'You didn't think to mention that to me at any point, Luca?'

Dom and Gino exchanged a glance. '*Uh-oh*,' droned Dom, grinning. 'Looks like Sophie and Luca had a prison date without Nic . . .'

'Shut up,' I hissed.

'*Calmati*.' Luca came back to himself and clapped Nic on his back. 'Don't read into it, brother. It was nothing.'

'Yeah. It was nothing,' I added, hardening the words.

Nic squared his jaw. He was staring at Luca like he might want to set him on fire, and I felt the tension in the room soar. Only Dom was finding it funny. An hour. I would have to wait an hour for this Council, whatever it was. And I would have to do it under this stupid cloud of testosterone.

I went to the bathroom to splash some water on my face and update Millie. I felt calmer, better, focused. I just had to stay alive and keep the people I loved close by until it was all finished – until Donata was dead. I tried not to dwell on the possibility that the Falcones might slip up – that their counter-plan, whatever it turned out to be, might not work, that Jack would rally in anger and still come for me. I tried not to think about Sanctuary being denied to me, about my mother and me having to face all of this alone.

When I made my way back to the foyer, everyone had scattered. I followed the hallway on the right, tracing the rumblings coming from the belly of the house. Halfway along the corridor, I pushed a door open, following the shouting. The room was huge, with an array of gaming equipment inside – dartboards, punching bags, a foosball table, a pool table and a stereo system. There were couches and beanbag chairs around the walls, and three large diamond-crossed windows looked out on to the swelling storm.

In the middle of the room, Dom and Nic were running circles around each other. Felice and Luca were leaning against the wall, watching them with the casual interest of passing spectators, and Gino was reclining in a beanbag chair, eyes half-closed.

'What's going on?' I asked Luca, just as Nic flipped Dom flat on his back. There was a heavy thump and Nic's triumphant laughter split the room apart.

Luca indicated the little muddle of testosterone. 'Relatively safe conflict management in a house of assassins,' he explained. 'Whenever we have an argument, we take it to the sparring room. When there's a winner, it's over.'

'What were they arguing about?'

Luca didn't answer me.

'Dom has a loose mouth,' supplied Felice. 'And you're an easy target.'

'Oh,' I said. *Asshole.*

Dom was back on his feet. He took a swing at Nic. Nic blocked his head with his hands and Dom used his distraction to swipe his foot across Nic's legs, almost toppling him off balance.

'Watch your knees, Nicoli!' shouted Luca, betraying how interested he really was in the scrapping. 'Don't worry about your face, *bel ragazzo*!'

'No helping!' yelled Dom, coming at Nic again. This time he was shoved backwards, his shoes squeaking across the wood as he tried to keep from falling.

Felice was entranced by the fight. 'Nic's too heavy-footed,' he muttered to Luca.

'He's stronger than Dom,' Luca countered. 'Soph, what do you reckon?' he asked, turning to me. I had been checking the time on my phone, trying to keep the anxiety from fluttering into my throat. It was getting late, the humidity was tortuously high, and I wanted to get home before it broke. I wanted to be out of Cedar Hill before the storm came.

Did he just say *Soph*?

'I think Nic will win,' I said, trying to appear calmer than I felt just then. 'But that's mainly because I want Dom to lose.' I was hoping Nic would knock him flat on his face and then I would point and laugh at him and shout *Ha! You suck, Dom Falcone!*

'Watch your knees!' Luca yelled again. 'That's his tactic!'

'*Stai zitto!*' Nic hissed, springing towards Dom and trying to tackle him at the waist. They started grappling with each other and I saw Nic's head snap up and register me for the first time. He pulled backwards, balancing on the balls of his feet like a boxer.

Luca dipped his head close to mine, and I watched Nic's face change as he glanced over. 'Maybe if Dom shakes his head hard enough, he'll spill enough of his hair gel to trip Nicoli up,' he muttered. 'And then I'll be down a hundred dollars.'

My laugh escaped me in a loud, obnoxious wheeze and I had to clap my hand over my mouth to stop the noise. Nic was looking at us again.

Luca raised two fingers and pointed them at his eyes. 'Focus, brother!'

It was too late. Dom had rounded on Nic, and was coming at him from the side. He clasped his head underneath his arm and wrestled him to the ground. 'Tap out!' shouted Dom, his order flying away with laughter. 'I got you! I win!'

Nic's forehead was pressed against the ground. After several fruitless seconds of struggling he tapped out. Cursing, he sprang to his feet and started brushing himself off.

Luca pushed off the wall and stalked towards him, his hands raised in aggravation. 'What was that? I told you to focus. You're too distractible.'

'*You* were distracting me!' I was taken aback by how angry Nic was. I knew he had lost, but it was just a game and it wasn't like he had gotten hurt.

'Stop acting like a baby,' said Luca coolly. 'You lost me a

hundred dollars.'

'Why don't *you* fight me, then?' said Nic, squaring up to him. 'If you're so knowledgeable then you'll beat me.'

Luca waved his request away. 'Don't be so childish. We have to go now anyway.'

Nic pushed the matted hair from his eyes. 'We've got time. Since you're so concerned about your money why don't you try winning it back? Five hundred dollars for the winner!'

Five hundred dollars. Whoa. I would have fought him for five hundred dollars. I had gotten beaten up by his uncle for much less. And that would go a long way to helping me skip town.

Luca wasn't biting. 'You're so wound up,' he said. 'Calm yourself.'

I recognized the look in Nic's eyes – that blazing defiance. *Uh-oh.* He kept coming at Luca; it was as if something inside him had been triggered and there was no backing down. 'You're too soft, are you? How can you run this family if you can't even block a punch?'

Dom and Felice were exchanging loaded glances.

'What is this?' asked Luca. 'What's gotten into you?'

For the briefest second, Nic's gaze flicked to me. 'You know what it's about.'

Luca was shaking his head. 'Brother, you have gone mad.'

'Or maybe you've gone soft.'

'Ooooh,' said Dom, riling them both up. 'That's fighting talk. Are you going to let him disrespect you like that, Luca?'

'Do you ever shut up?' I snapped at Dom. 'Seriously. Grow up!'

Dom's lips smacked together in a disgusting air kiss. 'This is

253

your fault, *bella puttana*.'

I flipped him the middle finger. '*Vaffanculo!*'

Felice laughed. 'The *Americano* knows Italian!'

The atmosphere didn't seem so playful any more, thoughts of earlier bets dissolving in the heat of Nic's aggression. He prodded Luca in the chest. 'You're too weak,' he said. 'You're cooped up here with Valentino like some glorified bodyguard. You've lost your edge. You've been on the sidelines too long.'

Luca stepped back. 'Careful,' he warned. 'You don't want to go down this road.'

'I get it,' said Nic, pushing into his brother's personal space. 'You don't want me to embarrass you.'

He kept going. Dom was chanting at them now and Felice was laughing, his attention glued on the brothers.

Luca snapped.

'Enough!' he shouted, and the searing rage surprised us all. He was feral, heaving, dangerous. I pressed my back against the wall, wishing I could rewind time and not have come inside, setting into motion whatever this was. 'If you say one more word, Nicoli, I'll knock you out. *Non mettermi alla prova!*'

Even Dom was starting to look nervous. Felice had stopped smiling. An air of hostility descended and I felt the dark cloud of something else looming towards us. This was Luca unhinged. This was pure, palpable anger. It turned him into something else. *Don't say a word, Nic. Just keep your mouth shut.*

Nic was all energy. He was putting on a show. His face broke into a grin, thirty-two bright white teeth glaring at Luca. 'You're all talk, Luca. You couldn't knock Ignacio over.'

Luca lunged at him and their bodies connected with a thud. Luca took the first punch in the side of his head; it knocked him sideways and my stomach lurched. I shouted at them to stop but they were engrossed in one another, trading hits like they were punching bags.

Luca was much quicker than Nic, his movements turning to streaks of black as he whipped around him. It seemed easy for him, like being set to fast-forward was second nature. His retaliation came in six lightning jabs to Nic's stomach and one to his chin. They almost knocked him clean out but he struggled upright, swaying on his feet.

They broke apart and I got the sense Luca was giving him time to recuperate, dancing wide circles around his brother. Nic roundhouse-kicked Luca, catching him heavy in the shoulder and forcing him off-kilter. Luca rallied, darting around Nic and grabbing him by the neck. Panting, he forced him to the ground, his black hair falling in strands across his eyes. Nic kicked against Luca's side with his feet and he crumbled backwards, cursing. His gunshot wound. What a low blow! I had the sudden urge to slap Nic on the side of his head, and felt a twinge of surprise at the strength of my anger. They were being as immature as each other. It was a fair fight.

Dom and I were both shouting now. Luca tackled Nic at the knees and they went flying backwards, crashing against the wall. Nic slipped towards the ground and Luca seized his unsure footing, looping his arm around his neck and clamping him in a headlock.

They fell to the floor together. Luca flipped Nic over, pressing his knee against his brother's back and pulling his arm towards the ceiling behind him. Nic was wedged between Luca and the floor, his whole body twisted on itself. He was panting, his face turning red from the pain. Luca would snap the bone if he wasn't careful.

'*Basta*,' he growled in Nic's ear. 'OK? Enough.'

Nic gurgled something. Luca had won, but he didn't seem any happier about it than we were. He released his brother and Nic flopped across the floor, holding his arm gingerly.

Nic shot to his feet and tried to wrangle Luca's neck. He mistimed and Luca swivelled, his face contorted with fury. He threw himself at Nic, knocking him to the ground again and landing on top of him, planting a leg on either side of his torso so Nic couldn't get back up. They were screaming at each other in Italian and now Dom was getting involved too. He tried to pull Luca away, but he didn't have the strength, and my attempts weren't helping either. Felice remained as he had been all along – spectating.

Nic spat across the floor. Luca whipped out his switchblade, flicked it open and drove it into the wood beside Nic's head. He pulled back, heaving, and I could see the shock coursing through Nic, the speechlessness slapped across his face. The knife glinted less than three inches from his head.

'Enough.' Luca's teeth were bared. 'You've had your show.'

He got to his feet, this time being careful not to turn his back on Nic again. The fighter in him disappeared almost immediately and he returned to his previous sense of calm, fixing his T-shirt and rolling his neck around until it cracked. He was beat – his shoulders sagging and his torso dipping more to one side. I could tell his wound was hurting but he would never admit it.

Nic got up. His cheeks were flaming red and he was panting hard. He didn't look at me. He didn't look at anyone. Without saying a word, he ducked, like a football player about to tackle, and charged full-force at Luca. He knocked him backwards and together their momentum surged, carrying them towards the window. We were all yelling then, but Nic was frenzied with anger, an animal buzzing for the kill. He kept running at Luca until, with his own twisted war cry and the mingling of our screams, he released him and Luca went crashing through the window. The glass shattered into a million pieces that rained over him as he slid backwards over the ledge.

I shrieked as we rushed towards him. Nic just stood there, peering out of the window at his brother, who was lying in a bed of glass shards stained with his own blood.

'*Sei fuori di testa*,' said Dom, turning on Nic. 'What the hell were you thinking?'

Luca's eyes unglazed as he sat up, taking in the trickles of blood along his bare arms. His face was cut up too, crimson dripping down his cheek and on to his neck. He pressed a hand against the wound in his side. I hoped it hadn't reopened from all the fighting.

Felice came to stand between us, his hand clasped over his mouth as he watched Luca sway unsteadily to his feet. He shook his head, tutting loudly. 'My window,' he sighed. 'That was Venetian glass.'

CHAPTER TWENTY-EIGHT
THE LOOK

Luca climbed back through the window. I balked at his casual return, studying all the thin lines of blood that were streaking his body. He didn't look at Nic again and Nic didn't apologize to him. He was too busy arguing with Dom.

Luca shrugged off my concern and pushed by us.

'Hey!' I called after him.

'I'll go get cleaned up.'

'You're hurt,' I said to the back of his retreating head. 'You need to go to the hospital.'

He swatted his hand in the air as he disappeared into the hall. 'I'm fine.'

Like hell he was.

I left the room and followed him up the marble staircase,

trying to decipher the feelings that were lurching inside me. There was worry – sure, his face was bleeding and his arms were cut up. There was anger, too, at Nic, because he had been a royal asshole for targeting Luca's wound and then for throwing him through that window. But there were other things that I couldn't place and they swirled inside me, filling me with anxiety. I wondered at the eagerness of my steps on the floor, desperate not to lose Luca as he climbed higher and higher with no regard for my shadow.

I kept staring at him, at the way he clutched his side, at the weariness in his slow steps. He had started to pick the glass out of his arms, breaking apart his skin and removing the shards without so much as a flinch. He was many things to his brothers – a constant, protective presence, wise and focused, and loyal. He was so important to the family and yet, wounded, he retracted into himself.

It wasn't right.

He had opted to leave Nic without verbal or physical retaliation, both of which I knew he was capable of. The thought made me want to scream at someone. Why was no one coming to see if he was OK? Why did he feel it was perfectly acceptable to walk this off and to endure it by himself when any sane person would go to the emergency room to get the glass out of their skin?

He disappeared into a room on the third floor. I lingered beside the stairs, wondering what to do. He wouldn't want me to follow him in there. But this wasn't about letting him save face, this was about making sure he didn't need stitches, that all the bleeding had stopped and that he was going to recover just fine. This was about showing him the care he

deserved and not leaving him to suffer it in some unnecessary stoic silence.

I knocked on his door.

He opened it hesitantly. He was using a cloth to dab at the
blood on his face. He paused with it pressed against his jaw
as his eyes widened. 'Sophie?'

I didn't wait for him to stand back and allow my entry.
I barged inside and, without stopping to notice the size of
his room or the bed or the colours on the walls or the
closet space or anything else that might have mattered to
me at another time, I turned to face him, running my
words together before he could kick me out. 'I know you said
you're fine and I'm sure you are but I'm not just going to
wait downstairs when I've just seen you go through a
freaking window. It's not right that you should be up here
alone and I don't care if you tell me to leave but I had to
see for myself that you really were OK and that you didn't feel
. . . you didn't feel . . . what? Why are you looking at me like
that?'

'Like what?'

His gaze was so penetrating it was like he was trying to pick
apart the threads of my soul. I realized then why the blue in
his eyes seemed so striking, why they stood out in a room of
twenty Falcones and why they seemed bluer than any other
pair of eyes I'd ever seen. There was a thin ring of black
around the irises, a dark perimeter caging in all that bright
cerulean so it wouldn't spill over. 'You're just . . . you're
staring at me,' I said in a voice much quieter than I meant it to
be.

A muscle feathered in his jaw. He swallowed. 'I'll stare at

you if I want to.'

Why did I feel so hot all of a sudden? It was like my lungs weren't filling up properly any more. 'Did you get all the glass out?' I asked, changing the subject.

Luca dropped the cloth so I could see the scrape just below his cheek. It wasn't deep but it was still bleeding a little. 'I don't know,' he said softly. 'I can't see.'

I rose to my tiptoes, and without really thinking or meaning to, I moved closer to him, teetering unsteadily as I tried to examine the wound. His aftershave rolled over me and I inhaled the scent.

'Well?' he asked, his voice suddenly husky. 'Will I live?'

'I'm not sure. Let me take a closer look.' I bit back my smile and craned my neck but swayed on my toes, falling into him. I pressed my palms against his chest to steady myself and his hands shot up, covering mine. I could feel the unsteady thump of his heartbeat beneath my fingertips.

I stared at our hands – my paleness beneath his smooth olive tan – his fingers dwarfing mine. My whole body faltered. I could sense him watching me, waiting for me to look into his eyes.

I couldn't step away from him. In fact, the closeness of him wasn't nearly enough. Slowly I raised my gaze. Luca's smile tugged softly at his lips.

'Maybe I am looking at you,' he whispered. 'Maybe I always have been.'

And then he kissed me.

It was slow and gentle at first, our breathing unsteady, as he combed his fingers through my hair, pulling me closer. My lips parted, and I felt his tongue brush against mine, searching, wanting more. Desire made us braver, fiercer, and I fell into him as our kiss deepened. In that moment, with the warmth of his lips on mine and his heartbeat hammering against my fingertips, it felt like coming home.

CHAPTER TWENTY-NINE

THE INTERRUPTION

A knock on the door shocked us apart. We jumped away from each other, eyes wide, and panting.

What the hell were we doing?

This was weird. This was so weird.

But it hadn't *felt* weird.

Nic charged into the room. 'Luca, what the hell is taking you—' He almost toppled me over. 'Sophie . . . there you are . . . What are you doing in here?' he asked, surprise warping his voice.

'Me?' I said, hearing the high-pitched squeal in my words. *Oh, just betraying you.* 'I was checking the damage *you* did.' I cleared my throat, wondering if my cheeks were still red, if my lips were swollen. 'He's OK, no thanks to you.'

'It's fine,' said Luca. He was scrubbing a hand through his

hair, trying to tame the unkempt strands. It was hard not to blanch at how *un*composed he sounded now, how flighty his breathing still was. 'She took the glass out.'

'Right,' said Nic, eyes narrowed. 'Sorry about that.'

There was a very long, very deep silence, during which time I imagined Nic barging in five seconds earlier and decapitating Luca. What was I doing? What was I feeling? Everything. My whole body was pulsing with every possible emotion all at once, and it was making me forget myself, and the danger my family and I were still in.

Stupid. I was being stupid.

'Don't worry about it,' said Luca. He flicked his gaze to me. It was unreadable.

It had been less than a minute since we were gasping between deep, lingering kisses, and now it felt like he barely knew who I was. Did he regret it? Did I? Was he freaking out too?

'Let's go,' said Nic, standing between Luca and me, so that his brother left the room ahead of us. 'Everyone's waiting downstairs.' He looked at me when he said, 'You're going to be fine. We won't make you and your mother face the Marinos alone. You don't have to look so worried.'

'Worried' was a colossal understatement.

I had just kissed Nic's *brother*.

I was going to hell.

I pressed a trembling hand to my heart. I was swirling in a pit of my own foolishness and trying to keep my mind from replaying the kiss that had swept me out of my world and made me forget my name.

Holy crap.

I had kissed Luca Falcone.

Luca Falcone had kissed *me*.

What . . . ?

We were on the second floor. When had we come down the stairs? Luca was still in front of us, his shoulders sloping away from me as he walked down another flight. 'Where's Valentino?' he asked over his shoulder.

'In his office,' said Nic, with a shrug. 'Something urgent came up.'

Luca nodded without turning around, his feet falling quick and light on the steps as he hurried away from us. When we got to the bottom of the stairs, the foyer was swarming with mafiosi. I stalled with my hand clutched tightly to the banister. Old men with gnarled faces and engraved walking sticks milled beside younger counterparts with severe eyebrows and pursed lips. The level of attractiveness was definitely unnatural. There was an abundance of enviable olive skin and luscious dark hair.

And all this for little old me.

Before my life got sucky and dangerous, I barely answered my mother's calls and I rarely checked my voicemails. The Falcones, on the other hand, seemed to be entirely reachable. They had come at once. Now they stood shaking hands and greeting one another in the foyer as the sound of their laughter echoed around them. It was hard to listen to what was being said – what greetings and stories were being exchanged – because most of the Falcones, especially the older ones, spoke in Italian. No one noticed me as I stood at the foot of the stairs. This was power and family rolled into one, and the strength of their bond seemed to fill the mansion up, reminding me of just how alone and vulnerable my mother and I truly were.

Councils, Nic had told me, were a common occurrence, but Sanctuary was not. In the history of the Falcone dynasty he had heard of only one appeal for Sanctuary – a wealthy bootlegger back in Sicily who was in trouble with a rival mob and came seeking refuge for his young family from Luca's great-grandfather. But I was a Gracewell, with no wealth to offer. I wasn't even Sicilian. And the cherry on top of the murdery cake was my ever-present status as niece of the man who had likely stabbed Calvino Falcone and daughter of the man who had shot Angelo.

Luca got lost in the crowds, shaking hands and kissing cheeks, widening that ever-growing space between us and leaving me wondering whether I had imagined our entire moment upstairs. Gino and Dom passed me by. Dom winked and I flipped him the middle finger.

Felice appeared and started to usher everyone down a hallway. Luca was leading the pack, making niceties with an old man with white candyfloss hair, his arm offered to a stooped lady with leathery dark skin.

Nic stuck by me and that only made it worse. I sent a quick update minus-the-kiss to Millie while guilt twisted like a knife in my gut. Still, there was so much distrust between Nic and me already that part of me rebelled at the idea that I should feel bad at all.

I was shuffling after him, following the procession of Pantene hair and expensive suits, when someone called my name.

I turned on my heel.

Valentino was in the middle of the foyer.

Nic lingered beside me until Valentino waved him away, and then he disappeared, dutifully, like the good soldier he was.

Valentino's gaze was hooded, his lips drawn tight; his mood wasn't good. Felice had obviously delivered news of the Marino plot to take his family out.

He was dressed well, in a dark suit and tie. He wore a thick gold ring on his right hand. I noticed it when he used his finger to beckon me towards him. I went, because he was the boss, and we both knew I needed something from him.

'Hello,' I offered, realizing he wasn't going to break the silence first. I stood far enough away so we could look at each other straight on.

'Hello?' he repeated, his mouth twisting to a frown. 'Is that all you have to say?'

OK. He was mad.

'Look, I didn't realize my coming to you for help would cause all of this.' I gestured behind me. 'That really wasn't my intention. I just had to try something. After what Donata—'

'Sophie,' Valentino cut in. 'Did you really think I wouldn't find out?'

I brought my hand to my mouth and covered it. Were my lips still red and swollen? Had he seen somehow? Were there cameras in this place? 'W-what?' I stammered.

'And you have the gall to sit in that room with the entire Falcone family and expect Nic to vote for your Sanctuary.'

'I—I, no, I haven't. Nic wants me to be safe, just like I want him to—'

'You know, I suspected something,' he said, cutting me off

267

again. His voice was acidic. 'But until just now, I didn't know what it was.'

'Look, I'm here for one reason only. I've given your family information, and I'd really like if we could keep the topic to that, and that alone.' My chest was full of butterflies frantically beating against my ribcage.

Valentino rose from his chair, stretching his back and cracking his neck. It clicked, the sound echoing in the silence. 'I won't keep this secret for you. Not in a thousand years.'

Well, fine. He could tell Nic. I needed the damn Sanctuary, and that's what mattered. 'OK,' I said. 'I get it. You're mad. The others will probably be mad too. But I've come here for my mother and me, and that's what I'm focused on right now.'

'*Sei pazzo.*' He was looking at me like I had sprouted horns. He pointed behind me to where the others were waiting. 'If you walk into that room, I can't be responsible for what they'll do to you.'

OK, harsh much? Nic might be pissed when he found out, but I doubted a ton of the other Falcones would revolt. Did they really care that much about each other's outside relationships? Or had I misread how deeply their codes ran? My mind flicked back to my mother, to how Donata had bent her over that sink with a gun to her throat.

'I'll take my chances.'

'Felice might shoot you point-blank in the head.' His response was so dramatic, I thought it was a joke but there wasn't an ounce of amusement in his voice – it was musical and lilting, yet his words were ice cold. He was expressionless, studying my reaction as he added, 'I won't stop him.'

'Felice?' Alarm quickened my pulse. I was starting to get

the feeling we were on different planes. 'Why the hell would Felice care?'

'Don't be so ignorant, Sophie. You've insulted my intelligence enough already.' Valentino's sneer did ugly things to his face. Luca's face. He was ruining Luca's face. 'Felice will care the most.'

I knew I could never predict the temperature of Felice's reactions – or his actions, for that matter but something definitely wasn't adding up. The hostility in Valentino's gaze was too strong, his words too severe. 'Wait . . .' I said, edging closer, watching him as he was watching me. 'What are you talking about?'

He didn't miss a beat. He didn't even blink. 'You know what I'm talking about, Sophie.'

Did I? Unease grumbled inside me. I steeled myself, determined, afraid, ready to get this over with. It was just one kiss. One stupid mistake. If he had something else to say then he could say it, but I wouldn't play this game with him, not while my mother was at home waiting for me. 'Just let me plead my case.'

'You will have to, now that I have you.' Valentino's eyes narrowed as he came towards me, the wheels of his chair gliding soundlessly over the Falcone crest beneath us. 'You've sealed your death sentence by coming here.'

'Maybe,' I said, turning to follow him and trying not to show my fear at his words. 'Maybe it was sealed either way.'

Without turning around, he said, 'There's blood on your face.'

In the darkness of the long corridor, I furiously scrubbed my cheek with my fingers, removing the smudge of Luca's blood that had imprinted on my skin during our kiss.

At the very end of the hallway Valentino tapped once on the door. He dropped his voice, and in barely more than a whisper, he said, 'For these last minutes, you have your secret and your life. Enjoy them while they last.'

Goosebumps rippled along my arms as I shuffled into the room after him, and I wondered again, with rising panic, whether Valentino was really talking about the kiss at all.

CHAPTER THIRTY

THE SECRET

The meeting was held in a room at the very back of the house. A huge table made from varnished dark wood stretched the entire length of the room. The oil painting from the Priestly house in Cedar Hill – Valentino's rendering of the avenging angel – hung in the middle of the room, and framed pictures of other Falcones, all dead, ranged along a shelf underneath. Calvino's picture was nestled between Angelo's and that of an old man with no hair – Rico Falcone, I guessed, since he was the most recent Falcone casualty.

Valentino stopped at the head of the table, and one by one, like a domino effect, every single Falcone – women and men, elderly and teenaged – formed a procession leading towards him. He held his hand out, his lids falling lazily as they each bent low and kissed his ring, murmuring Italian greetings as they turned to take their seats again. I pressed my back against the wall.

The Council was called to order. Felice sat on Valentino's left, Luca on his right. He hadn't looked in my direction once. He was facing forwards, the muscles in his jaw grinding. Nic winked at me before turning his attention to his oldest brother. I wished I could have shared his confidence.

Valentino cleared his throat. 'Welcome, everyone, to what promises to be a memorable meeting.' He flicked his gaze to me. I looked into those azure eyes and saw my own hope-lessness reflected back. 'Today, we remember those who have given their blood to protect this family.' He placed a hand on his chest and dipped his head. 'We think of Calvino and Rico. *Ora riposano in pace.*'

Quiet murmurings echoed along the table as the other Falcones pressed their hands to their hearts as Valentino had. '*Ora riposano in pace.*'

Valentino snapped his head up and the tender moment was gone. He looked straight at me when he said, 'We are here today to discuss a serious matter, which concerns Donata Marino and the Marino family.'

There was a hiss from somewhere at the far end of the table. Elena pulled her lips back, her teeth bared, at the mention of her sister. Valentino pointed towards me. 'For those who are not aware, I present to you Sophie Gracewell, daughter of Michael Gracewell.'

Luca looked at me for the first time. His expression was shuttered.

'She has come to us today seeking the order of Sanctuary, for the protection of her mother and herself,' Valentino added with a sneer.

A man with a heavy white beard seated part way down the table, said, 'Such ceremony for small matters, Valentino. Of course we offer Sanctuary – it's nothing for us.'

'So it would appear,' muttered Felice.

Outside, the storm clouds were sinking lower and lower. The room was charged, and the hairs on my arm were standing up. The urgency of the situation licked at my consciousness.

'It's ludicrous,' Elena cried. Her hands rose into the air, gesticulating above the heads around her. 'These people are the family of the man who killed your father, Valentino. They certainly do not deserve Sanctuary.'

A man with puffed-up white hair and a face creviced with wrinkles clapped his palm on the table. 'We do not punish innocents,' he said in a voice croaky with age. 'Elena, you are letting your personal feelings override your duty to protect. That is the Falcone cause.'

Her voice turned hard. 'That has not been our cause for a long time, Tommaso.'

I was watching Valentino. He and Felice had their heads bent together. His lips moved hurriedly, and every so often Felice's eyes would grow very large. He glared at me, and I felt like there was a sniper rifle trained on my forehead. Luca sat apart from their huddle, his mouth set in a hard line as his twin angled his body towards Felice, continuing their hushed conversation.

Dom was speaking at the other end of the table. 'I say we send her back to Donata. We've got all the information we need. What Sophie does now shouldn't concern us.'

'Exactly,' said Elena in an exasperated voice. 'At least one of my children sees sense.'

I couldn't place the look on Felice's face, but it was utterly mirthless. He was staring so hard at me I felt the heat underneath my skin. I lifted my chin, determined not to break under his attempts to intimidate me.

Someone slammed their fist on the table and I was startled back into the conversation. Gino's glass of water had toppled over and spilt on to his lap. Luca was standing up, his palms pressed against the table. 'I owe Sophie Gracewell my life. Is that really *nothing*, Mother? *Con tutto il rispetto, si sbaglia.*'

'That doesn't excuse her blood ties!' shouted someone else, his voice joining with the heat of others. 'We just buried Calvino. Are we all so quick to forget how and where he died? Are we all so quick to forget his death at the hands of Jack Gracewell?'

'The girl is just a teenager. *Una innocente,*' Paulie said, and my heart swelled with gratitude. 'We must believe she is here to assist us. She brought news of Donata's plotting.'

'Unreliable news,' said a young man with a shaved head and a severe nose. He fiddled with the gold chain around his neck. 'Who knows if it was made up just to get us on side?'

'Donata has Sophie in her sights,' said Luca. 'We don't know what she plans to use her for. We don't know if she plans to kill her.'

Well, he mightn't have been able to stomach looking at me properly after what had happened upstairs, but at least he was fighting for me. I exhaled a quiet sigh of relief. The word of the Falcone underboss would carry a lot of weight in this room.

'Donata won't have time to use anyone for anything,' said Gino. 'Because we're going to kill that Marino bitch and mount her head above the fireplace.'

'*Dio*,' muttered an old woman right across from me. 'Is this what we have become?'

'Gino,' cautioned Elena. 'Watch your language.'

He snapped his head down, folding his arms in a childish huff. 'You weren't complaining when Nic dumped Sara into the lake with all that *cazzate* on her skin.'

I felt a sudden whack of nausea. It was *Nic*. Nic threw Sara Marino in the lake. *He* had carved those words on to her body. I covered my mouth and concentrated on not getting sick. I had come here willingly. I had known discovering more horrible truths was a possibility. It was *their* world. But this . . . I had never expected *this.*

I stared at Nic. He was shouting at his brother, his eyes flashing with rage, his chest heaving violently. No one around the table seemed remotely surprised. God. Who was this boy? This was so much bigger than me and him now. This wasn't about his heart – this was about his soul. Maybe the nagging voice in my head was right, maybe he was beyond saving. Maybe they all were. I felt a sudden, crushing sadness inside me. It took every ounce of strength to stay on my feet, to keep my mouth shut.

'Settle,' said Valentino, gesturing at Nic, who was still yelling at Gino in Italian. 'Nic was following a direct order. Gino, you're steering this off course.'

Of course, Valentino had ordered the carving and the water burial. And still he presided like an angel over the gathering: clean, clear, beautiful . . . deadly. He really was the worst of them all. A puppetmaster: all head, no heart.

Luca's voice soared above the rising commotion. 'We have the upper hand thanks to Sophie. I think it best to remove her and her mother from Cedar Hill.'

'We'll hide them,' interjected Nic. 'And give her father protection from Franco Marino in prison.'

'Her *father*?' screeched Elena. 'Have you gone *mad*, Nicoli? What *nonsense*.'

'It's Jack we want,' said Paulie.

Elena's chair screeched backwards. She stood now too, leaning across the table. 'Who are we to trust a Gracewell after everything they've done? Who are we to trust the words my own sister has said to her? Donata has never spoken plainly in her life. Everything is a trick with her.'

'Sophie is not Donata,' said Paulie, calmly.

'She speaks for her.' Elena curled her lip. 'Do you forget your brothers so easily, Paulie?'

Paulie clapped his palms off the table but his voice remained deceptively careful. 'Do not use my brothers against me, Elena. I know very well what we have lost.'

An old man with liver-spotted skin and a large bulbous nose was clinking the side of his glass with the end of a switchblade. '*Silenzio!*' he called out in a heavy, rolling accent. '*Calmatevi, tutti voi.*'

Valentino raised his hands and quiet descended. Elena and Luca sat down.

'Ignacio,' Valentino said. 'You have the floor.'

The old man dipped his head in gratitude. He pulled back and looked at each of the members as he spoke. 'When my brother Gianluca was alive, he would not allow Councils to descend into such chaos. We have a clear-cut decision to make. The fate of this girl's safety, whoever she may be, has been entrusted to this family. What is the point of squabbling like *bambini*? Let someone speak for her virtues and then let us decide like adults. I will not sit here and be subjected to such childish disorder.'

'Wise words,' said Tommaso. 'Sophie Gracewell seeks to align herself with this family and gain Sanctuary. Who will speak for her?'

Valentino shifted in his chair, pulling out an envelope and handing it to Felice. Without taking out the paper inside it, Felice peeked in. He glanced back at Valentino, his expression grim.

Nic stood up. He held a steady stance, his hands folded in front of him so that he loomed over the rest of the Falcones like a soldier standing guard. 'I'll speak for her, since I know her the best.'

'And 'cause you're doing her!' shouted Dom, his words peeling into raucous laughter. Gino shook with childish titters and I felt my face grow hot.

'*Vaffanculo!*' hissed Luca. 'Have some respect!'

'Let the truth reign,' Dom returned with a sneer. 'He wants to make her his *comare*!'

I didn't know what a *comare* was, but I could tell by the blazing anger in Nic's expression that it was meant to be offensive. I felt the overwhelming urge to launch across the table and punch Dom's stupid face in.

'*Smettila!*' said Nic. 'Or I'll come over there and stuff my fist down your throat.'

'Speak!' said Ignacio. He pursed his lips and the resulting frown was so severe I felt a trickle of fear creep down my spine.

Valentino gestured towards Nic, rolling his hand in a circle. 'Go on,' he said dispassionately. He was staring at me again. I could almost see the cogs turning in his head. I looked at my hands. If he was going to say it, he should just *say it*, and stop lording it over me like this.

Luca's mouth was set in a hard line, his penetrating gaze fixed towards the side of Nic's face as he spoke.

'We know of Donata's movements, but Jack Gracewell is still hard to pin down. He might not come back to Cedar Hill at all now he has the Marinos to do his bidding. If it comes to tracking him down, Sophie is the best tool we have. We'd be fools to set her loose while she has so much to offer.'

'And, don't forget, you're doing her!' Dom catcalled. This time Luca leapt out of his seat and lunged towards him, grabbing his shirt collar and tightening it around his neck.

'Luca,' cautioned Valentino, a frown drawing his eyebrows together. 'What are you doing?'

Dom's face was turning purple. '*Calmati*,' he wheezed. 'What's it got to do with you anyway?'

'Act your age, *idiota di merda*.' Luca pushed him away and fell back into his chair with a sharp curse.

'Nic, are you done?' asked Valentino.

Nic was looking unsure of himself. That made two of us. Did he mean all that stuff about using me and exploiting my allegiance? Or was he saying what he knew they wanted to hear? He was so nebulous, his family's mission twined so tightly in his core that it was difficult to separate the two.

'Yeah,' he said, rubbing the back of his neck as he sat down.

'What else is there?'

'Can we just vote already?' CJ was the youngest in the room and he appeared to be monumentally bored. I guessed his murder of Sara Marino had earned him his place at the table.

'Wait.' Luca stood up and walked alongside the table, stopping behind Paulie and pinning his attention on his mother. 'Nic shouldn't have to plead Sophie's case by presenting her as a weapon at our disposal. Sophie seeks what is good and just in this world, just like we do. Her loyalties are decided not by blood but by right and wrong. She has never betrayed this family, and when times have questioned her allegiance she has stood beside the Falcones. She risked her life to save mine. Now we can repay her. This isn't a matter of her use but of our collective conscience, and whether we are going to do the right thing.'

The room had fallen silent. Valentino's eyes were closed, his frown deepening bit by bit. The words were not sitting well with him; I could feel it. I could feel it coming towards me, like a tidal wave. Beside him, Felice's gaze was hooded with caution.

'Eloquently put, Luca,' said Paulie. 'You truly are your father's son.'

Elena tapped her nails along the table and heads turned in her direction. 'Eloquent or not, my son,' she said. 'There is still the question of whether she will betray us.' Her exhale sounded disconcertingly like a warning whistle, and it snapped something inside me.

I had had enough of my name being bashed. Plus, I had stayed silent for what must have been a world record for me. I stepped forward, clearing my throat and intending to clear my name too, before she stomped over it any more. 'I'm not a snitch. I know the importance of *omertà*. I've never spoken to a cop about anything to do with you or my uncle. I came today with information hoping you might give my mother and me something in return. I've never tried to betray any of you, despite your actions – which have, in the past, been pretty shady.'

'Shady?' grumbled the young man with the shaved head.

'Case in point: my kidnapping and attempted murder.'

That shut him up.

I stamped down the quiver in my throat. 'I love my mother more than anything. Donata Marino is threatening to split us apart if I don't do what she wants. Jack has installed himself in the Marino family. His vendetta against this family is stronger than ever. They are coming for me and they are coming for you. I've come here for your protection because I can't protect myself. But that doesn't make me weak; it makes me smart.'

'So you propose we offer you our protection for *nothing*?' snapped Elena. 'You will deplete our attention and our reserves because you've involved yourself in something that was none of your business in the first place?'

'*We* are the reason she's *involved* in this,' interrupted Luca.

'No.' The word was so small it almost got lost in the rising argument. But I had been expecting it. I had been waiting – like a lot of other people, apparently – for Felice to finally open his mouth.

Luca rounded on him. 'What do you mean, "no"?'

Felice stood up, his sudden height commanding all of the attention in the room. He fixed his tie with one hand, his

280

other clutching the envelope Valentino had handed him. 'I mean we are not the reason she has been sucked into this world.' His voice was utterly emotionless, his words quietly sure as he flicked his attention to me and said, 'Sophie has been part of this world since birth.'

One by one, every head turned in my direction.

There was a cavernous silence.

Nic broke it. 'What?'

Echoes of '*What?*' followed.

'What?' I added, just for good measure.

Valentino was sitting back in his chair, fingers steepled in front of his mouth. 'I gave you ten minutes, Sophie. I gave you the opportunity to come clean on your own, but you wasted it. So, you can say it now,' he offered with blithe indifference. 'Or you can let Felice tell them.'

I was suddenly keenly aware that Valentino was not talking about The Kiss, and that whatever was in that envelope was not evidence of what had happened with Luca.

'Valentino . . .' I began, trying not to focus on thirty pairs of eyes burning through my skin. 'I really have no idea what you're talking about. I think there's been some confusion . . .'

'Oh, there has been confusion, Persephone,' said Felice. 'Why don't we alleviate it right now? Tell us, *bugiarda*, at what point in your pathetic relationship with my nephew were you planning on telling him that you are, in fact, *a Marino*?'

The accusation landed like a slap in the face. I jerked backwards, halfway between a laugh and a splutter, as incredulity washed over me. My mouth fell open, as I grasped for a response. It was a struggle to find the right words to aptly communicate just how insane Felice was being. This was character assassination at its worst. 'Stop,' was all I could manage. 'Just stop.'

The silence sizzled as Felice leant across the table towards me. 'I *thought* I knew those eyes from somewhere.' He pointed directly at me and I noticed, dimly, that everyone else leant closer too. 'Those are Vincenzo Marino's eyes. Those are the same eyes I looked into when I pulled the trigger and shattered his skull.'

There was a collective intake of breath.

I almost smiled. His plan was so stupid, so *outlandish*, it would never work. He could never discredit me like that. I rolled my eyes – my *incriminating* eyes – so they could all get a good look at how dumb their *consigliere* was.

'What is this, Felice?' Elena asked. 'What are you saying?'

'You've said it yourself countless times, Elena. There is something *off* about this girl. You saw it that night in the hospital.'

Elena rose a little in her seat, latching on to Felice's ridiculous diatribe. 'Yes . . . but this . . .'

Felice glared at me. 'I will ask you only once. Are you, or are you not, the granddaughter of Don Vincenzo Marino?'

'You know I'm not,' I gritted out. 'Cut the crap. You know who my father is.'

'I know *now*,' he boomed, the sudden loudness shocking me a little. 'Though it's taken me far longer than I would have liked, I've finally found the missing Marinos.'

I lunged towards him, stretching across the table as my lungs burnt with all the names I wanted to call him. 'You're sick,' I hissed. 'To make up lies like this after I brought you real information that would help your family. It's low, even for you.'

Murmurings began – sceptical, hesitant, as heads whipped back and forth between Felice and me.

'At first it didn't make sense,' Felice continued, turning to his family now and leaving me discarded in his periphery. I straightened up, composing myself. I would not go crazy. I would not stoop to his level. 'Why would Donata Marino welcome Jack Gracewell into her fold? We have long known how private the Marino family is. Their allegiance makes no sense. Her interest in this girl makes *no sense*. And yet her final words to her were *Fidelitate Coniuncti*! Incredible!'

'Felice,' Luca growled. 'You're going too far.'

Felice's eyes were flashing, desperate, searching. He turned to Valentino. 'Tell them,' he implored. 'Make them see.'

Valentino knitted his hands together on the table, his ring flashing beneath the lights. 'Before our father was killed, he had been looking into Michael Gracewell's past. I've found files that show his growing interest in the Gracewell family, but almost half of them are not directed at Jack and the Golden Triangle Gang. He seems to have been piecing together a puzzle, and Jack was only part of that.' He ran his tongue along his teeth, pausing, deliberating in his head. Everyone – including me, despite the absurdity of it all – was hanging on the next word from their boss. 'There's no record of the Gracewells as children. Michael Gracewell first appears as a junior in a high school in Milwaukee at sixteen years old. A transfer student from Chicago with no background. Until now I didn't know what any of this meant, or what my father was pursuing at the time of his death. Most of us had forgotten the legend of the missing Marinos.'

'Not all of us,' said Felice, his voice deathly quiet.

Valentino ignored the interruption. 'I never thought to make the connection between my father's research on the Gracewells and the Marinos until Jack Gracewell turned to Donata Marino, of all people, for protection from us. Until Donata Marino opened her doors to a simple *Americano* with a languishing drug trade. Then I started to wonder.'

'This is ridiculous!' I said, looking around at matching expressions of incredulity. 'I know exactly where I come from. Jack and my dad had to move to Milwaukee when they were young to live with their grandmother. Their parents died in a car accident when he was—'

'Sixteen,' said Felice, getting to his feet. 'I know. I was there.' He made the sign of a gun with his finger and thumb and pointed it at my head. 'But it was no car accident, believe me.'

I shook my head. This guy was utterly deluded. There was no way he was taking me down like this. Not when I needed Sanctuary. Not when I had my mother to think about.

'You know, Vincenzo's boys weren't there that day,' he said to me. 'The two of them were gone before I could finish the job.' He clicked his fingers. 'They had vanished in a puff of air.'

'Jack and my father aren't twins,' I countered.

Felice shrugged. 'Neither were the Marinos. Twins make it a better story. It seeks to justify the Marinos' hit on my own father on the day Luca and Valentino were born.'

'You're clutching at straws,' I said. 'You know you are. Everyone can see it.' I was starting to sound less sure of myself, but only because he was so convincing. That didn't make him right. He was a lunatic.

'You're either a good liar or a dumb fool,' said Felice, coming closer. I watched his hands, anticipating the appearance of a real gun, but he kept them where I could see him, raising them as he asked, 'Do you know why your father murdered my brother? Because I think I finally understand now.'

'It was an accident.' I blinked back the tears pooling in my eyes.

Felice was losing his composure. His voice was shaking. 'Don't you think it *strange*?'

'He came for Jack that night,' I said, repeating what Felice had told me all those weeks ago. 'You said it yourself.'

Felice turned to the others. 'Who here believes Michael Gracewell's hit on Angelo was an "accident"?' he said, making air quotes.

There was a stony silence. Nic deflected his gaze. Luca wouldn't look at me either.

Felice turned back to me. 'Haven't you ever asked yourself what your father was truly capable of?'

I declined to answer, offering him my most contemptuous glare instead.

'I made my own assumptions, but I didn't know. The truth is, my brother never told me where he was going that night. I knew he was up to something so I had to follow him, like a *scarafaggio*!' He was starting to perspire. The lie was breaking through. 'Your father killed Angelo because he knew who he really was! Angelo was going to break apart your perfect little life.'

Thirty heads rolled back towards me. There was a general

sense of wonderment – dark Italian eyes widening in surprise, mouths going slack. A flurry of whispers scuttled along the table. They were falling for it. They would vote against me.

'You're lying!' I shouted. 'Stop it!'

Luca shot to his feet so he could stand between Felice and me. 'Drop this now, Felice,' he warned. 'It's not right what you're doing.'

'Luca.' Valentino's quiet interruption killed the commotion. It was remarkable; whenever he spoke, the whole room dangled on his word. Luca backed away from Felice and stood, instead, by his twin's shoulders.

To Felice, Valentino said, 'Show them the photo.'

Felice didn't take his eyes off me. 'With pleasure.'

He pulled a page from the envelope he was holding, and slid it across the table. I stepped forward tentatively, staring over Gino's head to look at it. We were all craning to look at it.

'Stateville biometrics,' narrated Felice for those who couldn't see. 'They make a record of their prisoners' identifying markers when they're brought in. Valentino pulled some strings. He received this email thirty minutes ago.'

Felice's words droned in the background of my attention. I was too busy staring at a photo of my father. It was like his mugshot but in this one, his shirt was off, and there were three images, one of him side-on, the shamrock on his arm small and blurry. He'd told me he had gotten it with a friend on his eighteenth birthday – a cautionary drunk tale. His back was bare, and in the photo of his front, right over where his heart was, was a crest with a black handprint inside it. Beneath it were the words *Fidelitate Coniuncti.*

Donata's final words to me.

'Loyalty binds us,' translated Valentino. He wasn't anywhere near the photo, but I'm sure he had already stared at it long and hard. 'The Marino family motto.'

'That,' Felice's index finger stabbed the tattoo on the page, 'is the Marino crest. Every Marino since the dawn of *Cosa Nostra* has had this crest engraved on their person. Many of us in this room have seen them first-hand on their corpses.' He sucked in a gulping, excited breath. 'He's covered it since, smart boy. But *these* he can't get rid of.' He moved his finger and pressed it over my father's grainy, lifeless eyes. '*These* are Don Vincenzo Marino's eyes.' He lifted his head and moved his finger until it was an inch from my face. 'And so are those.'

CHAPTER THIRTY-ONE

THE LIFE

I pulled back from the table. I was finding it difficult to stay calm, more difficult than it was to believe what Felice was saying. I had seen that crest a ton of times, on hot days when my father worked in the garden, when he got out of the shower in the morning. He had told me he and Jack had gotten the same one as teenagers – as a way to always remember each other no matter where they ended up in the world. So they would never forget where they came from.

So they would never forget where they came from.

The room was deadly silent. I stumbled backwards, pressing myself against the wall and feeling its coolness through my tank top. I was going to pass out. I was going to get killed.

Felice seized the stunned silence. 'If you examine the records, collated with Angelo's research, you will see that the prison-recorded birthdate of Michael Gracewell matches exactly that of our own dear Vince Marino Jr, the boy who disappeared on me all those years ago. The missing Marinos might not legally exist any more, but they are still living right under our noses. And I'd bet my own blood and bones that their nearness to this family is no coincidence. I put a bullet in their parents, so little Vince Marino put a bullet in Angelo, and Antony put five stab wounds in Calvino in Eden. All this time, we wondered what Gracewell was offering Donata. It was simply his true identity. A Marino always sticks by their own.'

At that, the seated Falcones broke into a rush of frantic murmurings. The tide was turning. Felice was winning. Chaos was rising. I was going to drown in it. 'No,' I insisted, shaking my head violently. 'No, it's not true. It can't be true.'

'Liar!' Elena sprang to her feet. 'We've caught you out. Admit it! Admit your father is Vince Marino. Admit your uncle is Antony Marino.' She jabbed her finger at me. 'Admit that *you*, Sophie *Marino*, are a rotten liar.'

'I'm not a liar!' I shouted. 'I don't know anything about this!'

Dark gazes pressed against me. They were waiting for me to say something, to justify the insanity of walking into their house and expecting to live.

They'd never believe my innocence. Not now. How could I not know where I came from? How could I not know who I was?

How could I not know?

How could they not tell me?

'It's not true,' I said weakly, hearing the doubt in my words. 'It can't be true.'

Luca turned to his brother. 'Valentino?' he said quietly. His expression was thrumming with unexpected vulnerability. It

289

made me want to slam my head against the wall. 'Is this true?'

The room fell deathly silent. Valentino nodded. '*È la verità.*'

Luca turned, slowly. His face was shuttered again. He was in commander mode. To me, he said, as simply as if he were asking my age, 'Are you a Marino?'

'I—'

'You heard Valentino,' said Nic, who had become markedly dishevelled in the last minute. He threw his eyes to the ceiling, his hands raking through his hair. 'She's a fucking Marino.'

I backed towards the door.

'So we're agreed?' Felice yelled above the rising commotion. 'I can kill her?'

'No!' said Luca, arms outstretched towards him. 'Keep your head, Felice.'

'Everyone be quiet and don't move!' said Valentino, and the room fell silent again. 'We must come to a decision.'

Run, said a voice in my head. *Run and don't stop. Don't stop even if they shoot your legs out from under you.*

'Nicoli.' Felice's voice was shrill as a bell. 'Let's let Nicoli decide her fate.'

'Felice,' Valentino warned. 'This is not a game.'

Felice pulled out his gun and waved it above his head. 'I want to know which is stronger,' he told the room. 'Loyalty or love.' He pointed the gun at my head and cocked the trigger. 'I want Nicoli to tell me what to do to the Marino in our midst.'

'*Basta*,' said Luca, his voice little more than a growl.

'Felice,' said Paulie.

Valentino said nothing. So Felice kept his gun high.

Nic stepped towards me, but without blocking Felice. He cocked his head, his expression unreadable. 'She can stay if she proves herself. She has to kill a Marino. We can use her connection to them.'

Luca came to stand by Nic, the two brothers shoulder-to-shoulder, both of them looking at me as if they had never truly seen me before.

Maybe they hadn't.

'Go,' Luca mouthed. 'Now.'

I seized their makeshift shield – whether they meant it that way or not – flung open the door and ran as fast as I could. I didn't turn around to see if they were following me, or to listen to the rising shouts and screeching chairs. I sprinted and sprinted until my chest burnt and my legs shook, and then I pulled out my phone and called Millie.

My mind whirred as I ran. It couldn't be true. Fate wouldn't be so cruel. My own parents wouldn't be so dishonest as to keep something like this from me. The secret was too huge. Too impossible.

And yet that tattoo kept flashing in my mind. Forgotten arguments from long ago undusted themselves – all those times when my parents thought I was asleep, all those times my father looked over his shoulder, or stood at the windows of our house, watching the darkness. The clawing sense of wrongness in what he had done to Angelo Falcone. The anxiety that rested behind his eyes now he was in prison, the sense that something bigger was coming and he couldn't stop it. Puzzle pieces were shifting all around me . . . and somehow, somehow the impossibility of it didn't seem so big at all.

I'd escaped from the Falcones with my life just now. But I knew that once Donata realized what I'd done, it would be forfeit either way. If loyalty was supposed to bind us, then I was the worst Marino in history, because I had just unravelled it completely in the course of one afternoon, and laid her imminent plans to move against the Falcones right on their doorstep. I was stuck between two bloodthirsty crime families, and over the course of one day I had made enemies of them both.

Millie pulled up when I was almost a mile outside Felice's house, forcing myself along the main road, staying close to the thicket of trees in case an offending SUV rolled by and put a bullet in my head. I threw myself into her car and doubled over, covering the back of my head with my hands. I was half-crying and half-choking.

'What happened?' Millie asked. 'What the hell happened in there?'

'Just drive, please,' I begged her. 'I have to get home.'

She crushed her foot on the gas pedal, and after a minute I sat up and blinked into the darkening sky. It was later than I thought. She was waiting for me to speak.

There was only one thing to say.

I had added it up in my head. The tattoo. The Marinos' interest in Jack, in me. Sara's dimples. The sense of kinship I felt with her. Donata had yelled for Antony that night at Eden. He was already standing behind her, trying to entice me into their family, their business. He was my only uncle, and I didn't really know him at all.

Everything I thought I knew was changing.

There was only one way I could ever know for sure. Only one person who would tell me the truth. And she was at home packing up our lives so she wouldn't have to face it.

'Millie.' I heaved a shuddering breath. 'I think I'm a Marino.'

'*What?*'

'I think my dad's real name is Vince. I think he and Jack are the missing Marinos.' I started to hyperventilate, my hands clutching around my throat as I tried to gather myself. 'Say something,' I pleaded. I needed it to go away. I needed my life to be normal. I needed to calm down. 'Say anything.'

'Wait,' gasped Mil. 'Wait, wait, wait, hang on. Wait. Does this mean that you and Nic are somehow . . . related? Have you been like . . . incestuously making out this whole time?'

OK. Anything but that. '*Ew. God. No.*' I reeled backwards, disgust warring against my rising freak-out.

'OK, sorry, my bad,' she said, raising her hand in placation. 'But in my defence, these Mafia family trees are incredibly complicated and I really only concern myself with the hot members.'

'I'm not related to Donata,' I said, realizing the small mercy in that at least. 'She married into the family.'

'But isn't she, like, the Marino boss now?' Millie released a low whistle. 'Damn, that lady is ambitious.'

'Mil,' I groaned as I stuck my head between my knees and shut my eyes. 'My whole life is literally turning upside down, and I really just need you to talk about something else. Anything else. Please, just distract me. I need you to make it stop.'

'OK.' I heard her suck in a breath, and after a moment of consideration, she said, 'Did you know a baby puffin is called a puffling?'

PART IV

'A truth spoken before its
time is dangerous.'

Greek proverb

CHAPTER THIRTY-TWO
THE KEY

I burst through my front door, half expecting my mother to be waiting for me. She was in the sitting room, a mug in one hand, her phone in the other.

'There you are!' She sprang to her feet, spilling tea across her shirt. 'I've been calling you. You said you'd only be a couple of hours, Sophie. I was worried.'

Rage rumbled inside me. I took a deep, steadying breath.

'Am I a Marino?'

The mug smashed at my feet. The pieces nicked at my ankle, drawing blood. I turned from her and marched upstairs.

'Sweetheart,' she spluttered, following me. 'Hang on.'

'You lied to me,' I shouted over my shoulder. 'All my life you've been lying to me.'

I crashed into her room and dragged the chair by her vanity table over to the wardrobe.

She stood in the doorway, alarm warping her voice. 'What are you doing?'

I climbed on to the chair and started flinging my father's old clothes out of the way, searching through his side of the wardrobe. I was looking for a half-forgotten memory from my childhood. A box I found once when I was trying to find my Santa presents two weeks before Christmas. I had come across a black box, frayed at the edges, that my father had yanked off me. A box he told me never to open.

Well, guess what? I was damn sure going to open it now.

'Stop.' My mother was beside me, tugging at my arm. 'Can we just talk about this?'

I whirled on her, flinging another set of shirts on to the floor. 'What do you want to talk about? How Dad is one of the missing Marinos? How his real name is Vince? How we've been part of the mob this entire time and no one thought it was a good idea to tell me? Is that what you want to talk about?' I yelled. 'Because I can't imagine how you're going to explain all that to me!'

Her eyes grew big in her pale face. 'W-what?'

'I know!' I told her. 'I know what I am.'

She stumbled backwards, collapsing in a heap on the bed. I kept rifling through my dad's closet, shelf by shelf, searching for that box.

'You were never supposed to find out,' she said, her voice barely more than a whisper now. 'Your father left that life behind a long time ago . . . He never thought it would catch up with him.'

I fisted a pair of jeans in my hand, turning to her. 'But it did, didn't it?'

She couldn't look at me. 'Jack didn't get as far away from that world as your father did. He was drawing suspicion. And then . . . then Angelo Falcone started looking into them and—'

'He murdered him.' I rested my head on the top ledge of the wardrobe as the chair wobbled beneath me. 'Dad killed him on purpose that night and you knew!'

'Sophie . . .'

'Don't lie to me! Stop lying to me!'

'He told me before they took him in,' she admitted. 'He said he had to do it, to keep you safe, Sophie. He couldn't risk it getting out. He wanted you to live a happy life. Not the one he had. He lost his parents to that world.'

'You knew he murdered him,' I cried. 'And you were OK with it!'

'I'm not OK!' She scrambled to her feet. I looked down at her tear-streaked face and saw the desperation in her eyes. 'Why do you think I don't visit him? Why do you think I don't answer his letters? Why do you think I can't *stomach* looking at him any more, Sophie? It terrifies me. I can't stop thinking about it. I hate that world. I hate everything it stands for.'

Where was that damn box? I grabbed their wedding album from the top shelf and flung it to the floor. 'Then why did you *marry* him?'

'I didn't know his past when I married him! He and Jack were taken away by their grandmother. They legally changed their identities. He was a Gracewell when I met him.'

'OK,' I said, forcing calmness into my body. 'When did you find out he was the heir to a bloodthirsty crime family?'

'After a few years.'

I fought the urge to take her by the shoulders and shake her. 'Then why the hell did you stay with him?'

'Because I was pregnant!'

The chair wobbled again. I shot my hand out and grabbed the shelf to steady myself.

'I was pregnant and I was in love,' she said. 'I didn't want to punish him for where he came from. He was making an honest name for himself. He hadn't seen his family in years. Nobody was ever going to find out. Sophie,' she added, her voice turning hard, 'I fell in love with someone who wanted a destiny different to the one he was born with. A man who was kind and funny and loyal and protective. And when the truth came out, I was still in love with him, because my knowledge of who he was didn't change anything about who he had become. I loved him, Sophie, in spite of his family. Do you find that so hard to believe?'

I faltered, my words catching in my throat. She fell in love with a mafioso.

Was that really so hard to believe?

No. It was easy to understand. Too easy.

I turned back to my search. 'You were supposed to tell me everything after Donata left yesterday,' I said. 'She was sure you would.'

'I know,' she conceded.

'And you didn't.'

She raked her hands through her hair, greasy tendrils swiping across her forehead. 'I didn't know what to do, Sophie. Your father made me swear to him that I'd never reveal it. That I'd hide it with every last breath. But then . . .

300

Jack got in hot water and he went to . . . he went to Donata, of all people, and he broke open the secret. And suddenly she had her eyes on you. She knew who you were. She said she was allowing me the courtesy of telling you. I told her I would.'

'You really thought you could hide it from me?' I asked her.

'I had to try,' she said, her words cracking. 'I had to try.'

'What were you afraid of?' I asked, feeling marginally less angry now. It wasn't so hard to understand my mother's position. No wonder she hadn't been coping well. She was chewing on a secret so big it was destroying her. 'Telling me wouldn't have ended the world.'

She shook her head. 'You can't bury something if you keep digging it up. We had to keep going, keep living the life we'd made. I was afraid you would go to them. That they would pull you in and you would see a family with money and protection and support, a family you never really had. And then Jack cut us off and the bills started piling up, and when Donata came I thought she would tell you, and you would leave me for betraying you.'

I reached down and clasped her hand. 'I would never leave you!'

'I wanted to do the right thing, the *best* thing . . .' She shook her head, her expression filling with sadness. 'But I couldn't tell what it was, Sophie.'

'What do you mean, Jack cut us off?'

'Jack handles the diner money,' she said. 'He's stopped sending us our share, and you weren't well enough to go to work. I've been too frazzled to finish my own projects . . . and . . .'

'I would have gone back, Mom. You should have told me sooner.'

301

'Your health is more important to me.'

I rose on to my tiptoes and returned to my search, feeling a mixture of triumph and fear as my fingers brushed against something hard and dusty at the back of the closet. I pulled the box out, balancing it carefully as I heaved it down. I climbed off the chair and dropped it on the bed.

'Sweetheart . . .' she began, 'I think we should take this slow . . .'

I opened the box and dumped its contents on to the bed. 'We don't have time for "slow".'

My father's past fluttered on to the duvet.

'God,' I breathed, as I picked up the yellowed birth certificate from Northwestern Memorial Hospital and read the faded writing.

Vincenzo Alessio Marino

D.O.B: 12th of September, 1971

Father: Vincenzo Carmine Marino

Mother: Linda Mary Harris

I brushed my thumb over my father's birthdate.

My father, Vincenzo Marino Jr.

I swallowed hard.

My eye fell on a newspaper clipping. I picked it up; the article was marked 14th November 1987. I scanned it, trying to detach myself from the gruesomeness, from how close to home it really was.

TWO DEAD IN MOB HIT. THE BLOOD FEUD CONTINUES.

The bodies of Vincenzo Marino, Mafia boss of the Marino crime family, and his wife, Linda Harris, were discovered in their home in Hyde Park yesterday afternoon. They had been shot execution-style. Their sons, Vincenzo Jr and Antony were not on the premises at the time of the shooting.

Vincenzo Marino was born in Sicily, but relocated to Chicago with his family when he was a young teenager. Linda Harris was a Wisconsin native of Irish descent, who had studied art in New York before she met and married the infamous Mafia don.

Head of an organization nicknamed the Black Hand Mob, Vincenzo Marino was widely referred to as the 'Iron Hand' due to the successful steel business he owned and operated with his brothers. Gangland rivalry is suspected to be involved in the killing, with a source close to the FBI pointing to the rival Falcone crime family as having carried out the double hit.

The Marino deaths are the latest in a series of Mafia-related killings and disappearances over the last year. The suspected blood feud has claimed the lives of eleven Falcones and sixteen Marinos since its eruption. The investigation continues.

Beneath the article, there was a grainy photograph of Vincenzo Marino and his wife, Linda Harris. My grandparents. They were dressed formally and smiling at something off camera. She was beautiful. He looked just like my father. In all my life, I had only ever seen one picture of them – a holiday snap from when my father was a child. He said the other pictures were too painful for him to look at. But now they were spread out below me, tens of Polaroids of the Marino boss and his wife, of Jack and my father, smiling and laughing, wearing silly hats and blowing out candles and doing all the normal things that normal happy families do. These were not deadbeat parents, the way I'd always been told.

'Where were Dad and Jack?' I asked, sifting through the photographs. 'The article says they weren't in the house when they were killed.'

I was all too aware of my mother hovering behind me, her heavy breathing filling up the silence. She was panicking and trying not to show it; I was trying not to scream at her. It was a delicate dance.

'Linda's family hid them. They were already in Milwaukee before the murders. Your grandfather suspected there was a hit out on him and he didn't want to take any chances. Linda wouldn't leave her husband's side.'

'And she died for it.'

'She did.'

She died for love.

For stupidity.

'Do you call Dad "Vince" or "Michael"?'

'He's only ever been Michael to me.'

I laughed, but there was no amusement in it.

'Sophie . . .'

'Why did Dad come back to Chicago?' I cut in. 'Did he have a death wish or something?'

She sighed. 'I was in college here when we met. I wanted to stay and raise a family, and by the time I found out about his past, he said the danger was over. The Falcones would never find out who he was.'

'Still, why risk it?'

'I don't know, sweetheart.' She sat down on the bed, disturbing a group of photographs. I picked up the key underneath. It was heavy and brass, with a thick loop at the end, where the metal broke away into connecting swirls. 'He wanted to be Michael Gracewell. He believed we'd get away with it.'

'Well, we haven't,' I said, bitterness twisting my voice as I twisted the key in my hand. It was fancy, important-looking. It opened the safe in the diner – I'd bet my life on it. Something lurched inside me. What the hell was it doing in my father's closet?

'Just because Donata told you doesn't mean the other families will find out.'

I lifted my gaze. 'Donata didn't tell me.'

She screwed her face up. 'What?'

I stood up, still clutching the key. 'The Falcones did.'

I don't know why I revelled in the surprise on my mother's face in that split second, why it made me feel good to know that there were secrets she didn't know either. It was petty and small, but that's how I felt. Stupid. Untethered from my own identity.

She shot to her feet. 'No.'

'Yes,' I said.

She shook her head. 'But how?'

I crushed the key in my fist and threw the rest of the photos off the bed. Anger surged in me now that I had seen it all, now that I knew for sure. 'Because I went to them,' I said, hot tears welling in my eyes. 'Because I thought they were our only hope! Because I thought we had to be protected from the Marinos! I went to them thinking they would help us, and I left with Felice Falcone screaming "Marino" at me.' The sobs came thick and fast, choking me.

'No,' my mother half-shrieked. 'They can't know.'

'Everybody knows!' I yelled. 'Everybody knows and we're stuck here like rats, waiting to be killed or used in this stupid blood war! You should have told me!'

'I wanted to protect you!' She was shouting too. Panic had seized us both. We saw our fate mirrored back at us – hopeless, inevitable. We had burnt all our bridges. The secrets had cut us down. 'I've been tearing my hair out thinking about it. How could I risk telling you? After the warehouse . . . after how close they got to us, and you were so brave and so good. The Falcones weren't looking at you any more – they *owed* you. I thought we could walk away. I thought our secret was still safe. How could I tell my baby girl the family she comes from is sick and twisted, after everything we've come through? How could I break your heart like that?' She was crying harder than me.

'I never had a choice,' I said, a violent sob rattling my shoulders. 'All this time I was living a lie. I never had a way out, and you all knew it!'

'We wanted to *give* you a way out,' she insisted. 'I wanted to more than anything, sweetheart.'

Something shifted inside me as Nic's forgotten words rose to the surface, wrapping around me. The world got very dark all of a sudden. 'I'm bound by blood, Mom.' My voice fell deathly quiet. 'There *is* no way out.'

'Oh, Sophie.' She dragged her hands across her face. 'Do you know that you're the most important thing to me in the whole world? I love you.'

'I know,' I said, defeated. 'I know that. I love you too.'

I sank to the floor and she sank with me. The key fell to the carpet between us. 'I was trying to protect you,' she said, clasping my hands in hers.

'And I was trying to protect you,' I told her. 'And now we're screwed.'

She wiped her cheeks with the back of her hands. 'No.' She got up and pulled me with her. 'We're going. We have to go. We have to go tonight.'

'They'll find us, Mom. There's no way out of this life. Don't you get it? Jack's got all that money in the diner. He's got all the resources in the world.' I picked up the key and brandished it between us. 'He's got his damn safe in *our diner*. Donata's watching us. I don't know what the Falcones are going to do any more than you do, but I know we don't have enough to get away from them. We won't be able to hide. I was supposed to choose, and I chose wrong.'

Nic's words rang in my head. *She's a fucking Marino.*

The look on Luca's face.

My mother took the key from my hand. 'Well, then, let's get the resources,' she said, her voice spiking. 'If they're going to treat us like Marinos then let's act like them.'

I eyed the key. 'No way.'

'Yes way,' she said. 'It's the only way.'

'We can't take their money!' I hissed. 'Are you crazy?'

'Yes! I'm crazy with worry and this is the only way out. Let's take it and get the head start we need.'

I shook my head. 'Dad would never—'

'Your father isn't here!'

We huddled around that key, scrolling through all the ways tonight could blow up in our faces. The underworld was moving around us. We had to go. Eat or be eaten.

'It's too dangerous,' I whispered. 'The Falcones are watching the diner. They'll kill us.'

'No, they won't. They won't suspect us. They're looking for Jack, remember?'

'You didn't see them.' I thought of the horror in Nic's eyes. The moment he had looked at me like I had betrayed him. 'You don't know what they're capable of.'

She stuffed it in her pocket. 'I know the stakes, Sophie. We've got a little time. Donata thinks you're on side, remember? She said she'd come here first to brief you. And she hasn't yet. "Soon" is not tonight.'

'I'll go, then. You keep watch and I'll go in.'

She shook her head. 'You're not a thief, Sophie.'

'Neither are you!'

'This is my job. I'm supposed to protect you. I'm supposed to keep you safe.'

I had a sudden flash of Sara Marino trying to claw the blood out of her arms at Eden.

There's this blood in us.

'No. I'm the Marino, remember?'

She shut her eyes tight. 'You're not going in there, Sophie.'

'Fine,' I huffed. 'Then neither are you.'

'Sweetheart . . .'

'It's way too dangerous. Let's just get in the car and go. Leave the money where it is. We'll find another way.'

There was a heavy silence. She chewed her lip, thinking. And then, at last, her shoulders dipped and she said, 'Pack a bag. We'll discuss it when we're in the car.'

I left the pieces of my father's past, the broken secret he had kept from me, and went into my bedroom and threw my whole life into a suitcase.

I was fishing a pair of shorts out from underneath my bed when the front door slammed. My heart slammed too.

My mother had reversed out of the driveway by the time I got downstairs. She sped away from me, leaving me screaming at the back of her car as the first drops of rain began to fall, heralding the storm.

She was going to rob the safe.

They were going to kill her.

CHAPTER THIRTY-THREE

THE SAFE

I didn't care about the rain on my cheeks or the wind whipping through my hair as I charged through the darkness. I didn't think about the lightning ignite the sky or hear the thunder clap like drumfire. Houses passed in blurs, the trees streaking green beneath the street lights.

I ignored the crippling need to stop, to bend at the waist and vomit. My exertion ebbed, vibrating like needle-points in my legs as I pushed myself towards the diner, towards my mother. I was running faster than I ever had before, every step pulsing through my ribs, calling old wounds to the surface.

I skidded into the parking lot. My mother's car was parked in the furthest corner of the lot, nestled where the street lights weren't shining. It wasn't exactly the perfect disguise, but she had hidden it, at least. There was no sign of the Falcones but I wasn't dumb enough to think they weren't there somewhere, if they weren't already inside Gracewell's. If I had learnt anything these past few weeks, it was to expect the unexpected.

And trust no one.

I ran towards the diner, conscious of eyes on my back. I swung open the front door under the awning, groaning at the fact that it wasn't locked. Locking it behind me, I followed the sound of frantic rustling behind the counter and into the kitchen. My mother was flinging pots and pans out of the cupboards.

'I told you not to come!'

She snapped her head up. She was wild-eyed, her hands still scrabbling against the wood. 'Where's that damn safe?'

What the hell had gotten into her?

'No,' I said. 'No way. We are not taking their money. We need to get out of here.'

'Sophie, stop, *think*,' my mother urged. 'We've been backed into a corner. You said it yourself, you're bound by blood. We both know what that means. They'll come after you either way. At least this way we'll have a fighting chance.'

I glanced around the kitchen. It was eerily quiet, the sounds of our breathing mingling with the dripping of the tap. I could hear my own heartbeat.

'We can't, Mom. They'll kill us. They'll kill you.' The idea swarmed behind my eyes and vibrated in my throat. 'I can't lose you too.'

'They won't catch us.' She gestured out on to the diner floor. 'They're not here, sweetheart. Look around you.'

'The Falcones—'

'The Falcones don't care about the money.'

I faltered. I knew that was true too. They had more money than they knew what to do with. This was about Jack for them.

'Where is the safe?' my mother pleaded. She was panting, and the panic between us was rising. 'I know you're scared, I know this isn't the right thing, but it's the only way we can do this. Jack's been bleeding us of money for years. We're only taking what's owed to us. We're only taking enough to disappear. You're my baby. You're my whole world. I won't let them take you from me.'

I looked into her watery blue eyes, at that faltering smile, and I caved. We'd never make it far enough away without that money, and we both knew it. We were here now, and the damage was done.

'We have to be quick.' I stuck my hand out. 'Give me the key.'

The cabinets stretched along the back wall, above the prep area, ending just before the back door. You could fit a whole person inside. Millie and I often debated trying it, but most of them were usually locked and Ursula always got angry when we tried to climb on stuff. She almost fired Millie the time she caught us playing 'The Floor is Lava' in the kitchen.

I hoisted myself above the stove, balancing on the edges of the countertops as I swung open the furthest cupboard and peeled away the lino wallpaper to find the safe. It was a wide, hulking thing, with a thick brass keyhole.

'Oh my God.' My mother was below me. 'It's huge.'

'Can you keep watch, please?'

I turned the key three times and a resounding click echoed

through the kitchen.

Of *course* my father had known about the safe. I was officially unsurprised.

I heaved the door open, and cursed into the echoey din. Inside, a smaller metal safe stared back at me, a thick, circular dial dominating its face. I almost smashed my head against it. 'You've got to be freaking kidding me!'

'What is it?' My mother's voice sounded a long way away.

'Another safe!' A fitting ode to Jack's prevailing paranoia, not to mention his constant status as one giant aggravator in my life. 'This one has a combination!' I called out. The stupid key was no good without the combination. I was ten seconds away from grabbing my mother and getting the hell out of there.

I unstuck my head from the cupboard. My mother was hovering between the kitchen and the diner, squinting through the rain-spattered windows into the darkness. If the Falcones were out there, they obviously didn't see us as a threat. I didn't know whether to be thankful or mildly offended.

'Try your birthday,' she called back.

I tried my birthday with shaking hands. I tried Jack's birthday. I tried my father's birthday. I tried my mother's birthday. 'No!' I thumped my head against the cold metal. 'No no no!'

Dammit. Panic was raging inside me. My fingers were shaking and there was no moisture left in my throat. It had to be something important. If Jack and my father both had a key, then it had to be something that linked them. Surely. *Surely.* Like the tattoo I was convinced they both had.

I pulled back and a dim light went off.

313

The date their parents were murdered.

I racked my memory. The newspaper article had been dated November 14th.

I keyed in 111387. There was a series of loud clicks. 'Yes,' I said as triumph flooded me. I pulled the handle and the safe heaved open. I backed up on my haunches as the door swung outwards. 'Got it,' I shouted. My voice echoed inside the metal din as I plunged my head into the depths of Jack's and my father's secrets.

Inside, the money was arranged in little towers. I guessed there were at least five hundred thousand dollars, but there were so many stacks, it could have been double that, or even triple. More money than I would ever see again. It was like something out of a movie.

'Holy crap,' I muttered. My hand hovered over a stack of bills. How much was in just that one? Ten thousand dollars? Twenty thousand? I dropped it on to the countertop. We'd just take one. They'd hardly notice, I said to myself. Besides, we were dead either way. At least this way, we wouldn't die poor.

OK, maybe two stacks, then. I took out another one, pushing away the feeling of panic.

I brushed the rest of the money out of my way and stuck my head back in, trying to ignore the stale mustiness. Dirty money smelt bad. There were other things in the safe. I lingered, staring wide-eyed as I grappled with bits of paper. There were switchblades. Falcone switchblades with names I didn't recognize. Ernesto. Alberto. Piero.

What the hell?

I lifted a piece of paper to the light. There was a list of

names scrawled in my father's handwriting. I recognized most of them. *Felice, Evelina, Ernesto, Alberto, Piero, Angelo, Paulie, Calvino, Elena, Gianluca, Valentino, Giorgino, Dominico, Nicoli.* There were different marks beside some of the names, the darkest one beside Evelina.

Behind the switchblades, at the very back of the safe, was a ring. It was a ruby ring – blood-red and still shining even in the darkness. I plucked it from the shadows of the safe and pulled it into the light so I could read the word engraved inside it, between a swirling E and F.

Evelina's ring.

I swallowed the bile rushing into my mouth and without thinking, I shoved the ring in my pocket. My legs gave out and I stumbled backwards, falling from the chair and whacking my hip bone on the stove. When I picked myself up, I was staring right at my uncle.

He was standing in the doorway between the kitchen and the diner. My mother was bundled in a ball at his feet.

'You'd better not be doing what I think you're doing,' he said, calmly.

'Mom!' I darted across the room and crouched beside her unconscious form. 'What the hell did you do to her?'

The rain and wind were so loud I hadn't heard him come in. If there had been a scuffle, he had ended it quickly, and I had been too busy sticking my head into a safe to notice.

Jack – *Antony* – looked down on me, his eyes dark and hooded. 'She was going to scream. I didn't want her drawing any attention to us.'

'You knocked her out!' I glared up at him. 'What the hell is wrong with you?' I pulled her limp body into the kitchen, away from Jack's muddy boots, and propped her up against the island. 'Mom?' I said, nudging her gently. 'Wake up, Mom.'

'So, I see you found your father's key,' Jack muttered. 'I suppose you know everything.'

'Just when I thought I couldn't be any more disgusted,' I hissed. 'I know all about you, *Antony*.'

'Good. It's about time.' He pushed past me, undaunted by my use of his real name, and unfolded a duffel bag from under the counter. He picked up the stacks of money I had dropped on the counter and held them up. 'I see you decided to rob me.'

I channelled every drop of venom into my response. 'I'm a Marino, right? Why not take what's mine?'

He barked a laugh. 'A true Marino would have cleaned the entire safe out.'

'Well, I guess I'm not good at being a depraved criminal.'

'You're so dramatic.' His movements were hurried as he shoved the money into the duffel bag in thick fistfuls.

'Don't forget the switchblades,' I snapped. 'What charming keepsakes. I'm sure all those Falcones are turning in their unmarked graves.'

'That's your father's business,' he huffed, climbing up on the counter to reach further inside. 'The revenge was always more his thing. I just want to make money.'

Oh my God.

'He's been involved all along?' My voice sounded impossibly far away – hollow, quivering. I swallowed the rest of my reaction. Not here. Not now. That brand of betrayal ran too deep. I would deal with it later.

Jack stopped his rustling to glance over his shoulder. He shrugged heavily, and something peculiar flashed in his eyes. 'They took everything from us, Sophie. I thought you'd be able to understand that.'

I kept my voice as steady as I could. 'I *understand* that you're going to get killed pretty soon, and you know what? I think you deserve it.'

I patted my mother's cheek. A welt was rising on the top of her head; Jack had hit her hard. I couldn't drag her out, could I? Maybe I should just whack my head on something too and go with her, into dreamland, where I had a name and a family that still made sense.

I was trying really hard not to think about the ring in my pocket. Trying not to think about my father with his greying hair and melancholy eyes, rotting in prison. Where he deserved to be, as it turns out. And I was *really* trying hard not to cry in front of my uncle.

He heaved another tower of money into the duffel bag and swept his hand inside the safe, checking that everything was out. 'And what about your dad?'

'Leave him out of this.' I didn't have anywhere near enough energy to open that box of broken promises. I wanted to twist my hands in his collar and scream at him. But I could never get to him. He was behind bars. Safe.

Another wheezing laugh escaped Jack. He slammed the heavy brass door shut and locked it. 'Newsflash, Persephone, we're all fucked up in this together. Your father and I are blood-red with guilt. You can't pick and choose which one of us to hate.'

My mother still wasn't stirring, and I was starting to grow desperate. Slits of white pushed against her drooping eyelids. I brushed her hair back and felt for the pulse in her neck. It was weak but steady. 'I need you to wake up,' I whispered as tears pooled in the backs of my eyes. 'I really need you to wake up now.'

Jack covered the safe behind the lino and shut the cabinet. When I looked up, he was right above me. The duffel bag was slung on his shoulder and his eyes were flashing with some new crazy purpose.

'Just go,' I said, pushing it out with all the strength I had in me. I was not going to think about the switchblades. I was not going to think about what that list meant. Or where the ruby came from. I was not going to think about how many lies my father had told me.

Jack had the audacity to laugh. 'We both know I'm not leaving here without you, Soph.'

'I can't help you kill the Falcones. Donata won't—'

Jack barked an incredulous laugh. 'You don't really believe Donata expected you to *kill* anyone, do you?'

I blanched. 'She said she wanted me to help her.'

'You don't even know how to use a gun, let alone kill a man. For Christ's sake, you're seventeen years old.'

'But then how was I supposed to—'

'Don't worry about it,' Jack interrupted, amusement still colouring his tone. 'You've already done it, Soph. You've already helped her.'

'I—' The words fell away from me. 'She knew I'd go to them,' I realized. 'She wanted me to go to them.'

She played me.

But why? I didn't get it – I couldn't grasp the scope of her plan. I was too close to it, and it didn't make sense. But I knew I had slipped up.

'Donata is a very intelligent woman,' Jack said admiringly. 'You shouldn't underestimate her.'

My mother was groaning, and I was beginning to realize that the two of us getting out of here together and without Jack was going to be impossible.

As if reading my thoughts, he said, 'You can't run, so don't try.'

'Why?' I asked, hearing the childishness in my own voice. 'Why do I matter so much?'

'Because you're family,' said Jack. 'And family stick together.'

'We don't want to stick with you, *Antony*, we're fine by ourselves.'

'Well,' he said, still ignoring my use of his real name, and looking past me out the window into the storm-swept parking lot. 'Donata's collecting Marinos. She wants you in the fold where she can keep an eye on you. So you know what that means?'

'What?'

'It means tough shit.'

We glared at each other as my mother twitched beside me – Don Vincenzo Marino's eyes mirrored back at each other, shooting mistrust.

The rain thudded relentlessly against the roof. Thunder groaned, rumbling ever closer as the windows rattled in their frames. I could feel my heartbeat in my fingertips. Dread was uncoiling in the pit of my stomach as a new comprehension dawned on me: there was no one left to help us. I had to call the police. I had to take my chances.

'You should have told me,' I said. 'I deserved to know.'

'I vowed I would tell you if one of us ever came out of hiding.'

'You are out of hiding.' Subtly I slid my phone out of my pocket.

'I tried to tell you at Eden but you wouldn't listen,' he said irritably. 'What does it matter, anyway? You know now. We've been running for too long. It's time to stand up and fight.'

'I don't want to fight.' I unlocked my phone.

Jack's attention flicked between the parking lot and where I was crouched beside my mother. His eyes narrowed at something outside.

I started to dial, the phone hidden by my side, but Jack whipped around and snatched it from me. He brought his hand down hard across my face. 'What the fuck are you doing?' he spat. 'Calling the police – are you crazy? Do you *want* to get killed, is that it?'

I lunged at him, but he caught my fists as I slammed them against him. 'Just go!' I yelled. 'What are you waiting for?'

'Calm down!' he snapped. I thrashed against him but he held firm, dragging me towards the server line behind the till. He pulled his phone from his pocket. Whoever he was calling answered on the first ring. He spoke low and quickly, his eyes darting around the diner, ignoring my mother as she started groaning. 'They're on the move,' he said. 'Three.' Another pause, and then, 'Watch the front, but I'm guessing they'll come around the back.'

I glanced over my shoulder. Through the window, in the distance, a flash of lightning illuminated three dark shapes at the very far end of the parking lot. The Falcones were coming. We were caged in.

Jack pulled me back into the kitchen. A strange part of me was glad my mother was out cold for this. If our doom was rising to meet us, at least she wouldn't have to suffer the terror of it. At least she hadn't seen those switchblades, the ring, the truth. At least she didn't realize how depraved her husband really was – how we had both been conned. At least her heart was still whole.

Across the kitchen, the back door was shut and locked. It was heavy and metal – and impenetrable.

'What are you going to do now?' I asked, trying and failing to pull him back to the serving section of the diner – to the diner phone.

'We're going to kill them,' he said. 'And finally teach you the meaning of loyalty.'

His eyes were fathomless pools, polluted with his scheme. I tried to twist out of his grasp but he clamped down harder. He stalked to the other side of the kitchen, through to the serving area, so he could glance through the windows again. Sheets of rain crashed against the windows, but outside all was still.

Or so it appeared.

I had to get out. If I could get out, I could flag someone down. I could get us out of there. I struggled against him.

'You can go,' he said. 'But you'll have to take your chances with the assassins outside.'

There was a deafening crash from the kitchen – something

was colliding against the metal door. Jack had been right – the Falcones had come around the back, where their attempts to get at him would be hidden in the darkness of the alleyway.

I seized this distraction and bolted into the serving area. The furious thudding of Jack's pursuit jolted me faster. I sprinted across the floor, pulling tables behind me as I went, hoping to slow him down. He bounded over them with wild abandon.

I reached the front door and managed to free the lock with fumbling hands. Jack grabbed my T-shirt. We tussled and he yanked me backwards, clenching my shoulders. 'They'll kill you!'

I stomped on his foot. 'Let go!'

Two loud cracks rang in the air outside. Closer than thunder, more frightening than lightning. I stumbled backwards, hitting my head against Jack's chest. He gripped my arm again and pulled me with him, knocking over a table.

Another crash rang out back in the kitchen, the door clanging against their attempts to demolish it.

They were everywhere.

The front door swung open in front of us and Donata Marino swept into the diner, bringing a flurry of wind and rain with her.

'There you are,' she said, holding her gun high. 'By happy coincidence you are already exactly where I want you to be.'

'You lied to me!' I spat. 'You used me!'

'Like a carrier pigeon.' She took a step closer, blocking my way. I could see the beads of rain sliding down her face. 'As if I would ever expect you to betray the boy that gives you flowers and looks at you like you're worth something.'

I gaped at her.

'I have eyes everywhere, Sophie.' She shook her head. 'And I am no fool.'

'*Why?* Why send me there?'

'Don't you understand power structures, silly girl?' She lowered her gun and tucked it in her pocket. Her smile was a patronizing slash of red lips. 'Our strike tonight is only as good as the highest-ranking member we kill.' Her smile grew as she saw comprehension move across my features.

She knew she could never get to Valentino. But Valentino was one half of a whole.

So . . .

'Luca is the target,' I whispered.

She nodded. 'I wanted the underboss to know we were coming so he would come out of that mansion and stand with his brothers, where I can get at him.'

As she shut the door behind her, I caught a glimpse of Gino Falcone slumped against the doorframe, his gun held limply in his hand as rivers of crimson pooled across his T-shirt.

I knew in that split second that I had made the gravest mistake of all, and that tonight we would all pay for it.

CHAPTER THIRTY-FOUR

THE GAS

Donata seized me by the collar and dragged me with her like a dog. 'The others are at the back door?' she asked Jack. There was another bang from the kitchen and she smiled, her question answered. She indicated behind her with a flick of her wrist. 'Giorgino Falcone was too busy playing with his phone to see me. *Imbecille*. Libero and Marco will cover the front now. The others are en route. The Falcones have backup, so we'll have to be quick.'

God. There were so many of them moving around in the darkness, seizing the storm and harnessing its protection.

I struggled out of Donata's grasp and tried to crane my neck to search the doorway again. She pushed me back into the kitchen, where Jack was lifting the bursting duffel bag on to the island. My mother's eyes were closed but she was still groaning softly, reality filtering back to her, piece by piece. Donata ignored her.

'Sophie, I am going to do for you what I could not do for my sister many years ago. I am going to get those demons out of your head. Tonight is the beginning of the life you were meant to have. Tonight you will become a Marino.'

The door heaved again, and this time a dent formed in the centre of it.

Jack stretched his body over the stove and flicked the gas on, one burner at a time. I watched the air above them start to ripple.

'What the hell are you doing?' The realization came upon me like a bed of nails in my back. Before I could scream at them, Donata had clamped her hand across my mouth, suffocating the air as I tried to suck it in.

'Family business,' she said, and I felt the whisper of her smile in the hairs on my neck. 'Let me explain something to you, Sophie.' She was breathing so heavily I couldn't hear myself think. 'When I was a little girl, my sister stole my favourite doll while I was at school and cut all her hair off. When I got home, I seethed for two days and two nights. Then on the third day, I told her that in revenge I was going to go out to our garden shed, open the hutch inside it and take the head off her pet bunny rabbit.'

I struggled harder, but she clamped down, speaking faster. 'Elena was terrified. She wanted to know when I was going to do it. As a matter of fairness, I told her I would do it in two weeks' time, on the fourteenth day, and that I would wait until she was asleep so she couldn't stop me.'

The gas was filling up the room with frightening speed. I

could already smell the sulphuric burn sticking to the inside of my nostrils. There was another crash – and this time Nic's voice rang out above the thunder and the rain. 'Marino, you coward! Open up!'

Nic. I shut my eyes tight. *Dammit.*

Donata was still talking. 'Instead of coming on the four-teenth day, she spent every single one of those nights camped outside in a sleeping bag, waiting for me. Once she knew I was going to do it, she couldn't help herself. She couldn't stand the suspense, the idea of not truly knowing when or how I would strike. Her protective instincts drove her to that cold, damp shed, and her fear kept her there. It deprived her of sleep, of sanity . . . and still, when the day came, I took the head as I swore I would.'

Jack was circling the kitchen. He had unstuck the cork noticeboard and wedged it beside the stove, and now he was dropping everything flammable he could find on to the floor, throwing tablecloths and napkins around the countertops like he was playing with streamers.

'You see, Sophie,' said Donata, 'Elena has always been calculated, cautious . . . *predictable.*' I could feel the smile in her last sentence. 'Gianluca Falcone is every bit his mother's son. He will always place himself where the threat is greatest. And that's how I know he's outside that door right now.'

As if in answer, the door clanged again and this time a hinge crumbled.

Donata's laugh rang out. 'The underboss is Valentino's highest protection. He only comes out of his brother's shadow when he knows real, palpable danger is near. Caution has brought him here tonight, and his predictability will get him killed.'

I shut my eyes tight. Luca wouldn't leave Valentino in the middle of a blood war.

There's no way.

We were facing the caving metal doorway from across the kitchen. Behind us the passage was free, safe from the destruction Jack was cultivating. As the full horror of their plan crystallized before me, Jack's psychotic laugh surged through the kitchen, rising up with the gas.

'Come on in, boys!'

CHAPTER THIRTY-FIVE

THE EXPLOSION

I knocked my head backwards, smashing it against Donata's collarbone.

'Stop it,' she hissed, wrangling me against her. 'Or I'll split your head against the stove and leave you here to burn with your boyfriends. If you're not with us, you're against us.'

Across the room, my mother stumbled to her feet, one hand clamped on her head and the other clutching her stomach. Watching the glazed expression on her face and the way her mouth was twisting with pain, I felt only dread.

'Sophie?' she slurred. She barely reacted to the fact that I was being restrained by Donata Marino. She double-blinked, flinching. 'What is this?'

Her eyes grew as she noticed the acrid smell. She sniffed the air, her lip curling. 'Oh,' she gasped, whirling on Jack.

'What are you doing?' She staggered past my uncle, making a beeline for the stove.

Another metallic thump sounded and the floor reverberated. The lock on the door came unhinged.

My mother reached one of the burners. Jack dived at her. He grabbed her by the elbow and jerked her backwards, slamming her head against the island. She slid to the ground, leaving a streak of blood against the wood.

I screamed so hard into Donata's hand that I almost suffocated myself. My knees buckled but she held me up, propped against her.

Jack yanked the gas line out from behind the stove and ripped it from the wall. It popped with a hiss and the air around it started furrowing. Coughing with violent force, Jack grabbed me and pulled me backwards, floundering across the kitchen, away from the fumes as they surged around us.

Donata took the duffel bag and retreated into the serving section as my uncle crushed me against him. My mother was lying in a sprawled heap between the stove and the island.

'Let me go!' I shrieked. 'Let me help her!'

He held me inside the kitchen doorway, our backs to the diner, our faces to the metal door as it swung open. Through the thickness of the gas, Luca and Nic appeared in the doorway and every shred of hope inside me shrivelled up and died.

The alleyway stretched into the darkness behind them, where the dumpster had been tipped on its side. Trash was strewn everywhere. Wind and rain swept into the room, and the raging storm grew piercing and loud around us.

The Falcone brothers raised their guns.

In a flash, Jack manoeuvred me in front of him until I could feel his chin against my head, his noisy exhales rippling through my hair. 'Go on,' said Jack. 'Shoot at us, why don't you?'

Luca lowered his gun.

Nic hesitated.

The moment seemed to stretch interminably. In that instant, when even the thunder seemed to quell, my whole life rested at the mercy of Nic Falcone's trigger finger. I looked inside the barrel of his gun, studying those two black circles, one delicately poised above the other, and felt the nearness of my own death.

'Nicoli,' warned Luca.

Nic's arm was twitching. 'I can still get him.'

'Nicoli.'

My eyes were spiking with tears. 'The gas,' I rasped. 'The gas is on.'

Nic's gaze grew wide with understanding. Finally, he noticed the smell, the thickness in the air, and he flinched. He lowered his gun.

The door slammed shut behind them, teetering on broken hinges.

'You're scum, using them like this,' said Luca to Jack. He was inching forward, moving without trying to make it look obvious. 'You'll have to walk out of here sooner or later, and when you do we'll get you.'

'You wouldn't risk her life.'

He raised his eyebrows, his feet sliding soundlessly towards us. 'And you would?'

Jack's grip tightened, his arm clamped against my throat

until I was choking. The lights in my brain were flickering, the edges of my vision blotting with black smudges.

Dimly I saw my mother's hand clutching the island as she tried to lift herself from the floor. Her hair was streaked with blood but her mouth was moving, slowly, testing out syllables.

'Do you want to find out what I'm capable of, filth?' said Jack.

Luca curled his lip. 'I'll gut you, Marino.'

Jack shifted with alarming speed, pushing me backwards through the door. I tumbled into the main diner as he slammed the kitchen door behind us.

'Mom!' I screamed as Donata appeared from the darkness behind me and flicked her Zippo lighter through the server window.

The blast erupted in a flash of bright orange. It ripped across the kitchen, exploding in a resounding boom that shattered all the windows. The walls shook and I was thrown backwards, across the till counter and on to the diner floor.

CHAPTER THIRTY-SIX

INFERNO

The kitchen was bursting with flames. Dark, grey smoke billowed out through the serving window. The wood was crackling, breaking off into huge splinters that plummeted towards the floor.

Behind me, Jack and Donata had made it to the front entrance with the duffel bag. My uncle's hair was singed, his face blackened from the blast. He was doubled over, clutching the doorframe. 'Come on!' he panted at me. 'We have to get out of here!'

'My mom's in there!'

I stumbled towards the kitchen, screaming.

Howling.

Shrieking her name.

'She's gone, girl,' Donata shouted.

Jack's voice arced above hers. 'Come on!'

I ignored them, and this time my uncle didn't come back for me. They charged into the night, their bounty won.

Through the serving window I could see a thick wall of flames splitting the kitchen in two. It was licking the right-hand side by the stove and spreading along the wooden countertops, devouring the tablecloths and cork board. I pushed closer, my eyes watering against the scalding heat.

Nic and Luca were slumped against each other on the other side of the room. They had been flung backwards in the explosion. Luca's head lolled against his shoulder. His eyes were glazed. Nic was doubled over beside him. He wasn't moving either.

My mother wasn't with them. She had been close by the door when the explosion hit, and I strained to see if she had made it into the darkness, but the alley was impossibly far away and my vision was blurry from the thickness of the fire. I called out to her but the flames rallied against my words, swallowing them.

Grabbing a cloth from under the counter and holding it over my face, I wrenched the kitchen door open and the fire surged towards me, knocking me backwards. I covered my face as I skidded across the ground, hitting my head on the back of the counter. The doorway was a block of thick, black smoke, rolling over my head and out into the diner.

I rose to my knees and pushed through the doorway, keeping my head bent low beneath the smoke, and the rag tight against my mouth. The air was torturously dry and my lungs felt like they were crumbling inwards, blackened and parched. My mother wasn't inside – I couldn't see her through the flames and the smoke. I realized that soon she would be looking for me. I had to get out before she came back in. I ignored the burning in my chest and set a course for the boys, keeping left against the wall as I crawled across the hot tiles.

The fire roared like an untamed beast, surging ever closer as I pulled my body across the floor, cutting my hands on glass as jars popped and splintered around me. The back door had been blown off its hinges in the explosion. The alleyway beyond winked at me through crests of amber.

When I reached the boys Luca was half-conscious, his head bobbing off his chest as he tried to lift it. Nic was still crumpled in half. I grabbed Luca by the shoulders, shaking him.

'Luca!' I slapped him across the face. 'Wake up!'

He started to stir, his eyes igniting with a dull flicker of recognition.

I shook him again. 'Get up! We have to get out.'

The fire was creeping closer to our huddled circle, the flames growing hot against my back. Pots and pans were clanging to the ground, rolling against my ankles, and putrid smells were filling the air.

Luca was coughing violently. I pulled him by the shoulders and he pitched forwards, dragging himself to his knees.

We turned to Nic, scrabbling on either side of him. Luca lifted his brother's crumpled torso up so that he was facing forwards. His eyes were shut and his forehead was mussed with black. Luca shook him, his movements frantic with dawning horror. What if he didn't wake up? What if the blast had been too much for him?

I squeezed Nic's hand to try and rouse him. Luca was shouting, but I couldn't hear what he was saying. I grabbed Nic's wrist and struggled to find his pulse. It ebbed faintly beneath my fingers.

There was an almighty smash behind me, and I lurched forwards as a light fixture split in half and came crashing to the ground. Shards embedded themselves in the backs of my arms.

I still couldn't hear Luca, but I could read his lips. 'We have to move him!'

I crawled over Nic's body and grabbed his left arm as Luca took hold of his right. We heaved together, falling on to our haunches and dragging him with us. I gritted my teeth, spluttering as smoke choked the oxygen from our lungs. We pushed backwards, where the flames were charring the presses above the stove. Nic was impossibly heavy. His arms and legs splayed against the floor, lolling over ash and dust as we inched towards the doorway. My eyes were so sore I could barely keep them open, but I could feel the coolness rippling somewhere nearby. We were almost there. If we could just make it to the threshold, my mother would help us pull him outside.

A cupboard burst into an explosion of orange and red and I jumped to the side. Luca twisted and fell against me. Nic's legs began to twitch. He lifted his head and it fell backwards until he was staring up at the ceiling. He blinked quickly, trying to orient himself. His mouth was falling open, and his chest lurched as he spluttered black mucus on to his shirt.

I could feel the cool air on the back of my neck. *Just five more steps. Ignore the heat. Don't think about the pain.* And then we were out, stumbling backwards into soaked trash and splashing puddles. Nic was on his side, his hand pressed against the dirt, trying to steady himself as he retched. Luca had doubled over against the dumpster.

I lifted my head, squinting into the darkness. All I could see was red. The fire had robbed me of my senses. I blinked hard. There was nothing but trash, and me and Nic and Luca. And . . . there was no one else.

'Mom?' I floundered into the alley as I scanned the darkness, the flames still imprinting in my vision like stencils. 'Mom?'

There was no moisture in my throat, no energy left to move my tongue. She couldn't hear me, not over the thunder and the fire and . . . it didn't matter. Because she wasn't here – she wasn't outside. She wasn't here!

I turned around. The doorway was half-enveloped by flames but I could see a way into the smoke. I was small enough to clear it. I charged, throwing myself into the amber hole and spreadeagling myself across the ground.

Behind me, Luca was screaming my name.

I set my sights on the island in the centre. Hungry flames were choking down its wooden base. There was a narrow passageway but the unlit space was dwindling rapidly. I started crawling towards the island, circling the pocket of fire. Already, my cheeks were scalded red-raw and my eyelids were beginning to droop. My head felt heavy, rolling forwards from my neck. But I could swear I heard a voice, a quiet tinkling amidst the inferno. Was she calling my name?

I forced myself further into the heat. Was that her shoe, right there, through the flames? Had she been wearing sneakers? I forced my eyes open, searching for the mirage. I was beaten back again, the heat pouring over me like boiling water. The fire was at my elbows, stabbing me.

I reached the other side of the island. Someone was definitely calling my name. Was it her? Was I close? I could only see the floor, tiles mussed with smudges of black. The countertops had collapsed on themselves, shooting splinters of wood into the centre of the kitchen. Knives and forks nipped and jabbed at me as I crawled over them. Trickles of blood trailed down my arms and sizzled in the heat.

There. That foot again. I was trapped behind the flames, and the spark of white rubber was unmoving.

'Mom,' I called out, but there was nothing but smoke spluttering out of me. The room was pressing down on me, pinning me to the floor.

Somewhere over my shoulder, someone was yelling at me. It wasn't her. It was harder, deeper, further away. I was fixating on the shoe, trying to keep my eyes open. It was impossible. Everything was amber. Searing, white-hot, burning, shrieking amber. I was choking, but if I could just get to that shoe, I could grab her leg. I could wake her up. She would come back to me. We would crawl out of here together.

The shouting soared above the fire. There was so much screaming and it was closer now. Was it coming from me? From her? I could barely tell.

Where did the shoe go?

There!

I lunged but the fire soared, whipping at me, and I collapsed behind the flames. My lungs filled with smoke and I gasped, my body lurching for fresh air. There was none. I pulled my head up, searching, but it was too heavy. It flopped back down.

Her foot had disappeared behind streams of red and orange. Had it been a foot at all?

Something cracked and I was forced down, my cheeks smashing against the floor. I had lost direction. It hurt to suck in what little air was left. The flames were surrounding me in a circle. Which way was out? I scrabbled across the tiles, shrinking tight into a ball. I could feel the flames licking at my bare skin.

'Mom!'

Nothing came out.

'Someone help us!'

Clammy hands grabbed my ankles, pulling me backwards. Was she behind me? I couldn't remember what direction she was in. Voices surged around me. There was yelling, arguing. The hands didn't belong to her – these hands were coarse, their grip tight against my seething skin.

I clawed forward again, dropping my body against the floor. The hands were pulling me back. They moved to my waist and then my shoulders. I coasted backwards, my body scraping off the tiles.

'No,' I gasped. 'No. No.'

A sliver of warm air rushed into my lungs, but everything was still glowing. The ground was cool against my cheek. My eyelids drooped. I would rest here, just for a moment. I would let sleep take me from this nightmare. I was in a dream, and the dream was scalding me alive.

CHAPTER THIRTY-SEVEN

SIRENS

Wind beat down on my weathered body. I lurched and something rolled down my chin. The air was too cold to choke in. My head felt like it was splitting in two. Aches pulsed through my limbs, sticking me to the ground.

Think. Concentrate. I tried to switch my brain back on.

The ground was rough beneath my legs. The pressure was gone from my chest. The back of my head was scratching against something. I was on my back. Yes.

The lights behind my eyes were still blazing, but the roaring was somewhere behind me. The heat was close, but not like it was before. Wind was pushing hair across my face. It stuck to my lips. Drops of water pricked my cheeks. It was raining. I was outside. Yes. There was a chorus of new sounds soaring into the night.

Sirens. I tried to imagine what a siren was. *Ambulances. Fire trucks. Police cars.* We were safe.

'Sophie!' That familiar voice, silky like honey. *Nic. Yes, that's right. Nic is here.*

There was more noise – clanging, shouting. There were discussions – serious, angry discussions. A female voice. 'Sophie? Sophie, can you hear me?'

My mother?

No. Not her.

There were more words, important words, falling around my ears. I strained to listen. Smoke inhalation. Gas leak. Explosion. One more. One more left. *One more left inside.*

My attention snapped. I was falling away from reality, into something else. My limbs stopped aching. Everything was weightless. The voices were drifting far away from me, the warmth barely reaching me now.

I fell down, down into blackness.

And then light was flickering. My mother's voice beckoned me towards her. The fire surrounded her, but it wasn't hot any more.

'Sophie? Can you hear me?'

I stumbled forwards, falling at her feet. She knelt down to me, her big blue eyes swarming with tears. Her lips were moving but I couldn't hear her voice. 'Sophie, can you open your eyes for me?'

She pulled me into her. I wrapped my arms around her neck, expecting the softness of her hair and the gentle scent of her lavender perfume. Her arms were like reeds, slimy and cold. They fell away, withering to the ground. I frowned, pulling back. Her hair was stringy and damp, her perfume like wet earth. I tasted ash in my mouth. I blinked and her face disappeared. I turned and the blackness engulfed me.

'Sophie?'

Inside, my body cracked and splintered. Heat surged through me, scalding me. Outside, my arms and legs sprawled in puddles, shaking with cold.

Where was she?

Where was I?

CHAPTER THIRTY-EIGHT

TRAGEDY

GAS EXPLOSION DESTROYS FAMILY DINER; OWNER'S WIFE PERISHES IN FIRE

One person was killed and three more were injured in an explosion and resulting fire that levelled local family diner, Gracewell's, in Cedar Hill on Sunday night.

Celine Gracewell, wife of owner Michael Gracewell, was present at the time of the explosion, and was pronounced dead at the scene. Her daughter, along with two of her friends, was also inside the restaurant. It is reported that Gracewell's daughter attempted to go back into the fire to rescue her mother, but was unable to.

Preliminary investigations suggest a gas leak was to blame for the destruction, setting off a fire which spread rapidly through the rest of the building. Police have yet to determine an official cause for the explosion, and investigations are ongoing. They are also looking to talk to Jack Gracewell, acting manager of the diner, who has been not been contactable since the incident.

Located on the corner of Foster and Oak in downtown Cedar Hill, Gracewell's has been a favourite family establishment for over fifteen years.

Celine Gracewell, 43, a local dressmaker and part-owner of the establishment, was standing close to the gas leak at the time of the blast, and lost her life on impact, it has been reported. Since the explosion, neighbours and friends have been leaving tributes at the site. As city workers and electric utility experts tore through the rubble this morning, many gathered in the street to pay their respects.

Ursula Nguyen, assistant manager at the diner for ten years, was inconsolable as she laid her wreath among the others. Of Celine Gracewell, she said, 'She was a wonderful person. Always smiling, always happy. It's such a loss for the whole neighborhood. I'm devastated for her daughter.'

Rita Bailey, long-time resident of Cedar Hill, was visibly stunned as she visited the site to see the destruction, commenting, 'I'm reeling. How could anyone have seen this coming? This is such a tragic thing to happen.'

Details of Celine Gracewell's memorial service have not been released. It is not known whether the diner will be rebuilt.

PART V

'I come to lead you to the other shore;
into the eternal darkness;
into fire and into ice.'

Dante Alighieri, 'Inferno'

CHAPTER THIRTY-NINE

DARKNESS

They told me I was in shock.

I didn't feel the shock. There was just emptiness, like someone had tipped me over and rattled me until everything fell out. My arms were red, the skin behind my wrists rising in angry blisters towards my elbows. I couldn't feel it. I studied the white gauze as it encircled my flesh, pressing against the angry wound. A nurse cut the ends of my singed hair. They put salve on my ears. I hadn't noticed they were burnt. They gave me tablets and I took them.

When they talked to me, their tones dipped, and I watched chapped lips moving around exaggerated syllables. *Is there someone we can call?* Brows creased. *Do you understand what I'm saying to you, Sophie?* A gentle hand laid on top of mine. *Do you have someone you can stay with?*

A policewoman escorted me to my house. I don't remember what time it was when I shut the door behind me. I trudged upstairs, my brain still thick with fog. I sat beneath the showerhead, feeling cold beads sprinkle away the smoke that clung to my skin. My body was blotched with red. The shampoo lathered away the rancid scent of rotting and I emerged, naked and zombie-like, into an empty house without understanding why it was empty.

As morning dawned, grief reached its fingers inside my head and plucked me from my deadened sleep. Understanding hit me like a slash of sunlight through my curtains and I sprang into wakefulness, coughing black sludge across my pillow.

Screams ripped from my chest as the pain soared, every memory colliding at once until she was everywhere, her face etched behind my eyelids when I blinked.

I collapsed on to the floor, curling my arms tight around my knees until I was as small as I could make myself. Tears pooled inside me, blooming across my chest, but I couldn't get them out. I couldn't weep or cry and the tears bled inside me, icy and unshed.

I slept alone. I missed the soft padding of my mother's slippers in the hallway, the appearance of her face at my doorway wishing me goodnight. The darkness was a gift, but the silence that came with it was crushing.

CHAPTER FORTY
THE PHONE CALL

The ceiling blurred in and out of focus. I rolled out of bed and stood in front of my wardrobe. The grief resurfaced with sharp urgency, jabbing at my sides. I sank to the ground, anchoring myself against the carpet, and waited for the tears that never came. Instead they puffed up inside my chest, pushing outwards like a thousand tiny hands.

There were voices downstairs. It was late and the sun was starting to dip. It took me a minute to recall what day it was – Saturday. I used to love Saturdays. Pots were clanging in the kitchen. Mrs Bailey was making dinner again. She wasn't a good cook but she had come by every day since it had happened. She had rallied, and I felt bad for judging her so harshly in the past. Millie was downstairs. She had stuck by me every day and even though I could find little to say to her

– to anyone – the familiarity of her accent wafting through the house brought me some comfort in the darkest moments.

I scrolled through my phone. They had found it in the parking lot after that night. They said it got separated from me in the blast – the technology somehow miraculously surviving intact – but I knew better. He had left it there for me. *Don't think about him.*

I had four missed calls from an unknown number. I clicked back into the home screen. My mother and I stared back at me, flashing identical cheesy smiles, our heads touching against each other so that our hair blended into one golden halo.

The pressure on my chest tightened. I stowed my phone away and scrambled back into bed. There was no point in getting up when the day was already disappearing. I turned on to my side and stared unblinkingly at the wall. Flames started to creep into my mind, the searing hotness pulsing through my bandaged arms. I blinked until my head pounded from the effort and the flames melted away.

The house phone was ringing downstairs. A fit of coughing seized me, and I spluttered into my pillow, trying to stifle it. I came away from the fabric feeling woozy. The pressure intensified, closing around my chest until my lungs felt like they were being crushed into small papery balls. I shrivelled up, pulling my knees into my chest and bowing my head against them.

'Are you asleep?' Millie was at my door. I raised my head and blinked her into focus. Her hair was piled on her head, her face drawn tight with exhaustion.

'I'm awake.'

She edged inside, the phone clutched in her hand. 'It's your dad again . . .'

'No.'

She perched against my bedside table. 'Soph, you need to talk to him.'

I shook my head. My voice was unsteady. 'I can't, Mil.'

Her face crumpled, the concern turning to anguish. 'You need each other right now, Soph. You can't go through this alone. You shouldn't have to.'

I imagined what it would be like to have my father there with me, to hug him and not have to worry about prison guards pulling us apart. What a wonderful thing to stand against the tide of grief and anchor ourselves to each other. But that was before everything. Now, when I pictured him, I saw Vince Marino. I saw a liar.

'I'm not alone,' I mumbled. 'I have you.'

She clutched my hand in hers. 'I don't know what to do, Soph. I don't know how to make it better. Please.' She squeezed my hand. 'You need to let him in.' It sounded reasonable, but Millie didn't know what I knew. She hadn't seen what I had seen inside the diner. The switchblades. The ruby ring. My father had been feeding me lies my whole life. He wore his mask so carefully I had never thought to look beneath it.

She replaced her hand in mine with the cordless phone. 'Talk to him,' she urged. 'He doesn't get a lot of time on these calls and he's been trying you all week, Soph. Please talk to your dad.'

She left, and I looked at the phone in my hand, listening to the faint droning of a man I didn't really know at all.

'Soph? It's Dad. Are you there?'

I opened the locker drawer and took out Evelina's ring. I had stuck it in my pocket during a moment of madness at the diner. It was the only thing that had made it home with me. Everything else was rubble and ash.

'Soph? I know you're there. Can you pick up, please?'

I studied the ring as it glinted in the palm of my hand. The ruby was blood-red. *Sempre*. But nothing lasts for ever.

'Come on, Soph.'

I pressed the receiver to my ear. 'Hello, Vince.'

I caught the end of his sharp inhale. 'Soph—'

'Hey, here's a funny thing,' I interrupted. 'I'm a *Marino*.'

'I know you're angry—'

'And did you *know*,' I continued, my voice rising, 'there was a secret safe in the diner?'

My dad's breathing quickened, and I could almost feel his panic thundering down the line. 'Listen, I've applied for furlough. I'm going to try and get out so we can—'

'And did you *know*,' I said, my voice rising higher still, 'that before your Marino *family* burnt down our livelihood, I found a bunch of Falcone trophies? A switchblade for every unmarked grave, I'd bet.' I drowned out his answers, getting shriller and louder. 'Did you know there was a ruby ring in there? Did you know that ring belongs to Felice Falcone's missing wife? Did you know there's a list of Falcone targets written in your handwriting? Did you know Angelo Falcone was actually murdered? And did you know that all my life you've been one *huge fucking liar?*

His reply was lost in the air. I hurled the phone at the wall and it broke, falling to the floor in bits of plastic.

I slammed the ring down on my bedside table. I thought that would have made me feel better, but it didn't.

But at least now he knew.

Now there were no more lies between us.

CHAPTER FORTY-ONE
THE UNWELCOME

Millie crept into my room half an hour later. Her eyes flicked to the broken phone, narrowing in understanding as she stepped over it. 'So . . . that didn't go well, then,' she surmised.

'You have no idea.'

She huffed a sigh and cocked her head, studying my pathetic, crumpled form. Eventually she said, 'I think you should try and get out of bed.'

This was not the first time she had suggested this. It wasn't even the tenth time.

I stared at the white flecks in my fingernails. 'What's the point?'

She sat down at the end of my bed. 'Living, Soph. *Living* is the point.'

'I am living,' I mumbled.

'No. You're existing.'

I flicked my gaze up, but I couldn't manage the half-smile I was going for. 'What's the difference?'

'You know the difference,' she said softly. She seemed so small and tired at the end of my bed. Her hoodie sleeves were pulled over her hands and her face was drawn. Guilt swelled inside me.

'You don't have to spend all your time here with me, Mil.' I gestured around me – at my messy room, my messy life. 'I know it's depressing. I know I'm not exactly performing in the friend department. I haven't been for a while.'

'Soph,' she chastised. 'You know I'm not going anywhere. What kind of friend would I be then?'

'The kind I'm being?' I shrugged. 'You shouldn't have to be in the darkness with me.'

'I think the whole point of being a good friend *is* being in the darkness. I'll be your light, until you can be it yourself again. How about that?'

I mustered a smile, and for a moment it felt like my heart was swelling just a little. 'You're very good at this,' I told her.

'Well.' She flashed me a grin. 'I do like to overachieve at all the important things.'

I leant back against my pillow and let the silence fall around us. Millie shifted, examining me in the falling light, and I knew it was coming even before she said it – the inevitable. 'So,' she began, tracing circles on the duvet. 'School starts back next week.'

She might as well have dropped a fresh heap of trash on my face. I grimaced. 'I'd rather gouge my eyes out and eat them.'

'It's our senior year. It'll be fun.' There was little, if any, conviction in her reply.

I imagined the dull thud of my feet in the hallways, the thunderous clanging of lockers between classes, the mindless nattering filling the air, the soul-destroying existence of my life inside those walls. If I was a source of interest before, I'd be the main attraction now. 'I'm not ready.'

Millie gripped my leg through the duvet. 'You have to *make* yourself ready, Soph. You have to grit your teeth and do it, you know? It's the last year. And then everything changes. You can do it. We both can.'

I didn't answer her. The conversation had tired me out, and I didn't feel like wading into the matter of school just then. After a while Millie accepted defeat and rolled off the end of my bed. I burrowed further in, feeling vaguely embarrassed by my petulance. She got up and crossed over to the doorway. I could feel her hovering, her fingers scratching lightly on the wood.

'What is it?' I asked.

She measured her words, starting out slowly like she was still unsure of whether to say anything at all. 'I know you told me you don't want to talk about that night yet. And I've tried to respect that. But I don't see how I can keep this from you any longer . . .'

I sat up. 'Keep what from me?'

'The Falcone boys are downstairs. They've been here for a while, actually, but I knew you didn't want any reminders of . . . of what happened . . .' She trailed off, examining her shoes. 'I wasn't going to tell you, but I think you should know. They won't go away. They don't want to leave you unprotected . . . in case . . .'

In case he *comes back for me.*

Millie had thought me crazy for not telling the police about Jack and Donata. I had considered it, in my darkest moments, but I wanted two things that snitching couldn't assure me: a fate worse than prison for them, and my own survival.

Millie looked uneasy. 'Nic says he won't leave until he sees you. Mrs Bailey has been swatting him with tea towels all week.'

All week.

I frowned at my duvet, zeroing in on the swirls. The pain had regressed to a dull thud in the base of my chest again. I hadn't thought about Nic much since the fire, but there were things that needed to be said, and maybe it was time to deal with that. 'Can you tell him to come up?'

Millie bounded into the hallway and down the stairs. 'Nic?' she called, and for the first time I registered the low timbre of a new voice and realized it had probably been there all along.

When Nic appeared in my doorway he was paler than I'd ever seen him. His hair was messy and his jawline was marked with the dark shadow of week-old stubble, making him seem much older. He had a bandage running the entire length of his arm and another wrapped around his hand.

He didn't move to come inside, though I could tell by the quiet shuffling that he wanted to. What must I have seemed like to him? A wild animal waiting to pounce, or something wounded and caged?

He fiddled with the cross around his neck, pulling it up and down the chain so that it made a faint grinding noise in the silence.

'How are you?' The words rasped in his throat. The smoke had gotten him bad.

I spread my arms wide by way of explanation: I looked like I had been dragged through a field of manure backwards and then dressed in a dumpster by a blind person.

'I'm sorry,' he said softly. 'I'm sorry she's gone.'

Don't think about her. I scrunched my thoughts down and looked at Nic instead. It was impossible not to think about the last time I had seen him. I remembered the dumpster-groove in the kitchen's metal door, the way Nic's eyes had flashed as he faced off with my uncle. *Don't think about Jack.*

I had dragged Nic's lifeless body away from the fire that destroyed my life . . . *Don't think about the fire.* I had gone to help him instead of making sure my mother was safe. I should have checked, but I didn't. I should have helped her first, but I didn't. *Don't think about her.* He had pulled me away from her white sneakers when I was almost close enough to touch them.

'Sophie?' Nic's body was dipping across the threshold, his fingers digging into the doorframe.

'What?'

He blinked, surprised by my bluntness. 'I'm worried about you.'

Now that he was standing across from me, I realized I didn't want to see him. All our memories were bad ones – I couldn't remember the good ones, couldn't pretend his kisses would make all the darkness go away. Everything was too clear now.

'You don't have to be a Marino any more,' he said quietly. 'Not if you don't want to be.'

'I was never a Marino,' I shot back. 'You know that.'

He looked away, sheepish. He had thought I lied to him all along – I could see it in his expression.

'And I sure as hell am not a Marino now,' I added, hearing the venom in my words.

'Come back with me,' he said. 'We'll avenge your mother together. We'll kill them for everything they've taken from us. You'll have your revenge, I promise.'

What a way to comfort someone in the depths of grief – to promise death and destruction – and yet I felt charged by it. This was Nic – there were things he could never give me, empathy he could never really feel, but this, *this* was his world and of all the promises he had ever made and unmade, I knew he would keep this one. And that brought its own set of complications, because as much as he would do this for me, deep down it would always truly be for him.

'Gino,' I remembered. 'They shot Gino.'

Nic's expression darkened. 'He's in hospital. He's hanging in there.'

'Oh.' I nodded, the barest trace of relief rising inside me. A small mercy. 'Good.'

'They'll pay for that too,' he said, his voice hard.

I looked at him – at every part of him, really, wholly – for the first time. I looked past the cheekbones, the searing eyes and the gentle curve of his lips. I had seen his body come alive, his fingers constricting around throats, his hand wielding a knife, his actions charged with murderous intent.

His T-shirt was creased slightly above his waistline. Even now, in times of mourning, he carried a loaded gun. He was an assassin – he had killed before and he would kill again and he wouldn't lose any sleep over it. Nic was raw, heart-thudding passion personified, and he couldn't measure it out for certain parts of his life and deny the others. He cared about me, sure, but he cared about other things, too. And they were darker, violent things that made up who he really was at his core. He had dumped Sara Marino in the lake. He had carved words of warning into her skin. And here he was, glittering in the duskiness – an angel sprung from hell.

Yes, I *would* say something to him; I would say the only thing pushing against my brain. I would say the thing that needed to be said.

The words came out clear and loud. 'You hesitated.'

'What?'

'You didn't drop your gun.'

'What are you talking about?'

Carefully, I extracted the memory from That Night. 'In the diner, when you and Luca came in through the back door, you both raised your guns. I looked inside the barrel of yours as you aimed it with full confidence at my head.'

Comprehension moved through Nic's features, relaxing them. 'But I wouldn't have shot you.'

'My head was in the way.'

'My aim is very good.'

'That's the wrong answer.'

'What's the right answer?'

'The fact that you don't know says it all.'

'I'm a good shot,' he protested.

I glared at him. 'I'd like to be alone now.'

'What?'

'You've seen me. I'm clearly alive. I am not communicating

with any "fucking Marinos" as you call them. I am putting food in my mouth and consuming water regularly. You can go home now.'

'But I want to help you, Sophie. This isn't good—'

'Nic.' I sighed. 'There's nothing you can do for me.'

'I love you,' he said, pleadingly.

The words hit me right in the chest. He had never said that to me before, and now here it was, laid bare, in the lowest moment of my life. There was nothing but truth between us – the cold, hard truth, and those three little words that suddenly felt so huge. I had wanted to hear that for as long as I could remember. I had wanted someone to look at me the way he was looking at me just then. But now that I had it . . . it felt hollow. It felt wrong. And I knew, deep in my gut, that I wasn't in love with him. I never had been. I'd been infatuated with the idea of love, and at a time when I had so little of it in my life, he had waltzed right through my defences and become that idea. I didn't know what or who he really was beneath that.

'You don't know me,' I said quietly. 'Not really, not properly. Our whole time together has been about trying to make it work against all these crazy odds. It's been about obstacles, not about each other.'

'I know what I feel,' he said resolutely.

A little broken part of me wanted to laugh. 'You couldn't even *look* at me when you heard I was a Marino.'

'I was caught off guard,' he protested.

'When you love someone, you don't lie to them. You don't point a gun at their head. And you don't turn your back on them when they're at their most vulnerable.' I swallowed hard. 'That's not love.'

He shook his head.

'I think you love the idea of me,' I whispered. Saying the words out loud hurt, but there was a tinge of relief in it too, as if the twisted fairy tale I'd been trying to make work was over, and I was OK. I had stopped trying to change him, trying to change myself to fit with him. 'But we're not right for each other, are we? We end up lying to each other, *hurting* each other.'

Nic ground his knuckles against the doorframe. 'I told you. I would never hurt you.'

'There's more than one way to hurt someone.'

'Yeah.' His face twisted, from confusion to something else that I couldn't place. 'There is.'

I scrubbed my hands across my face, feeling exhausted all of a sudden.

'We can talk about this again,' he said quietly. 'When you're feeling better.'

I didn't want to look at him any more. How could I, knowing I had gone to him when I should have gone to my mother? How could I lean on him with the image of his pointed gun burnt into my mind? He would always put his duties before everything else. He was a soldier first and a person second.

When I didn't reply, he sucked in a breath and said, 'We've heard your uncle and Donata are in New York meeting suppliers. I don't know what their plans are, but when you're feeling up to it, I think we should talk about your safety.'

'He won't come back here,' I said. 'Not after what he did. There's too much heat on him.'

'I wouldn't be so sure.'

I slammed back against my pillow, fear and rage competing inside me. 'I need to be alone right now, Nic.'

'I'll come back when you're feeling better.' He hovered in the doorway for a moment longer. 'And Sophie? Thank you for saving my life.'

In place of hers, I thought, as bitterness twisted inside me. What was I supposed to say to that? *You're welcome*? It didn't matter. He had disappeared into the hallway. Something sour curled in my stomach. Skirting around that night had opened the gates, and the images were slithering into my mind like snakes, and I had to shut them out and block my ears to keep them away. *Not yet. Not now.*

I waited until I heard the soft thud of Nic's feet reach the bottom of the stairs, then I buried my head between my knees and rocked back and forth in my bed, trying to calm my thoughts. *Think of something else. Think of anything else.* It was so hard; every part of me was bound up in my mother, in the diner, in my uncle. I dug my nails into my palms and concentrated on the little half-moons of pain. The minutes ticked by, slowly, and the cloud inside me got heavier. The sun had disappeared. It was getting dark and there was a quiet touch of relief in it.

CHAPTER FORTY-TWO

THE BREAKDOWN

'Sophie?'

I snapped my head up.

Luca was standing in my room. He was so close to me his knees were brushing against my bed. How had I not sensed him before now?

I sat up, shrouded inside the bedcovers. His hair was swept back from his face so his blue eyes shone unnaturally in the duskiness. His mouth was quirked to one side, frowning, but otherwise he looked well. Smoke inhalation obviously agreed with him.

I didn't have the strength to be indignant. 'I want to be alone, Luca.'

He glanced at the door, his teeth nipping across his lower lip. 'Why have you fashioned yourself like an Eskimo?'

'Excuse me?'

He gestured at the duvet pulled over my head and around my shoulders. 'That can't be good for your burns. You must be incredibly overheated.'

'I'm fine.'

He pinned me with his gaze. 'Are you?'

'I don't recall inviting you up here.'

He lowered himself to the floor and sat on my carpet, leaning back on the palms of his hands. 'Come on, Sophie. You should know well enough by now that I make a habit of showing up to places I'm not invited.'

His gaze was appraising. I had the horrible sense that he was leaning right over the waters of my soul. It occurred to me then, rather inappropriately, that this was the first time he had spoken more than a few words to me since he had twined his fingers in my hair and crushed his lips against mine. *Stop.*

I regressed further into my Eskimo-blanket. 'What do you think you're doing here?'

'I'm waiting,' he said.

I shook the duvet off and tossed it behind me. 'What are you waiting for?'

'This.'

'*This?*'

'Conversation, Sophie. You need to talk to someone.'

For one precious, golden minute, there was nothing but incredulity filling me up. '*Now* you want to talk to me?' I said.

He screwed his face up. 'What do you mean by that?'

'Nothing's changed,' I said. 'I'm still a Marino.'

He gestured at himself. 'And I'm a Falcone. Who cares?'

365

'You did, Luca. That day at your house.' I wasn't really mad about that – it made sense, given everything – but it bore mentioning, especially since I sure as hell wasn't going to mention the *other* reason he acted so weird at the Council. '*You* cared,' I repeated, trying to shake off the sting that came with the memory.

He leant closer. 'You're damn right I cared,' he growled. 'I cared that the Marino standing in front of my entire family with a red target on her forehead was the only Marino in the history of the world that I have ever and will ever care about.'

'Oh,' I said. Beneath the dull thud of grief there was something else flickering inside me. 'You didn't care about the . . . the name.'

'Not the name.' He held my gaze, unfaltering, unblinking. 'Just the girl.'

I looked at my hands interlocked on top of the duvet. 'You really aren't like them,' I murmured.

'No,' he said. 'I'm not.'

I thought of my own family. The safe, the switchblades, the ring. Evelina. God. The things I knew. The things I wished I *didn't* know.

I shook my head. 'If you knew how badly I'm tangled up in this Marino thing . . .' I trailed off, my words falling into breathlessness. It was too much to think about.

He offered me a conspiratorial smile. 'If you knew how badly I'm tangled up in this Falcone stuff . . .'

I grimaced. 'You know what I mean.'

'I'm not going to judge you,' he said. 'You're the same person you always were. So please,' he leant back again and this time his smile was soft, 'don't worry about all that other stuff, Marino.'

'OK, Falcone.' I scowled at him and he scowled right back. 'But I really just want to be by myself right now, so if you think I'm just going to sit here and spill my guts to you about what I'm feeling, then you're wrong.'

'That's fine.' He shrugged, looking past me towards the slivered gap in my curtains. 'Did you know it's going to be a blood moon tonight? You should open your curtains so you can see it.'

'Are you being for real right now?'

He raised his eyebrows, the movement making his eyes seem impossibly huge and bluer than ever. 'Have you never seen one?' he asked. 'The moon looks like it's been dipped in red paint and it glows so bright you can barely see the stars. It's one of those phenomena that remind you how—what? Why are you looking at me like that?'

'OK, Mufasa. I get it.'

Luca's mouth dropped open and I had the absurd feeling of laughter catching in my cheeks. 'Excuse me for trying to enlighten you about the wonders of this universe.'

'Don't waste your breath on me, Nature Nerd. Save it for the space documentary you so obviously want to make.'

He shook his head. 'See what happens when I try to be sincere? You stomp on my dreams.'

'I'm not stomping on them, I'm making fun of them. There's a difference.'

'Is there?'

'It's very subtle.'

'So are you going to let me finish?'

I was pulled back into myself, the amusement draining

from the ache in my cheeks. Had I been smiling? I frowned, scolding myself. I rubbed at my chest, trying to soothe the sudden roaring pain inside it, demanding to be felt.

Luca was talking again. What was his game plan? Did he really think I was interested in astrology at a time like this? 'What are you still doing here?' I interrupted. 'I mean, seriously.'

He fell out of his sentence. I watched him weigh his words, surprised at how accustomed I had become to the subtleties in his body language. 'We went through a big thing, Sophie. *You* went through a big thing.'

'So?'

'*So*?' he repeated with emphasis. 'I'm worried about you.'

'Don't.' The pang was growing deeper. I lay back and looked at the ceiling.

'You saved my life, Sophie. *Again*,' he added after a beat, like he couldn't quite believe it. I wasn't sure which shocked him more, the fact that he kept almost dying, or that *I* kept saving him.

'That's 2-1 to me,' I said, without feeling any amusement. 'You owe me a grand gesture.'

'I thought it was a bouquet.'

'One is a bouquet. Two is a grand gesture.'

'Name it.'

'Go away. Is that grand enough for you?'

'That's too grand.'

I exhaled noisily at the ceiling.

'So what's going on with that old lady in your kitchen? She's been here all week. I asked her if she was your grandmother and she called me a worthless heathen and told me to mind

368

my own business. Millie had to force her to let us inside and when Nicoli tried to make a sandwich she threw a fork at him. As someone who has thrown many forks at my brother I wouldn't advise it. He has a very bad temper . . .' Luca kept talking, filling the space with words upon words, waiting for me to bite.

I unbunched the duvet and pulled it over me again with a groan. He could sit in my room for ever and burn a hole in my carpet, but if he thought he could get me to open up to him he was wrong.

He changed tack. 'What did you say to Nicoli earlier? I've never seen him look so contrite. Was it the whole beard thing? It makes him look creepy, doesn't it? A couple more days and he'll turn into Rasputin. That's a historical reference, by the way. It's very funny, I assure you . . .'

I had done a history project on Rasputin. I smiled despite myself, then bit the inside of my cheeks and concentrated on the soreness as I made myself remember my mother's face.

Finally Luca fell silent, defeated by my stillness. I could still feel his presence. I smelt the faintness of his aftershave in the air. I was keenly aware of his every exhale, his every quiet movement.

He didn't budge, didn't even take out his phone. He just sat staring into the darkness, and for what? After ten minutes I sat up again and burrowed over my duvet, freeing myself from its clinging heat. I sat facing him on the bed. 'Can't you take a hint?'

'I can,' he said. 'But that doesn't mean I have to follow through on it.'

'Well, it's inappropriate for you to be here. This is my bedroom.'

He lifted his brows. 'You've been in *my* bedroom.'

There. So he remembered. He didn't seem to care, but at least he hadn't forgotten about it. 'Sorry,' he said quickly, dipping his head and running his hand across his jaw. 'I shouldn't have said that.'

We sat in silence. After a little while, he turned away from me and lay back against the carpet, folding his arms behind his head. I studied his profile, the sureness of his brow line, his straight-edged nose. Then I turned away too. What a time to be so superficial and distractible.

I thought of my mother again. I remembered being six years old and missing the ice cream truck when it came by my house. I had chased after it and just as it disappeared around the bend at the end of my street, I tripped. I started to cry as blood dribbled down my legs. My mother was on the phone to one of her clients at the time and had been watching from the window. She rushed outside and folded me into her arms. I could smell lavender and sunscreen. *Don't cry, sweetheart.* We drove to the corner store and filled a basket with every colour popsicle imaginable. At home we packed the freezer until it was overflowing. She smiled at my blue-frozen lips. *Now you'll always have backup, so you don't have to chase the truck if you miss it.*

There – that pain again, sharp and twisting. I gasped, falling back into myself.

'Are you thinking about her?' Luca asked.

I didn't answer.

I heard him shift and caught his outline in my peripheral

370

vision. He was sitting up. 'They say internalized grief takes longer to heal.'

I opened my mouth and then shut it again. I had nothing to say.

His voice twisted into something soft and sombre. 'When my father died I didn't cry for three weeks. It's not that I wasn't sad. I was sadder than I ever imagined a human being could be. It felt like something was burrowing inside me, trying to claw its way out. Even gunshot wounds pale in comparison.' He smiled a little, wryly. 'But for some reason I couldn't talk about it, I couldn't cry about it. It's like everything was trapped inside me, and the longer it stayed that way the more it felt like it was ripping me up. I kept wondering what was wrong with me, why I couldn't grieve the way my brothers were. Why I couldn't just feel it and . . . let it out.'

'Why couldn't you?'

'I don't know,' he said. 'I think I was too scared to cry. I never knew how much grief felt like fear. I was terrified of my life without my father in it. He was a part of my identity, and when he left it was like he took a chunk of me with him.'

'The best bit,' I whispered, feeling a deep thud of empathy.

'Yes,' he murmured. 'The best bit.'

'Do you think he did?'

'Maybe.' He jerked his head. We still weren't looking at each other, but I could see most of his face now. His brow was furrowed. He was lost in another time and place. 'But at the time I never considered that he had left behind a part of him, too, in me.'

'His best bit?'

I caught the corner of his smile. 'I like to think so.'

Slivers of moonlight were peeking through the gap in my curtains, streaking across the carpet. I could see Luca's hands bathed white beneath it.

I found myself moving closer, straining to see him and wishing he would look at me. 'Does it get easier?'

'I don't know,' he admitted. 'They say it gets better but I think the pain becomes bearable not because it's quieter or lessened, but because you get used to it being there. Life goes on, and you go with it.'

I frowned, rubbing the pain beneath my chest. 'I can't imagine I'll ever get used to this,' I conceded.

He turned to watch me in the darkness. The moonlight fell across his face, alighting the deep cobalt in his eyes. 'You'd be surprised at what you're made of.'

'I don't think I will be.'

'I do.'

My throat was starting to feel wobbly. 'How do I do it?'

Luca got to his knees so that we were leaning towards each other at eye level. He didn't touch me, but something inside made me feel like maybe he wanted to. I wanted him to. His hands were hovering close to mine. 'You embrace the pain, Sophie. Don't fear it. Let it wash over you. Use it as fuel to spur you on.'

'I don't want to think about that night.'

'You have to, sooner or later.'

'I should have saved her.'

'You couldn't have.'

'I didn't try hard enough.'

'Sophie.' Luca came closer still. I was overwhelmed by his smell, fresh and familiar. My fingers were starting to shake. I could feel the walls starting to buckle, the things I had kept hidden beginning to emerge once more. 'When I pulled you out of that fire you were nearly dead. Even if you had gotten to her it would have been too late for both of you.'

I gaped at him, and something flashed at the back of my mind. I remembered the feeling of hands on my ankles, my shoulders, my waist, dragging me from her. '*You* pulled me out?'

He fell on to his haunches. 'Who did you think it was?'

'Why didn't you let me get to her?'

'You wouldn't have been able to.'

My voice changed. 'Why did you take me away from her?'

His voice changed too. Anger, fear, insistence strained his words. 'Because you were burning alive. You did the thing I told you not to do. You jumped off the cliff.'

'I was trying to save her!'

'You were killing yourself!'

The walls were coming down and my mind was exploding with that night. 'She was calling out to me.'

Luca's movements changed. They became slower, more deliberate. 'She wasn't calling you.'

'I heard her.'

'The fire does strange things to your senses.'

'You're wrong.' I kept thinking about those white sneakers.

Luca placed his hands on either side of my legs, his fingers curling in the sheets. 'Sophie,' he said softly, 'your mother lost her life in the explosion. She was too close to the stove when it happened.'

I rose up, away from him. I was disconnecting, the room spinning as memories crashed into me. 'I could have saved her but you took me away from her!'

He was shaking his head.

The fire burnt inside my mind. My arms were stinging. I could taste singed hair across my lips. Before the fire there was the explosion, before the explosion there was the gas and before the gas there was Jack. Before that . . . there was everything else. A raging war. I grasped at the thread of understanding. 'They lured you to them. They knew you'd come to protect your brothers.'

'Yes.'

How could he remain so calm? Wasn't he thinking about all the things that I was? Wasn't he feeling the heat of the memories like flames?

'You're supposed to be smarter than that.'

'I know.'

'My mother is dead.' That was the first time I ever said it out loud. It felt like I was flaying myself. The backs of my eyes were stinging.

'I know,' he said gently.

'They wanted to destroy you. They wanted to teach me a lesson. And they killed her to do it. She wasn't supposed to be there.' Everything was colliding and I felt the white-hot edge of rage burn inside me. The words sprang from me, strung together in hurried sentences. 'If you and Nic hadn't come in they wouldn't have done it. I told you Donata was coming. I told you she was planning something but you couldn't walk away – you couldn't back down! You had to risk everything for some stupid game of honour that means nothing in the end! If you hadn't been there at the diner, *watching*, waiting for them, trying to *hurt them* instead of trying to protect yourselves, then this wouldn't have happened. If you Falcones hadn't murdered Sara Marino – if you didn't *insist* on killing *everything and everyone* – then my mom wouldn't be dead now. You shouldn't have followed them. You shouldn't have forced your way into the diner. Why couldn't you have just left it all alone?'

Luca was getting to his feet.

I stood up, too. 'You don't get to leave before you hear this,' I shouted.

He just stood there, his chest squared towards me. His gaze was unfaltering. 'I know,' he said. 'Say whatever you need to say.'

'Don't patronize me!' My face was wet and I realized with surprise that I was crying. Tears were dripping down my neck, soaking into the collar of my T-shirt. 'Ever since your family came into my life, everything has gone wrong!'

'I'm sorry.'

'And now I have nothing.' I was sobbing so hard the words were catching in my throat. I coughed and it turned to wheezing, and I doubled over, spluttering, on to the bed.

Luca moved his hand towards me but I slapped it away. 'You've destroyed my whole life.'

'That was never our intention, Sophie.'

I backed up, hitting my knees on the bedside table. I dragged my hands across my face, wiping away the moisture. 'You've obliterated me.'

He edged towards me. 'I know what it's like, Sophie.'

'No.' I prodded his chest. 'You don't know. You gamble with people's lives all the time. You've probably taken as many as you've grieved. You are used to the possibility of death, you live inside the nearness of it. My mother and I lived in *this* house, in *this* peaceful place where we worried about pork chop dinners and making rent and getting the car fixed and making sure the dishwasher didn't break down again! She didn't deserve to die the way she did.'

'I'm not trying to—'

'You have brothers and cousins and uncles and a mother who loves you!' I cut in. 'Even with all the bad things you do, you have a whole family to turn to, and I don't have anyone.'

'Sophie—'

'I thought you'd protect us from them,' I choked out.

'We *will* protect you, Sophie. Come home with me,' he urged, 'where he can't get to you any more.'

'Don't you see?' I said, hearing my voice rise to a manic level. 'He's *already* gotten to me.' I pushed Luca and he stumbled backwards, clutching at his side. His wound. Pain flared behind his eyes.

'Just get it out,' he said, gritting his teeth. 'Get it all out.'

'Get it out?' I said. 'Get out my "feelings", is that what you mean? How about this—' I pushed against him. He faltered, his hands clutched harder around his torso. 'I.' I shoved him again and he turned sharply and backed against the wardrobe. 'Hate.' I pushed him. 'You.'

He ground his teeth. 'OK.'

'Not OK,' I shouted at him. 'NONE OF THIS IS OK.' I curled both my hands inside his T-shirt, scrunching the fabric in my fist. 'Why did I save you? Only to have it lead to this!'

I shoved him and he hit his head against the wardrobe. His eyes grew, two big expanses of startling blue, shadowed by his frown. I felt a flicker of something unpleasant – regret,

376

remorse? I hadn't meant what I'd said – not really – but the words weren't coming from a logical place.

'I'm sorry,' he said, breathless.

I stared at my hands still curled in his shirt. I fell back from him, examining my fingers. They were twitching in and out of fists. I looked at Luca. His body was dipping towards his injured half. His lids were at half-mast. How many ways had I hurt him? How far could I go? He was *letting* me – even though he could stop me easily, he hadn't. I had come at him with every drop of venom I had in me and I felt none of the relief I had expected. I felt like a damaged version of myself. My mother was gone, and in her absence I was bitter and cruel.

A familiar feeling of panic took hold of me. I didn't know what to do, how to make him go away, how to tell him this wasn't really about him at all. It was about her. The tears were breaking through a second time, coming harder and faster down my cheeks. Strangled cries sprang from me and I realized I was hyperventilating. *I am breaking down,* I realized with horror. *I am losing myself.*

Luca pushed against me and I thought he was finally going to retaliate, to do to me what I had just done to him. But he didn't. He rounded on me, pulling me into his chest and crushing his arms around me. I collapsed into him, feeling the weakness in my legs. I was so startled I let him hold me, feeling the hardness of his body beneath my cheek, the frantic thrumming of our heartbeats pressed against each other.

He was talking to me, his voice low and urgent against my hair, but I couldn't hear him. Something inside me was breaking; he had pricked the balloon in my chest and the pressure was draining. My cries were muffled against him, my tears staining pools across his T-shirt. I was inhaling his scent, my fingers pressed across his collarbone, and his hands were on my back holding me together as sobs quaked through my body.

And it wasn't enough. I needed to be closer to him; I needed to forget myself. I lifted my head and he brought his hands to my face, his thumbs gently wiping the tears from under my eyes.

'It's going to be OK,' he murmured, the pads of his fingers warm against my skin. He touched his forehead to mine. 'I won't let him hurt you again.'

My breath hitched in my throat. I gripped the collar of his T-shirt and lifted my chin. His lips brushed against mine.

'Sophie,' he breathed. 'We can't—'

'Please,' I said, moving my hands around his neck. 'I need this.' Whatever he was about to say got lost between us, because suddenly I was crushing my lips against his and he was twining his fingers in my hair, kissing me so hard it knocked the breath from me. This. This was what I needed. I pressed my body against him and dragged my fingers through his hair, pulling him closer, breathing him in. He groaned as he pushed his tongue into my mouth, deepening the kiss and gripping my waist as he spun me around. His hands found mine, our fingers splaying together as he lifted them above my head and pinned them against the wardrobe. He leant against me as he sealed every last inch of space between us with his body and took all the bad memories away.

He gasped for air against my lips, and I smiled as all the

pain and darkness burnt away inside our kiss. He made me dizzy. He made me forget.

It ended too quickly. Suddenly, he was pulling away from me and panting, his hand clutching his chest.

'I'm sorry,' he said, eyes wide. '*Cazzo.* I shouldn't have done that.'

'I did it,' I said, heaving an unsteady breath as I unstuck myself from the wardrobe. 'It was me.'

'I can't do this.' He backed up. 'It's not right.'

I backed away too. What was I thinking? What was I *doing*? I looked a mess, *was* a mess. I hadn't slept properly in days. 'You don't want to,' I said, feeling the pain resurface sharply, grief and anger mingling in a cocktail of embarrassment and regret. 'It's fine.'

'Of course I want to,' he said, his voice spiking. 'I want to more than anything. I *always* want to. That's the problem.'

I forced myself to look up at him.

His expression was pained. 'I won't take advantage of your grief, Sophie. I'm not that guy.'

I nodded, feeling the numbing effects of his kiss melt away. Memories charged back into my head and the clouds regathered, heavy and unyielding inside me. I was too wrung out to fight it.

Luca was still talking. My body was shaking.

I could see my mother's face, her sprawled legs, her glazed expression. And I hated it. I hated him and his family and everything they had done to me and he was holding me again and I realized I was crying more tears even though I shouldn't have had any left and his arms were too strong for me to move and I felt like I was suffocating and that made me want to hurt him and yell at him and tell him to get away from me. And I knew it wasn't about Luca and I wanted to tell him that too but in the end I couldn't tell him anything. I pushed away from him, stumbling backwards and falling in a heap on my bed.

'Sophie.' His voice was gruff. I could sense him pacing by the bed, though I wouldn't look up at him.

'Go away,' I pleaded. 'Just go away. Please. I need to be by myself. I need some time.'

'OK,' he relented finally. 'If you need anything—'

'I'll be fine,' I said hastily.

Luca pulled his switchblade from his back pocket and laid it on the bed beside me. 'Just in case,' he murmured.

I fingered the engraving, the swooping letters that I knew so well. *Gianluca.* 'A Falcone switchblade for a Marino girl,' I whispered. 'Is this really what your grandfather would have wanted?'

He pulled something from his back pocket. 'I'm not my grandfather.' He held his hand out between us, and my gaze settled on Evelina's ruby ring, resting in his palm. 'And you are not your father.'

I glanced at the empty bedside table. He must have picked the ring up when I was sulking. God. He knew. *He knew.*

'Life has dealt you a rough hand already,' he said quietly, closing his fingers around the ring. 'You don't have to pay for his mistakes as well, Sophie.' He moved to the door, pausing on the other side of it. 'When you're ready, come to us. We'll give you Sanctuary. I'll vouch for you, to the family and to my brother.' He touched his head against the frame, and smiling sadly, he added, 'Don't forget, I still owe you that grand gesture, Marino Girl.'

My smile was watery. Why was it so damn difficult to look at him? I shut my eyes. 'Please just go.'

And he did.

CHAPTER FORTY-THREE

THE BLOOD MOON

When they had all left, I let the memories engulf me. This time I didn't push them away. The tears had come, and with them, some release. I showered and got dressed. Feeling stifled by the piercing silence, the constant feeling of loneliness inside me, I grabbed a hoodie and let myself out into the garden. I sat on the grass and pushed my thoughts outwards, beyond myself. The blood moon hung low above me, red ripples making grooves inside it. Patches of grey blotted the exterior, curving away into rivers of crimson. I lay back, burying my hands behind my head. My mother's flowers dusted the air with sweetness, banishing the acrid memories of ash and dust.

Thoughts of the fire, of Jack, of rent and guardians and futures balanced on the edge of a knife, melted away.

Memories of flames and smoke filtered into the balmy night air and the essence of my mother settled around me, gently this time, like a blanket laid across the earth. I looked up, past my house and the sadness in its walls. I was so tired, every muscle spent from being wound so tight. I had to plan, I knew that, but my thoughts were bleeding into the darkness around me. There was only the moon and the soft whispering of a warm breeze. And in the quiet comfort of the great big world and the beauty looking down on me I drifted asleep.

When I woke the sun was high in the sky. The backs of my arms were imprinted with grass blades and my hair had dried in crimped waves behind my head. My phone was buzzing. 'Unknown' flashed on the screen as I swiped my finger across it.

My voice was groggy with the dregs of sleep. 'Hello?'

'Sophie?'

I almost crushed the phone inside my fist. '*Jack?*'

'I need to talk to you.'

'Are you kidding?' I sat poker-straight on the grass, blinking my surroundings into focus as my head threatened to explode. 'The police are looking for you,' I said, my voice turning thick and watery. 'Mom is dead, did you know that, you selfish son of a bitch?'

Jack's tone was businesslike. 'It was an accident,' he said briskly. 'You know I didn't want that to happen. The situation got away from us.'

I clutched my stomach, fighting the urge to vomit. 'You let it happen. You're a murderer.'

His reply was woven inside one long sigh. 'You're grieving, I understand, but there'll be time for that later. I need you to meet me somewhere.'

He was wired to the moon and floating out of reality if he was dumb enough to think I would ever want anything to do with him again. '*Are you crazy?* Have you actually lost your mind?'

'Donata wants me to bring you in now. Important things are at play. We're Marinos, Sophie, don't forget. And Marinos stick together.'

He *had* lost his mind.

'How could you leave it so long to call me? How could you run like that? How could you do that to her?' Why was I bothering? There was nothing he could say, no words to take back what he did.

'I've been trying to get through to you all week.' Jack was drawling and I realized he was probably high or drunk, or both. 'There's been too much heat in Cedar Hill, but it's dying down. Listen,' he said. 'I'm your guardian. I've spoken to Donata; I've talked her around. You were scared that night, you didn't know what you were doing, you're just a kid still. We have a job for you. We'll take care of you – you'll have money and protection. And we need you, too. A young girl who no one would suspect, just like Sara was. You're going to be our secret weap—'

'Don't you dare come near me,' I cut in. 'You're poison, Jack.' I choked on the rest of my sentence. How desperately I wanted to put my hands around his throat and watch him suffer. I thought of Nic's promise to me, and something flared inside me. I wanted to make Jack pay.

'We'll talk about this,' he said. 'You don't have to be by yourself any more.'

'That's how *you* made it!' I hissed. My nails were digging grooves in my palm. I was shaking, every part of me livid with hatred so deep I thought I might be sick.

His voice rose. 'I'm sorry about your mom. I was sure the fire would finish the Falcones but I miscalculated. I made a mistake, Sophie. There's still time to make it right. Trust me, I'm trying to protect you. I want to make sure you're safe. The future can't be avoided. If you're not with us, you're against us, and Donata won't stand for anything less than your full compliance. Not after your hesitance in the diner. Don't make it harder than it has to be.'

I hung up and slammed my phone against the ground. Rage and fear ripped through me. He wasn't going to stop. He was drugged up, profit-hungry and corrupt, and I was in his sights. Nic was right. Either I would join him or the Marinos would skin me alive.

How far away was New York? How long did I have? I remembered the cold stare of Donata Marino. What would she do to me if I refused to help her?

I locked the back door behind me and thundered upstairs. I would no longer be a sitting duck. I would not suffer the fate of my mother.

CHAPTER FORTY-FOUR
THE ESCAPE

I was in the upstairs bathroom squishing my moisturizer into an already full rucksack when I heard a car door slam outside. I burst into my mother's room, ignoring the stale feeling of depression that clung to the lavender-scented drapes inside. I edged towards the window, peering over the doorstep, where the top of my uncle's head was visible. He had already left New York when he called me. I never had a head start.

I was too late.

Crap. I slid back into my room and stuffed Luca's switch-blade in my pocket. The doorbell rang, followed almost immediately by several loud thumps. My phone was buzzing in my pocket.

By the time I was halfway downstairs, there was a key

turning in the lock of the front door. I almost bit off my tongue as it swung open in front of me, swallowing a curse. Jack stomped inside and I froze with one hand on the banister, the other across my heart.

We stared at each other. Every bone in my body ached to hurl myself at him, wrap my hands around his throat and watch the light drain from his eyes. I hated him, and the heat of my rage felt like it might burst through my skin and rip me apart. Would he take me by force or could I run? I had to think, to focus. I couldn't mess this up.

Slowly I came towards him, forcing one foot in front of the other, pulling the tendrils of raw fury back into my body and stifling them. I had to compose myself, to squash the hostility long enough to get away from him. And I would do it, even if it destroyed a part of me to do so. I would not let my emotions sell me to Donata Marino. I would not let them keep me from avenging my mother.

Jack's frame seemed to press outwards against the narrow hallway. There was no space – no place that his shadow didn't touch. 'Sophie.' One word: not quite angry, but stern.

'Jack.' *Antony*, I reminded myself. But no matter what the truth was, he would always be Jack to me. A liar. A coward. The word Antony tasted too bitter in my mouth. My fingers squeezed into my palms until their tips bent back on themselves.

He shut the door behind him. 'You didn't answer me.'

I felt my voice vibrating with fear, so I forced it higher, louder. 'I was upstairs. Can't you wait, like, two minutes?'

There. That teenage indignation. Jack huffed a sigh and I watched his shoulders dip. He thought this would be easy; he

387

thought I would come around. *Idiot.* He stepped closer, and it took everything in my power not to attack him. 'Are you ready to come with me?'

We both knew it wasn't a request; he was just allowing me the illusion of free will, for old times' sake.

'Do I have a choice?' Surly, but not unbendable. It was a delicate line.

'No. Either you come or she'll kill you.' A sigh, a flicker of the man I used to know. 'And we've lost enough already.'

We've. I contemplated lunging at him and clawing his eyes out. I might get one before he wrenched me off him.

'You'll have to come now,' he said.

Focus. I stamped my foot. 'This is *so* unfair.'

'Hurry up and pack a bag. I'll wait down here.'

I jutted out my chin. 'Can't we just stay here?' The idea of having him anywhere near the last place my mother had laughed and lived made me want to scream, but he would expect some opposition to the move, and if I didn't dig my heels in, he'd get suspicious and trail me while I packed.

'We're going somewhere nicer,' he said impatiently. 'Somewhere closer to the trade.'

'Where?' I whined.

'Will you just pack? I'll tell you later. Libero and Marco are waiting in the car.'

I couldn't escape. *Double crap.* At least he hadn't brought that murderous skeleton near my mother's house. I didn't know how much more my wavering restraint could take, and the idea of coming at Donata Marino with a kitchen knife was just too tempting.

'Fine.' I trudged back upstairs, blinking back the tears of

rage that spilled freely down my face once I was turned away from him.

I hovered in my bedroom, staring out the window as hopelessness wrapped itself around me. My eyes fell on the wooden trellis crawling up the back wall – the last of my mother's garden projects. Slowly, carefully, the threads of a plan unfolded in my head. I'd have to go out back. It was my only chance – my last chance.

I opened the window in my room and swung my already-packed bag out, angling my arm so that it landed in a bush to the right of the kitchen, away from the window. Then I stuffed an old rucksack with towels and sweatshirts to make it appear full. I stomped around for a while, slamming my feet against the floor above Jack so he'd think I was having a tantrum.

After ten minutes, I came downstairs. He hadn't moved from the hallway. He stopped scrolling through his phone and registered the bag as I dropped it by his feet, taking care not to be any nearer to him than I had to be. I scooted backwards, arms folded across my chest. 'There.'

'Good,' he said, stowing his phone in his pocket. 'You're cooperating. I knew you'd come around. It was all just a horrible accident, Soph. The wrong person died, but don't worry, we're going to take another run at those bastards, and this time they won't get out alive.'

I sneered internally. He obviously didn't know I was the one who had rescued them. Man, he was such a moron.

I forced a shrug. 'Whatever. I can't make rent by myself, and we both know I have nowhere else to go.'

The ghost of a smile flickered across his face, and I caught myself wondering what it would be like to cut it out of him and watch the colour drain from his lips. I smiled too as the image danced in my brain. One day I would find out.

Jack unclasped the front door and lugged my bag over his shoulder. 'Ready?' he asked, his tone already lifting.

I stalled. 'I need to pee.'

His brows lifted. 'What? Why didn't you go upstairs?'

'I was too busy rushing for you!'

'Fine. Hurry up.'

I locked myself into the bathroom under the stairs and assessed the window. It was too small to fit through; I had overestimated my tininess. Dammit. I ran the tap and cursed loudly enough so he could hear me. Then I shouted through the door, 'Can you please get me a toilet roll from the cupboard in the upstairs hallway?'

My heart thudded in my chest.

Please please please.

There was a loud, pointed sigh and then the heavy plodding of his feet on the stairs. I eased open the bathroom door, shut it quietly behind me and darted into the kitchen and out the back door. I had seconds at best.

I grabbed my rucksack from where it had landed, and catapulted towards the end of the garden. I threw the bag over the wall and started climbing, my feet scaling the trellis, my hands clawed tight against the concrete. I was halfway over the wall, my feet scrabbling against wood on one side and my fingers clutching stone on the other, when Jack's voice rang out behind me.

He was running and I was struggling, heaving my body over the wall until it scraped along the top as I slithered over it. And then he was below me, lunging for my foot and wrapping his fingers around my ankle. With a primal shriek, I kicked out, anchoring myself with my hands as I bucked against him. He held firm. With my free hand over the wall I grabbed Luca's switchblade from my back pocket and flicked it open. Jack yanked me by the ankle. I slipped towards him with the blade outstretched, and slashed it as hard as I could across his face.

He fell backwards, shrieking as blood pumped from his eye and coated his fingers as he held them tight to his face. He lunged blindly for me, but I had re-straddled the wall and was rolling over it, falling away from him.

I landed with a thud on the other side. The drop was high and the fall jolted the wind from my lungs. I re-stashed the blade, ducked and rolled, grabbing my rucksack and stumbling into a small line of trees that hid me as I pressed against the wall that bled into another, larger street of houses. Jack's screams of agony hung heavy in the air behind me, and I seized the surge of adrenalin they gave me.

I sprinted along an endless row of boxy homes, hopped into a nearby garden and weaved my way behind a squat wooden house with a dilapidated porch. At the back of it I lost myself in an expanse of shrubbery and threw my rucksack over wall after wall, chasing the sun as it sank away from me, until I was too tired to do anything but wedge myself behind a garden shed somewhere along the endless row of houses. I tucked my limbs inside my body, shrank into a ball and waited for the darkness to hide me from Jack and his Marino assassins.

I took out my phone and called Millie.

'Soph?' She cleared her throat, waking her voice up. 'Is everything OK?'

'Yeah,' I said quietly, conscious of the fact that I was trespassing on someone else's property. 'I just wanted to tell you I'm leaving town for a little bit.'

'What? Why? What's happened?'

'Calm down,' I said quickly, cutting off the freak-out. 'I'm just living, Mil. I'm living like you told me to.'

Panic vibrated in her voice. 'Soph, you're freaking me out. What are you talking about? I didn't mean "leave town" when I said that, I meant "get up and go for lunch with me" or something. This is definitely not what I meant.'

'I know.' I smiled against my phone. 'I'm not going off on some big soul-searching adventure.'

'Oh,' she said, relief colouring her tone. 'I thought you were about to ditch me for the pyramids or the Grand Canyon or something.'

'Jack's back in Cedar Hill.'

She sucked in a sharp inhale. 'Shit.'

'Yeah,' I concurred. 'I'm going somewhere he can't get to me . . . until I want him to.'

'What exactly does that mean?'

I tempered my response. There were some things she would understand, and some things she definitely wouldn't, and the truth of what I was planning was in the latter category. 'It means I'm going to lie low, just until the danger dies down.'

'Then lie low here, Soph. You know you're always welcome at mine . . .'

I had to smile, because we both knew it wouldn't work, and

still she had offered because that was the kind of person she was. Unafraid. Loyal. 'You really are an amazing friend, Mil.'

'So are you,' she shot back.

'I think you're definitely winning in the friendship stakes right now.'

Her laugh tinkled down the line. 'You've had your moments too, Gracewell.'

Gracewell. I bristled. That word. That lie.

It stood for nothing.

'We'll deal with this together,' she said, filling up the silence and pulling me from the impending spiral of rage and disappointment I was becoming all too used to.

I ignored her unfailing optimism, a part of me wishing I could believe it. 'I think the whole point of being a good friend is not putting your friend or her family in danger when you don't have to.'

'I'll be fine.' She didn't sound sure, but I didn't need her to be, because *I* was sure about two things now: Jack was incredibly angry, and he was also incredibly dangerous. That made him unpredictable. And if Millie sheltered me, she'd be in his firing line too, and I would never let that happen.

'I'm not taking that chance,' I said firmly. 'And you know that.'

'Where are you going to go? What are you going to do? Where are you now? Did Jack—?'

'Mil,' I interrupted. 'I have a plan, don't worry. I promise I'll fill you in as soon as I can, OK?'

'OK,' she relented after a short silence, her voice turning sceptical. 'But whatever happens, just don't leave me behind.'

Even the thought of it made my chest seize up. 'Never.'

'Because I *cannot* do senior year without you. It'll break my spirit, Soph. It'll suck the soul out of me.'

'I know,' I said, soothing her through a bubbling laugh. Her drama was the only kind I would freely welcome into my life. 'Don't worry,' I teased. 'I'll go into the darkness with you.'

'Good,' she said, matching my tone. 'Because you're my light.'

'You're so sappy.'

'You love it.'

'I know.'

CHAPTER FORTY-FIVE

THE BEGINNING

I waited on the doorstep at *Evelina*, counting the heartbeats it took for the door to open. Nineteen.

'Sophie.' Luca stepped out of the darkness.

'I was hoping it would be you.'

He smirked. 'What can I say? I *am* most people's favourite.'

I bit back the retort I would have offered him under normal circumstances – *Can your entire ego really fit in this house?* Instead, I offered him the apology I owed him. 'Listen, I didn't mean any of that stuff I said to you in my room. I was just so sad and panicked and angry about everything. And, well, you were there and I couldn't stop everything from bursting out of—'

'Sophie.' Luca raised his hand, frowning. 'Please don't apologize for the way your grief chose to be felt that night.'

'But I was so rude.'

'Well, you usually are rude, so I'm used to it.'

I shot him a withering glance and he swallowed it up with a grin. I'd forgotten how disarming his smile could be. It was his greatest weapon.

'Jack came back for me,' I said.

His expression darkened. He ran his gaze along my frame appraisingly. 'Did he hurt you?'

'No, but I think I cut his eye out with your switchblade.'

His eyebrows disappeared under black unruly strands of hair. 'Is that right?'

The reason for my visit rested between us. He knew what it was, but I knew I had to say it. I had to make it real in order to move forward. And he had to hear it.

'I'm on my own now,' I said quietly. The realization was a sting, and saying it aloud seemed to take all my energy with it. 'For the first time, I'm really, truly on my own.'

Luca came a little closer, like he was trying to enclose us in a bubble where the badness couldn't reach me. We could have been anywhere in the world just then, because I could only see him. 'Do you want to stay here?' he asked. 'With us?'

This was it – the first step. I was turning away from the sun and facing my destiny. I had to say the words. I had to make them real.

Unflinching, unblinking, I said, 'If you let me stay, I'll help you kill them.'

He gaped at me. 'Is that a joke?'

'I've never been more serious about anything in my life.'

'Marino,' he said, his voice twisting. 'That's dark.'

I held his stare, ice-blue and blazing. For the first time ever

I had a purpose edged with steel and fervour. I knew what I had to do. I had made my choice. The path *was* dark, but there was no going back.

This was my world. It had always been my world. It was time to stop fighting it and start living in it.

With drops of my uncle's blood still staining my fingertips, I stood on the threshold to the criminal underworld, facing the Falcone underboss, and sealed my destiny.

'I don't want to be a Marino, Luca.'

He stepped backwards into the foyer, and I followed him inside.

'OK,' he said, his eyes still locked on mine. 'Then be something else.'

We stood facing each other on top of the Falcone crest as a strange new warmth bloomed in my chest.

'Any suggestions?' I asked.

'I can think of one.'

ACKNOWLEDGEMENTS

Mom, this book is for you. Thank you for the Tooth Fairy letters, for the library visits, for the magical trips and the musicals. Thank you for dressing me up in a little velvet dress and bringing me to *Swan Lake* when I was three years old. I know you got a lot of strange looks from people for bringing a child as your date, but I remember every second of it. Thank you for always encouraging me to be creative, to follow my dreams and to embrace the zanier parts of life.

Dad, you are one of the zanier parts of my life. Thank you for being kind and intelligent, and funny and weird as hell, all at once. Thank you for teaching me how to live with humour and sensitivity, and to laugh often. I think I've taken all those years of your ridiculous (but impressive) accents and your (frankly worrying) preoccupation with sweets, and rolled them into these books. You really are the best dad in the world, and now it's in print, so that means it's true!

Colm and Conor, you are my favourites. Thank you for being so kind and supportive and fun throughout this journey. Colm, you are the voice of reason in my life, unerringly positive and generous with your time and advice, and I thank you for that. Conor, you're hilarious and really strange, but in a good way. We both know you're going to end up in one of my books one day, so I look forward to a time when we can toast to that (and also to you not suing me). You are the best brothers I could ever ask for: the perfect combination of humour, intelligence, kindness . . . and just a dash of shadiness.

To my agent, Claire Wilson, thank you for always being in

my corner, and for keeping the excitement and enthusiasm alive every step of the way. It comes as no surprise to me that you have acquired an entire coven of avid supporters. Thank you also to Lexie, and to everyone at Rogers, Coleridge & White, for championing this series and helping to spread the mafia love!

I don't know much about covens, but I have an inkling that Claire's Coven is one of the best out there. Thank you all for the inspiration, friendship and general brilliance, particularly my Stag Sisters Alice Oseman, Lauren James, Melinda Salisbury, Sara Barnard and the beautifully kind Alexia Casale and the hilarious Gary Meehan.

To everyone at Chicken House, I will be forever grateful to you for offering such a warm home to Sophie and her journey, and for welcoming this kooky author along with her! Barry Cunningham, you jumped right out of my college thesis and were even more magical in person. Thank you for making my dream come true! Rachel L and Kesia, the most formidable editing team, thank you for reading my first draft, discussing it, and then coming back to me with my favourite response: 'but then, what if THIS CRAZY THING happened?!?!' No idea is too grand or intimidating with you both on my side! And, more importantly, on Sophie's side! Rachel H, Jazz, Laura M and Laura S, thank you a thousand times for your unwavering enthusiasm and support for these books. And for putting up with my countless emails – encompassing everything from types of font to shipping allegiances in *The Vampire Diaries* – with such patience and kindness!

This book is as much about friendship as it is about love. I wouldn't have had the confidence to start writing or the drive to keep going without the incredible friends in my life – my 'Millies', and the best platonic romances I've ever had! Jess, thank you for being both sister and friend to me. I don't know what I'd do without you in my life – I wouldn't get tagged in all those raccoon videos, but I know I'd be a lot less happier than I am. Katie, twenty years and you're still not rid of me yet! Ha! Thank you for being the kind of friend who calls me up just so I can listen to you cry and scream while you try to kill a daddy-long-legs in your room. I treasure that trauma, almost as much as I treasure you. Susan, you are hilarious – a real burst of colour and joy. What would I do without those voice messages where you just meow at me over and over again? Don't ever change. EVER. Becky, expert sailor, ballroom dancer, runner, yoga-doer-person, and probably something else random by the time this gets published, I'm so glad we had that 'sister-sister' moment at summer camp all those years ago. You bring so much adventure and positivity to my life. Sheila, there is so much I could write here about our friendship, but a lot that I probably shouldn't ... What can I say? I'm not superstitious, but I am a little stitious. I'll never forget the day we locked eyes over that science table, and I thought to myself, 'That girl looks like a pixie,' and directly following that, 'She's hilarious. I'm going to force her to be my friend.'

Aidan, I know YA books about crime and romance are far from your usual interest in hard-hitting sports biographies of random people I've never heard of, but I really appreciate you embracing these books and for investing in the characters. It makes me happy to know they are now all committed to your (disconcertingly) infallible memory. I know you're a hotshot solicitor now, but you'll always be a sweet kid to me. Steph, when you turned upside down and balanced on your head to convey the word 'bat', you taught me the true value of Extreme Charades. Wherever you are in the world, and whatever new thing you are accomplishing, you always make me immeasurably proud. Thanks for 'Lego-head'! And thanks in advance for the castle you're going to design for me. Please consider this a binding contract. Katie O'B and Becca, thank you both for being so supportive and excited from the very beginning of this whole process, for spreading the love and for being a part of every step. Aoife, I love the scope and excitement levels of our chats – dragons, fantasy, films, imagined lands and general mutual fan-girling. I can't wait to see what the future holds for you and your immense talent. Louise, I know our livers are mortal enemies, but you are the most wonderful friend. I can't wait to retire to our castle together, where we will live reclusively and obnoxiously.

To Sam and Mims, thank you for the mad (and very tasteful) adventures. From discovering dinosaur tracks and the world's largest pecan, to hot-air balloon rides, remote cabins and Friendsville, there's no two people I'd rather get trapped in an elevator in the middle of the night in Nashville with than you. I'll always treasure our bond, and those eighty-six elk that joined us on our travels.

Sinead, thank you for helping me shape this book, for really understanding the characters and for discussing their journeys at length with me. There's really no better combination than Nutella waffles and murder-chat! Thanks for letting me pick your brain. Over and over and over again. Long may it continue.

I would write a book-length of acknowledgements if I could. Thank you to all of my friends, and friends of friends, and friends of family, here and abroad, who have supported this series since it came out, sent pictures, updates, reactions and messages of goodwill. I am so sincerely fortunate to have you all in my life. And to my family, my amazing aunts and uncles and cousins (and second cousins and third cousins), you really are some of the best and coolest people I know, and I feel very proud (and very smug) to be able to say I am related to such an incredible group of people.

When I was at Dominican College, Taylor's Hill, I was incredibly fortunate to have two brilliant English teachers. Thank you to Miriam Maher and Geoff Drea, for showing me how to embrace the power of stories, and the importance of creativity. I didn't know how lucky I was to have you as my teachers when I was at school, but I know now, and I thank my lucky stars for it.

Gerry Morrissey, fire fighter extraordinaire, esteemed Hazelwood resident and owner of the cutest dogs I've ever seen, thank you, firstly, for selflessly devoting your time to such a brave and important profession, and secondly, for talking me through the intricacies and details of fires, and not tiring of my many many many questions.

Finally, to the bloggers, booksellers and readers who embraced *Vendetta*, here at home and abroad, I owe you all an ever-growing debt of gratitude. Thank you for shouting about it online and offline, for spreading the love and keeping it alive during the wait for *Inferno*, and for all that you do for the love of reading and the general awesomeness of books. I love being part of such a wonderful, passionate culture.

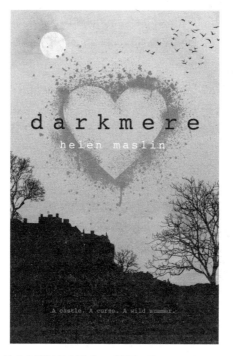

DARKMERE by HELEN MASLIN

Outsider Kate has a crush on the coolest boy in school, Leo. He's inherited a castle, a menacing ruin on the rugged English coast. When he invites her along for the summer, she finally feels part of the gang.

But Darkmere's empty halls are haunted by dark ghosts. Two centuries ago, Elinor – the young wife of the castle's brooding master – uncovered a dreadful truth.

As past and present entwine, Kate and Elinor find themselves fighting for their lives – and for the ones they love.

'A contemporary take on the gothic . . .
I romped through it.'
FIONA NOBLE, THE BOOKSELLER

Paperback, ISBN 978-1-910002-34-6, £7.99 • ebook, ISBN 978-1-910002-75-9, £7.99